Fatal Harvest

Vicki Wootton

Published by Stargate Publishing

Vancouver, Canada

Dedication

This novel is dedicated to the planet Earth, our mother and our home, in the hope she will survive long enough for us to come to our senses.

***

Author's note

The inspiration for this novel came largely from reading a book by Laurie Garrett called "The Coming Plague" (Farrar Straus Giraux, 1994). It is a well-researched and alarming book, a dramatic account of what could happen in the near future if we don't take action soon.

Part One - The City

"Disease is the retribution of outraged nature."
Hosea Ballou

Chapter 1

I was doing my homework while Mom and Dad watched a drama on the video-net when the program suddenly went off and was replaced by one of the news announcers. "We interrupt this program to bring you a special bulletin."

I turned from the computer to watch the video screen. Whenever they broke into a regular program—as had been happening a lot in those days—it usually meant trouble.

"What now?" My father shifted in his chair.

"Shh! Listen," Mother said.

". . . an outbreak of plague. We take you now to Valerie Cope at St. Paul's Hospital. Valerie, what can you tell us?"

The scene changed to the inside of the hospital. In the corridor behind the reporter, hospital personnel could be seen going about their work.

"Thank you, Pamela." The reporter turned to face the camera. "Doctors have confirmed that the young man who was brought in this afternoon, and who passed away half an hour ago, was a victim of plague. I have with me Dr. Amrik Mohajer, an epidemiologist. Dr. Mohajer, what can you tell us about the man who died this evening?" She turned to a dark-skinned man with glossy black hair and beard.

"Well, his name was Kevin Free. He was found lying on a pile of cardboard in an alley near the docks. He was obviously very ill, so someone called the emergency services and he was brought here."

"How long was it before you discovered he had the plague?"

"Naturally, as soon as he arrived in Emergency, they knew he was suffering from something unusual, so they began to take precautions immediately to isolate him."

I don't remember exactly what was said, but they went on to explain what caused the plague—how the forest fires of the previous three years had driven rodents that carried the plague bacteria, *Yersinia pestis*, into populated areas, and how the situation was exacerbated by the strike of sanitation workers and the unusually hot weather.

I saw Mom take Dad's hand and shivered in spite of the heat.

That's how the epidemics started. I was thirteen years old at the time. It has taken me almost twenty years to reach a point where I can write about it, or even think about it with a degree of detachment. The things that happened during the next few years were so horrifying that after a while, we became numb. It might seem as if we stopped feeling things but as everyone knows who lived through that time, there is only so much horror a person can endure before the only way to survive is to suppress the feelings altogether. Even writing about it now has brought to the surface many painful emotions, but I feel the story should be recorded so that our children will know about the mistakes made by their ancestors, the actions or lack of action that led to current conditions.

It was the first time since the worldwide influenza epidemic of 1918 that an epidemic had resulted in such a high death toll in this country. We were used to hearing about alarming outbreaks of diseases like cholera, plague, dengue fever and Ebola in other countries—in Asia or Latin America or Africa—but we never expected it to happen here. Once started, it spread rapidly all over the continent, and in spite of quarantines, bans on travel, and the closing of ports, it was soon out of control. We began to hear horror stories from Europe, Japan, Russia, and Australia, all of which suffered similar outbreaks.

Chapter 2

Kate, come and see this!"

I dashed downstairs and followed my mother into the living room where my father was sitting in his chair, leaning forward towards the video screen.

". . . in several parts of the city." The announcer was standing across the street from a burning building. Behind him, police were struggling to force back an angry crowd of demonstrators while firefighters battled to douse the flames with streams of water and foam.

The scene changed to a studio set. "Thank you, Chris." The announcer somehow managed to smile and look grave at the same time. "That was Chris Andreyev at the scene of the latest drugstore attack. We now take you to police headquarters for a word from police spokesman, Constable Jackie Wing." The scene changed once more to the exterior of the Police building. Constable Wing was a hefty-looking Chinese officer. He cleared his throat and looked down at a sheet of paper in his hand. "Chief of Police Harper has issued the following statement. . ."

I don't recall his exact words, but the statement, like many others we were to hear in the coming days, asked people to remain calm, the government had everything under control. Any further terrorist attacks on pharmacies and clinics would be severely dealt with.

Every day, there were stories of demonstrations outside government buildings and hospitals, frightened, angry people demanding something be done to stop the epidemic. Pharmacists, terrorized by hold-ups for medicines and just plain vandalism, started barricading their stores and closing down. The big chain stores like London Drugs built barricades of sandbags around their stores and hired platoons of armed guards to protect them. Soon, signs appeared in the windows of many stores declaring that they did not stock antibiotics.

More and more deaths were reported every day, but after the first few weeks of the plague epidemic, they stopped reporting the death toll. It only made things worse.

People were scared, and angry. Why was this happening to us? Why isn't someone helping us?

Mobs of irate people roamed the streets at night, drinking and screaming slogans. When they started breaking shop windows and looting, the city council declared a curfew, but it was hard to enforce because of the shortage of police personnel. They asked for help from the RCMP, but it had more than they could handle dealing with similar problems in those suburban communities that had no police forces of their own.

Finally, Premier Chin announced that an emergency meeting of the legislature in Victoria had voted to declare martial law.

There was a look of profound sadness on her face as she made the announcement. "We have no other alternative if we are to maintain civil order. I have consulted with the Department of National Defense and have been assured that we will receive their complete cooperation in this matter. As of tomorrow, October 29, members of the armed forces will be patrolling all major communities. You will be required to stay indoors from six p.m. until six a.m. unless you are part of the emergency services. Employers will issue official passes to those who need to be out because of their occupation."

There were more details, but what it boiled down to was that a rigorous curfew was going to be enforced to stop the rioting and mayhem. What we didn't expect was the amount of force that would be used to quell infractions. They shot to kill.

I'll never forget the look on Premier Chin's face as she said good night. Tears glistened in her eyes. I wonder if she had a premonition that she would be the last premier for many years. I didn't hear until later that both her parents had already succumbed to the plague.

Even as they were putting into effect those drastic measures, the worst of the civil disturbances were over. People seemed to be starting to accept the inevitable and no amount of shouting and tantrums would make any difference. A feeling of depression and apathy settled over everyone.

Chapter 3

I heard the I-Com chime in my parents' bedroom as I was getting ready for school one morning near the end of November. Everyone else had left, so I answered it.

"Celeste?" It was Gran speaking in her precise English accent. "Is your mother there?"

"No, she's gone to school already. What is it, Gran? Is something wrong?"

"It's your grandpa. He's not feeling well." Her voice sounded shaky, as if she were trying to keep herself under control.

"He's not . . . it's not, you know. . .?"

"Plague? I don't think so. This is different." She hesitated. "Can you get a message to your mother to call me as soon as possible?"

"All right. I'll see her at school; I'm just about to leave. How are you, Gran? Are you okay?"

"I'm fine. How are you and Paul?"

"Fine. I'll tell Mom. I hope Grandpa feels better soon."

I put the receiver down with a hollow feeling in my stomach, a sickening premonition of catastrophe. My beloved Grandpa. Tears welled in my eyes. *So it's come at last,* I thought, *we aren't going to escape after all.* I tried to convince myself I was exaggerating and he'd probably caught a flu virus. All the way to school the thought kept running in my mind, *my Grandpa's sick, my Grandpa's sick . . .* I was so distracted by the thought that I reached school without even realizing I'd walked there from my house.

I had a few minutes to spare before my first class started, so I went to look for Mom in her lab. I caught her attention through the glass door panel and beckoned to her. She said something to the students and came to the door.

"Hi, Celeste. What's wrong?" She looked frightened. "It's not Paul, is it?"

"No, Mom," I wiped my eyes with the back of my fingers. "Gran just called. She says Grandpa's sick. She wants you to call her."

"What's wrong with him? Did she tell you?" She gripped my arm. Her face had gone white.

"She didn't say, but she doesn't think it's plague."

The bell rang for change of classes, startling us.

"All right. I'll call her right away." She looked at her watch.

9

"I gotta go, Mom. See you at lunchtime—I want to know what she says. I hope Grandpa's okay."

At noon, I went to wait for her outside the staff room "Are you waiting for your mother?" asked the school secretary who was just coming out of the office next door.

"Yes, I was supposed to meet her here. "

"She's left. She asked me to give you the message."

"Did she say where she was going?"

"She said her father's sick and she was going over there to see if she could help."

"Thanks."

I turned to leave, feeling a shiver of fear. What was wrong with Grandpa? Was he going to die? He always seemed so healthy and full of energy. Sometimes he spent up to ten hours a day in his printing shop. I couldn't imagine him being ill. Maybe he'd been overdoing it and needed a rest. But Gran wouldn't have called Mom if that were all it was. I couldn't stand the anxiety of not knowing, so I left the school grounds to find a pay phone where I could call my grandparents' house. Mother answered.

"Mom? Is Grandpa all right?"

"It looks pretty bad, Celeste." Her voice was huskier than normal.

"What's wrong with him?

"I don't know; I think it's something new."

"Does he have to go to the hospital?"

"No. Gran called the doctor—Grandpa's too sick to go to the office—the doctor said it sounds like a virus that's going around and he should stay home and get plenty of rest."

"Why doesn't he go to the hospital?"

"There's no room, Celeste. The hospitals are all full. There's not much they could do for him that we can't do at home, anyway."

"Are you coming back soon?"

"I'm going to stay and help your gran, she's been up all night. What time does your last class finish?"

"We have phys-ed at two-thirty so I should be out by about three-fifteen. Why?"

"I want you to go straight home afterwards and look after Paul until I get there. I have to go now."

"All right, if I have to. Bye, Mom." I loved my little brother, but sometimes he could be a pest, getting into my belongings and always needing baby-sitting, keeping me from doing things with my friends.

My mother still hadn't come home when Dad returned from work, so we ate our dinner without her. We were just clearing the table when the I-Com chimed. Dad answered it.

"Kate? What's the matter?—Oh, no!—that's unbelievable . . . so fast. What was it, do you know?" He sat down on a kitchen chair. I watched him, hanging onto every word, an icy feeling going through me.

"I know. Are you coming home?—All right, I'll see you in the morning . . . Of course we can." Dad put down the receiver.

"Dad. What happened?"

"Your Grandpa died a few minutes ago. I'm sorry, Celeste." He put his arm around me. "I can't believe it happened so fast. He was at work yesterday and now he's gone."

"Where's Grandpa gone?" Paul asked, looking up from his construction set with big tears in his eyes.

I pulled away from my father and ran up to my room. I threw myself face down on the bed, grasped the covers in my fists, and cried into the pillow. I couldn't believe I would never see him again, never feel the tickle

12

of his mustache when he kissed me or hear his loving, "Here's my princess," whenever I came to visit. I realized mother had lost her father and Gran her husband, but I couldn't imagine they felt worse than I did. I was angry too. What the hell was happening to us? Why were so many people dying? You heard people saying it was a judgment from God because we had become so wicked. Sometimes I was tempted to believe it, except when good people like Grandpa died.

The day after Grandpa died, a girl collapsed in the washroom at school. She shook uncontrollably and blood trickled from her nose and mouth. She gasped for breath.

"Ugh! Gross," someone said.

"What's wrong with her?"

"Somebody call the nurse."

"Let's get out of here," another girl shouted, leading a rush for the door.

The sick girl was taken away in an ambulance and we never saw her again.

With the onset of cooler weather, a new virus had appeared on the scene. It had the medical profession baffled, although initially they'd thought it was a particularly lethal mutation of the influenza virus.

Whatever it was, it was deadly—far more deadly than the plague. It attacked the mucus membranes and peripheral blood vessels, rapidly breaking down the tissues, causing hemorrhages and the destruction of lung tissue, leaving the victims coughing up blood and fighting for breath. Purple-red patches appeared all over their bodies from broken capillaries. In some cases it attacked the digestive tract, and others—rarer, but much more painful—the membranes covering the brain and spinal cord. There was very little that could be done once a person was infected. The victim would have a raging fever, often bleeding from the mouth, nose, and anus. They were unable to swallow food, and within forty-eight hours, would probably be dead. It appeared to be an air-born virus, which made it even more lethal. The few people who did survive an attack were usually healthy young adults whose immune systems were strong enough to fight it.

This new disease terrified people even more than the plague had and, in spite of warnings from the government, they started flocking from the city. Whole families packed whatever they could carry in their cars and vans and rushed away to what they imagined would be safety, leaving their homes and most of their belongings behind. Even the soldiers, who had until now kept some order, disappeared. Every night, the video-net carried reports and pictures of the traffic jams on the highways out of town. We saw hundreds of the abandoned cars along the roadsides that had run out of fuel or broken down. If people thought they would be safer in the countryside, they were in for a nasty shock. The residents of the farms and the small rural towns and villages were heavily armed. They put up manned roadblocks to prevent city-dwellers overrunning them. And to show they meant business, demonstrated no reluctance to shoot strangers. In spite of seeing reports of the chaos and danger that awaited them in the countryside, people still kept leaving the city. I suppose it was the human tendency to be doing something, anything, even something dangerous, rather than sit around waiting for fate to overtake them.

Early on, some people thought they might find safety in the offshore islands that crowd the coast, but they were ruthlessly discouraged by the islanders when they tried to put ashore. Several small craft had been sunk before outsiders were convinced that they would find no safe harbor there.

Chapter 4

Mom and I got up early so that we could get to the gas station, before the rush started, to fill up Dad's gas-powered car. He'd taken mom's electric Duet to work.

"Hurry up, Celeste."

"I'm ready." I wound a scarf around my neck and followed Mother to the car. "Let's go!" I said, pulling on my mittens

It was nearly seven o'clock in the morning and the sky was just getting light. The air was so cold, our breath made small clouds. Mom unlocked the car doors and we slid inside, flinching at the coldness of the seats. The windows immediately steamed up. She pressed the starter and the ignition responded with an abortive click.

"Damn! Don't tell me it's going to give me trouble."

"Maybe it's just cold," I suggested uselessly. "Try it again."

She put her foot down on the gas pedal and pressed the button again, this time there was a brief sputter. After several tries, the engine started to vibrate roughly, shaking the whole car then it died again. "I don't want to run down the battery," Mother said as she gave it another try. The engine caught this time and kept running, shakily at first, but gradually becoming smoother.

"Phew! That's a relief."

The streetlights were out and the sky had lightened considerably by the time we reached Hastings Street. We turned towards the city center and started to look for a gas station that didn't have too long a lineup. The traffic was noticeably lighter than it had been a few months earlier.

"We might as well try this one." She turned into a service station that only had about forty cars lined up waiting for their turn at one of the six pumps.

A large hand-lettered sign informed customers that they were limited to twenty liters per vehicle. The price had gone through the ceiling since deliveries of fuel had stopped. The pipelines to the refineries were still operating and the refineries were running, albeit at a slower pace, but distribution was severely curtailed due to the ban on inter-regional transport and a shortage of drivers.

This was our weekly trip to refuel the car so that we could go shopping. By now, we were used to the wait and brought a thermos of tea with us and books to read while we waited.

We heard car doors slam loudly up ahead, then men's enraged voices. Two angry men stood face to face near the pump while an attendant watched helplessly. Such confrontations were not uncommon. We rolled down the windows to hear what it was about.

"You pushed in front of me, fucker."

"It was my turn, you jerk. Get that heap of junk out of my way, asshole, before I . . ."

"What? Come on, try something—I dare you . . ." The speaker was a beefy, red-faced man in work clothes.

"Come on guys, you're holding up the line." The young woman attendant looked nervously from one to the other.

People in the lineup started honking their horns and yelling at them to get on with it. A tall, heavyset man came out of the service bay wiping his hands on a dirty rag. A handgun poked conspicuously from his overall pocked. Seeing him, the two combatants got into their cars and slammed the doors.

"All right. *You*," he pointed at one of the drivers, pull back. And you, get your gas and go. No more trouble, you hear?"

"But I. . ." The driver who had been asked to wait made a feeble effort to assert himself.

"I don't want to hear it," the big man interrupted. "Just do as I say or leave now." He watched for a moment to make sure they'd taken him seriously returned to the service bay.

About fifteen minutes later, we got our weekly ration of fuel and went back onto the street.

"Where are we going today?" I asked.

"*Celebrity Foods.* It's a big warehouse where they sell bulk foods. I want to stock up on rice and flour and stuff like that. But first I need to go to the bank and get some money."

There was a lineup at the bank as well. Banks had started to cut back on their hours of operation until they were only open three hours a day, four days a week. This forced people to use the banks' ATM machines, and led to longer waits every time we tried to draw out some cash. Either Dad or Mother made a habit of going every night to draw out their daily limit of four hundred dollars. They had already used the I-com to transfer their savings into their operating account. I think they were afraid the bank would run out of money and wanted to make sure we had enough to live on during the crisis.

"Shit, the damn things closed down," a woman ahead of us complained. "Come on, Tasha, it's no good waiting.

There's nobody in there to get it going again." She grabbed the hand of her little girl and left the line-up.

"Must have run out of money again." Another woman turned away in disgust. "I suppose we'll have to come back later after the bank opens."

The other people in the line went to the window to verify that it really was closed, then with sighs and curses, turned and left.

"Not to worry," Mom said, "I've brought *some* money with me. I hope it's enough."

There was such a large crowd at the food warehouse that they had opened the loading bay doors at the back for people to enter, and had them exiting though the front doors by the cash registers. There was a chain across the doorway, which was lowered every five minutes or so to allow a few more people in. Most of the customers were women, and all were wearing facemasks. There was very little conversation as we waited. People glanced around suspiciously, avoiding meeting one another's eyes. If it hadn't been necessary to buy food, I'm sure they would rather have stayed safely at home. A few of them had brought children with them, taking on the added burden of trying to soothe their whining and keeping them from getting too close to other children.

When we got inside, we found large signs on the shelves saying, *Limit - one bag per customer* or *Two cans per customer*. The shelves were beginning to look decidedly empty as well and, as with gas, the prices had soared. We came away with two ten-kilo bags of flour, ten kilos of rice, ten of salt, some dried beans and a large pail of honey. There was no sugar left and very few spices or dried fruit. We also got a large bag of rolled oats, a four-liter can of cooking oil, and some baking soda.

"It's looking bad," Mom said as we stowed the purchases in the back of the car. "We're going to have to make this last. I don't know when they'll have any more supplies delivered."

"What are we going to do, Mom? I mean, if we can't buy?"

"We'll find a way to manage somehow. People lived for thousands of years before they had supermarkets. They grew their own food and traded with one another."

"But—you know—we can't grow wheat and stuff like that. How can we live on just vegetables?"

"We'll have to make some major adjustments in our eating habits. We rely on so much stuff that's imported from other countries; coffee, oranges and bananas, tea and rice. We won't be able to get those things any more.

We'll have to get used to eating the things that are produced right here. We're lucky in one respect—there's plenty of fish and game in this region, and it's a good climate for growing things, even with the changes in the weather."

"But it won't go on like this forever, will it? I mean, everybody is always talking about when things get back to normal."

"It may take a while, Celeste. The way things are going; so many people getting sick and dying, things could get even worse."

For the next few weeks, Mom and I kept busy shopping. We concentrated on canned and dried foods, durable clothing, camping equipment, basic medical supplies, tools, seeds, and batteries. We also bought some old-fashioned oil lamps and paraffin to fuel them. Everything was stowed away in an empty room in the basement with a strong lock on the door. This latter precaution filled me with apprehension, suggesting intruders and other dangers.

Mother was sick for a while with a fever around Christmas, scaring us all, but she pulled through with antibiotics and rest at home. By some miracle, the rest of the family stayed healthy.

Chapter 5

I was supposed to be doing some schoolwork on the I-com computer, but I had become bored with it and started playing a game.

"I'm going to tell Mom you're playing games," my five year-old brother Paul threatened.

"You do and I'll hide your game disks. Just mind your own business."

"I'll tell." He wasn't very original.

Suddenly, all the lights went out and the computer screen went blank.

"Hey turn the lights on," Paul yelled.

"What happened to the lights?" The computer was on a table near the window, so I leaned over and pulled aside the curtain. There wasn't a light to be seen anywhere outside.

"Looks like a power failure," Dad said, coming over behind me to peer out. He turned towards my brother. "Are you all right Paul?"

"Yeah. When are the lights going to come on?"

"I don't know. Stay where you are, your mother's lighting the lamps. We'll be able to see in a minute."

"I was on the computer, Dad, when the power went off. Will it damage the programs, going off like that?"

"No, they'll be okay. You'll lose any work you didn't save though."

"She was only playing a game."

"Thank you, little brother. Why are you such a twit?"

"Don't call him names, Celeste."

"He can be such a pain sometimes."

"Will you two stop arguing?" Mother entered carrying a couple of lamps. She put one on the bookcase and the other on a cabinet near the door then joined Dad at the window. "I hope this doesn't last long. I wonder why the power went off, there's no storm or anything to bring down the power lines."

"The power company is probably falling apart like everything else. Not enough people to do the work and keep things going."

"But there are so many people out of work—why don't they hire some?"

"It's not that easy, Kate; you can't replace skilled workers with unskilled. They wouldn't know what they're doing and would only make things worse."

"I suppose you're right. It's just so discouraging. Things are getting worse every day."

"Why don't we turn on the radio, maybe they can tell us what's happening?" I suggested.

"You need electricity to run that." Dad turned from the window.

"I know, but I've got batteries in my portable. I'll go up and get it."

"Here take this." Mother handed me one of the lamps.

I went up and brought the portable radio down to the living room. Dad turned it on and started turning the dial to find a radio station that might have some information. All he could find was music and announcements about the current crisis, or statistics of the latest casualties. We kept it tuned to one of the news stations until someone came on with the announcement about the power outage.

"Most of the north and eastern sections of the city and suburbs are without power at this time due to a power failure in part of the power metropolitan grid. Hydro company officials say that, in spite of severe staff shortages, every effort is being made to restore power as soon as possible. The cause of the failure is unknown at the present time.

"Jeez, what else is going to go wrong?" I complained.

"That didn't tell us much," Dad said, switching off the radio. "We must save the batteries."

"What are we going to do?" I asked.

"There's nothing much we can do but wait." Mother looked at her watch. "And I think it's time for you to go to bed, young man," she said to Paul.

"Oh, Mom. You always say that. Can't I stay up a bit longer? I'll be ascared upstairs in the dark all by myself."

"You're such a baby," I said.

"Leave him alone, Celeste," Mother said. "It might be a good idea for all of us to go to bed. There's not much point in sitting around in the dark."

Chapter 6

Hey, Dad, what's happened to the I-com?" I was trying to call Pam but the line was dead.

"Did you check to make sure it's plugged in properly?"

"Of course, Dad." I sighed. "Shall I go over to Pam's and see if hers is working?"

"Good idea. If theirs is working, call the phone company and report ours is out of order."

I put a sweater on and ran over to Pam's house two doors away. Her grandmother answered the door. "Hi, Mrs. Kumari, is Pam around?" I asked.

"Come in," she replied. "She's in the kitchen having breakfast."

I loved the spicy smell of cooking in the Kumari house and wondered what they would do when they ran out of their exotic Indian spices. I went back to the kitchen and found my friend sitting at the table. "Hey, Pam, is your I-com working?"

"I don't know. Why? Is something wrong with yours?"

"Yes, the line's dead."

"Wait a minute, I'll try it." She lifted the receiver from its panel on the kitchen wall and put it to her ear. She jiggled the button then shook her head. "No, ours isn't working either. Don't tell me the phone's going to be off now like the electricity."

"Let's go and find a payphone and see if it's working," Pam suggested.

Although almost every home and business was equipped with an I-Com—short for *Integrated Communications System*—the public pay terminals handled only basic telephone service without video. This was to avoid vandalism of the expensive equipment. Our I-com, which was linked to the computer, allowed us to send and receive faxes, order merchandise, pay bills and transfer money in bank accounts, download and upload school assignments, and even get simple medical diagnoses and prescriptions. We were also linked to the Internet and many public databases.

"Finish your breakfast first," Pam's grandmother said.

She put a mug of tea with milk on the table for me. I spooned some honey into it and took a sip.

"Would you like a chapatti with your tea?" Mrs. Kumari asked.

"It's all right, Mrs. Kumari. I just had my breakfast. Thanks anyway."

I finished the tea and put the mug in the sink. Pam, who had finished eating, went to fetch her coat and put her boots on. We closed the back door and hurried down the street to the corner grocery store, which was now boarded up and abandoned. There was still a pay terminal on the wall outside. A man was using it when we arrived. He pushed a few buttons, shook the receiver, put it to his ear again, then slammed it back onto the hook and turned away.

He walked away, muttering, "Damn thing's not working either."

I looked at Pam who shrugged. She picked up the receiver and listened, then shook her head.

"Let's put some money in and see if that makes it work," I suggested. I took some coins from my pocket and put them in the slot. Still nothing. "That's it then. I suppose we'll have to manage without I-Coms now." I pushed the button to get my coins back and turned away.

"What do you want to do today?" I asked

"I don't know. God, I never thought I'd miss school. It's so boring with nothing to do."

"Shall we go and see if Eric and Mike want to go somewhere?" Eric and Mike Chan were our neighbors. Eric was two years older than me and Pam, but Mike was our age. We sometimes hung around together.

"I guess so."

"Maybe they'll have some ideas about the I-Com. We could go downtown and try to find one that works."

"My dad doesn't like me going downtown after . . . you know."

"Sorry. Dumb idea." Come to think of it, it wasn't too safe for Mike and Eric either. "We have to do something. I'm getting stir crazy."

"We could walk down to the library."

"If it's open," I replied. "Anyway, let's go and see what Eric and Mike are doing."

"You like Eric, don't you?" Pam looked sideways at me and I felt my face turning red.

"He's okay I guess. How do you feel about Mike?"

"He's just a kid," she replied.

"He's older than you."

"Two months."

"Well. . .?"

"He's all right I suppose." She shoved her hands in her pockets and started walking faster. I had to hurry to keep up.

"I have to go to my house to get my jacket," I said.

When we reached our house, we found my father had left for work—he usually left about ten o'clock and was home again by four. There wasn't enough work for him to put in a full day. Mom had returned from her errands and was putting things away in the kitchen.

"Where've you two been?" she asked.

"The I-com wasn't working so we went to try a payphone."

"Oh no! Any luck?"

"No. It's probably going to go just like the power."

"What are you planning to do today? Besides your school work, that is."

"We're going to see if the library's open."

"Can I go?" asked Paul who was sitting at the kitchen table with his coloring book and crayons.

"No," I replied. "You just went out with Mom. You'd only slow us down."

"Aw, Mom, it's not fair," he pouted. "I never get to go anywhere."

"While you're out, there are a few things I'd like you to look out for," she said, ignoring Paul's whining. "We need some more paraffin for the lamps. If you find any,

31

get as much as you can—there's no telling how long we're going to need it."

By this time, we only had power for a few hours each day on a staggered basis. Sometimes we had lights in the evening, other times the power came on in the daytime and once in a while, the middle of the night. We had to adjust our cooking to fit the power supply.

Mother gave me a list and a handful of money. "See what stores you can find open, and check to see if there's anything useful being sold on the street. Don't buy anything that's not on the list. Look out for fresh fish," she added. "Keep the money in your money belt out of sight, and be careful. Don't forget to wear your mask."

"I know, Mom. We're going to see if Eric and Mike want to go with us."

"Good. You'll be safer in a group."

We crossed the road to the Chan's house and knocked on the door. Inside, running feet thudded down a flight of stairs, then the door opened and Mike peered out at us.

"Hi!"

"Hi! Do you and Eric want to come out with us? We have to get a few things for Mom, and we thought we might go to the library afterwards." I pulled down my mask.

"Come in. I'll ask Eric." He shut the door behind us and yelled, *"Eric!"* He went towards the back of the house. "Come to the kitchen, it's warmer there."

It was. The Chans had had the foresight to buy a wood-burning stove for heating and cooking when the power was off.

"Where's your Mom?" I asked.

"She took Amanda to Chinatown with my Aunt Rita and Grandma Loh." When Eric appeared in the doorway, Mike explained, "They came to see if we want to hang out with them,"

"Sure, why not?" Eric went over to the stove. "Wait a minute, before we go, we ought to put some more wood on the fire. Mom'll kill us if we let it go out."

Eric went outside and came back with an armful of fire logs. He put a couple in the stove and left the rest in a box on the floor. "Now, where did mom put the new masks?"

After finding a couple of masks, the two boys put on their jackets and boots. As we were closing the Chan's front gate, we saw Lia leaving her house next door.

"Hey! Where are you going?" she asked. Her real name was Cecilia, but she hated being called that—especially the way her father said it: *Checheelia*—so everyone called her Lia. He also pronounced my name *Chelesté*, but I didn't mind. Lia was twelve years old, a very pretty girl with large brown eyes and dark, curly hair. Her father, Tony Purcello, was a baker. Her mother worked at the hospital and her brother, seventeen year-old Rick, helped his father at the bakery.

"Nowhere special, just around," Mike said.

"Can I come with you?"

Beside me, Pam sighed. I think she was a bit jealous of Lia and, in spite of her protestations of indifference; she resented it when Mike paid attention to her.

"It's okay by me," Mike replied.

"Let's go," Pam said irritably.

We went up the road and turned towards Hastings Street. Most of the shops were closed and had their windows boarded up, having been forced out of business when their stocks ran out and there was no hope of fresh supplies being delivered. People always used to complain about having to rely on suppliers back east—now we were in a situation that brought home to us the danger of concentrating most of the country's manufacturing in one area. Not that many local goods were moving either—we did have some manufacturers here, but even they were closing down because of lack of materials and power to run the machinery.

Some people had set up tables along the sidewalks, or spread items for sale on the ground. We stopped by a woman sitting on a folding chair with children's clothing and toys spread out before her. She had a worn, troubled face and I wondered if she had lost a child—or maybe more than one. A little girl of about ten sat by her side with two puppies in a cardboard box.

"Are the dogs for sale?" Eric asked the woman.

"Yes. Either that or barter.

"It might be a good idea to get one," Eric said. "I have a feeling we may need a watch dog if things go on the way they have been. What breed are they?" he asked

"As far as I can tell, they're a Lab-Shepherd mix. The mother was a German Shepherd. They'll make good watch-dogs," she added hopefully.

"What do you want for them?"

"A hundred dollars each," she looked down at her daughter. "We might be able to exchange them—she needs some new boots and a warm jacket." The little girl was wearing a jacket that was much too tight and her thin wrists stuck out several centimeters from the sleeves. She had a worn pair of running shoes on her feet. "We need food as well—you know, flour, salt, sugar, that sort of thing."

"What size shoes does she take?" asked Pam who was small for her age.

"Shoes . . . what size are those, Tracy?"

"I think they're twelves, but they're real tight. They pinch my toes." She reached down and pressed the toe of her shoe to demonstrate.

"So she'd probably need thirteens, or ones might be even better," the mother replied.

"I might be able to get some of my old things—my grandma always keeps everything, even when it's too small for me." She looked at the rest of us for approval then added, "Could we get both dogs for some clothes and boots? I have some shoes as well if you want them."

"It depends what condition they are in. Bring them over and we'll see," the woman replied.

"I bet my things would fit her," Lia interjected.

"Come on, let's finish what we have to do first, we can come back later." Mike urged us.

"If you're still here when we get back, I'll see if I can get some things." Pam said.

"I'm going to ask my Mom if I can bring some of my old clothes," Lia turned back towards home. She ran across the road and disappeared around the corner.

"Trust her," Pam said grumpily. "She always wants to be the center of attention."

"Come on, Pam," I said, taking her arm. "It doesn't matter."

By the time we finished shopping, I'd managed to get half a dozen eggs, some fresh fish sold from the back of a pickup truck, and eight litters of paraffin.

I took the food and paraffin home and met the others back on the street. Lia was there with the new puppy in her arms. She told us that when she got back to the mother and daughter, there had only been one dog left.

"Is it a boy or a girl?" Mike took the puppy from Lia's arms. "Here, let's see."

Eric looked at the puppy, which Mike was cradling on its back in his arms. "It's a girl,"

"What shall we call her?" Lia took the dog back from Mike. It squirmed in her arms and licked her face, making her giggle.

Vicki Wootton

"I dunno," Eric answered, "It's your dog."

"No, I want us all to share it. How about <u>Blacky</u>?" Lia suggested because the dog's fur was mostly black.

"Not very original," Mike replied.

"What about <u>Greta</u>?" The name seemed to me appropriate, given her German Shepherd origin.

Nobody objected, so the new dog was named Greta. The next problem was finding somewhere to keep her.

"We'll have to build a dog house."

"It's too cold to leave her outside. Can't she stay in somebody's house?"

"I don't think my Mom and Dad'll let us keep her at our house," Eric said.

"We can keep her at my house," Lia offered. "I'll ask Mom. We can make a doghouse for her when she gets bigger. The weather will be warmer then."

Chapter 7

I was woken up in the middle of the night by the sound of terrible coughing and my parents' voices, talking

38

softly, but urgently. I got out of bed and peeked through the open door and saw lamplight spilling out into the hall from Paul's room. I crept out and looked in through his door. Dad was standing by the bed in his bathrobe running his hand through his hair in helpless bewilderment. Mother, wearing a mask, sat on the edge of the bed holding Paul and wiping his face with a wet cloth. Paul's breathing was very noisy and made a sort of whistling sound. He was having a hard time getting his breath and coughed weakly. The cough had an awful bubbling sound as if it was coming through a pipe filled with water, and a trickle of blood ran out of the corner of his mouth. His eyes were closed and his head was lolling back on Mother's arm. I went cold with dread.

"He's burning up." Mother said.

"Mom, what's wrong?" I started into the room.

"Don't come in," she said sharply.

My eyes filled with tears and I stepped back.

"I'm sorry; I didn't mean to yell at you. Paul's sick and I don't want you to catch it, so please stay outside."

"What are we going to do? Shouldn't we take him to the center?" Father paced to the door and then back to the bed.

"There's not much choice. I think we'll have to," she replied. "Go and get dressed, then bring the car to the door. And put a mask on. I'll get him ready."

"Mom, what's going to happen to him? Is it the—you know—that virus?"

"I don't know, dear. He's a very sick little boy. His only chance is to go to the medical center." She looked exhausted, her forehead creased with worry. "Go back to your room and try to get some rest. One of us will come back to be with you as soon as we get him settled."

I went back to my room where I sat down on the bed and watched through the open doorway. Mother passed by, hurrying towards the stairs carrying Paul wrapped in a blanket from his bed.

That was the last time I saw my little brother.

Paul fell ill shortly after his sixth birthday. We had been keeping ourselves relatively isolated from other people, but it was hard to deny him some kind of birthday celebration, so we had a small party with a few of his friends. That may have been how he caught it.

Dad came back from the medical center around six o'clock, just as it was starting to get light and made himself some coffee. I hadn't been able to go back to sleep after they left and was sitting in the living room in front of the blank video screen. I was very scared.

"How is he?" I asked as he slumped down on the sofa across from me. "What are they doing to him?"

"He has an IV going with medication, but it doesn't seem to be doing much good. They've got vaporizers to try to help clear his breathing passages, and your mother's sponging him to bring down the fever. There's not much else they can do except hope he is strong enough to fight it. And pray." He rubbed his eyes and took a sip of coffee. "Your mother won't leave him alone there. They only allow one person with each patient—to help with the care, I suppose." He got up from the sofa and came over to where I was sitting. "How are you feeling?" he asked me anxiously. He put his hand on my forehead to see if I was hot. He had dark shadows under his eyes and he looked years older than he had a few months ago. His hair seemed thinner and had more grey in it.

"Fine." I did a mental assessment of my body and couldn't discern anything unusual. As if this self-conscious attention had sparked it, I had an unbearable urge to cough. I coughed. This brought a look of alarm to my father's face.

"It's all right, Dad. It's nothing, just a tickle in my throat."

"You'd better drink some fruit juice and take your vitamins," he told me, evidently unable to think of anything else that could prevent my being attacked by the same microbes that had got Paul.

I cooked Dad and myself some oatmeal for breakfast, but after taking a few spoonfuls, we both lost interest in eating and sat lost in the silence of our own thoughts. Finally, Dad roused himself and went out into the back garden where he started digging the area we planned to turn into a vegetable garden. I washed the dishes and put them away, then went upstairs to tidy the bedrooms and make the beds. I left Paul's room as it was, just closing the door on it. I was not very enthusiastic about housework, but I needed something to occupy me just as Dad did. I had just finished cleaning the bathroom when I heard a car door slam outside. I dashed to a window at the front of the house and saw Dad standing beside the car holding Mother in his arms. She was crying.

Like all casualties of the epidemics, Paul had to be cremated. There were so many deaths at the time that it was impossible to hold a separate ceremony for each family, so they had funeral services for several victims at a time. I don't remember much about Paul's funeral except that we were in a room with several weeping strangers in separate, tight little groups. A man read some prayers while a woman played something melancholy on a piano in the background. We were stunned. It had all happened so quickly. I regretted not being nicer to my little brother.

Ironically, the temporary medical center where Paul died had once been his school.

A few days later, I was sitting on the front steps when I saw the Chan's car drive up to their house across the street. The front door of the house opened and Mike and Eric came out. Mr. and Mrs. Chan climbed slowly from the car. Mrs. Chan was weeping loudly. With her husband supporting her on one side and Eric on the other, she slowly made her way up the path to the house, leaving poor Mike standing by the car looking lost and bewildered. I got up and walked across the road.

"What happened, Mike?" Tears glistened in his eyes.

"It's Amanda. She's . . ." He wiped his shirt cuff across his eyes. Amanda was his five year-old sister.

"Oh, Mike, I'm really sorry." With tears running down my face, I put my arm around him and we hugged each other. His body felt so bony and frail.

Chapter 8

One event stands out as the turning point, the moment when I realized that our lives would never be the same again and whatever future I had imagined for myself would never happen. My father arrived home from work one day at noon, looking stunned. He was carrying a plastic shopping bag filled with books and things. Mother, who had been in the garden hanging some washing on the clothesline, followed him into the house.

"What's the matter, John?" she asked. "You're home early."

"Yes. Marshall's packed it in. No clients. No job. And now, no paycheck." He dropped the bag and his briefcase on the floor and slumped down on a kitchen chair.

"Oh, no!" She stood behind him and put her hand on his shoulder. "I thought it was bad enough when the schools closed. What are we going to do now?"

"I don't know." He sounded so hopeless.

"We'll think of something until things get back to normal. We'll just have to use our imaginations. I'm sure there's . . ." Her voice trailed off as if she realized she was only speaking meaningless platitudes.

"Things won't get back to normal, not in our lifetime. It's gone too far. Anyway, whatever happens, I doubt there'll be any call for computer programmers."

The subject of work came up one evening while we were eating supper. Gran was eating with us. She'd moved into the basement apartment in our house when Grandpa died. She was still working at city hall.

"The city's looking for workers you know, John."

"What sort of work?"

"Just laboring I'm afraid.

"What would they be doing, Mother?" Mom asked.

"At the moment, they're looking for people to join the cleanup crews."

"You mean the *death squads*?" I used the grisly nickname we'd adopted for them.

"I wish people wouldn't call them that." Gran replied. "Somebody has to do the work; you can't leave dead bodies lying around."

"Aren't they afraid of getting sick?"

"The city provides protective clothing. You must have seen them."

"You mean those things that look like space suits?" I turned to my father. "What do you think, Dad?"

"I don't know." He sighed. "Do you think I should try it, Kate?"

"It would give you something to do and we could certainly use the extra food. It's up to you though. I don't want you to do it if you feel uncomfortable about it."

"I don't think comfort comes into it," he replied.

"You know what I mean."

"I suppose I could check it out."

* * *

As I went carefully down the basement stairs, which were only dimly illuminated by the light from the window in Gran's kitchen, I heard a scuffling sound coming from the bathroom.

"Gran? Is that you?"

I was sure Gran had gone to work. I'd seen her leave earlier. I wondered if she'd come home early. The sudden crash of breaking glass startled me and I ran back upstairs to our kitchen where Mom was making dinner.

"What's the matter?" She looked up from the pot she was stirring. "Did I hear something break?"

"I think there's someone in Gran's kitchen."

"What do you mean? How could anyone get in without us seeing them?"

"The window's open, I think."

"Let's take a look." Wiping her hands on a towel, she rushed out the back door and around the side of the house.

I followed her and saw her bending down near to the tiny bathroom window, tugging a small boy through the opening. He struggled and yelped as she pulled him out and set him down on the path. She kept a firm grip on his arm.

"Here's our little burglar," she said. "He somehow managed to squeeze in through the bathroom window, but he got stuck coming out."

She knelt down in front of the boy holding both his arms. He had stopped struggling and stood mutely with tears streaking his grimy face. He was very dirty—not the kind of dirt little boys get from normal, everyday play, but the ingrained dirt of someone who hasn't washed in a long time. His hair was a straggly mass of dark matted curls. He looked about seven or eight and was very thin with a pinched little face that emphasized his big hazel eyes.

"What were you doing?" Mom asked.

He didn't say anything, just stood with his eyes downcast.

"Where are you from? Do you live around here?"

Still no answer.

"Are you hungry?"

He raised his eyes and looked at her. His eyes flicked over to me, then back to Mom. He licked his lips, but remained silent.

"Would you like something to eat?" Mom asked gently. She smiled at him.

Not taking his eyes off her face, he nodded his head once.

"Come on then." She stood up and took his hand.

We went back into the house and closed the door.

"Would you like to wash your hands before you eat?" Mom asked the boy.

He tucked his hands up in his armpits and looked sullenly at the floor.

"Never mind then. Here sit down at the table." She pulled a chair out for him. "Get me a bowl, Celeste. He can have some of the stew."

"But, Mom, he's so dirty."

"It doesn't matter. Can't you see he's starving and scared half out of his wits? Let's get him comfortable first."

She ladled some stew into a bowl, set it in front of him and handed him a soupspoon. She poured some water from a bottle into a glass and gave it to him. He started to blow on the stew, frustrated because it was too hot. After a few minutes, he began to shovel it into his mouth as if he was afraid it would be snatched away. Mom sat at the table opposite him and drank some water.

"Why don't you go down and get the tomatoes?" she said to me. "And while you're down there, see what was broken."

A flicker of fear passed over the boy's face. I ran down the basement stairs and looked in Gran's bathroom where I found a broken glass on the floor near the sink. After picking up the glass, I got a can of tomatoes from the storeroom and I hurried back upstairs.

"It was only a glass," I said.

The boy, who was eating a cookie, looked at me defiantly then lowered his eyes.

"What's your name?" Mom asked. "My name's Kate and this is Celeste. Will you tell us your name?"

He shrugged.

"Where do you live?"

Still no reply.

"Where are your mom and dad?

Tears welled up in his eyes and slid down his face. He wiped his cheek with the back of his hand, leaving muddy streaks. Mom went over and put her arm around him.

"Would you like to have a warm bath and put on some clean clothes?"

"I need to go to the bathroom." His first words were spoken gruffly as if his vocal cords were rusty from non-use.

"All right. Let me show you the way." He slid down off the chair, and then Mom took his hand and led him out of the room. I started to follow.

"Stay there, Celeste. I think too many people make him nervous. Put some water on to heat up."

I filled a couple of large pots with water from the pails by the door and placed them on top of the wood stove that now stood beside the electric range, then I added a couple of logs to the fire box. We now bathed in the kitchen, which was the warmest room in the house. It took too much water to fill the bathtub upstairs so we had acquired a zinc tub about a meter long and half as wide. Mom returned with the boy carrying a couple of towels, a pair of jeans and a tee shirt that I'd outgrown, and some of Paul's underwear.

"Bring the tub in please, Celeste."

I went out to the utility room and took the tub down from its hook on the wall, then set it down on the floor by the stove. When the water was hot enough, Mom poured it into the tub and added some cool water from another bucket. We didn't have any shampoo, but we had plenty of plain soap. She put a bar of soap in the water and pulled over a chair to hold the towels.

"Here you are," she said to the boy. "You'll feel much better after you have a bath. Leave your dirty clothes on the floor. Don't forget to wash your hair. We'll leave you alone now to give you some privacy. Yell if you need anything. Okay? Come out here and tell us when you've finished."

He nodded his head without meeting her eyes. Before we left the kitchen, Mom locked the back door and put the key in her pocket. We went into the living room, closing the kitchen door behind us.

"What do you think he'll do? I asked.

"I hope he'll have a bath," she replied. "Go and listen at the door, see if you can hear anything. Don't let him hear you though. I want to try to gain his trust and he won't trust us if he thinks we're spying on him."

I put my ear to the kitchen door, but I couldn't hear anything at first apart from a rustling sound, then I heard a small splash. I returned to the living room.

"I couldn't tell." I shrugged. "How long are we going to wait?"

"The water will be cold in about half an hour. If he's not out by then, I'll take a look and see what he's up to." She picked up some knitting.

I got one of my schoolbooks and tried to complete a lesson, but my heart wasn't in it now that I couldn't use the computer. I put the book down and picked up the notebook I used as a journal. I wrote a few lines and riffled back through the pages, reading some of the past entries.

We both looked up when the kitchen door opened. He stood in the doorway, water dripping from his hair. He was wearing the clean jeans and shirt, both of which were a bit too big for him.

"Feeling better?" Mother put aside her knitting and stood up. "Come on, let's dry your hair." In the kitchen, she picked up one of the towels and started to rub his head briskly. "Can you empty the tub, Celeste?" She handed me the door-key.

I dragged the tub across the floor to the back door. The water was now cloudy beneath the dirty scum on the surface. At the open door, I scooped the water up in an empty pail and poured it into a barrel outside. We saved all our washing water for the garden. When there was only a little water left, I picked up the tub and emptied the remaining water into the barrel then I hung it back on its hook and returned to the kitchen.

The boy was sitting at the table looking down at his hands folded in his lap. His hair hung in tight curls. Now that he was clean, I could see that the darkness of his skin was not all dirt; he was naturally dark skinned. He was a very attractive but sad looking little boy. Mom made some tea and put three mugs on the table. We both sat down.

"Do you feel like telling us your name now?" she asked.

"Tate." His voice was barely audible.

"Tate. Do you have a first name?"

"I told you—Tate."

"I see. That's a very nice name. What's your last name then?"

He shrugged.

"Where are your parents?"

"Gone."

"Don't you know where they are?"

"No. They're just gone." I thought he was going to cry again.

"Do you mean they're, you know. . ." I said. "Did they get sick?"

"My mom did."

"What about your father?" Mom asked.

"Don't know."

"Where do you live?"

"Around." Another shrug.

I felt sorry for the poor kid. He wouldn't last long if he'd lost both his parents and had nowhere to live.

"Mom, can he stay with us?"

"Have you got anywhere to live?" she asked Tate.

"Uh, uh." He shook his head.

"Would you like to stay with us? I'll have to get my husband's okay, but I'm sure he'll agree. You'd have to help with the work if you do."

"Okay." He looked up at her then lowered his eyes again. His legs were swinging nervously under the table.

That's how Tate came into our lives. We found out later, when we could get him to talk more, that he was nine at the time. He stayed with us for a few weeks, then surprised us one day by saying he wanted to go and live with Peter Hetherington, one of our neighbors.

"Did he invite you?" I asked.

Tate shook his head.

"Well how do you know he wants you there?"

He shrugged, looking a little deflated.

"I'll have a word with him," Dad offered. We were just finishing breakfast and Dad hadn't left for his new job yet. "But you're welcome to stay here as long as you like."

All I knew about Peter at that time was that he was an artist of some kind—later, I learned he was a graphic designer—and also played the guitar and wrote songs. He was in his late thirties or early forties with thick brown hair and a beard. He had once had someone living with him, but she'd been gone for a couple of years and he now lived alone. In the evenings that summer, we sometimes gathered with the neighbors on someone's front porch and Peter would play and sing for us, encouraging us to join in. Tate seemed to enjoy the music and was fascinated by the guitar, so I suppose that's what attracted him to Peter.

Peter said he had no objections to Tate living with him, as long as he helped with the chores. In fact, he would welcome having someone to talk to.

Chris Valentine, another neighbor who was a nurse, brought a little girl home to live with her around this time. The girl had lost both parents in the epidemics and had nowhere else to go. Jackie was eleven. She had red hair and green eyes with very pale skin and freckles. She was a timid, sad little waif.

Chapter 9

One sweltering night in the middle of July, I woke up in a sweat with terrible stomach cramps. I drew my knees up in an effort to ease the pain, but it didn't help much. A wave of nausea overwhelmed me and my mouth filled with saliva. I struggled out of bed. I couldn't straighten up because of the cramps so I hurried, doubled over, to the bathroom. After throwing up everything in my stomach I still continued to retch, bringing up nothing but acrid bile. I was freezing in spite of the heat and began to tremble uncontrollably. I rested on the edge of the bathtub for a moment until an urgent pressure in my bowels sent me rushing back to the toilet. It seemed as if my body was purging itself of all its fluids. Too weak to lift the pail of water and flush the toilet, I just sat there shivering.

A light appeared in the hall.

"Are you all right, Celeste?" My mother pushed open the door. "I heard you moving around. . ."

"Mom!"

"My God! Are you sick?" She came into the room and put the lamp down on the counter. I was still sitting on the toilet. "You look terrible. Do you want me to help you?" She didn't say anything about the awful stench.

"I'm sorry, Mom." Tears began to run down my cheeks.

"It's all right, love. Come on, I'll help you up." She took my arm and helped me off the toilet. When I tried to straighten up, I doubled over with the cramps again. I swayed weakly on my feet and clung to Mother.

"Good lord, you're freezing, put this around you." Mother wrapped a bathrobe around my shoulders. "Sit down here while I flush the toilet." She lowered me to the edge of the bathtub and poured water into the toilet.

"How do you feel now?"

"Awful." I licked my lips. "I'm so thirsty."

"Come on, let me get you back to bed, then I'll go down and get something for you to drink."

When we reached my room, she opened one of my drawers and took out a clean nightgown. "I'll get some water so you can wash."

Once I was cleaned up and back in bed, I drank some of the tea Mother had brought for me. The moment it hit my stomach, I vomited, then I had rush to the bathroom to empty my bowels again. I couldn't believe fluid could pass through my body that fast.

58

We were terrified, fearing it was another strain of the deadly virus that had plagued us for the past eight months, but the symptoms were different. It didn't take long for the beleaguered medical profession to realize that they had a cholera epidemic to deal with. Luckily for me, the attack wasn't fatal, but it left me feeling weak for a long while.

* * *

Unknown to our parents, my friends and I started scavenging in empty houses. It wasn't very difficult for us to discover which houses had been abandoned, and it was easy enough to gain access to them. Sometimes the doors were left unlocked, but if they weren't, we simply broke the basement windows and got in that way. We would probably have been doing this much earlier, but it took us a while to for need to overcome our reluctance to trespass. We learned early to avoid refrigerators after opening a few and discovering the putrid remains of rotting food. We carried away cans and any dehydrated foodstuffs we could find, such things as rice, cereals, beans and flour. Not that there was much left in most of the houses, especially the ones where the owners had died or left more recently, after the food shortages. We weren't the only ones doing this, of course—there was fierce competition often leading to fights.

The first time I brought home some of the scavenged food—a couple of tins of soup—my mother wanted to know where it came from.

"I found them," I told her.

"You don't just *find* food lying around waiting to be picked up," she replied. "I want you to take them back where they came from. Right now."

"But, Mom, they don't belong to anybody. We need food."

"Unless you tell me the truth about where they came from, I don't want anything to do with them, no matter how hungry we are."

I walked to the window and looked out. It was getting dark and the sky was taking on a ruddy glow. "I found them in an empty house," I mumbled.

She didn't hear me and told me to speak up. I ended up telling her about our forays into abandoned houses. I was surprised by her reaction. Instead of the anger and punishment I had been expecting, I saw her eyes fill with tears. She sat down at the kitchen table and covered her face with her hands.

I went to her and put my hand on her shoulder. "Mom! What is it, Mom?"

She sighed and took my hand. "It's . . . I can't believe we've come to this." She shook her head. "It's so dangerous, Cel. I don't want you to get hurt. I think we should have a meeting with the others and talk about this."

Mother organized a meeting of the remaining people on our block. There were Don and Debbie Harris, a couple in their thirties with their eight year-old son, Jason. They were both on the heavy side with dark blonde hair. Don was a bus driver, and Debbie had been a secretary until the company she worked for went out of business. Both Don and Debbie had been smokers, but now that cigarettes were no longer available, Don had taken to sticking stalks of grass in his mouth and chewing on them.

Other survivors on the block included the Chans, Pam and her father and grandmother, Peter Hetherington, Chris Valentine—the twenty-nine year-old nurse—Tony Purcello and his daughter, Lia. Tony's wife had died earlier in the year and his eighteen year-old son, Rick, had left home. The remaining members of the group were Marvin Litsky, a heavy-set, morose man in his fifties and his creepy son Albert. Mr. Litsky had lived alone until Albert turned up one day, to everyone's regret. I remember vaguely that there had been a Mrs. Litsky when I was younger. Marvin was a carpenter.

Although he always seemed distant and uncommunicative, a gentler side of his nature had been revealed a few months earlier when he'd found a sick kitten and nursed it back to health, patiently feeding it with a medicine dropper until it was strong enough to eat by itself.

The result of the meeting was that scavenging became part of the routine life of the community. We became more methodical, and had adults along to protect us and recommend things to look for. In addition to food, we began to look for tools, household linen and durable clothing, any medications and any first aid equipment we could find, as well as batteries, soap and camping equipment.

I was surprised that Mother and the other adults faced up so quickly to the reality of necessity. There was some opposition. Debbie Harris thought it was sinful to rob the dead, but she always had a tendency to dramatize and overreact. Mrs. Kumari, Pam's grandmother didn't like the idea very much either, but they soon came around when the alternative appeared to be starving.

* * *

"Hey, Mom, come and look at this."

"What?" Mother came and stood beside me at the bedroom window.

It was early evening, just starting to get dark. Our house was situated on a hill with a clear view to the west towards the city center where clouds of red-tinged smoke poured into the sky. Several of the tall buildings downtown were ablaze.

"My God, look at that!"

"I wonder how they got started," I said.

"Who knows? One thing's for sure, they won't be able to put them out." She sighed.

After that night, we spent many autumn evenings watching the city burn.

Chapter 10

It was almost dark as Pam and I emerged from the alley. We were still a distance from home and were slinking in the shadows, keeping to back-alleys where there was more cover. Suddenly a group of dark figures loomed up in front of us, taking us by surprise. We had our spray cans in our hands and had the presence of mind to use them. After squirting pepper spray at their faces, we turned and ran. Followed by their angry yells and curses, we fled down the alley.

They recovered quickly and came tearing after us. Just as I thought we were going to get away, I tripped on the uneven pavement and fell. Before I could get up, they piled on top of me.

"Run, Pam, get help" I saw her fleeing form disappear round the corner at the end of the alley before my face was smashed into the ground.

"Get up, you bitch." I was yanked up by the hair. "Let's take a look at you."

I stood spitting dirt from my mouth while they shone a torch on me.

"Look at this." one of the said. "Fresh meat! "

The others snickered, filling me with terror. "You're not. . . *no*," I screamed, struggling to free myself.

They all laughed uproariously at this, holding their stomachs and slapping one another. I wondered if they were overacting for my benefit. Two of them still held onto me in a vise-like grip, however.

"She thinks we're going to eat her," one of the youths laughed. "No, darlin', we just want you to come with us and . . ."

I felt a hand on my breast then others started pawing my body. "Let me go," I sobbed. "What do you want? Take this stuff; you can have it if you let me go." I kicked the things I had dropped when I fell.

"We'll have them anyway," another voice said. "And you as well." He put his arm around my neck and pulled me towards him, forcing his mouth against mine. I struggled and tried to bite his lip then spat at him in disgust. A stinging blow on the face jerked my head backwards. "You can cut that out. You better be nice to us, or else we'll. . ."

"Come on, Blue, let's get out of here."

They dragged me on a brief journey through some more alleys to a large building that looked like an abandoned warehouse. It was quite dark by the time we arrived and there were no streetlights, so I couldn't see any details. They shoved me into the space behind a large trash container and moved aside a plywood panel against the wall of the building, then pushed me through the gap. They followed me in and replaced the panel. The interior of the warehouse was partly illuminated by a fire in the middle of the floor, which threw spectral shadows on the walls. There were piles of rubbish lying everywhere.

"What you got there?" A female voice drew my attention to two wraithlike figures sitting on what looked like piles of rags near the fire.

"Look at the sweet young thing we found. Watch out though, she bites and spits like a cat." He shoved me forward towards the fire.

I turned around and looked at my abductors. There were four of them, dressed all in black with moldy-looking leather jackets. Their heads were shaven. I wondered where they found razors to keep them like that. They all had pieces of metal poking through their ears and one even had what looked like a paper clip stuck through the side of his nose. I saw the two by the fire were dressed and adorned the same way and, with their short cropped hair, it would have been hard to tell whether they were male or female were it not for their voices.

"Sit down, you," the tallest boy ordered with another shove. "Tie 'er up while we have something to eat."

Two of the boys pressed me to the floor and tied my hands behind me then they tied my ankles together.

"Give us something to eat," the older boy said, dropping to the floor to sit cross-legged by the fire. "We'll keep her for desert," he added with a snicker.

"Hey, you know what? The stupid bitch thought we were going to eat her!" They all laughed. "Fresh meat!"

The others sat down beside him then the two girls picked up some mismatched bowls and served them something from a steaming pot on the fire. They ate their food noisily, slurping and belching. They didn't offer me any, but their table manners and the awful smell of the food would have put me off if they had. I was too scared to be hungry anyway. I looked around, hoping to see a way to escape.

When they had finished eating, they spent a moment picking their teeth with their dirty fingernails then the boys started drinking some foul smelling liquid and became increasingly rowdy and silly. The joking and laughter came to an abrupt end and I noticed their eyes were all fixed on me.

"Who's going to go first?" one of the boys nodded in my direction.

An icy bolt of fear shot through me. I could barely breathe. I tried to scoot backwards, away from them.

"Who do you think, dummy?" the biggest boy said. He looked about eighteen and had black stubble on his face and head. I saw his eyes glistening in the firelight. "Get her ready," he ordered the two girls.

"Come on," one girl said, grabbing my arm. "Get her other arm, Tiff."

I screamed.

Suddenly, there was a crash by the entrance and several shadowy figures rushed through the opening. It wasn't light enough to see who they were, but it was obvious they were armed.

A familiar voice called out, "Are you in there, Celeste?" It was my father.

"Daddy!"

The gang members cursed and tried to scramble away into the shadowy corners.

"Don't move, any of you. Stay where you are." That was Don's voice. "These guns are loaded and we don't need much provocation to use them."

They froze in place.

While the others held their guns on the punks, my father came over to where I was sitting near the fire. "Did they hurt you?" he asked, kneeling down to cut the bindings on my arms and ankles.

I couldn't answer, but when I started to sob, he may have taken that as confirmation that they had. He helped me to my feet and put his arm around me. "You're all right now. You're safe," he said gently, leading me towards the opening. "Wait here, I'll be right back."

I saw my father turn towards the others—Don Harris, Peter, Tony Purcello, Mr. Chan with his shotgun, and Marvin with the rifle. Don was holding his handgun and Tony and Peter were armed with metal bars. The four boys who had attacked me were cowering on the floor.

"We didn't mean no harm," one of them whined.

"We just wanted to have a bit of fun. We weren't going to hurt her."

"No! *Please . . .*"

A shot rang out and the dark boy—the gang leader—jerked and fell backwards, bloods seeping from a wound in his shoulder. As if the shot had released something in them, the others fell on the boys, kicking and clubbing them.

The two girls started screaming, as they cowered behind a pile of refuse.

"Let's finish them off" Don Harris pointed his gun at one of the boys.

The boys renewed their whimpering and tried to scuttle away, nursing their wounds. All but the one who had been shot. He hadn't moved.

"No!" I cried. I don't know why, but I just couldn't bear the idea of killing them in spite of the fear I'd felt.

"Leave them," my father added. "If we kill them, we'll be as bad as they are. They've learned their lesson." He angrily kicked one of the boys in the groin.

"If we ever see you again, we will kill you. On sight," Don kicked another boy in the head.

We walked away from the pathetic group. They didn't look so frightening now.

I shivered uncontrollably as we walked home, my teeth chattering noisily. My father took off his jacket and put it over my shoulders. He didn't say anything, just walked beside me with his arm round my shoulder. I knew I had had a very lucky escape. I couldn't bear to think about what would have happened if I hadn't been rescued when I was.

When I got home, Mom and Gran opened the door before we even got up the steps.

"Celeste, oh my little girl, thank God they found you," Mom sobbed, taking me in her arms. "Are you all right. Did they hurt you?"

She held me by the shoulders away from her and looked at me. The pain and concern in her eyes started me crying again.

"What did they do to you?" Mom asked sharply when she saw my tears.

"Nothing, Mom." I fell into her arms again, sobbing. "I was so scared, Mom. They tied me up..."

"It's all right, love. You're safe now."

"Maybe Celeste would like a hot bath, Kate," Gran suggested. "And something warm to drink."

I was grateful for her interruption. It gave me time to calm down a bit. I did feel dirty, defiled, and a bath was what I needed before anything else.

Later I heard how Pam had run home to tell my parents what had happened and how my father had called on the neighbors to help search for me. They found the warehouse by the flickering lights visible through windows high up near the roof. They'd been looking for a way into the building and had just discovered the hole behind the dumpster when they heard me scream.

Chapter 11

Our second Christmas after things started to fall apart was a joyless season with few treats. It was the first

Christmas without Paul as well, which made it doubly bleak for our family. As the new year started, Dad was still working on the *death squads* although the number of disease victims had diminished and fewer patrols went out. Now they were clearing up the corpses of people who had died of exposure and starvation, not to mention those killed in senseless violence.

One unusually cold January afternoon, Mother, Gran and I were huddled in sweaters and heavy socks around the wood stove in the kitchen. Gran had been laid off from her job because the city no longer had funds available to pay employees.

A pot of stew made from dried beans and a few root vegetables was simmering on top of the stove. We no longer had electricity. Mom was reading by the light of an oil lamp, Gran had some sewing and I was trying to do some schoolwork. Occasionally one of us glanced at the clock or the window.

"I wonder where your father is. He should be home by now," Mother remarked. "We'll wait another half hour and if he isn't here by then, we'll eat without him."

Finally, we ate our supper and spent the rest of the evening alternating between watching the clock and peering hopefully out of the front window, but Father didn't come home. I caught Gran looking at Mom a few times, as if she had something on her mind, but couldn't bring herself to say it.

"Maybe he's stayed over with someone from work," I suggested.

"It's not like him, Celeste." Mother couldn't sit still; she jumped up again and went to the front door to look down the street. She came back, bunching up her shoulders and rubbing her arms. "You go on to bed, love, I'll wait a bit longer."

I went to my room reluctantly and snuggled under a pile of blankets and quilts. I had that empty feeling you get when you know something awful has happened or is about to happen—as if your whole insides have emptied out to make room for the anguish and pain to come. I lay listening for a long time, hoping to hear the back door open and footsteps sound in the hall. When I went downstairs the next morning, Mother was curled up on the sofa, wrapped in a quilt, alone.

Neither Mother nor I felt like eating anything that morning. As soon as it was light, Mother put on her jacket and boots, preparing to go out.

"Where are you going, Kate?" Gran asked.

"I'm just going to look around. I can't sit around here doing nothing."

"Do you want me to come with you?" I asked.

"No, you stay here with Gran in case he turns up while I'm out."

Her reply didn't make much sense, but I didn't question it. I knew she wanted to be alone.

She returned about an hour later. I didn't have to ask whether she'd had any luck, her face told me all I needed to know. She suddenly looked shrunken and older, her eyes filled with despair. When she'd removed her outdoor clothing, she accepted a mug of tea from Gran and sat by the stove holding it with both hands.

I knew it was best not to say anything. Mother wasn't the sort of person who shared her emotions easily—a legacy from her English parents, probably. When she put the mug down, I reached out and took her hand, fighting back tears. Gran came and put her hands on our shoulders. We sat quietly for a few moments then mother stood up with a deep sigh.

"I have to find him," she said and began to put her boots on again.

She persuaded Don Harris and Peter to go with her to the department where father worked, but the only thing they could tell her was that his crew had failed to return the previous afternoon. They said they had lost several units over the past few months.

"What do you mean, lost?" Mother asked sharply.

"We think they might have been hijacked by criminal gangs after they were emptied. They take them for the fuel and parts."

"What happens to the crews? What's happened to my husband?"

"I'm sorry, I can't tell you that. We don't know for sure. Sometimes the crews are killed; sometimes they just disappear. I'm sorry."

My mother looked even more pale and defeated when she returned. All she got out of the trip was a couple of bags of food. Small consolation for the loss of a husband and father. She spent the rest of the day in her room and wouldn't come down for supper; Gran took her something on a tray.

The next morning, she brought the tray down with the food untouched. She laid it on the table then put her arms around me. "I'm sorry, love. You're hurting too, aren't you?" She held me tightly, pressing her mouth on my head.

My eyes filled with tears. "He may still come back, Mom" I replied. "Don't give up hope."

He didn't, of course. I missed him terribly. I cried myself to sleep many nights, remembering happier times before everything started to go wrong. Sometimes I would wake up with a start, my heart pounding, consumed by a feeling of dread.

Mother was withdrawn and lethargic for a long time after my father disappeared. She seemed to have become a grey shadow of her former self, never going out or participating in any of the household activities.

* * *

"Can you smell something burning?" Mother roused herself from her reverie.

I tested the air. "I smell smoke."

"Let's take a look."

She opened the front door and we went out onto the porch. The house on the corner was in flames. We heard a crash of broken glass followed by a shout then three shadowy figures ran from the house and disappeared into the darkness. Other neighbors came out onto the street. We joined them, forming a huddle in the middle of the road, and watched the house burn. Luckily, no one lived there. The house had been abandoned since the previous summer.

"It's getting closer," Don Harris said, putting his arm around Debbie's shoulder. "We're not safe in our own homes anymore."

"My God, Don, we've got to do something about this. We can't stay here . . .," Debbie cried in a panicky voice, pulling away from him. "What about Jason? It's not safe."

"Maybe it's time we thought of moving somewhere safer." Peter Hetherington said.

"Where would we go?" Debbie Harris looked from Don to Peter.

"One thing I do know, we should try to stay together. We all know one another and we'd be more secure as a group," Peter said.

We watched a while longer as the house burned and gradually collapsed in on itself. It was far enough from the next house that it didn't pose a danger of spreading. Firefighters were a distant memory by then, and even if they had been working, there was no way of calling them without telephones or I-Coms. And we couldn't rely on the sporadic water supply for fighting fires. When a building caught fire or was deliberately torched like this one, it was left to burn itself out. More and more fires were springing up every day. The night sky was often a lurid red from the blazing buildings. Our district had been relatively free of them until recently, but as Don pointed out, they were coming closer.

"Maybe we should have a meeting and talk about moving," Edward Chan suggested.

"I think that's good idea," Peter said.

"Just say where and when. We'll be there," Don Harris agreed.

"Why not come to our house tomorrow afternoon— say around one? That'll give us time to get finished before it gets dark," Mr. Chan adjusted his glasses, glancing at his wife for agreement. Mrs. Chan nodded.

"That's fine by me," Peter replied.

"We'll be there." Mother turned to me, holding out her hand. "Come on, Celeste, let's get back inside, it's too cold to stand around out here.

The group of neighbors slowly broke up and dispersed.

The next afternoon we and our neighbors straggled into the Chan's house. Mom and a couple of other people brought small bags of dry tea so that we could have a hot drink without depleting the Chans' meager rations. A fire blazed in the fireplace of their basement recreation room, which was the largest room in the house. We settled down, some of us sitting on the carpeted floor, others on chairs and sofas.

"Where's Tony?" Don Harris looked around.

"He said he'd be late. He's gone to try to find some flour," Mr. Chan was standing by the fireplace holding a kettle of water. "I think everybody's here. Emily's bringing down some mugs for the tea then we can get started." He bent down and suspended the kettle from a hook above the burning logs.

"Maybe we should move out of the city altogether," Don Harris suggested.

"How could we do that? We've got no way of transporting our belongings very far. We'd have to leave everything behind," Mr. Chan said. "Besides, look what happened before when people tried to leave."

"Ed's right. I'm sure we can find a safer place than this, not too far away," Peter combed his beard with his fingers.

"We'll be all right as long as we stay together and watch out for one another," Mother said.

"What we need to find is a place where it's not so open on all sides, somewhere we could defend."

"Like a fortress?"

"Maybe that's going a bit far, but . . . well, why not?"

"I suggest a few of us go and look around—see if we can find a suitable place where we can all live close together," Chris said.

"How about nearer the mountain? The mountain behind us might give us some protection then we'd only have to watch the front," Eric put in.

I still couldn't get used to seeing Eric in his new gold-rimmed glasses. He'd always worn contact lenses, but his mother had insisted on getting him glasses, saying that contacts weren't practical and were too easy to lose.

"Sounds like an idea," Peter replied.

"So who's going out to look for a place?"

"We could all go in small teams, not all at once. We could take turns. When somebody discovers a suitable place, the rest of us could look at it and decide."

"How are we going to move all our stuff?" I asked.

"Let's find a place first then worry about that. We'll find a way. Don't forget, Celeste," Peter winked. "Necessity is the mother of invention."

Several people groaned at his use of the old cliché.

"Another thing," Marvin said. "I think we should have somebody keeping lookout at night, so nobody comes and burns down our houses while we're asleep."

"I agree with Marv," Don Harris said. "Maybe we should take it in turns to stand guard—two hours at a time or something."

"Where was Greta? She should have warned us strangers were around." Peter commented.

"Sorry, she was sleeping under my bed," Mike looked a bit sheepish. "Well, it was too cold for her outside."

Greta perked up and wagged her tail, knowing we were discussing her.

"It's no use having a watch-dog if she doesn't watch," Mr. Chan sounded cross. "From now on, she must stay in her dog house at night. She's got an old rug to sleep on."

"I'm scared somebody might try to steal her," Mike replied.

"I'm sure she's big enough to take care of herself."

They discussed the idea of having night patrols for a while and made up a preliminary schedule for keeping watch. The men refused to allow any women on watch with the excuse that they were too vulnerable.

Chapter 12

It was a warm day in early spring with misty rain hanging in the air. Dressed in slickers and old rubber boots, the Chan brothers, Pam and I made our way over to the local branch of the public library. Making sure nobody was around; we started exploring the building, looking for a way in. It was a one-story structure with wood and brick siding and large windows facing the street. Apart from the glass entrance doors at the front, which were chained and padlocked on the inside, the only other door was an emergency exit at the side. The exit door was flat and featureless with no way to open it from the outside. We would have to find a way in to open it from the inside. Around the back, we saw what we were looking for: two small frosted glass windows set high up in the wall that must be the washrooms.

Eric Chan looked around and found a small rock on the ground. "Stand back!" he warned. He threw the rock at the window and broke the glass.

"How are we going to get in that?" Pam asked, "It's too high up."

"We are going to boost you up and you, my dear, are going to go in."

"Oh, no! I'm not going in there by myself."

"You're the only one who's small enough to get through the window," Eric sounded exasperated.

"What about me?" Mike offered. "I'm not scared."

"Okay! Come on, Celeste, give us a hand." Eric looked up at the window. "Wait a minute; you'll need something to clear away the broken glass."

Eric found another rock and gave it to Mike then he signaled me to crouch down beside him, so that Mike could stand on our shoulders. We slowly raised ourselves upright lifting Mike up to the level of the window. When he jabbed at the broken glass, we all wobbled and Mike lost his balance and fell down.

"Shit, this isn't going to work." Eric brushed mud off his jacket. "What we need is something firm to stand on. Let's look around and see what we can find."

We looked at the row of houses across the lane behind the library, glanced at one another, and took off across the weed-strewn yards. Even though the first house we approached had the blank look of abandonment, we were cautious.

"Let's try the garage, there might be a ladder," I suggested.

The wood was swollen from dampness and the garage door was hard to open, but we managed to push it open wide enough to squeeze through.

"God! What's that awful stink?" Pam covered her nose with her hand.

"Smells as if something died in here," Mike forced his breath out through pursed lips.

"Fuck! Look at that," said Eric, pointing to a pile of litter in the shadowy corner.

Once our eyes adjusted to the dim light, we could see the swollen carcass of a dead dog lying on a pile of rags.

"How could anyone be so cruel as to leave the poor thing locked in like that?" I commented.

"It probably came in through that hole," Eric replied, pointing to a gap in the corner. "It was probably starved and knew it was going to die."

"Let's get out of here. There's no ladder anyway," Pam said, backing away.

We thankfully pushed our way back out into the fresh air.

"Let's try the one next door."

After a short search, we found an old, paint-speckled stepladder and took it back to the library. This time it was easier for Mike to climb up and clear away the glass. He squeezed through the window and dropped from sight inside. We heard a loud crash followed by an outraged curse.

"You okay, Mike?" Eric looked up at the window.

"Landed in the fucking can," Mike replied. "I'm okay. I'm going to look at that door now."

We went back around the side of the building. There was a muffled clatter from inside, then the door opened. We entered the twilit interior, greeted by the familiar smell of dust and old paper. There was a bleak chill in the air inside the library. The main room received enough light from the clerestory windows for us to be able to see fairly well. Out of habit, we spoke to one another in hushed voices as we made our way through the rows of shelves. After picking out as many books as we could each carry and stowing them in the plastic garbage bags we'd brought along, we left by the emergency door and pushed it closed behind us. We left the ladder under a tool shed near one of the houses behind the library.

Mom and Peter came with us on our next trip to the library and helped pick out more books. Primarily, we were looking for anything about medicine and healing, especially what was then called alternative medicine; growing and preserving food; building and carpentry; and crafts such as sewing, knitting, pottery making, and weaving. We also picked up a couple of books about alternative power sources—how to make things like wind generators, using water power for running mills and generators, solar panels, and so on.

Early on, while the libraries were still operating, Mom and Dad had borrowed quite a few useful books. By the time they thought about returning them, the libraries were closed, so we still had them at home. We added a few volumes about history, chemistry, mathematics, physics and biology as well as art and music to Mom's small supply of textbooks. Mike and Eric were especially enthusiastic about the science books and offered to take charge of them.

Peter and Marvin went out one night and returned with some tools, which they said they had liberated from the ruins of an abandoned building supply store. In the following days they made several more such excursions bringing back an assortment of hardware and fittings as well as some lumber then they went to work building a couple of sturdy carts. The only problem with these vehicles was that we had no method of moving them apart from our own muscle power, and once they were loaded with our belongings, they were very heavy. Although our new home was only about three kilometers from the old one, it was up-hill most of the way.

Marvin, Peter and the Chan boys tinkered for days with various contraptions trying to improvise some kind of motor, but we ended up pulling and shoving the carts to the new home ourselves. Fortunately, they had thought to provide them with strong brakes so they didn't run back down the hill when we stopped to rest. It took us a good part of a day to take each load even though we had already taken a lot of things on our bicycle carriers. We all had bicycles, some of which had little carts on wheels attached to the backs.

The place chosen as our new home was a small townhouse complex on the edge of Burnaby Mountain. We had no idea why it had been abandoned, but the houses were not too badly damaged and it would be fairly easy to fortify.

The city had become very depressing by this time. Residential neighborhoods that had once been horticultural showplaces with beautifully maintained flowerbeds and neatly trimmed lawns had turned into a weed-filled, overgrown wilderness. It was only by constant watering and cultivation that people had been able to maintain their exotic shrubs and colorful flowerbeds. Many of the trees and shrubs had died and been replaced by wild native plants—fireweed, purple vetch, and goldenrod had taken the place of the marigolds, lobelias and petunias. The ubiquitous blackberry brambles were thriving everywhere, tangling themselves around fences and hedges, with vine maples and sumac shooting up in their midst. The houses had fared little better than their gardens. Most of them had broken windows, fallen roof tiles and faded paint—a general air of disrepair. Some houses even had grasses and vines growing on their roofs and out of chinks and crevices on their sides. Many of the abandoned homes had burned to the ground and the ruins were almost obliterated by tangles of vines and weeds.

From early spring to late autumn, the air was filled with the humming of insects and singing of birds, while the usual city sounds of motors, machinery and loud music were seldom heard. Dogs and cats seemed to have become almost extinct. They'd either been eaten, or had run wild, taking to the ravines and thickets to avoid being hunted and killed by hungry people. We guarded Greta as if she were a member of the family, and never let her run loose.

Chapter 13

Once we settled in our new home, we set about preparing a garden and fortifying the complex. Fortification meant stringing fishing line at knee and shoulder level between the trees on the hill above the houses and hanging clusters of empty tin cans to warn us if anyone tried to approach from that direction at night. We also dug a couple of traps across the hill— trenches covered with twigs, leaves and grass, with glass shards and broken bricks in the bottom. The idea was not to seriously hurt anyone, but to create enough pain and aggravation that any would-be attackers couldn't help crying out. The warning would give us sufficient time to prepare our defense—if the traps didn't discourage them.

Marvin, Don and Peter raised the height of the fencing all around the complex and put metal spikes along the top. Windows and doors facing the street were boarded up on the ground and second floors, leaving only the third floor windows for lookouts. Many windows faced onto an inner garden, so we still had enough light. We had accumulated more firearms and a small supply of ammunition by then, and were prepared to shoot anyone who persisted in attacking us. At least the men said they were, and I had already seen one instance of how they could react if one of us was in danger. There was always someone keeping watch at night.

We all contributed to the vegetable garden, digging, planting and weeding. During our foraging, we had accumulated a supply of seeds—we weren't sure whether they would germinate, but they were all we had. Shortage of water was another problem we faced. We carried most of our water from a small lake on a nearby golf course. At least it had been a golf course at one time, now it was wild and overgrown with brambles, bushes and long grass. It used to be the favorite summer home of enormous flocks of Canada geese and mallard ducks, but they had been nearly exterminated by hungry hunters.

It still rained occasionally, so we rigged up pipes from the roof gutters to collect the runoff in barrels. We also got into the habit every time we washed ourselves, or dishes and clothing, of carrying the water to the garden afterwards.

Summer and autumn passed relatively peacefully. We harvested our garden and preserved what we could for the coming winter. We foraged for wild edible plants and fruit, using one of the books from the library as a guide, looking for edible mushrooms, blackberries, wild ginger and other roots. We learned to roast chicory and dandelion roots to make a beverage resembling coffee, which we called root coffee. Occasionally we came across vegetables that had re-seeded themselves in abandoned gardens and obtained a few more carrots, potatoes and onions to supplement our own produce.

Whenever we had to leave the compound to forage or fetch water, we went in groups with at least one armed adult for protection.

Chapter 14

During the summer, I realized Mother and Peter were spending an unusual amount of time together, sometimes disappearing for several hours. Once in a while, I noticed she wasn't in her bed at night. This made me feel angry and resentful, and I started avoiding her, only speaking to her when absolutely necessary. It didn't take her long to pick up on my behavior.

"What's the matter, Celeste? You're always pouting these days and snapping my head off over nothing."

"Nothing," I replied sullenly.

"It has to be something. What's upsetting you? Is it something I've done?"

I shrugged and looked away, out of the window.

"Don't turn away from me, Celeste. There's only you, me and Gran left now and if we start to turn against one another . . . ." She tried to put an arm around me but I shrugged it off. "I love you, Celeste." Her voice became plaintive.

"What about Dad?" I glared at her. "He could still come back, you know."

"Is that what you're upset about? You miss your father? I miss him too, Celeste."

"You don't act like it," I retorted angrily.

"Is it Peter you're angry about, love? I'm sorry if it upsets you. What can I say? Your father's been gone for eight months. I'm sure he would have returned by now if he were still alive. I'm not too old to need companionship and Peter's a good man. You'll understand one day, Celeste."

I didn't dislike Peter, but I was resentful because I thought she was being disloyal to my father. I still expected he would turn up some day. I'd left a note at our old house to tell him where we'd gone in case he returned there. I refused to give up hope.

I suppose I was being selfish and hypocritical as well, but I was only fifteen and I did understand to a certain extent. I was more than a little attracted to Eric Chan and always seeking opportunities to be with him. I think he felt the same way about me because I would sometimes catch him gazing at me in a strange way. I couldn't imagine what he saw in me, I thought I was most unattractive with my straight brown hair and uninteresting blue eyes, and I was so skinny with hardly any signs of developing into a woman. I envied Lia her lovely dark curly hair and Pam's glossy black hair and dark eyes.

* * *

The city was burning. The fires spread rapidly, engulfing entire neighborhoods—months of hot dry weather left the wood-frame buildings tinder-dry. From our vantage point, we could see clouds of black smoke spreading from the south all the way across the west to the north. At night flames reflected on smoky orange haze that filled the sky. We felt we were witnessing the death throes of our once magnificent city and were finally forced to admit that our survival might be threatened if we remained there much longer.

While it was relatively peaceful in our small enclave, it was getting worse outside. We didn't know what was happening most of the time as there was rarely anything to be heard on our battery operated radio, but we could see the signs plainly enough. The fires came closer and closer to where we lived. It looked as if the whole city would be swallowed up in the conflagration. We realized it was time to move again.

"We can't go now, it's nearly winter," Debbie Harris objected. "We'll freeze to death."

"I'm not going anywhere," Mrs. Kumari folded her hands in her lap and looked resolute.

"Me neither," Gran added. "I'm too old to go trekking all over the place."

"Oh, Mother, you have to come. You're as fit as any of us, and you're not that old," my mother replied.

"Wouldn't we be safer on one of the islands?" Chris asked.

"How would we get there?" Peter replied, "And besides, don't you remember how the islanders reacted last time anyone tried to land there?"

"Look, let's keep to the topic, okay?" Edward Chan was all business, as usual.

"I think we should start getting ready to go right away before it gets too cold," Peter said.

"Surely we aren't just going to pack up our stuff and wander off into the countryside in the hopes of finding a place to live," Don Harris looked around at the others.

"Of course not. Some of us will have to go out and find a suitable place, then come back for the rest of you."

We were gathered in the Harris's living room, sipping root coffee and trying to come up with a plan. Eventually, they decided that Peter, Don, Marvin and Eric would take off on their bicycles the next day and scout for a new home. Each had a pack with enough supplies to last for several days and some camping gear. Don and Marvin also carried a rifle each for protection.

Debbie wept as she said good-bye to Don. She clung to Jason's hand as if she was afraid he'd disappear too. The poor kid looked as if he didn't know whether to cry or not as he glanced from his mother to his father.

Mother looked worried as they disappeared down the road. "It'll be all right, Mom, they'll be okay," I said, as much to reassure myself as anyone.

We spent the next few days waiting anxiously for sign of the men returning, going outside a dozen times a day to gaze hopefully down the street. Debbie came over three or four times a day for reassurance. In the afternoon of the fourth day when nobody was looking out, we heard an unusual clip-clopping noise outside. Pam and I dashed to a window and were amazed to see Peter and Marvin coming up the street on horses followed by Eric and Don on bicycles. They were back!

Everyone rushed outside to meet returning scouts.

"Where did you get the horses?"

"Did you find a place?"

"Thank God you made it."

"Where are your bikes?"

Peter and Marvin climbed down and tethered the horses to the fence where there was plenty of grass for them to munch on.

"Hey, give us chance to get inside." Don grinned and hugged his tearful wife. He took Jason's hand and the three of them went indoors.

"Let's go inside where it's warm and we'll tell you everything," Peter turned to me. "How about bringing some water for the horses, Celeste?"

I dashed off to fetch a bucket of water while the others helped the travelers bring their packs and the two remaining bicycles inside.

"Here, let me help you." Eric came up behind me and kissed the side of my neck.

"Oh, Eric, I was so scared something would happen to you." I put the bucket down and threw my arms around his neck.

"Well it didn't, but I'm glad you care," he said, kissing the end of my nose. "Come on; let's water these horses so we can go inside."

In the house, bowls of hot stew and warm drinks were passed around while the men told us about their trip.

"Did you find a place?" Edward Chan got right to the point.

"Oh yes. We left the freeway when we got to the river, and, instead of going over the bridge, continued eastward along the river bank," Peter went on with his narrative.

They had come to a smaller river that emptied into the Fraser from the north and followed it upstream. Avoiding any places with smoke coming from the houses, they eventually reached an abandoned village on the riverbank. It was only about a dozen or so houses with a small wooden church. The four men spent the night there and searched the area the next day. It seemed ideal to them. It was isolated and there was some cleared ground for planting a garden. It was protected by rocky outcroppings of the mountains to the north. There was plenty of bush nearby for hunting, and the river for fishing. The bonus was finding the two horses grazing near the village although there was no sign that anyone lived there. They must have been let loose from a stable behind one of the houses because the men found bridles and saddles there.

The horses were to make our journey to the new home so much easier. The carts Peter and Marvin had made were extended and fitted with shafts so that the horses could pull them using contraptions of ropes and straps to attach them to their harnesses.

One morning a few days before we were due to leave, Pam knocked on our door and came in, her eyes red from crying.

"Pam, what's the matter?" I asked.

"It's my grandmother." Tears filled her eyes again. "She absolutely refuses to go, so Dad says we'll have to stay here with her."

"What choice does he have?" Mom asked. "She's his mother; he can't just abandon her."

"I want to go with you. I was looking forward to it. I don't want to stay here." She slumped down in a chair with a sob and covered her face with her hands.

"Mom, it's not fair." I said. "Why can't she come with us? Couldn't you ask Mr. Kumari? She'd be okay with us; we could look after her. Please, Mom."

"It's none of our business, Celeste."

"But, Mom, it's not fair. Besides, how can they live here all alone? "

"Do you know what your father plans to do after we leave?" Mother asked Pam.

"He says he'll try to find an Indian community and take us there to live." She sniffed and wiped her nose. "I don't want to live with strangers; I want to stay with my friends."

"You realize that if you did come with us, you might never see them again," Mother reminded her.

"I just wish my stupid grandmother wouldn't be so stubborn. Why can't she just come with us?"

"That's not entirely fair, Pam. She's already left her native country and come thousands of miles to live here among strangers. You can't blame her for wanting to be near her own people. She must be lonely."

"I know, but why should I have to give up my life just because she's lonely?"

"I'll go and talk to your father. I don't promise anything, but I'll see what he says. You stay here with Celeste."

"Oh, Mom, will you? That's great." Pam and I hugged each other, sure that Mother would be able to persuade him.

Mother put on a sweater and went next door to talk to the Kumaris. About forty-five minutes later, she came back looking upset.

"What did he say, Mom?"

"She can go with us if that's what she really wants." Mother sighed. "Your father is not happy about this, Pam. The only reason he's letting you go is that he feels you may have a better chance of survival away from the city."

Pam's face had lit up with happiness when Mother started talking but, by the time she had finished, my friend didn't look quite so pleased. It was hard for her to leave her family, but her father said he'd try to come out and see us when things settled down a bit and it was safer to travel.

Chapter 15

On the original journey, the scouting party had gone south, around the hills behind our home into the industrial district of Coquitlam, before turning east into the rural area of the Fraser Valley. On their way back, they'd come by the shorter route around the north side of the hills along the edge of the Burrard Inlet that projects about twenty kilometers inland from the coast. As they didn't encounter any danger on the way back, we decided to go the shorter way to the new home.

We set out early on a chilly but clear day at the beginning of November, a motley caravan of bicycles and two horse-drawn carts, winding down the residential streets to the highway out of town. The party consisted of five men: Peter, Marvin, Tony Purcello, Don Harris, and Edward Chan; six women: Debbie, Mother, Gran, Emily Chan and Chris; six teenagers: Eric and Mike Chan, Pam, Jackie, Lia and me; and two children: Jason Harris and Tate. Nineteen people altogether.

We managed to reach the small town of Port Moody at the head of the inlet by dusk and set about finding a place to spend the night. The town seemed to be sparsely populated and, although we caught sight of several men with rifles at various points, no one bothered us. We found a sheltered spot in a former park to make camp for the night and unloaded our camping and cooking equipment. The kids were sent to gather firewood around the nearby trees and soon a fire was lighted to heat some food. After unhitching the horses and giving them some water, Marvin tethered them to a nearby tree to graze then joined us at the fire.

"This is like the old pioneers," Chris said.

"Yes. Except instead of going west, we're going back east." Don replied.

"And they only had to face hostile Indians. Everybody we meet could be dangerous," Debbie added. "I still don't think this is such a good idea." She added automatically.

"Are we going to be cowboys?" Jason asked.

"I don't know, son," Don brushed his hand over Jason's head, then plucked a grass stem and stuck it between his teeth. "It certainly looks as if we're going to be farmers. For a while, at least."

Eric signaled across the fire with his eyes and stood up. I got up and stretched, then went around to join him. As we started to walk away, his father said, "Don't go too far away."

"We're just taking Greta for a walk." We unhooked her chain from the side of the wagon and strolled hand in hand down to the shore. While Greta romped and did her business, we sat down on a log and watched the moonlight reflected in the water of the inlet. Everything had gone well that day and the night was so peaceful, it would have been easy to believe the worst troubles were over.

Then Greta started to bark and tug at her chain. When we let her go, she ran back towards the wagons. We got up and followed her apprehensively.

Two men with rifles stood near the campfire. One of them said, "I hope you aren't planning to settle here."

"We're just passing through on our way east," explained Peter. "We're only stopping the night; we'll be on our way tomorrow."

"That's good," replied the man. "We just want to make sure there's no problems. I see you've got kids with you, so I don't expect you're looking for trouble."

"I understand," Peter replied.

"By the way, I don't suppose you've got anything to trade have you?"

"What sort of things?" Don asked.

"You know, salt, tools, things like that."

"What are you offering in trade?" Mother stood up and joined the group.

"We've got some surplus smoked salmon, apples, a few vegetables, and stuff like that."

"We haven't got any salt, but maybe you could use some sewing needles." I was surprised to hear her lie, but we had to be careful not to let go of anything we might need later. Besides, the men did have guns and could have easily taken what we refused to let them have by barter.

"I don't know, what do you think, Al?" The two strangers conferred for a few minutes and came back

"Okay. We can always use them to trade. Anything else?"

"I guess we could spare a couple of pairs of scissors, too, and some buttons."

"What do you want to trade for?"

"I don't suppose you've got any honey?"

"No, but I heard you can get some farther up the valley."

"Oh well. The smoked salmon sounds good."

It was a new image of my mother. *The trader!* I was proud that the others trusted her to do the bargaining, but then, she was the one who kept the inventory, so she knew what we had to spare. We ended up getting a shoebox-sized package of smoked salmon and a jar of preserves for the needlework equipment. Not a bad bargain on the whole—something of lasting value for something with immediate survival value.

After the men left, we unrolled our sleeping bags and settled down to sleep. Next morning we were awake at sunrise. It was another cloudless day although the air was decidedly nippy, making it a little difficult to get out of our warm sleeping bags. A hot beverage and some fried potatoes flavored with flakes of smoked salmon for breakfast soon warmed us up then we were eager to get moving again. We hoped to be able to reach our destination before nightfall.

Because of the topography of the area—we had to go around another mountain spur—the next leg of the journey took us through Coquitlam. This made us nervous because it was a semi-industrial zone mixed with low-grade residential housing—just the kind of place where gangs might lurk.

The men loaded the firearms and concealed them on the wagons within easy reach. Don tucked his handgun in his belt under his jacket. We rode our bicycles close together with the children and younger females on the inside, glancing nervously about as we went. Occasionally, we saw smoke coming from a building in the distance, but the only people we met were two couples on bicycles who waved to us as we passed.

Around noon, we left the buildings behind and came to the river flowing from the north. We were now in open country. Almost. When we crossed the bridge over the river, there were fields on both sides of the road, but in the distance, we could still see signs of the subdivisions and shopping centers that had been eating up the farmland for the past fifty years or so. Along the highway were abandoned fast food outlets, empty car lots, and defunct garden centers. About half a mile past the bridge, we turned left onto a side road going north towards the mountains. The road was narrow and filled with potholes sprouting weeds and small bushes. Vegetation was encroaching on both sides of the road too, narrowing it into a single lane track. It was easy to see how it could disappear altogether in a few years.

Once off the highway, we stopped to rest and have some lunch. Clouds were gathering in the west and it looked as if the weather was about to change. As long as it didn't rain, it could be a change for the better. At that time of year, it was usually colder on clear days than when it was cloudy.

Marvin disappeared with a bucket down a path through the bush towards the river and returned with water for the horses. After lunch, we hastily packed up to resume our journey.

"Not far now," Peter informed us. "Just another three or four kilometers."

Mom helped Gran to her feet. "How are you making out, Mother?"

"I'll probably never walk again after this," Gran, who was the oldest member of our group, limped over to pick up her bicycle. "I'm using muscles I didn't even know I had."

"Would you like to ride on one of the carts?" Peter asked, "We can move a few things and make a space for you to sit."

"That would be wonderful if it wouldn't be too much for the horses."

"I don't think it would make that much difference. We'll be there shortly then they can rest."

We put on a spurt of speed for the last leg of the journey bolstered by anticipation and a desire to have it finished. We passed a few abandoned houses, some little more than shacks, with no signs of life. We really were off the beaten track, and I could see why the scouting party had thought this would be a safe place to set up a new home. As we came around the final bend in the road, Don Harris, who had been in the lead, stopped his bicycle and signaled for the rest of us to stop.

"Uh oh! Seems we have company."

Part Two - The Country

Chapter 16

It looks as if the place wasn't abandoned after all," Peter said. We could see smoke rising from the chimney of one of a small cluster of wood-frame houses up ahead. "Wait here, we don't want to frighten them with a lot of people. Two of us can go and find out who they are, and how many; the rest of you can wait here."

"I'll go with you," offered Tony Purcello. It was a good offer—nobody could look less threatening than Tony who was about five feet nine inches with warm brown eyes and a good-natured smile.

"All right, but we'll take one of the rifles, just in case." Peter leaned his bicycle against a tree and hung the sling of the rifle over his shoulder. "It would be better if we went on foot."

"Can I come, Poppa?" Lia begged.

"No. You wait here with the others," Tony replied. "Don't worry, we won't be long."

We watched anxiously as they went down the road and disappeared from sight near the house with the smoking chimney. The silence was broken by nothing more alarming than the occasional snorting of the horses, and the creaking of the carts as they moved restlessly. There were no gunshots, no shouts, but Peter and Tony seemed to be gone for what like hours. We waited on the grass by the road, fidgeting with our packs and gazing towards the village.

Finally they appeared again accompanied by another, smaller figure. As they came closer, we saw that it was an old man who wore his long grey hair in braids. He was shorter than Tony and wore a jacket that looked as if it was made of animal skins. His high leather boots had thongs wound around them. We moved to meet them as they approached.

"This is Joshua Henry," Peter said. "He lives in the house down there."

Joshua Henry was a native. He quietly looked us over and nodded his head then he turned to the horses and stroked their foreheads.

"Okay!" he said in his quiet, husky voice.

Peter let out a long breath as if he had been holding it until he got an answer. "Mr. Henry says it's all right for us to live here. He's the only person left in the village now."

Several more deep breaths were expelled and some of us cheered, then we thanked the old man.

"How come we didn't see you when we came here before?" Eric asked.

"I was away working on my trap lines," he replied. "I just got back yesterday. I knew somebody had been poking around, and the horses were gone."

"Are they your horses?" Mother asked.

"They belonged to my nephew. He's gone now so I watch out for them."

"We're sorry," Peter said. "We wouldn't have taken them if we'd known you still lived here. We thought they'd been abandoned."

"They wouldn't stay around long if they was abandoned," Mr. Henry replied. "You can use them if you like, long as you help take care of them."

"Is it all right if we start to . . . you know . . . get settled?" Debbie asked anxiously. "It looks like it's going to rain and . . . you know"

"Help yourselves," he replied.

"Can we look at the houses and find which ones we can use?"

"Sure. Nobody else needs them."

"What's the name of this place?" Mother asked, as we walked down the road.

Joshua uttered a multi-syllabic Indian name which he translated for us as *Little Home by the River of the Salish.*

"Do you mind if we call it *Salish* then?" Salish was the only part of the name we knew. It was the name of a First Nations tribe that had inhabited the whole coastal area before Europeans came and took over.

Joshua shrugged. "Up to you," he replied.

We trooped into the village where Marvin and Eric unhitched the horses and let them loose in the field by the river. There were about fifteen houses, built on two intersecting streets with the church at the center. After we parked our bicycles, we scattered around the village, opening doors and searching houses, most of which were so dilapidated and dirty that they weren't fit to live in, although there were three that looked promising. They would need some cleaning up and repairs to make them livable, but each would accommodate a small family.

There was one other building in addition to the houses and church, a combination general store and gas station. At least it had been—it too was abandoned and empty. The screen door was hanging from its hinges, and the lock on the entrance was broken. While the grownups were examining the houses, we poked around the gloomy interior to see if anything useful had been left behind by the former owners. On one of the dusty shelves, we found a box containing some Christmas cards and calendars from 2015, a card of disposable lighters, and several piles of old magazines and newspapers. The boys discovered some cans of paraffin in the back room—the only really useful items apart from the lighters. Next to the store was a garage where a mechanic had probably worked at one time. Two fuel pumps stood in front of its wide door. We couldn't get the garage doors open, but when we peered through the dusty windows, it didn't seem to contain anything interesting. We left it to be checked another time and joined the others who had gathered at the church.

The main room of the church, a large meeting room, was empty. There were two smaller rooms at the back, one of which appeared to be a storeroom and the other a kitchen. There were also two toilets beside the kitchen.

The meeting room was big and drafty, but it had a big wood-burning stove halfway down one side.

"What do you think, Marv?" Peter asked. "We should be able to fix this up easily enough."

Marvin scanned the room carefully. "Looks to be in good shape, just needs a bit of insulation."

"Do you think we could build partitions to make some smaller rooms down the side? Peter asked.

Marvin nodded gloomily. "And maybe we could find something to put over the windows to keep the weather out."

"It would make a good place to have our meals and use as a sort of social center." Mother commented.

"Some of us will have to live here as well," Peter added. There isn't room for everyone in the houses. I think we ought to let the families have the houses and the rest of us live in the church for the time being."

"We'll all have to stay here tonight at least, until we get the houses cleaned up."

Before we started unloading the carts, we swept out the meeting room. The two younger boys were dispatched to gather firewood for the stove while Marvin checked to see that the stovepipes were connected properly and vented safely outside the building. The rest of us unpacked the carts and brought the supplies inside where we piled them neatly against a wall along with our packs.

By the time it was dark, we had a fire going in the stove. Mr. Henry had returned while we were getting settled with the gift of a leg of venison. This was cut up with some potatoes and onions and put in a pot to simmer on top of the stove. We brought in several pails of water from the river for our washing and drinking. It seemed unlikely that the water would be contaminated this far upstream—as far as we knew, there were no settlements farther up, nevertheless, we took the precaution of boiling it before drinking any, just as we always did in the city.

We spread out our bedrolls in groups around the room. Pam and I had put ours close to Mike and Eric at first, but Gran saw what we were up to.

"Come over here by me," she said, "You too, Pam."

Pam and I rolled our eyes at each other, shrugged, and moved the bedrolls to the place Gran had indicated. I saw Eric and Mike grin at each other.

We were all so exhausted that we could barely finish eating before we rolled into our sleeping bags and fell asleep. Sometime during the night, someone must have got up to put more wood on the fire because it was still alight next morning. We awoke to the sound of rain pattering on the aluminum roof of the church—the fulfillment of yesterday's threats. At least it wasn't as cold as it had been the previous day.

We no longer ate the same kind of food as we had before the disasters. For one thing, we couldn't get many of the foodstuffs we used to buy such as flour, sugar and cereals, so we couldn't have bread or pancakes or things like that. We had no poultry to supply eggs. One meal was pretty much the same as another now, whatever was in the pot from the night before was served for breakfast. If there was nothing left over from the previous day, we baked some potatoes in the coals of the fire and ate them with some dripping. Every time we cooked meat, we drained off the melted fat and saved it to use as a substitute for butter or margarine, and to make soap.

After we had eaten and had a perfunctory wash in one of the back rooms, we sat down to have a conference about the best way to proceed. Luckily, the church had some toilets that drained into a septic tank that were still functioning, although we still had to pour in water from a pail to flush them. We wouldn't be able to do much outside until the rain stopped, so the three families that had been allotted the houses went to clean and prepare them for moving in.

The Chans had one house, the Harris's another and our family with Gran and Pam had the third. Tate was going to live with the Harris's because he and Jason were about the same age and had become friends. Peter was to live with us. I was used to the idea of his relationship with my mother by then, and Gran seemed to approve, so who was I to object? Two of the useable houses were small with only a couple of bedrooms each, the third was a bit bigger—it had three bedrooms—so our family, being the largest, was allotted that one.

We drew brooms and tools from our supplies and went over to the house. The furnishings left by the previous owners were covered in mildew and rodent droppings, so the first thing we did was move them outside. We threw out an old sofa and an armchair, several damp smelly mattresses, and an assortment of moldy rugs, draperies and bedding. The kitchen was a terrible mess. Water that had come in through a broken window had seeped under the old linoleum making it buckle, and the floor underneath was rotted. The ancient electric stove was encrusted with spilled, burnt food and grease. It was useless to us anyway without power, as were the washer and dryer on the back porch, so out it went.

"I wonder if this is worth all the work we're going to have to do," mother said, leaning her back against the sink and brushing her hair off her face with the back of her hand. "Maybe it would be better to start from scratch and build a new house."

"It's too late to start building this year," Peter replied. "We'll have to make the best of it until we can get something better. I know it's discouraging, Katie, but it's better than nothing."

We kept at it all day except for a lunch break, gradually stripping away everything to the bare wood of the walls and floors. This meant taking up old linoleum and peeling off mildewed wallpaper. After all the debris was cleared out, we called it a day and returned to the church for supper.

Chapter 17

There were changes in the church when we returned. Someone had found a long table and brought it in, along with several benches. These were set up near the stove. While we sat around the table eating our supper, we talked about our progress and the problems we were encountering.

"I wish we had some *Lysol* or something to clean with," Debbie complained, "That place is so filthy, it's disgusting."

"I know what you mean," replied Gran. "It seems as if you'll never get it clean."

"Hey, guess what I found!" Mike interrupted.

We all looked at him expectantly. "Well...?" his father said.

"Another stove like that one," he nodded towards the wood-stove, "Only smaller."

"Where?"

"In one of the other houses. Lia and I were sort of poking around to see if we could find anything useful." He glanced at Lia and then looked down at his plate.

"You be careful poking around in those old houses, you might get hurt," Emily Chan scolded her son.

"Oh, Mom..."

"That'll be useful, Mike. You'll have to show us where it is in the morning, and we'll see if we can move it to one of the houses," Peter said. "Maybe we should search all the houses—carefully, of course," he added, glancing towards Emily, "See if we can find any more."

We slept in the church again that night and resumed our labors the following day. The rain was still falling in the morning, but it cleared up by lunchtime, leaving everywhere muddy and sodden. It took us three days to get our house in some sort of order and make it almost fit to live in. Luckily for us, there was a fireplace in the living room and once we had a fire going for a couple of days and replaced the broken window in the kitchen, the house dried out a bit and didn't seem quite so bad.

We decided to continue cooking and eating communally in the church. The families would use the houses for sleeping and when they felt the need for privacy. Marvin, with the help of Peter and Chris, had constructed several cubicles along one side of the meeting hall to accommodate those who didn't have houses. He found some lumber in the church basement, and had salvaged the rest from some of the unusable houses. Chris and Tony had paired up and shared one of the little rooms in the church. Lia and Jackie had another and Marvin slept in the third with his cat, Miranda.

I felt a bit sorry for Marvin because he was all alone. His son, weird Albert, had left one day while we were at the second home, much to the relief of the younger women. We didn't know him very well before the disaster so I have no idea whether Marvin had any other family and he never said much about himself. He was

120

quite taciturn, only talking when necessary, and seemed to enjoy his own company and be quite content to work by himself. Gran was the only other grownup without a partner and sometimes she and Marvin went for walks or sat together, exchanging a few words. Gran's personality was such a contrast to Marvin's. Whereas he was quiet and almost dour, Gran was usually cheerful and talkative. She was small, slender and energetic like Mom.

The basement of the church yielded some other goodies including storm windows for the main windows. There was also some furniture, mostly wooden tables and chairs and a few padded floor mats, which may have been used in the past for exercise classes or a day care center. These floor mats made good mattresses and were a very useful addition to our sparse supply of bedding.

While the rest of us were busy preparing our accommodation for the winter, Eric and his father, together with Don Harris and Tony, took the carts back to our old home in the city to fetch the rest of our belongings. When they returned four days later, they had another surprise for us. They'd bought two puppies from a half-starved boy they'd met beside the road. It was hard to tell what breed they were—certainly a mix— but they seemed to be about eight to ten weeks old and, although they were scrawny and undernourished, looked as if they were going to grow into large dogs. Greta began to fuss over the new puppies, sniffing them and uttering little barks. She licked each of them a few times and adopted them as her own.

When the puppies attached themselves to Jason and Tate and began to follow them everywhere, the two boys took it upon themselves to choose names for them. They decided on *Coke* and *Pepsi*—the names of two popular soft drinks that were no longer available. Although the boys probably didn't remember the drinks, they had seen the names on enough signs to be familiar with them. Jason and Tate were given the responsibility of cleaning up after the puppies if they made a mess indoors.

The grownups realized that the reality of our lives had changed so much that it was now necessary for everyone to learn how to use firearms. Of course, Debbie objected to having Jason take part, but gave in reluctantly when Peter explained that more people were harmed by not knowing how to handle firearms than by being deliberately shot. We didn't have enough ammunition to waste on target practice, but we all went through drills to learn how to clean, load, handle, and aim them properly, then we each got two cartridges to practice on targets. Some of us were more successful than others.

Joshua took the men into the bush with him occasionally to hunt for deer. He also showed us the best places to fish in the river and different methods of catching fish including netting and trapping. That part of the river was a great source of *steelhead,* a succulent kind of large trout, and in the late summer it virtually churned with salmon returning to their spawning ground farther upstream.

As the weather got colder, we were able to keep meat for several days by hanging it from the roof beams in an unheated part of the building where it would keep reasonably cold, if not freeze.

Early in December, just as we were settling in and becoming accustomed to our new quarters, there was a light snowfall. It had rarely snowed in the city and when it did, the snow melted as fast as it fell, but Salish was farther from the ocean and at a higher elevation, so we could now expect to see a lot more snow.

Both Peter and Eric were mechanically inclined and were always tinkering with machinery and mechanical devices they found. They were excited about an old generator they had discovered in the church basement and spent hours taking it apart, cleaning and reassembling it with the hope of being able to convert it to wind or water power as soon as the weather warmed up enough to work out of doors.

On the whole, we were happy that winter. We felt safer than we had in the past couple of years, and looked forward to a better life once we could start to grow our own food. There was naturally some friction from being cooped up together without much privacy and with very little to do. It was hardest on the ones who lived in the church. In spite of efforts to provide private spaces for everyone, they were never really alone unless they went out. We fortunate ones who had houses invited someone from the church to visit us occasionally.

Marvin and Tony looked at the rejected houses to see whether any of them could be renovated, but concluded that it would be no use trying until the weather became warmer.

We gathered in the church most evenings. Sometimes we would play games—we had a good supply of card and board games such as *Trivial Pursuit* and *Monopoly*. Other times we played hilarious games of charades or had sing-alongs accompanied by Peter on his guitar. We developed a wonderful feeling of warmth and community on those evenings together, with the dogs lying by the stove and Marvin's cat perched on top of a pile of boxes by the wall, eyeing everyone with regal disdain.

Chapter 18

In January, Mother announced that all the young people would have to start studying again.

"Ah, do we have to?" Tate protested.

"Don't think because there's no school life is going to be one long holiday," We had slacked off since we moved to Salish, being too busy with other things. "You need all the knowledge you can get, now more than ever before. Your survival might depend on what you know."

"I agree with Kate," Debbie said.

"Yes. You can't neglect your education," Mr. Chan added.

Emily Chan nodded in agreement while Lia, Jason, and Jackie made sour faces.

"But we haven't got any books to write in," Lia protested without much conviction.

"That doesn't matter, I'm sure we can manage. We've got some scrap paper and we can use boards to write on. We've got plenty of books to learn from. A couple of hours a day won't hurt any of you," Mother continued. "And it's not only the academic things you'll have to learn, you'll need practical skills if you're going to be any good in the new world. Things like carpentry, agriculture, nutrition, sewing and cooking."

"I hope us boys don't have to learn girls' stuff—sewing and cooking," Tate complained.

"Why not? What makes you so special? It won't hurt you. The more you know, the better off you'll be. So starting tomorrow after lunch, I want all of you here ready to get started with your lessons. Eric is going to help me with your instruction. Apart from the classroom, you can arrange with any grownup to learn whatever skills he or she has to teach."

The next afternoon, we assembled in the church to start school. Eric took the two younger boys, Tate and Jason, to one end of the table and started assessing their writing skills and knowledge of math. The rest of us gathered at the other end and received assignments from mother. She had decided to allocate one day a week to each subject: science, history, geography, mathematics, language and arts. We were given a passage to read and the following day, we discussed how well we understood it and what we had learned from it, then we did some written exercises. Eric, who had reached the highest grade level of any of the young people before the schools closed, helped us with math and science.

By helping Marvin, some of us learned some carpentry skills, Gran showed anyone who was interested how to knit and crochet, and Chris taught first aid and some health-care basics. We learned about cooking by helping prepare meals for the community; that was compulsory. Tate was learning to play the guitar with Peter.

Joshua Henry proved to be of enormous help to us, even though he tended to be reclusive. He taught us how to find edible plants and set traps for animals in the bush. At first the younger people were reluctant use this form of hunting because we thought it too cruel, but to our surprise, Joshua showed us several kinds of traps that were relatively humane. One was a kind of cage with bait inside to entice the animal in and a trip wire to close the lid once it was inside. We also learned the traditional native methods of smoking fish and game to preserve them.

We spent a good deal of time out of doors that winter, gathering firewood, scavenging, and just having fun in the snow, whenever it stayed on the ground.

Winter passed with no major mishaps and we managed to remain fairly healthy although we were a little emaciated. Debbie and Don, who had both been on the heavy side at one time, had changed the most. They were hardly recognizable as their former selves, but while Debbie looked quite svelte and much younger, Don became rather haggard and his skin seemed to hang in folds, aging him. Marvin was a lot thinner too, especially around the waist.

* * *

By March, our food stocks were almost depleted and we knew we had to do some serious hunting or scavenging if we were to survive until we could harvest our garden. This was where Joshua's knowledge was most useful. He showed us how to find and dig up the tubers of bitterroot—which we could skin and cook as a substitute for potatoes—wild onions, and fiddlehead greens from newly sprouting ferns.

A couple of grownups went out on horseback every day searching for overlooked caches of vegetables, or stray farm animals, but apart from a cache of potatoes and turnips in a root cellar, the only food they found was a few jars of preserves. We did obtain more seeds for our garden. We had been forced to do without flour for the past two years, so the potato, which is very versatile and easy to grow, had become our carbohydrate staple. We even made sweet rolls flavored with fruit, and a sort of bread from potatoes.

Everyone had to share in the hard work of turning the soil in preparation for spring planting. Marvin and Peter tried to make a plough from a pickaxe, but it snapped off in the hard ground when the horse started pulling it. They eventually succeeded in fashioning a crude plough from a piece of iron and some hardwood. Even with the horse drawn plough, it was still hard work turning the hard-packed soil filled with stones and old roots.

The rest of us followed after the plough with hoes and rakes to break up the clods of earth and remove tough roots and stones. We started in March while the soil was still wet and easier to work and, bit by bit, we transformed a weedy plot of land into prepared beds for planting vegetables.

Marvin built a cold frame with glass window-panes from derelict houses for growing seedlings and when it came time to set the seedlings out in the garden, he demonstrated how to pour a solution of water and soot into each hole to protect the tender roots from bugs.

Chapter 17

I put down the hoe I had been using on the garden and went over to listen to the men who were standing nearby discussing irrigation.

After the first seeds had been planted, the weather warmed up and the soil began to dry out quickly. If it didn't rain, our crops would not survive. Carrying water from the creek seemed like too troublesome a way of keeping the garden watered, so we had to come up with some other means of irrigation.

"See how the ground rises up there where the creek curves around." Peter pointed towards the rise above the garden. "If we could cut a channel through the bank there, we could get the water to flow down towards the garden."

"But that would only flood the garden," Don pointed out.

"No, wait. We could build a holding tank with a sluice gate so that we could release water to the garden slowly when it needs watering," Marvin suggested.

"That's a great idea," Peter replied. "We'll also need a way to spread the water around the garden so that some parts don't get drowned while others stay dry."

"I've got an idea," Eric put in. "We could dig little channels around each bed so that when the water starts to flow, it would run into them and spread all round."

"That should do it, Eric," Peter said, "How about you organizing that part?"

Eric smiled with pleasure, looking over at me. I realized then that he'd become one of the men. He was eighteen.

"Think it would be very hard to build a holding tank?" Peter asked.

"Well, the digging will be hard work, but once that's done, we can line it with boards so that the soil doesn't collapse into the water." Marvin scratched his head and thought for a moment, "We'd have to put a cover over it to keep out the animals, too."

"Sounds like a good project to keep us busy for a while," Don commented.

"If we have a tank filled with water, what's the chance of piping some of it into the church?" Mr. Chan asked.

"We could give it a try as long as we can locate some piping," Peter replied as the men started to drift off up the bank.

We spent the next two months digging trenches and tearing apart the old houses for boards to line the water storage tank. The most difficult parts were excavating a hole for the tank, and breaking through the rocky bank of the creek, but they managed it with a couple of pickaxes. It took several days for Marvin and the others to come up with a workable sluice gate. They were still unsure know how it would work once the water was in the tank. Luckily, they hadn't completely broken through to the creek yet.

Once everything was ready, a narrow channel was made from the creek, and the water flowed down the trench into the tank. We all stood around the tank watching as it gradually filled. The sides of the tank were raised above the ground to a level a little higher than that of the creek to prevent the water overflowing the sides, although there was no way to prevent some of it seeping through the cracks between the boards.

The next thing we had to do was dig up the yards around the houses and find pipes to bring the water down to the church. Before long, we had a gravity-fed water supply in the church and installed a couple of makeshift showers. It was such a relief not to have to carry every drop of water we used from the creek. Even though there was no hot water, it was still a vast improvement.

Planting and irrigation were only the first steps in the constant battle to grow food. As soon as everything was starting to flourish, we had to protect the tender plants from pests. The biggest threats came from wild animals—deer and rabbits. It wasn't possible to erect a fence around the entire lot, we didn't have enough materials, but the dogs took care of scaring away foraging animals before they could do much damage. We realized that we would inevitably have to share some of our bounty with insects, but we took what steps we could to minimize the amount of damage they did. Jason and Tate were given the job of going down the rows of plants, picking off caterpillars and grubs. They put them in small plastic pails and dumped them in the river.

Joshua and the other men disappeared from time to time, often returning with a few rabbits and the odd raccoon, and occasionally a deer.

* * *

I came downstairs one morning and heard someone retching in the bathroom. I waited for the bathroom door to open. When it did, mother came out, looking very pale. She pushed her damp hair back from her face, walked over to a chair and slumped on it.

"Mom, what's the matter? Are you sick?" I asked, barely able to conceal how scared I was.

"Come on, Celeste, let's go outside. I have to tell you something."

She stood up, put her arm around my shoulder, and took me out into the yard. The air was already sweltering, even that early in the morning. We walked over to a bench someone had set under a tree and sat down.

"I'm all right," she said. "I'm going to have a baby."

"No!" I cried, jumping up. "You can't."

"Celeste." She tried to take my hand, but I pulled away. "What's wrong? Why are you so angry?"

"It's disgusting. Besides, you're too old. You're not even married," I added as the clincher. "What will the others think?" I cringe now when I think about my irrational reaction that day.

"Honey, calm down. You know that Peter and I are as good as married, and you also know that marriage is not a prerequisite for becoming pregnant. Obviously I'm not too old because it's happening." This time she took my hand and held it firmly so that I couldn't pull away. She held my chin in her other hand and forced me to look at her. She had tears in her eyes as she continued. "Don't turn away from me now, Celeste. As for the others, I'm sure they'll be happy for us, as I want you to be. After all we've gone through together, all the dying and losses, you should rejoice at the thought of a new life coming into the world, into the family. I'm going to need you to help me get through it. You were right about my being old. It is dangerous for a woman my age to have a baby, but what can I do? It's happening."

I started to cry and hugged her. "I'm sorry, Mom. It's just—I don't know—everything's changed so much. I wish . . ." I sat down beside her.

"What, love?"

"Nothing."

"What about you? You're a young woman now. Don't you sometimes feel—you know? With Eric? I know you're fond of him"

I felt myself blushing and looked down at my lap. The problem was that the dangers of casual sex had been so firmly drummed into us in our education before the disasters that many young people like me were reticent about *going too far,* in spite of how we felt about each other. We were afraid of the sexually transmitted diseases that had become a problem of epidemic proportions. Of course we had the feelings and longings, but confined ourselves to a lot of heavy foreplay, relieving each other without resorting to actual intercourse. It wasn't ideal nor was it completely satisfactory, but we believed that unless we used protection, we could end up with some awful disease. It was the new method of birth control, replacing condoms and birth control pills. Fear.

I couldn't tell Mother any of this, no matter how frank she'd been about discussing sex with me, so I shrugged and said, "We're okay, Mom, don't worry." I stood up. "Let's go and have some breakfast."

"Wait. Celeste, you know that one of these days you're going to want to start a family yourself." She paused, searching for words. "What I wanted to say was that you can always come and talk to me. I'll be there for you, whatever you decide. And if you have any problems or fears, I want you to know that you can discuss them with me."

"Does Gran know?" I asked, changing the subject. "About you being pregnant?"

"Not yet. I wasn't sure myself until a few days ago. I'll tell her today, don't worry."

Chapter 18

The boys had gone off somewhere with the dogs and Mother and Gran were resting at the house. The others had gone fishing upstream with Joshua so we girls were alone, working in the garden.

"God, it's too hot for this," I said, picking up the basket of peas I'd just picked. Wiping my face for the hundredth time, I turned towards the church. "Let's put this stuff away and go for a swim."

Pam, Lia and Jackie followed me back to the church where we put away the tools and vegetables we'd picked. We grabbed a towel each and took off down the path beside the river.

The river was really more like a wide shallow creek edged with gravel and filled with smooth rocks and boulders. Above the village, it inclined sharply forming rapids, but farther downstream it leveled off. There were fewer boulders and the water was deeper and less turbulent. This was our swimming place. Willows and alder grew along the bank, screening it from the trail and giving us some shade from the hot sun.

In the summer, we wore shorts all the time with halter-tops made from scrap material, sleeveless tee shirts, or tanks tops, anything that would help us stay cool. By necessity, we recycled all our clothing, saving every scrap from worn out garments to piece together into something new. Sweaters were unraveled and re-knit or crocheted into socks, hats, and mitts for winter, and long pants were cut off to make shorts. The remaining fabric was made into storage bags for nuts, dried peas and corn.

The track led through bushes and clumps of wild flowers, yellow grasses gone to seed and patches of ripening wild blackberries. The air was filled with the buzzing of insects and the fragrance of vegetation.

"I'm going to skinny dip," Lia said when we reached the low strip of bank where we swim. She quickly dropped her top on the ground and scrambled out of her shorts, then jumped into the water. "Come on, it's great," she called.

"I'm not taking my clothes off," Pam said. "Somebody might come."

"Don't be silly, Pam. Everybody's miles away. Nobody'll see us," I told her. I knew the real reason for her reticence was that she was very shy, even with other girls, so I didn't push her.

She walked out into the water until it was up to her waist then started to do a sedate breaststroke. Jackie and I shed our clothes and splashed into the river to join the others. We swam for a while then floated lazily on our backs, gazing up at the cloudless sky. It was refreshingly cool in the water and for a while, we were oblivious to the difficulties of everyday life, and the hard work we had to do to survive. After cooling off in the water, we climbed back onto the bank and lay down on our towels.

I must have dozed for a while. I was awoken by a warm tongue licking my face. I opened my eyes and saw Greta staring me in the face, panting and wagging her tail. I noticed a movement behind her and looked up to see Mike peering through a gap in the bushes with a grin on his face.

I let out a shriek "I hope you're satisfied, Mike Chan," I said angrily, pulling the towel around me. "What are you doing spying on us?"

Lia sat up with a start and grabbed her clothes. Jackie was already dressed.

"I wasn't spying," Mike said. "I just followed Greta. I didn't know you were here, I thought she was chasing a rabbit."

"Yeah, I bet. Well I hope you enjoyed the view."

"Not bad," he replied.

"Where are the others?" Lia asked. She was holding her clothes clutched in front of her not covering very much.

Mike couldn't take his eyes off her, and I saw Pam scowling. She was fighting a losing battle with Lia for Mike's attention.

"They're coming down after they take the game back. We got a whole bunch of steelhead," he added.

"So. Turn your back so we can get dressed," I said.

"Might as well have a swim while I'm here." He removed his shoes and ran out into the river in his shorts.

"I told you," said Pam.

"No harm done," Lia said, stepping into her shorts. "Shall we wait here for the others?"

"I'm going back," said Pam, picking up her towel and setting off up the path.

"What's wrong with her?" Lia asked.

"I think she's a bit miffed because Mike was looking at you. I sometimes think you're quite shameless, Lia." I grinned.

Another task that kept us occupied that summer was cutting hay for the horses. They could graze outside most of the year, but we had to provide for those occasions when the ground was covered in snow. The men cut the grass with scythes, and the rest of us gathered it up when it was dry and carried it to an empty garage to store for the winter. There was plenty of grass around the village and in the orchard, so we didn't have to go far. I'll never forget those hot summer days, the air redolent with the smell of newly cut grass, lying on a cushiony pile of hay with a book, chewing on apples fresh from the tree.

* * *

We had a good harvest and it looked as if we would have enough food to see us through the next year if we supplemented it with fish and game. During the summer, Marvin had built a drying frame to dry some of the vegetables, so that we could store them. We had a fairly good supply of preserving jars for the things that couldn't be dehydrated like tomatoes, berries, and cucumbers. Root vegetables were stored in the cool, dry basement of the church.

In the fall, many hours were spent cutting and stacking firewood for the winter. The men went out into the bush and found dead trees, which they felled with axes and cut into portable sections, then dragged home with the help of the horses. They cut the wood into shorter logs with a Swedish saw, which was operated by two men, one at each end. After that, each log was split into small enough pieces to fit into the stoves and fireplaces. Everyone took a turn splitting logs, except Jason; Debbie wouldn't allow him to handle the ax.

Chapter 19

I was woken up by the sound of someone moving about the house in the dark. I got out of my sleeping bag. The house was freezing cold so I put my parka on over the tracksuit I slept in. I already had thick socks on my feet. I crept to the door to listen and heard a moan coming from Mother's room. I went out into the hall and pushed open her door. She was sitting on the side of her mattress with knitted shawl around her shoulders. A lighted candle stood on the box next to the mattress. There was no sign of Peter. She moaned again, bending forward clutching her swollen abdomen.

"Are you all right, Mom?" I asked timidly.

"Celeste? I'm sorry if we woke you." She looked up at me. "I think the baby's coming. Peter's gone to fetch Chris."

"I didn't think it was due until February," I said in bewilderment.

"It isn't," she replied quietly. A sad look crossed her face and was replaced by another grimace of pain.

"Is there anything I can do?" I asked.

"Help me up." She took my hand for support, and rose to her feet. "That's better. Bring the candle, we'll go downstairs. I'll have to light a fire to warm up this place."

"I can do that, Mom. Why don't you lie down and rest?"

"I can't rest, it's no good trying," she said.

We went downstairs, our shadows looming eerily in the flickering candlelight. She knelt in front of the fireplace and started raking the ashes from the previous day's fire.

"Will you get the kindling please, Celeste?"

I went to the back porch and picked up a basket of wood chips and dry grass. Mother laid some in the empty fireplace, put a few sticks and small logs on top then set them alight with a plastic lighter. She brushed off her hands and stood up, holding onto the mantle as another wave of pain overcame her.

"Can I get you anything, Mom?" I asked. "Shall I wake Gran?" I felt so helpless.

"No, let her sleep." She sat in a comfortable chair and watched the wood catch and begin to blaze. Her calmness impressed me, although I could sense she was feeling very anxious.

Just as the room was beginning to warm, the back door opened letting in a blast of cold air. Peter was back with Chris.

Peter went over to Mother and kissed her on the forehead. "How's it going, Katie?" he asked.

"I'm okay." She reached for his hand and held on to it.

"How are you feeling, Kate?" Chris asked calmly, pushing a blond curl up under her toque. She was muffled up in a parka and had a stethoscope sticking out of her pocket. After removing her jacket and dropping it on a chair, she went over to mother with the stethoscope. Turning to me, she said, "Tony's making some coffee, Celeste. How would you like to go and get us all a cup while I examine your mother?"

As I went through the kitchen, I put on my scarf and mitts then stepped into my boots. Glancing back as I closed the door, I saw mother lying on the homemade couch.

The sky was getting lighter, but the air was freezing outside, so I dashed across to the church and let myself in. Tony was stirring a large cooking pot on the stove. The coffee kettle was steaming next to it giving off the characteristic aroma of root coffee. Lia emerged from the back of the church with a trayful of mugs and placed it on the table.

"Morning," Tony said. "Coffee's ready. Come over here and get warm."

"Hi, Celeste. How's your mom?" Lia said.

"She's okay, I guess."

"Is she going to have her baby?"

"Looks like it."

I sat down at the table and sipped the coffee Tony had poured for me. He handed me a bowl of the corn and potato mush that we ate as a substitute for breakfast cereal, then put one on the table for Lia. We put some honey on the mush ate silently for a while. I was too distracted worrying about my mother to feel like talking.

"I'm going to take some coffee over for Mom and Chris now," I said when I'd finished eating.

I took my dishes to the back room and rinsed them in a pail of water, then returned to the main room where Tony was pouring the coffee into mugs on the board we used as a tray.

"Here you are," he said, returning the pot to the stove. "I put some honey in your mother's."

"Thanks Tony." I put my parka back on and zipped it up before picking up the tray. "See you later."

"Give my love to your mom. I hope everything goes okay," Lia said.

Outside, the sun had come up, bathing the landscape in a rosy golden glow. I saw lights flickering in the Chan's and Harris's houses indicating that they were up now, too. When I reached our house, I knocked on the back door before opening it. Peter was on his way to answer my knock, so I handed him the tray and took off my boots. He looked drawn and worried.

"Is everything okay?" I asked.

"I hope so," he replied. "Come and sit by the fire."

In the living room, mother had returned to her chair by the fire and Chris sat on the couch close to her. Peter handed around the tray of coffee then sat beside Chris. Nobody said anything for a while.

"Well?" I said. "Is everything all right." I looked at each of them.

Chris answered. "Your mother's labor has started," she said. "It takes time. We'll just have to be patient for a while."

"Celeste, why don't you go and wake Gran and Pam?" Mother said. She smiled reassuringly at me. "In a few minutes, we'll go over for some breakfast."

Peter put some more logs on the fire before we returned to the church. After breakfast, Mom, Peter, and Gran went back to our house. Chris told them to call her if anything happened.

I spent the rest of the day in a kind of haze. We tried to play a game of *Trivial Pursuit* for a while, but I couldn't concentrate. My mind was on my mother and what was happening at the house. After lunch, I asked

Eric to go out for a walk with me. We walked hand in hand down the path beside the river and checked the progress of the ice. It didn't look thick enough to skate on. We stayed out for about an hour. I can't recall what we talked about.

We were sitting by the stove with warm drinks when Gran came in, I saw the glitter of tears. She came over and sat beside me, putting an arm around my shoulder.

"What's the matter, Gran?" I asked in alarm. "Is Mom okay?"

"She's fine," Gran replied. "She's had a hard time, but she's all right."

"What about the baby?"

"I'm sorry, Celeste. It was already dead before it was born." She wiped her eyes again. "Poor little soul," she added.

"Oh, poor Mom." I turned and clung to Gran, feeling my tears welling up. "Was it a boy or a girl?" I asked.

"A little boy," she said. "Don't forget Peter," she added. "It was his first child. He's taking it very badly, poor fellow."

They buried my second brother the next day. He was so tiny; his cloth-wrapped body would have fitted in a shoebox. Peter made an inscription on a board to be placed up over the tiny grave in our front yard: *Aaron, son of Katherine Chandler Colbert and Peter James Hetherington. Born and died December 18, 2018.*

It took a long time for Mother to recover from the birth. She spent most of the time on the couch in front of the fire in the house, reading or just doing nothing, gazing sadly into the flames.

"I think I was just too old," she said with a sigh one day.

I found Gran a few days later packing up the little garments that had been made for the baby.

"What are you going to do with them?" I asked.

"I'm just packing them away. They'd only remind her. We'll keep them; there's bound to be more babies born."

A few days later, Debbie announced she was pregnant.

Chapter 20

Greta produced a litter of four puppies in January. She hadn't wasted much time once Coke became mature enough to be a father. She was allowed to keep them in the main room of the church so long as they stayed in their box. To ensure they behaved, Mike built an enclosure in one corner to keep them from wandering around and messing up the rest of the room.

We made more progress in the village that spring and summer. Peter and Eric provided us with a source of electricity with the rebuilt generator, some car batteries and a windmill. It wasn't enough to light up the village of course, but we could operate an electric grinder to grind up roasted roots for coffee, and corn to make cornmeal. Some evenings we were able to play music tapes on a portable radio-cassette player. We played around the radio dial once in a while, but never picked up anything other than the meaningless hiss of static.

We built a trading relationship with another small settlement nearby which provided us with honey in exchange for pelts and smoked fish.

In May, we heard about a neighboring farm that raised sheep and sold the wool, so Mother, Gran and Emily went over there with Eric to find out if they could acquire some in trade. It seems Emily had learned weaving when she was going to college and was eager to take it up again if she could obtain the materials. She thought it would make a good cottage industry. After some negotiating, we traded some smoked salmon for some wool that had already been spun into yarn. Marvin built a loom with Emily's guidance, and a new industry was born. The wool was a dull greyish-white color, so we experimented with vegetables and colored earth to see if we could find some dyes. We thought beets would give an attractive tint, but found that the color washed out. Eventually, we discovered through Joshua that sumac roots yielded a pleasant yellow dye and certain barks yielded a reddish brown color.

Debbie had a baby girl in July. She called her Carol-Anne. Tony and Chris cleaned up and repaired one of the houses for themselves and Lia to live in, and Marvin renovated the general store and made it his home and workshop. We continued to eat and socialize in the church, even though no one was living there anymore. It seemed more economical to pool our resources in that way. Improvements to the irrigation system provided running water for the houses.

By the end of August, preserving the harvest was well under way, and most of the hay was in for the winter. The catch of salmon from the river had been excellent, and we had a good supply of smoked fish to see us through the winter. We had finally reached a level where we weren't merely surviving, but were actually making progress and feeling optimistic about the future.

Eric and I started discussing the idea of making our relationship permanent, and maybe even starting a family of our own. I had turned seventeen in May and Eric would be twenty in December.

Chapter 20

How come you live all alone here? What happened to the other people?" Mike asked Joshua one day. We were sitting on the steps of Joshua's house, watching him pluck the feathers off a wild duck he'd caught.

"Most of them got sick and died. The ones that survived decided to go and live up country where they would be safer."

"Weren't you lonely here all by yourself?" I asked.

"It's peaceful, the way I like it."

"I hope we haven't spoilt it for you," I continued.

"Don't bother me none. Makes no difference either way, long as people leave me alone." He stood up and brushed the feathers off the front of his trousers. "'Sides, I can pass on some of our lore to you young folks. That way it won't be lost."

"I'm sure glad we found you, Joshua. I don't know how we would have survived without your help." I continued. "I mean you showed us how to find so many things we didn't even know you could eat, and medicine and stuff."

"Yeah, if it wasn't for you showing us how to trap animals, we'd probably starve," Eric added.

"That reminds me. We ought to check the trap lines tomorrow. It'll take us all day so bring along something to eat, and something to carry stuff in. We can pick some mushrooms and wild nuts while we're out."

Joshua laid the plucked duck down on the table on the porch and cut its head off with a sharp knife. After that, he spread its legs apart and made a slit in the lower belly. He then proceeded to pull out the bird's entrails through the opening. After sorting through the viscera, he set aside some of the organs—I guess it was the liver, the heart, and something else I didn't identify at the time—and dropped the rest into a bucket under the table.

We had become a lot less squeamish since moving to the country, and were getting used to seeing the reality of how our food is produced—not by picking it up neatly packaged from a supermarket freezer, but with real killing—blood and guts and all. And we'd learned not to waste much, keeping feathers and pelts to be cured and used in bedding and to make clothing. We saved the animal fats which, along with the lye leached from wood ash, we made into soap.

Eric, Pam, Mike and I left very early the next morning with Joshua. It was a beautiful sunny day with a warm breeze and an almost cloudless sky. We were wearing jeans, heavy shirts and our precious boots, and each of us carried a backpack. Joshua had his shotgun, but the rest of us only had hunting knives, which we carried in sheaths attached to our belts. We set off on the trail along the edge of the river until we came to an area of heavy bush, then we veered away into the woods. The plan was to go to the farthest point of the expedition, noting things along the way that we could pick up on the way back.

We had only gone about half a kilometer when we heard a bark behind us. We looked back and saw Pepsi coming up the trail. She gave her tail an experimental wave when she reached us, not quite sure of her reception. We had tried to get away without the dogs because they always frightened away the wild game, but she had obviously escaped, and now there was nothing we could do but let her tag along. She, like her brother Coke, had grown into a large handsome dog whose only identifiable ancestry was collie. Both animals had longish black, brown and white hair and long narrow muzzles.

We hiked until noon on a path that took us gradually uphill, then sat down to rest and eat the snacks we'd brought with us. We were hot and rather tired by then and had removed our warm shirts, leaving on the cooler tee shirts we wore underneath. We stretched out on the ground after eating until Joshua told us it was time to move on.

"This is far enough," Joshua said after we had hiked for another hour. "There are six or seven traps around here. Let's spread out and take a look."

Eric and I went in one direction while Mike followed Joshua. This was the part Pam hated. I could see her holding back as we moved into the trees.

"There's one," Eric said.

It was one of the cage traps and we could see the grey fur of the animal was trapped inside. Eric went over and carefully lifted the flap to peer inside. "A rabbit," he said. He reached inside and withdrew the trembling animal. I hated this part too and turned away while Eric killed it. We killed the small animals by breaking their necks or clubbing them on the back of the head. When I turned back, Eric was holding the rabbit by hind it legs. He tied some twine around its feet and hung it from his backpack. Before moving on, he reset the trap. We circled around the spot where we had separated, but found no more game in the traps.

We found Pam sitting by a tree where we had left her holding Pepsi by the collar. Mike and Joshua appeared from amongst the trees. Mike had a rabbit and a chipmunk, and Joshua a raccoon.

"Let's start back," Joshua suggested. "Keep your eyes open for mushrooms. I'll look out for hazels."

On the way back, we found a couple more small animals and a pheasant in the traps. Joshua showed us a small hazel grove. We shook the bushes to loosen the nuts then gathered them from the ground. Mushrooms were scarce at this time of year, but we found a few in damp, shady hollows. By the time we reached the river, we were well laden with things to supplement the larder.

When we came around a bend in the river out into the open, we saw thick smoke rising in the distance. Pepsi uttered a spine-tingling howl and the hairs on her back stood up. She took off down the trail with a sharp bark.

"It looks as if it's coming from our place," Mike cried.

"Come on, let's see what's happening," Eric shouted and began to run.

"Wait!" Joshua said. The urgency in his voice brought us up short. "Go carefully. We don't know what's happening."

A bolt of fear surged through me. I hadn't felt this scared since that night I was caught by the gang of punks. Everyone looked pretty shaken.

"Come on. Go quietly now." Joshua beckoned us to follow him.

We continued silently down the trail being careful to keep out of sight. More of Pepsi's howls and barks came from the distance. The feeling of dread grew as we got closer to the village. It soon became obvious that most of the buildings were burning. Joshua led us into a grove of trees and bushes on a small rise above the village where we could look down without being seen. The church was almost consumed by flames, and several houses were either smoking ruins or still smoldering. Billows of black smoke rose into the sky. There was no sign of life anywhere.

"Oh, God!" I moaned "What happened?"

"Where is everybody?" Pam grasped my arm and I could feel her trembling.

"Whoever did it is gone now," Joshua said. "Let's go down and take a look."

There was an eerie silence over the village, broken only by the crackle of burning timbers. The sudden crash of a collapsing building startled us. We could no longer hear Pepsi's cries; she had disappeared. Joshua went ahead, and we followed slowly, holding back, dreading what we would find.

Joshua came to the edge of the field where we grew vegetables, and we saw him bending over something in the dirt. We went closer and saw Marvin lying face down on the ground with a bullet hole in his back. His head was lying sideways and his eye was open, but it didn't move or blink. We knew he was dead.

"Oh no, not here too. . ." Eric cried.

Pam began to cry; I fought back tears. We clung to each other. Poor Marvin. He never had much to say, and he often seemed grumpy, but I remembered his gentle way with animals.

"Take off your packs and hide them in the bushes," Joshua ordered.

We followed him towards the burning buildings. The next body lay at the edge of the field close to the houses. It was Tony. His head was caved in and bloody.

Suddenly we heard an anguished cry from Mike who had wandered around the other side of the nearest house. We rushed around the building and found him kneeling on the ground beside the body of his mother. She had also been cudgeled to death. Mike's body was racked with choking sobs. His father lay close by, half his head blown away by a bullet. Eric gazed at his parent's bodies with a look of such profound despair, then knelt down beside his brother and held him. They clung together with tears running down their faces. I felt helpless in the face of such suffering. I touched Eric's shoulder, trying to offer solace then I realized they were completely oblivious to me, I left them alone.

I saw Pam leaning against a fence post, throwing up, and felt a wave of nausea pass through me. I took a few deep breaths to stifle the sickness and had a fit of coughing as the acrid smoke hit my throat. Fear and anxiety surfaced again. Where were Mom and Gran?

I turned around. Joshua was standing by the Harris's house, looking down. Don Harris was lying outside his house with his son, Jason in his arms. They'd both been shot. There was no sign of Debbie or the baby. We continued searching the village and surrounding area until it started to get dark. By then, the fires had died down to smoking ashes. Chris, Lia, Jackie, Tate and Gran were missing, and there was no sign of my mother or

Peter. I was dreadfully afraid they might have been inside the burning buildings.

The four of us sat forlornly on the ground at the edge of the village waiting for Joshua to return.

"Here he comes now," Pam said.

"What are we going to do, Joshua?" Eric asked with despair in his voice.

"Nothing much we can do tonight. Let's go back up to where we left the packs."

We stood up and started back up the slope.

"My God, I thought we were safe here," Eric raged. "I'll—if I ever find out who . . ."

"We may never find out who they were," Joshua replied. "There's so many bad people roaming around these days."

"If I ever find them, I swear I'll kill them." Eric's voice broke as he spoke. I squeezed his hand, tears filling my eyes.

"Shh! I think I heard something." Mike stopped and waved his hand to silence us.

A rustling sound came from close by then we heard a muffled sob. Pepsi burst out of the bushes and ran towards us. She gave a little bark and ran back into the thicket.

Eric whispered. "Wait here, I'll take a look." He walked cautiously towards the bushes and pushed them aside. "It's Tate!" he cried.

I was so pleased to see someone alive, I rushed over and crushed him in my arms. His face was streaked with tears and his hair tangled with twigs and bits of leaf.

"What happened?" I asked.

"Wait till we get up the hill and get settled down," Joshua urged.

We returned to the place where we'd left the packs and dropped to the ground. We were exhausted, emotionally drained. We had no bedding and nothing to eat apart from what we'd brought back with us. When Joshua suggested cooking one of the animals, nobody showed any interest.

"I'm not hungry," Mike said.

"Me neither," I added.

Joshua had brought a bottle of water, which we passed around to quench our thirst. He handed us the bag of hazelnuts. We each took a handful and cracked them with our teeth while we listened Tate's account of what had happened. Tate had grown into an attractive young teenager, strong and wiry. He usually had a ready smile, but he wasn't smiling as he told us about the raid.

Chapter 21

We didn't hear them coming," Tate started. "The first we knew they were there was when Lia and Jackie started screaming. They were over in the orchard picking apples."

"Who were they? Do you know?"

"Nobody I'd ever seen before," he continued. "They were dressed in that sort of stuff that has patches of colors, sort of green and brown, you know?"

"Camouflage," Eric interjected.

"Yeah, that's right."

"How many were there?" Joshua asked.

"I'm not sure. May be six or seven. They all had guns."

"What happened?"

"Well, when Jackie and Lia started screaming, Mr. Chan ran out of his house with his shotgun, but they saw him and shot him before he could use it. Then Mrs. Chan ran out and started yelling at them. Two of the men started trying to drag her away but she kept yelling and fighting them, so they started hitting her . . ." He stopped talking for a moment. "Sorry, I . . ."

Eric's clenched his fist. Tears rolled down Mike's face. I put my arm round Mike and pulled him close.

"What happened to the others?" Joshua asked Tate.

"I was down in the garden with Marvin picking beans. When the shooting started, he told me to hide in the bushes. Then I saw Tony running over to the orchard where he could hear Lia screaming. He was yelling at them to leave her alone, so they beat him up with their rifle butts. Then some guys grabbed Debbie and tried to drag her into the orchard. Don came out of the house with Jason and started to go after them. One of the men shot them both.

"What happened to my mom and Peter and Gran?" I asked.

"Didn't you know? Your Mom and Peter went off on the horses this morning. I think they were going to look for some parts for the generator."

"Thank God," I said. I was so relieved to hear Mom was safe that my eyes filled with tears again. "What about my grandmother?"

"I don't know. The last time I saw her, she was going over to the church with some vegetables from the garden." I went cold with dread.

"What happened to the others, Debbie and the girls?" Pam asked.

"They took them away with them. They took all the food they could load on the carts—our carts. They brought their own horses to pull it away."

"What I can't understand is how they managed to get so close without anyone seeing or hearing them," Eric said. "Where were the dogs?"

"I heard them barking in the orchard, then they went quiet," Tate replied. "I don't know why they stopped barking.

"They must have left their horses in the trees down the road then gone behind the orchard and crept up that way," Eric said.

Exhaustion took its toll and we gradually fell asleep tangled and intertwined with one another for comfort and warmth. When a muffled sob escaped from Mike, I stroked his back. My last thought as I fell asleep was of Gran, hoping she had somehow escaped.

We awoke early the next morning, cramped and damp from dew. It was only a moment before the horror of the previous day came back to me. I looked around at my companions who were stirring and stretching. No one spoke. Everyone looked haggard and stunned.

"What are we going to do?" Pam asked.

"We'll have to bury them soon as we can," Joshua said dipping his head towards the village. "But first we have to get something to eat."

We picked up our packs and the dead game we'd brought back the day before, and trundled down the hill towards the ruins of the village. A flock of black crows was swooping over the ground with raucous cries. We saw one bird standing on Marvin's body, pecking at the bloody spot on his back, another was pecking his eye.

"Get away!" Eric shouted, swinging his pack to scare to them off.

The crows cawed angrily and flew up to a nearby tree where more sat waiting to begin their grisly feast. Instead of going into the village, Joshua led us to the meadow by the riverbank and told the boys to gather some wood to make a fire. He instructed me and Pam to go to the garden and pull up some potatoes while he went alone into the village. The sun was up, so we managed to start the fire easily with some dry grass and a fire glass—a lens from an old pair of spectacles. Joshua returned with a sooty cooking pot, which he took down to the river and washed. He brought it back to the fire and started to skin the raccoon, telling Eric and Mike to prepare the two rabbits. Pam and I washed and cut up the potatoes, onions and carrots we'd pulled up from the garden.

While we were waiting for the food to cook, we went back to the village leaving Tate to keep watch over the cooking pot.

"Looks as if they took all the tools as well," Joshua informed us. "I had a look around and couldn't find any."

"Don't forget the hiding place," Eric reminded him. "It's a good thing Peter thought of hiding stuff, so that we wouldn't lose everything if . . ."

"Let's go and look. We'll need some spades to dig with."

Joshua led the way to the bushes in front of the low bluff overlooking the village. A cave-like hollow had been dug in the hillside behind the bushes. This was where the spare tools and implements had been hidden, greased and wrapped in plastic. Joshua and Eric started to pull bundles out of the hollow and pass them back to us. Mike, Pam and I unwrapped them and spread the tools out on the ground. There were some carpentry tools, hammers and saws, a set of wrenches and some screw drivers, knives, and scissors, as well as nails and batteries, but there were only two shovels and one pickax.

"These'll have to do." Joshua said. "Bundle up the rest of the stuff and put it back. We can sort it out later."

"Where are we . . .?" Mike couldn't finish the question. How can you talk about burying your parents?

"In the garden would be best," Joshua said, intuitively knowing what Mike had been about to ask. "The soil there is looser and easier to dig."

We walked back to the garden, averting our eyes from the swarming crows. Eric and Joshua chose a spot and started to dig. Suddenly Mike shrieked and rushed off waving his arms wildly at the crows around his parents' bodies. He picked up a branch and started flailing at the birds so that they scattered with strident cries and flew to perches on nearby roofs and trees. The crows glared at him balefully as he stood guard over the bodies. I saw him bend and brush something off his mother.

It was too painful to watch. I couldn't imagine the anguish he must have been suffering. I wandered over to the ruins of the church. They were still smoldering and too hot to touch, so I poked around the edges with a stick.

"What are you looking for?" Pam asked, coming up behind me.

"I ... Shit," I said. Tears started running down my face. "I wish I knew what happened to Gran." I threw the stick angrily into the ashes.

"Do you think she . . . you know, might have been in there?" Pam asked timidly.

"I don't know," I replied angrily. "How the hell would I know?"

I turned away and went back over to where Eric and Joshua were digging. They had already removed quite a pile of earth and I could see sweat dripping from their faces.

"Need a hand?" I offered.

"In a minute," Eric replied. "What happened to Mike?"

"He's over there by your house. He's keeping the crows off . . ."

Eric nodded and went on digging for a few minutes, then he climbed out of the hollow and handed me his shovel. "Here, you can do a bit if you like. I'm going to see how Mike's doing."

I watched him walk towards Mike who now had Pam sitting with him. I slid down the slope and started shoveling the dirt, the terrible rage I felt giving me impetus. The ground became harder as we dug deeper and finally Joshua climbed out and got the pickax.

"Get back," he told me, "I'm going to have a go with this, see if I can loosen it up a bit.

I climbed out and watched him wield the pick, marveling at the strength and endurance he displayed for an old man. He was at least seventy-five.

"Are you going to bury them all in the same grave?" I asked him. The hole was much wider than one body.

"Better that way. Quicker," he said, panting. "Have to get them buried fast as we can."

Just then, we heard the sound of horse's hooves approaching. In panic, I jumped into the hole and crouched down to hide, sure that the raiders were returning.

Chapter 22

It's all right," Joshua assured me, "It's your mother."

I peered over the edge of the pit and saw Mother and Peter riding slowly towards us. When they were a few meters away, they dismounted and continued on foot.

"Mom!" I climbed out of the hole. The look on her face changed from fear to relief when she saw me. I ran to her and threw my arms around her, sobbing. "Oh. Mom, it's so awful."

Peter went over to Joshua who was still standing in the hole. I saw them talking, then Peter went off towards the houses. Joshua climbed out of the grave and came over to where Mom and I were standing.

"I think the food should be ready now," he said, giving Mom a meaningful look and pointing towards the river.

We saw Tate coming towards us. Mom took the hint and urged me towards the riverbank where our stew was cooking. She took Tate's arm and turned him around to go back with us.

"Come on Tate, let's have some of that delicious food. I can smell it from here."

"There's nothing to eat off," Tate explained, "And no forks or anything. I was just going to see if I could find something."

"You go on with Celeste, I'll go and look," she assured him. "I won't be long."

I walked over to the pot that was cooking on the fire and gave it a stir. It did smell good and I was ravenous. We hadn't eaten anything, apart from a few nuts, since the snack we'd had at noon the previous day. I sat down on the grass next to Tate and put my arms around my knees.

"What are we going to do now, Celeste?" he asked.

"I don't know. We have to finish burying Don and Marvin and the others. I don't suppose we'll be able to stay here. There's nowhere to live." I turned to look at him. "I bet you were pretty scared yesterday."

He nodded his head silently. I saw tears in his eyes and looked away. "What about Jason?" he asked warily.

"I'm sorry, Tate. They killed him, too." I said. "I'm glad you're okay." I added.

I looked back towards the village and saw the others coming towards us.

"Okay, let's get this food served," Peter said when they reached us.

"We have to wash the bowls first." Mother took the pile of bowls from Peter and went down to the riverbank to wash them.

Her eyes were red and glistened with unshed tears. I wondered if she had found out what had happened to Gran. I got up and followed her.

"Where did you find the bowls?" I asked, crouching down to help her.

"The fire went out before it reached the back of the church where we kept the dishes and things. Everything is covered in soot and ashes, but we might be able to salvage some of them."

"Mom? Do you—I mean—I was wondering, you know, what happened to Gran."

"I think she's—Peter was poking around in the rubble and . . ."

"He found her?"

"Maybe. There's—it looks like a—a body."

I started to cry. "Oh, Mom. Poor Gran."

She was crying now, too. We clung to each other beside the flowing stream. *We're the only two left in our family now,* I thought.

"Come on," she said. "The others are waiting for their food." She pulled up the bottom of her shirt and wiped her eyes, then picked up the bowls and spoons. I followed her back to the fire, wiping my eyes on my sleeve.

We sat on the ground near the fire and ate our stew in silence, too stunned to talk. I noticed Mother picked at her food, but didn't eat anything. None of us could meet the eyes of anyone else for fear of the raw emotions we would see. After we had finished eating, we went down to the creek for a drink of water and to wash our bowls.

"Let's finish the burials," Peter said. "Josh? We can manage," he added as we all started towards the village."

"I want to help too. They're my parents." Eric said.

"Me too," Mike added.

"All right, come on," Peter said gently. "Why don't the rest of you look around and see what you can salvage? Be careful of the damaged buildings, though. We don't want anyone else to get hurt."

The sun was getting higher in the sky, but hadn't yet reached its zenith, so I guessed it was mid-morning when we straggled back to our ruined village.

"I'm sorry I yelled at you," I said to Pam when we were out of earshot.

"That's okay," she replied, touching my arm. "I guess you were upset about . . . your gran."

We poked around the ruins with sticks, but found nothing, then we looked around outside and found some plastic sheeting and a cooking pot that had been left behind the church. We collected some wooden boxes and a ladder in the orchard as well as a couple of sleeping bags that had been spread out on the ground. There was a whole line full of washing hanging behind our house, which included some sheets and towels as well as shirts and pants. Tate found a pair of boots under the Chan's porch and a collection of kitchen utensils in various places. The general store where Marvin had lived was not burned too badly, but when we went inside, we found all his tools were gone. His bedding was still there and a couple of books he must have been reading. That reminded me that all our precious books were gone, too. They had been kept in the church so that everyone would have access to them.

After about three-quarters of an hour, we heard Peter calling us and returned to the gravesite. Mike, Joshua, and Eric were adding the last shovelfuls of dirt to the grave and patting it down. Peter had found a board and was propping it up at the edge of the grave.

"We'll engrave it with their names later," he said by way of explanation. "We thought we would say a few words..."

We all stood solemnly around the grave with our hands folded in front of us, heads bowed.

"Who's going to speak?" Mom asked.

"I will, if you like," Peter replied when no one else offered. He folded his hands in front of him and continued, "Dear Lord, we ask you to accept the souls of our loved ones buried here today, to rest with you in eternal peace. Amen."

"Amen," we echoed.

"Anyone else like to say something?"

"Yes," Eric replied. "Mom and Dad, you were the best—we're—we're gonna miss you." There was a catch in his voice and he turned away quickly when he'd finished. He put his arm around Mike and they rested their heads on each other's shoulders for a moment. Mike had grown and was now as tall as Eric.

"I would like to say we'll miss our good friends, Don and Marvin, Emily and Edward, Tony, and poor little Jason," Mother said. "And my mother, Sandra Webb Chandler, I know they're in a better place now." She walked away and went towards the church ruins where she stood silently with her head bowed for a while.

"We can't stay here," Peter said a little while later when we'd all gathered under a tree to discuss what to do next. "It'll be winter soon and I don't think there's time to rebuild, even if it was worthwhile. Besides, they might come back. Who knows where they are? They probably discovered us when they saw the smoke from our cooking fire, so there's nothing to stop them seeing it a second time."

"Who do you think it was?" Eric asked.

"Sounds like survivalists," Peter replied.

"I wonder what they'll do to Debbie and the girls," I said with a shudder. "I hope they don't harm Carol Ann, or any of them."

"They must have been looking for women. There's probably a shortage of women in that type of group, so they raid other settlements and kidnap them."

"But why did they have to kill Mom and Dad and the others?" Mike asked angrily.

"It looks as if they resisted. From what I've heard, killing means nothing to them if you get in their way. They don't like opposition. The worst of it is, they believe—in a perverted way—that they're doing the

Lord's work." Peter turned to Joshua. "What do you think, Joshua? Do you know of a place where we would be safe for the winter? We don't want to go too far because we'll have to carry everything with us."

"There's several old farms around here," Joshua replied, scratching his head.

"We'd need something that's in fairly good shape. At least weatherproof."

"What about that farm where we found the potatoes and other stuff?" Eric suggested. "The house looked in fairly good shape."

"I'm afraid it might be too exposed," Peter said.

"There's an old house back over there a ways," Joshua said, pointing to a spur of the hill behind the village. "It's hidden by the rise back there."

"That sounds more promising, is it far? Maybe we ought to ride up there to and take a look at it." Peter said.

Joshua nodded and stood up. We all got up and looked around us, wondering what to do next.

"Kate, could you and the others start packing stuff ready to move? Some of you harvest as much as you can from the garden. We'll leave the root vegetables for later.

We can always come back for them." Peter nodded to Joshua, and together they left to get the horses.

We split up into two groups: Pam, Mike and I went to the vegetable garden and Mom took Eric and Tate with her to look at the supplies concealed in the cave. We found some plastic bowls in the back of the church and started to harvest the beans and peas that were ripe. Mike brought one of the wooden crates and filled it with tomatoes, cucumbers and lettuces. Every time we filled a bowl, we took it and emptied the contents into a large plastic sack. Some of the squash were ready to harvest, but the pumpkins were still quite small. We figured they would need another three or four weeks before they were ready. A lot of the plants were trampled down across one corner of the garden as if someone had ridden a horse across it, but the damage wasn't serious. It was mostly potatoes and carrots, which were safe underground. We worked silently, lost in our own thoughts, in contrast to our usual lively banter.

Joshua and Peter returned about an hour later.

"It might do," Peter reported. "It's an awful mess, but I think we could clean it up and make it livable. For the winter, at least. And it is well concealed."

Mother wrinkled her nose. "I suppose we'll be cleaning up spiders' webs and mouse droppings for the next two weeks."

"It won't be too bad if we all chip in," Peter replied. "Some of the windows are broken and need boarding up, but it looks fairly weatherproof. There's plenty of firewood . . ."

"It sounds like so much work. And I wonder if we can sustain ourselves now there are so few of us left. Maybe we should join another community." Mother said.

"It's an idea. What do the rest of you think?" Peter turned to us.

"We'd probably have a better chance of defending ourselves in a larger group," Eric said.

"Where could we go?" I asked.

"Well, we know a couple of communities; maybe we could join one of them." Mother replied.

"But would they have us? That's the question," Peter said.

"We've plenty to contribute," Mother said. "The horses, the vegetables from the garden, and they might be glad to have someone to teach their children, not to mention the extra hands."

"I think too much has happened today for us to make a decision. Let's stay here tonight and talk about it in the morning. We'll put everything up by the cave then we can make a temporary camp up in the clearing out of sight. We should be safe enough up there with Pepsi to guard us." He stood up and stretched.

His mention of Pepsi reminded Mike of the other two dogs. "Did anyone find out what happened to Coke and Greta and the puppies?"

"I'm sorry, Mike, I'm afraid they killed them too. I guess they didn't want them to warn us they were coming," Peter replied.

"How? I didn't hear any shots," Tate said.

"I'm not sure," Peter said. "There weren't any marks on them. Maybe they fed them some poisoned meat."

"Vicious bastards," Eric said.

The sun was dipping lower in the sky and we were starting to feel hungry again, so we went back to the meadow and finished off the remainder of the stew. After eating, we took stock of our bedding. We had five sleeping bags—Mother and Peter had taken theirs with them—Marvin's mattress and three blankets.

We climbed up the hill to the clearing and divided up the bedding. I shared a blanket and open sleeping bag with Eric, Pam, Tate and Mike were given a sleeping bag each and Mother shared a blanket and sleeping bag with Peter. Joshua spread the remaining blanket on a pile of dry grass to make himself a bed.

Chapter 23

The following morning, after washing in the river and eating a breakfast of fruit from the orchard, Mother and I started out to visit the community that had provided us with honey. We knew they weren't very friendly people, but they had never been openly hostile. They were usually polite and reserved, as if they wanted to be finished with our business and get back to whatever they were doing.

Their settlement was about three kilometers from our village if we went across country instead of taking the roads. We took a shortcut through some fields and came out on the lane leading to a cluster of houses dominated by a white church. There was an armed man on the road close to the settlement. As we approached, several dogs started barking. The man lowered his rifle when we were close enough for him to see who we were. Mother dismounted from her horse to talk to him.

"Good morning!" she said.

"Morning." The man's expression was one of suspicious curiosity, which didn't change when he spoke. He looked about sixty with sunburned, wrinkled skin and close-cropped grey hair.

Mother seemed to be at a loss for a moment, then she said, "Is there someone in authority we could talk to?" she asked.

"What about?" he asked.

"We need a place to stay."

"You should talk to the Reverend Eikhart."

"Where can we find him?" she asked.

"His house is down there right next to the church. The white one."

Mother remounted the horse and we rode slowly down the road into the little community.

When we reached the minister's house, we dismounted and tied the horses' reins loosely to a young tree. The house looked well cared for, although closer observation revealed some of the paint was flaking from the walls. The windows were clean and neatly curtained.

Even the smoke was rising from the chimney looked clean. We knocked on the door and waited. It was opened by a severe-looking woman with grey hair pulled back in a bun. She was quite tall and thin with steel-rimmed spectacles emphasizing her piercing blue eyes. She wore a grey cotton dress and black shoes of the kind that used to be called *sensible*.

"Yes?"

"Could we see the Reverend Eikhart?" Mother asked.

"I'll see if he's free. Just a minute." She closed the door leaving us standing outside on the porch.

Mother raised her eyebrows at me and I rolled my eyes. "Doesn't sound too friendly." I said.

The door opened again and the woman said, "He'll see you. Come in." She looked pointedly at our feet, as we were about to go in, so we removed our boos and left them on the porch. "He's in his study. In there." She pointed towards an open door.

Mother knocked on the door and entered the study, which, like the exterior of the house, was spotlessly clean and neat in spite of the large number of books on the shelves. Apart from the big desk and padded swivel chair, the only other furnishings were some hard wooden chairs. Above the small fireplace, which was empty and clean, hung a picture of Jesus surrounded by children. The man standing by the desk was shorter and plumper than the woman. His hair, what little remained, was white and fine, and his eyes were a frosty blue.

"Good morning," Mother said.

"Morning," he replied. "What can I do for you? Sit down." He pointed towards the chairs.

Mother and I sat down then he resumed his seat behind the desk.

"We live in the small community over by the river—Salish," mother started. "We've traded with you for honey, as you probably know."

He nodded.

"The day before yesterday we were raided. Most of our people were killed or abducted," she continued. "There's only seven of us left, apart from Joshua Henry. He's the old Indian—you may know him. Did you have any trouble here?"

"No. They came by, but when they saw we had good defenses, they left us alone. I think they come from down south, across the river." He stirred in his chair. He cleared his throat and thought for a moment. "Can I offer you some coffee?"

184

"That would be wonderful, thank you," Mother replied.

"Wait here, I'll get my wife to bring some." He left the room for a moment and we heard voices from the back of the house, then he returned and resumed his seat.

"What can we do for you? Is it funeral arrangements you want?"

"Oh, no, we've already buried them," Mother answered. "We are really looking for a place to live. We don't think we would be safe now that they know about our village, and there aren't enough of us to defend ourselves. Besides, all our houses were burnt down. We were wondering if you had room—I mean if we could come and live here. For a while, at least, until we can find somewhere permanent."

Mrs. Eikhart, the woman who'd answered the door, entered with a tray containing three steaming mugs. She put the tray down on the desk and left again.

"Help yourselves." The Reverend Eikhart nudged the tray slightly in our direction.

Mother and I picked up a mug each and wrapped our hands around it to absorb the warmth.

"What do you think?" Mother asked.

"Well, we don't take in outsiders as a rule. Willow Creek is a close-knit community. A Christian community. Everybody goes to church and lives by scriptures." He took a sip from his mug and replaced it on the tray, then folded his hands under his chin while considering what he would say next. "There are some empty houses that could be fixed up. How many did you say you are? Men? Women? Any children?"

"Seven altogether. This is my daughter, Celeste. There's one other teenage girl, two teenage boys, and two men."

"Hmm. If we let you in, you'd have to provide your own food and anything else you need."

"That's no problem. We still have a lot of the produce from our garden and we're used to hunting and fishing. We've got some tools we had hidden away, and our bicycles. We're not sure about the horses. They really belong to Joshua."

"Another thing," the Reverend continued, "You'd all have to abide by the rules of the community. Go to church and so on. Help with community work. The youngsters are what worry me. At their age, they start to get ideas—you know what I mean. Can't have them setting a bad example for the children in the village."

186

"Don't worry," Mother said. "They're good kids. They've lost their parents, but we'll look after them."

"Humph. I'll get someone to show you the houses." He stood up again and left the room.

"What do you think?" I asked.

"I suppose it'll be all right for a while. At least we'll have a roof over our heads and protection from raiders."

"I know, but—God—going to church . . ."

"Shh."

The Reverend returned several minutes later accompanied by another man. He was younger than the minister, probably in his forties, sturdily built with black hair and a beard. He was wearing denim overalls over a blue plaid shirt.

"This is Jack Newton," the Minister introduced him. "He'll show you to the empty houses. You can choose which one you want. Show them the Berry place and old Wong's house," He turned to Mother. "What did you say your names are?"

"I'm sorry," she replied. "I'm Katherine Colbert and, as you know, this is Celeste."

"Right. Come and see me when you bring your stuff. I'd like to meet the others."

More like look us over, I thought.

He got up and saw us to the front door where we put our boots back on. Mr. Newton stepped into his own rubber boots and started towards the road.

"Thank you very much," Mother said to the Reverend Eikhart as he closed the door.

"This way." Mr. Newton said, turning left on the street. "You were raided, I hear?"

"Yes, a couple of days ago."

"Yeah, they came by here, but we scared them off. You have to make a show of force if you want to be left alone. What happened?"

"Some of us were away from the village, that's how we survived. We had some dogs, but they're gone—all but one. They took some of the younger women and girls with them. They killed two women as well, all the men who were there, and one little boy. They burned all the houses."

"That's terrible. I'm real sorry." He shook his head slowly. "We saw the smoke. Thought somebody was in trouble."

"But nobody came to our help?"

"What could we do? By the time the fires were set, it was probably too late to save anybody. Besides, we didn't want to leave this place undefended with them around."

We turned a corner onto a side street and walked to the end where the empty house stood. Its windows were boarded up and the paint was worn off the exterior walls, but it didn't look too bad. We followed Mr. Newton up the walk to the front door, which was padlocked. He took a chain of keys from his pocket and undid the lock, then pushed open the door.

"There it is," he said. "This is the Berry house. They left about two years ago after their kids all died from the virus." He turned his gaze from the house and pointed back the way we had come. "Down there, see that blue house?"

We nodded.

"That's old Wong's. He used to have a general store here until he died in '09. You can have that if it suits you better. I got to get back to work now, so I'll leave you to it." He went down the front steps and started towards the road, then turned back. "When were you planning to move in?"

"Today, if possible," Mother replied. "And thank you for showing us the house. We'll see you later, I expect."

189

We went into the house. It was gloomy inside with the windows boarded up, so we left the door open in order to provide some light. The door opened directly into a large room with a fireplace that must have been the living room. It was empty and dusty, but in good condition. An archway at the back of the living room opened into the dining area beside a large kitchen. We went into the kitchen and unlocked the back door from the inside to let in more light and saw that the kitchen was also in good shape with ample cupboards. A raised metal plate on the floor at one end with a hole in the wall above it indicated the place where there may once have been a wood-burning stove. A door opened off the kitchen onto the basement stairs.

"It looks good," Mother said. "Let's look at the rest of it."

Returning to the front of the house, we opened the other door off the living room. It led to a small hallway with a staircase up to the second story. Upstairs we found three bedrooms and a bathroom. There was another room downstairs off the hallway, which had its own bathroom behind the staircase. This part looked as if it had been added onto the original house. We tried the taps in the bathroom, but no water came out.

"It's not going to be very comfortable without furniture," Mother commented. "But it doesn't need much work and at least we'll have a roof over our heads."

"Shall we look at the other house?"

"I don't think we need to today. This looks fine. Let's go back home and get the others."

Chapter 25

When we got back to Salish, they'd packed up quite a lot of the supplies ready to be transported. Everyone looked relieved when we told them about the house we'd been offered.

"It's not exactly ideal," Mother warned them.

"They look like a bunch of religious nuts to me," I blurted, "There's this really strict old minister. He seems to be in charge. He said we'll have to go to church." I shot Eric a look. "And no fooling around and setting a bad example for their kids."

"It won't hurt us," Mother said. "It's not all that bad, and the house is in good shape."

"I'm not going to church," Pam said defiantly.

"They'll probably think you're an ungodly heathen," Mike teased her.

"I don't care," she replied.

"We should get going," Peter reminded us.

"By the way, Peter, do you think we could manage to bring one of the wood stoves? There's a place for one in the kitchen, but someone's taken it out."

"I think the one in the Chan's house is all right. We'll have to come back for it. I wonder if the people in Willow Creek will lend us a cart to transport it and the rest of the stuff."

We took to the road with loaded backpacks and bicycle carriers and reached our new home late in the afternoon. Several children stood and watched as our sorry caravan entered Willow Creek. Faces peered out of some of the windows and curtains twitched as we passed, but no one greeted us.

After unloading the carriers and taking our baggage into the house, Peter and Eric went around and removed some of the boards from the windows. The glass was intact, and we had some light to see by. After that, we gathered some wood to build a fire in the fireplace ready to cook our evening meal.

Remembering the Reverend Eikhart's departing words, Mother suggested that she and Peter go down to his house and let him know we had arrived. I'm sure he already knew we were here, and many other details about us, but they wanted to keep on friendly terms with him, and also to find out where we could get water. The minister came back with them and was introduced to everyone. His face took on a sour expression when he saw the Chans and Pam, not to mention Tate. I don't think he was quite prepared for two Chinese, an East Indian and a mulatto, but if he was surprised, he made no comment.

On the way over, he had shown Mother where we could get water at a standpipe down the street near the intersection. Eric and Mike went to fetch water in the pails we'd brought with us. While they were gone, the rest of us cleaned out the kitchen cupboards then unpacked the things we'd brought with us and put them away. Pam and I helped Mother cut up some meat and vegetables and put them in the pot to cook over the fire then we were able to sit down and relax for a while. It would have been better to have kept busy; the moment we stopped working, all the horror of the past two days came flooding back.

While we were waiting for the stew, we heard a soft knocking on the front door. Mike, who was closest, jumped up to answer. Our visitor was a young girl of about thirteen or fourteen. When Mike invited her in, she entered the house timidly, looking down at the towel-wrapped object she was carrying.

"My mother thought you might like this," she said, handing the bundle to mother. "It's corn bread. Mom just made it," the girl added. She was a small and slender with dark blonde hair tied behind with a lace, pale skin and large grey eyes.

"That's very kind of your mother," Mom said. "And it's nice to meet you. My name's Kate, and this is my daughter, Celeste . . ." She went on to introduce all of us. "And you are . . .?"

"Rebecca Tomlinson," the girl replied. "I have to go now."

"Well be sure to tell your mother how grateful we are and I hope we'll get to meet her soon," Mother said as she closed the door.

During the following days, several of our new neighbors came to call with little gifts, including odd pieces of furniture, pots and pans, and food—mostly honey and preserves. Sometimes it seemed they approached us a bit furtively, as if they were afraid of being seen by their neighbors, but we were touched by their kindness. It would have been uncharitable to believe they were coming only out of curiosity. They didn't have much to say to us, reserving judgment I suppose, until they felt they could trust us, or if we fit in.

We brought the rest of the stuff from our old place. Peter had asked Joshua if he wanted to move with us, but he declined saying he would move into Marvin's place, which wasn't too badly damaged. He said we could still use the horses, and if he needed them, he'd come and fetch them. We left him plenty of vegetables for winter, and told him we would come over to go hunting with him.

That was one of the most miserable winters since the epidemics. Peter's guitar was gone and we'd lost all our books in the fire. The people in the new place were very reserved, so we kept to ourselves most of the time. We did participate in community work whenever called upon, and attended a church service every Sunday to listen to Reverend Eikhart's droning sermons filled with dire threats of hell and damnation for anyone who transgressed their narrow set of rules. These rules seemed to mainly concern bans on fornication and other—unnamed—perversions of the flesh. We used to secretly laugh about it at home, but didn't dare show our amusement in front of any of the congregation.

The children of the community were clean and well mannered, but seemed to lack spirit and spontaneity. Sometimes they would be playing exuberantly and suddenly, as if realizing they had transgressed some unspoken rule, they would calm down and continue more soberly. There were only about a dozen children under twelve, and eight or nine teenagers. The teenage boys worked alongside their fathers while the girls helped their mothers with domestic work.

When Mother offered to start a school, the Reverend Eikhart said he would talk to the parents about it. He also told her he would want to see whatever she proposed to teach—to make sure she wasn't corrupting them, I suppose. He told her she could open a school for the children under twelve, but the older kids could only attend after they had finished their chores. He allocated a room in the church hall to be used as the schoolroom. The church hall was also used for village meetings and an occasional social evening.

Poor Pam was particularly miserable in this new place. The older kids started to call her *the heathen,* just as Mike had predicted, because she never attended church.

"I hate it here, I wish I'd stayed with my father," she said tearfully one day. "I can't even go outside the house."

"I know," I replied. "It is pretty awful. Maybe we can find somewhere else to live as soon as winter's over."

"We were so happy in Salish," she continued tearfully. "Everything was going so well. I even miss Lia," she added.

"I wonder what happened to her and the others," I said.

"We don't even know if they're alive."

"I know. But I think they are, though. There's no reason for them to be killed. If they took them with them, they probably needed them for some reason."

"Why?"

"You know. What do men need women for?" I replied bitterly. I did hope that they wouldn't hurt them, but had serious doubts.

"You know, Celeste," Pam went on, "I've been thinking of going back to the city to see if I can find my father and grandma."

"But how would you find them?"

"I could go to the temples; somebody there might know where they are."

"You can't go by yourself, Pam. You might get killed."

"Maybe Mike would go with me."

"Wait a while," I urged her. "When the weather improves, maybe the four of us can go together."

"Okay. I suppose you're right," Pam sighed.

She moped around the house most of the time, when she wasn't preparing meals or helping me with housework and laundry—the jobs we'd taken over while mother was teaching school. Sometimes, the four of us would go for walks or bicycle rides, with Pepsi tagging along, to get away from the stifling atmosphere of the village.

It didn't take Pepsi long to find a mate in the village and by mid-December, she was showing definite signs of pregnancy. She gave birth to five offspring in January, three females and two males. Not a good ratio if we were going to keep the animal population under control.

Peter, Mike, and Eric built some furniture during the winter: a table and some benches for eating, and some storage chests, which also doubled as seats. One old lady in the village gave us a double bed mattress, which the rest of us insisted that Mother and Peter should have. Other neighbors gave us some old blankets, several of which we sewed into bags and filled with dry grass and straw to use as pallets for sleeping.

I think the parents of the children Mother taught felt they should pay her in some way because the children often brought little gifts with them to school. A pair of mitts, some outgrown boots, a jar of jam or an old sweater. We were grateful for everything they gave us. We were very needy, having lost most of our clothes and furnishings. We wanted to give them something too, but had so little to offer. Peter hit on the ideal solution when he borrowed a guitar from one of the men and used it to entertain them at one of the socials. After that, he was always welcome at gatherings to lead sing-alongs, and sometimes even some sedate dancing.

Winter finally passed and Willow creek started preparing for the spring planting. They had the good fortune of having a real plough to hitch up to one of their horses for turning the soil, and could therefore plant some grain as well as vegetables. Most people in the village planted their own vegetable gardens in addition to helping with large-scale community crops such as potatoes and corn.

Pam's desire to go back to the city caught our imaginations, and the four of us, Mike, Pam, Eric and I started to consider it seriously. There was little joy for us in Willow Creek after the warmth and friendship we'd known in Salish until the raid, and somehow, being so close to Salish reminded us of what we'd lost

Chapter 24

The four of us set out for the city on our bicycles the first week in April, carrying some camping gear and enough food to last us for several days. It had been warm and sunny when left Willow Creek. We also had our family's last remaining rifle.

We met very few people, and those we did see were usually some distance away, working in the fields or riding by. We reached the bank of the Fraser River by early afternoon and turned west. The roads were in much worse shape than they had been a couple of years earlier when we had left the city. There were now shrubs and sapling trees growing from cracks in the road, and the broken pavement was tilted this way and that, making bicycle riding tricky in places. Many of the abandoned vehicles—mostly private cars—along the sides of the road had been cannibalized for their parts, and quite a few were nothing but burned-out shells.

We had hoped to reach the outskirts of Burnaby before nightfall, but we were taking the longer southern route and had to go cautiously through these unfamiliar industrial areas. We'd decided to go that way because most of the Indian communities and temples were on the south side of the city and that would be the most likely area to find Pam's family.

When it started to get dark, we found a sheltered place near the old Patullo Bridge in New Westminster. It was surrounded by bushes, so we felt we would be relatively safe there. After gathering firewood, we'd lit a small fire and heated up some food. We were sitting on our packs, eating and discussing what we would do the next day when we were attacked.

We heard pebbles rolling down the bank and rustling in the bushes. Eric grabbed the rifle.

"I wouldn't, if I was you," a man's voice said.

We looked up and saw two men emerging from the bushes with weapons trained on us. Eric nudged me hard with his elbow, so that I lost my balance and rolled down the bank into the icy water of the river. As the current carried me, choking and gasping downstream, I heard Pam scream.

Before the river carried me too far, I washed up against an obstacle, either a root or tree that had fallen into the river. Whatever it was, it probably saved my life because I wouldn't have survived long in the icy water. I crawled out onto the bank and lay shivering, wondering what to do next. I had never been so cold. I wasn't sure whether it would be better to keep the wet clothes on or take them off and hope they would dry. I knew I had to find a shelter somewhere, but foremost in my mind was the need to know what had happened to the others. I hadn't heard any shots, but noise of the rushing water could have drowned the noise.

I got to my knees and pulled myself up holding onto the bushes, then sidled along the riverbank towards the place where we had set up our camp. I stopped to remove my outer garments so that I could wring the water out of them, shivering so violently that my frozen fingers could barely undo the fastenings. After I'd wrung out as much of the water as I could, I wrapped them around me again and continued stealthily along the riverbank, stopping to listen every few meters. There was no sound apart from the rippling of the river and the wind stirring the trees.

I must have washed farther downstream than I thought; I could find no sign of our campfire. Then the bridge loomed ahead. I had to climb up the bank to get around the pylons that supported it. Sliding silently down the other side, I found the campsite. The fire was still smoldering, the pan of food overturned beside it and my pack was still lying on the ground under the bush near where I'd been sitting, but there was no sign of my friends. I crouched close to the dying fire, hoping to absorb some of its warmth while I thought about what to do next. After adding a few more twigs to the fire, I opened the pack and took out the change of clothes I'd brought with me. Once I had changed into dry clothing, I unrolled my sleeping bag and wrapped it around me. After lying for a long time, shivering from the chill and starting at every sound, sheer exhaustion overcame my fears and discomfort.

I was awoken by a bird singing lustily in the bush above my head. I saw by the shadows and the pinkish-gold light that the sun was barely above the horizon. I started to cry when I remembered the previous night, fearing what had happened to my friends then I realized I was wasting time and energy. It was time to think about getting away from there. But where would I go? I wanted to find them, but I couldn't do it alone, even if I knew where they'd been taken. I realized that I'd have to go back to the Willow Creek. The prospect was dismal, but I had no choice now.

I repacked my backpack and looked around for anything else that had been left behind. The bicycles and the other packs were gone. My pack had been missed because it was hidden under the bush. I was alone with no transportation, a dangerous situation to be in. I still had the knife I always carried in my belt. I'd have to protect myself as best I could with that.

I hoisted the pack onto my back and started to walk along the riverbank where the bushes gave me some cover. After going a few meters, I realized I was hungry after all. I sat on the ground and rifled through my pack until I found some dried meat and corn bread. Putting them in my pocket, I resumed my walk along the bank, chewing on pieces of dry meat and a few bites of cornbread as I went. There was still some water in my canteen to wash down the food.

After about a kilometer, I came up against an obstacle, an old stone pier rising from the steep riverbank, and was forced to climb up to the road to go around it. I emerged cautiously from the screen of bushes onto the pavement. There was no sign of life apart from a few gulls, so I kept going on the road where it was much easier to walk.

After a while, I became aware of a strange noise behind me, gradually getting closer. I slid back down into the bushes to hide. The noise puzzled me—it sounded like the clopping of horse's hooves accompanied by a rhythmic squeaking sound and a metallic clanging as if a bunch of pans and pot lids were being shaken. There was another sound as well—someone whistling, quite merrily. I peeked between the branches and saw an amazing vehicle coming around the bend—a gaily-painted horse-drawn wagon with a canopy over it and pots and pans and all sorts of things dangling from the sides. The driver was wearing a leather vest over a striped shirt, and on his head was a brimmed hat with a feather in the crown. He sported a trim beard and had a smoking pipe in his mouth. He'd stopped whistling.

I was so busy goggling at the man and his vehicle that I lost my footing and, with a startled yell, crashed down the bank. I lay dead still, sure that he had heard me.

"Whoa!" the man cried. The wagon came to a stop. The squeaking and clattering were silenced so that all I could hear were the horses snorting. "Is somebody there?" the man called.

I kept still, hoping he would leave, but he pushed his way through the bushes and found me. I looked up at him as he gazed down on me.

"You all right?" he asked.

For some reason, I felt he wouldn't hurt me. I guess it was the way he had come down the road, so openly and noisily without any hint of stealth. That and his gentle grey eyes. I nodded.

"Need some help?" He held his hand out to me. I looked at it for a moment of indecision, then struggled to my feet and allowed him to help me up the bank.

"Thanks," I said, brushing the dirt and leaves off me.

"What are you doing out here all alone?"

I burst into tears and told him about the attack on our campsite. He listened attentively until I'd finished then said, "Would you like a lift? I have to be moving along."

"Where are you going?" I asked.

"Here and there," he replied.

"Why? I mean—who are you?"

"Come on, I'll help you up. We can talk while we're traveling." He took my pack and threw it into the wagon that was loaded inside with crates and bags and packages. He helped me to climb up onto the seat, then got up and sat beside me. With a flick of the reins and a click of his tongue, he got the horse moving again. "That was bad luck last night, running into those people. I don't think they'll harm your friends, I mean it's unlikely they'll kill them."

"Why did they take them?" I asked.

"They were probably looking for workers," the man replied. "There are some communities that make other people work for them, so they can have an easy life."

"You mean like slaves?"

"Something like that. If people won't work for them willingly, they kidnap them and force them to work. They've got plenty of weapons."

"Are they survivalists?"

"Not exactly, although there are some similarities. I avoid them, if I can. No, these are people who used to be rich I suppose, they got together with former government officials and, with military personnel to protect them, set themselves up in fortified towns. There's one out at Mission, on the north bank of the river, and another down by the border near Cloverdale. I hear there's a big one in Victoria. There are others who kidnap people for them. I guess they get rewarded with food and ammunition. Sort of like the press gangs that used to operate in old England."

"But how come you're safe? Don't these people ever bother you?"

"They bother me all right. Their existence bothers me. But no, I don't get molested very often by them. I'm a trader you see."

Chapter 25

A what?"

"A trader. A sort of peddler—some people call me a gypsy or tinker. I travel around the countryside trading with people, bringing things they need, distributing their products, and so on. They leave us alone because we're useful and don't do anybody any harm. Besides, we're the best source of news there is right now. I also carry messages and letters back and forth, so, in a way, I'm the postman as well."

I considered this for a while. I had never heard of such a thing before—our village had been too isolated— but it made sense. It sounded like an interesting kind of life. I looked around to see where we were and realized we had almost reached the turnoff to Willow Creek.

"Are you going to Willow Creek?" I asked just before we reached the side road. "We're almost there."

"What do you think? Will I be welcome?"

I smiled for the first time that day. "I think they'd be happy to see you," I replied. "You turn left here."

"Maybe I should tell you who I am so that you can introduce me when we get there," the trader said. "My name is Alexander Marcovic, but everybody calls me Tommy."

"Pleased to meet you, Tommy," I replied, offering him my hand. "My name's Celeste Colbert and people call me Celeste."

"Pretty name, Celeste," he said with a smile.

The village came into sight and soon we saw a couple of armed men standing in the road with dogs.

"You'd better slow down a bit," I advised. "It'll be all right. As soon as they recognize me, they'll know it's okay."

Tommy pulled back on the reigns and the horses slowed their pace. The two men were now standing in the middle of the road, and the dogs were racing towards us, barking.

I climbed down from the box. "It's okay, Mr. Tomlinson, it's me, Celeste. This is Tommy. He's a trader."

They asked Tommy a few questions and looked in the back of the wagon then, after exchanging a few words with each other, waved us on. I advised Tommy to stop by the church where I jumped down and went into the hall to find Mother. She was in the classroom with her young students.

"Celeste! That didn't take long," Mother said when she saw me. Then she must have noticed my expression. "Is everything...? What happened, Celeste?"

I burst into tears again and ran into her arms. "Oh, Mom." I wailed.

She propelled me out of the room into a little office where we could talk in privacy. I told her everything that had happened.

"My God, Celeste, that's terrible. I'm so sorry. Those poor boys. . . It's unbelievable on top of everything else that's happened to them." She sighed and brushed the hair back from her face. "When will this ever end?"

The sound of voices coming from outside caught her attention. "What's all the excitement?" she asked going to the window.

"I almost forgot, I met this man, Tommy. He's a trader. He gave me a ride back."

"I wondered how you got back so quickly. Let's go out there; I'd like to meet him. I'll just dismiss the children first, though." After telling the students they could go—to their obvious delight—Mother and I went out to the road.

A crowd of people was milling around Tommy's wagon, watched over by Reverend Eikhart. The cover of the wagon had been rolled back so that he could display his wares and make access to them easier. He explained to them that at present he preferred to trade for goods rather than money because that enabled him to keep stocked with merchandise, and many people he met didn't trust cash yet. Most of the merchandise was wrapped in packages and only identifiable by labels handwritten in black ink. There were a few bolts of cloth, plenty of pots and pans which, although they weren't all new, were in excellent condition. He had some glass jars of pickles and preserves, herbs and spices, a few tools, some yarn, shoes and boots, socks and other items of clothing. Most of the clothing was used, so there was no guarantee of finding a particular size or color. The commodity most in demand was salt, and he had a little, but it wasn't cheap.

When the distribution of goods broke down, salt was one of the things people missed the most then someone started recovering salt from seawater. This was a laborious process, which yielded only a small amount of salt, but soon others started doing it and a small supply began to trickle onto the market. The people who ran these operations must have made a fortune, because it was very expensive.

Tommy was glad to take honey in trade. It was very much in demand due to the unavailability of sugar—it is possible to obtain sugar from beets, but the processing required complex machinery, knowledge of chemistry, and other skills, so no one had yet had any success.

The biggest surprise was that he had a few bags of flour, something we hadn't been able to get for years.

"Where did it come from?" I asked him. I had taken up a proprietary position by his side and was helping him trade.

"There's a mill opened in Hope. It's run by waterpower. People who grow the grain take it there to be ground into flour."

He handed a small bag of flour to a woman in exchange for a bucket of honey. Some people who didn't have honey to trade brought clothes, eggs and other items, which Tommy assessed and came up with a value before handing over something in return.

When he had finished for the day, Mother asked him if he would like to come to our house for a meal. "You can stay the night if you aren't in a hurry," she added.

"That's very kind of you, Mrs. Colbert," he replied. "I'm sure Old Billy and Jane would like to get out of their harnesses for a while and have a rest."

Back at the familiar house, I was overcome with grief again. The house seemed so empty without Eric and Mike and Pam. It was then that I knew I couldn't stay there. There were too many memories of too many losses. It was unbelievable that out of our original group of twenty-one people, only four remained. Seven had been killed, eight had been kidnapped or disappeared and two had stayed behind in the city. I wondered if I would ever see any of them again, those who were still alive.

After supper while we were sitting around the fireplace, I brought up the subject of leaving with Tommy. "Could you use an assistant?" I asked him.

"Why? Are you applying for the job?" he replied with a laugh.

"I'm serious," I said. "I can't stay here, I have to get away and I thought . . ."

"Hmm." He looked at Mother and Peter then back at me. "I've no objection."

"Oh, thank you Tommy. I promise I won't be any trouble."

"Celeste, are you sure about this?" my mother asked. "It could be dangerous."

"It's not an easy life," Tommy warned. "Sometimes there's nowhere to sleep except on the ground, and keeping clean isn't easy. You have to take a bath when and wherever you get the chance, usually in a stream or a lake. You get soaked when it rains, frozen in cold weather, and baked in summer."

"I don't care," I said. "Anyway, we're used to roughing it."

"Are you thinking that you might find Eric and the others?" Peter asked.

"Maybe," I replied. "At least there'd be more chance than if I stayed here."

"We'll miss you," Mother said. "But if that's what you want to do . . ."

"I'll come back," I replied. "And you still have Tate."

"Not for long the way he's going." She ruffled his hair. "He's already got half the girls in town swooning over him."

"Kate!" He gave her a pleased grin.

"Yes," Peter added. "He's either going to be forced to marry one of them at gun point or else be run out of town by irate parents."

Chapter 26

The next morning I awoke early and packed my belongings ready for life on the road. Not that I had much to pack: a pair of sandals and a lighter set of clothing for the hot weather, some soap, a towel and a comb, a picture of my parents and Paul that I had managed to hang on to.

"I think you'd better cut your hair off," Tommy said at breakfast. "And you'll need a hat."

"Why?" I asked.

"Short hair so that we can pass you off as a boy if necessary, and a hat to protect you from the sun. I think I've got one somewhere you can use."

"But why would I have to pretend to be a boy?"

"It's not always safe for girls, as I'm sure you know."

I didn't mind the idea. I was fairly tall and certainly slim enough to pass as a boy and it might even be fun. When we lived in the city, after the plague, everyone had short-cropped hair for hygienic reasons, but I had let mine grow since then and now it was down below my waist. I reluctantly asked my mother to cut it all off.

"Be careful," Mother said when it was time to leave. She hugged me close for a moment then let me go.

"I'll be all right, Mom, honestly."

"Take care of her," she said to Tommy.

Tommy nodded and, as soon as I was on the box beside him, flicked the reins to get the horses moving

"Where are we going next?" I asked as we left Willow Creek.

"We'll go east on the highway almost as far as Mission, although we won't go into the town, then we'll cross over the river and continue up the valley on the other side." I took the reins while he lit his pipe. The smoke had a pleasant aroma.

"What are you smoking?"

"It's a mixture of herbs. There's not much tobacco in it."

One of the nice things about riding with Tommy was his comfortable silences. We could go for long stretches without feeling it was necessary to keep up a conversation. It gave both of us a chance to think. As we drove along the highway, I wondered why I felt so safe with him.

He wasn't very tall, maybe about five ten, and was fairly slim. His hair was a dark reddish brown with a touch of grey. His beard, which was a sort of ginger color, was also sprinkled with grey. He had a fine aquiline nose and was very tanned from constantly being out of doors. He was obviously intelligent and seemed well educated. I was curious about him.

"Tommy?"

"Hmm?"

"What did you do before you became a trader?"

"I was always a trader. Just a different kind of trader in the old days."

"You mean you owned a shop?"

"No, nothing like that. I was a stockbroker."

I only had a dim idea of what that meant. I vaguely remembered hearing about the stock market, and thought it had something to do with what rich people did with their money.

"Why do they call you Tommy?"

"I was named after a character in a musical. My friends associated me with this character."

"Why, what did he do?"

"He was a pinball wizard."

"A what?"

"It's a long story. I used to be married, but my wife divorced me. When the divorce became final, I kept telling everyone, 'I'm free', so they nicknamed me *Tommy*. It's a song the character sings in the musical." He turned and smiled at me. "Now tell me about yourself."

By the time I had finished relating everything to him from the time my grandfather died, we were approaching another community.

It was a cluster of houses in a bad state of repair. Several children were sitting by the roadside playing in the dirt. They wore ragged clothes and some of them had runny noses. They were all dirty. As soon as they saw us, they jumped up and ran towards us, yelling with excitement. Several grownups appeared from behind or inside the houses. They were just as bedraggled and unhealthy-looking as their children. The ground around was littered with broken machinery and rusted out car bodies. A few skinny chickens pecked in the dust watched over by a scrawny dog that raised its head wearily and growled when we came up, but didn't seem to have the energy to bark. A pig was rooting through some vegetable scraps in one of the yards.

"Not one of our more savory communities," Tommy murmured as we brought the wagon to a stop.

"Hey, Tommy!" one of the men greeted him. He took a swig from the jar in his hand before continuing. "How's business?"

"See you got yourself a new assistant," another one called.

"Yes," Tommy replied but didn't introduce me. "Charlie, Bert, how's life treating you?"

"Can't complain. Not much anyways."

"What have you got for me today?" he asked.

"A few gallons of good vodka," one man replied.

"Got some skins," the other added. "Jodie, bring those skins," he yelled and one of the women disappeared into the house. She returned with an armload of pelts and hung them on the fence. "Good skins," the man said, fingering them.

Tommy climbed down and went over to the fence. "Cured?" he asked.

"Yep. Did 'em myself." The man scratched his groin and spat on the ground. "Cody. Keep away from there," he shouted at a little boy who was sidling up to the horse.

"All right I'll take them. What do you need?"

"Got any ammo?"

"We need beans and salt," the woman said in a whiny voice.

"I know that," he told her. "But I need some ammo."

"All I've got is a few shotgun shells."

"They'll have to do I suppose. How about salt?"

The bargaining continued for about twenty minutes. We took on some pelts, several gallon jars of home-made vodka, and some dried herbs in exchange for dried beans, a little salt and some honey. Tommy also handed out some small sticks of dried meat to the children.

"Want to stay and have a nip?" a man asked Tommy, holding out his jar.

"No, thanks, Bert. Got a long way to go yet. See you in about two months."

He turned the cart around and went back to the highway.

"They looked so poor," I said when we got moving. "How do they make a living?"

"A little hunting, a little distilling." Seeing my puzzled look, he went on, "Their major industry is distilling vodka. It's quite a good product really for a cottage industry and they'd make a nice living if they weren't so lazy, and if they didn't drink away their profits."

It was a warm spring day with birdsong filling the air. The budding trees wore veils of misty green and the sky was cloudless. We stopped to have some lunch around noon, after we had visited another community. Sitting under a tree, we ate dried meat and corn bread, which we washed down with some apple cider. The cider made me feel drowsy and I dozed off for a while on the wagon after we got moving again.

We continued to see the hulks of old vehicles lying in the roadside ditches, rusty and overgrown with weeds and brambles. I supposed many of them belonged to people fleeing the city during the epidemics. *What had become of all those people?* I imagined that when they ran out of fuel and had to abandon their cars, they wouldn't have been made very welcome by the locals. *How would they keep going? Did any of them survive?*

We stopped for the night about ten kilometers short of Mission. Tommy drove the wagon off the road onto an almost invisible track that led into a field. Once the wagon was parked under a tree, he unharnessed the horses and let them loose. They made directly down the slope to a stream that ran along one edge of the field.

"How about finding some firewood so that we can cook something?" Tommy suggested.

After I'd brought some dry twigs and broken branches, he sent me to the stream to fetch water. Obviously, I was going to earn my keep, which made me feel better.

We had been given some rabbit meat on one of our stops, so Tommy made a stew with some potatoes and onions. We set about making a temporary camp while the stew was cooking. Tommy had a large tarpaulin rolled up in the back of the wagon. He brought it out and spread it on the ground beside the wagon, then lay his sleeping bag on one edge of it. He folded the rest of the tarp back and attached the other edge onto hooks on the wagon, making a sort of lean-to style shelter.

He looked up at me and grinned. "That's my shelter for the night. What about you?"

"Oh. I guess I'll..." I said lamely, looking around for an idea.

He laughed and stood up. "I was only teasing," he said. "You can sleep in the wagon, it'll be warmer up there. I'll clear a space for you."

We followed the stew with some root coffee and a small portion of honey cake that mother had given us. The cake was made from eggs, cornmeal and honey. It was sweet and tasty although the texture left something to be desired. The sky had clouded over late in the afternoon and as we finished eating, we felt the first raindrops.

"I'll put this stuff away," Tommy said, "While you rinse off the dishes."

I took my toothbrush and towel with me to the stream and had a quick wash after I'd cleaned the dishes. After running back to the wagon and putting the things away, I looked around for somewhere to relieve myself. We had become very aware in the past few years of the necessity to avoid polluting the water supply so I chose a clump of bushes well away from the stream.

Tommy was kneeling up on the box when I got back with his torso hidden inside the wagon. After a moment he withdrew and climbed down.

"That should be comfortable for you," he said.

"Thanks, Tommy." I climbed up and found he'd rearranged the interior to clear a narrow space across the width of the wagon near the front. I unrolled my sleeping bag and blanket and crawled in, thankful I didn't have to sleep outside. "Goodnight!" I called as I snuggled in.

We ate the remains of the stew the next morning before packing up and continuing on our way.

"We'll have to stop at a blacksmith today and have him take a look at the horses' shoes. Don't want to have one fall off on the road; we've got a long way to go this trip." Tommy informed me.

"That should be interesting," I replied. "I've never seen a blacksmith. Are there many of them?"

"I only know of a couple—this one and another across the river near Chilliwack. I prefer to use this one."

While we were waiting for the blacksmith to finish whatever he was doing to the horseshoes, we did some trading with the people in the area. It didn't take long for word to spread that the trader was there. I helped Tommy, keeping one eye on the glowing furnace inside the blacksmith's shed where the smith was hammering away on his anvil, his face and torso gleaming in the

224

firelight. He helped Tommy harness Billy and Jane to the wagon when he was finished, and we resumed our journey.

Chapter 27

Mrs. Johnson had a baby girl on April 20," Tommy announced.

"Good for her," I said. "What did she call her? And who's Mrs. Johnson?"

Tommy chuckled. "It's the sort of gossip I pick up and pass around. Tammy Johnson is the wife of Andy Johnson. They live in one of the small communities near here, and they called the baby Lesley Dawn. People like to hear news like that. It gives them a sense that life is picking up again."

"What else did you find out?"

"Al Kravitsky got drunk the other night and went on a rampage through the village trying to pick fights with everyone. His wife locked him out of the house so he had to sleep it off in the barn."

"The vodka, I suppose."

"Right, the vodka."

"Doesn't it bother you?"

"What else do they have to do? They've got to have some fun and most of these people haven't found anything else to replace television." We came to a side road leading towards the river and turned into it. "Time to cross the river."

"How are we going to get across?" I asked. The river was still very wide and rapid. It looked more than half a kilometer across to me.

"On the bridge. There's a sandbar in the middle of the river. The bridge goes across there."

The rain was still drizzling down and the river—a heaving mass of opaque grey—flowed swiftly below us. It reminded me of being washed downstream a few nights earlier. I shuddered. It was hard to believe it had only happened three days ago. It was already fading in my mind. I felt guilty because, in the excitement of being on the road with Tommy, I hadn't given much thought to my friends. I recalled a tender moment with Eric the night before we left and felt tears in my eyes.

Tommy, probably sensing that I was troubled, said, "Everything all right?"

"I was just thinking about my friends. Wondering where they are and when I'll see them again."

"Maybe we'll hear something on our travels. People tell me all sorts of rumors and gossip. Don't lose hope."

We had reached the south end of the bridge and the wagon rolled off onto the bank. "Bit of a climb here," Tommy said. "We'll get down and walk now to lighten the load for the horses."

The road was narrow with broken paving and holes filed with weeds and grass. It wound up from the riverbank for about half a kilometer to where it joined a wider road. There was a cluster of houses at the junction with smoke rising from the chimneys. As we approached, three or four barking dogs ran out to meet us. A man carrying a shotgun came out of the nearest house and called them off, then stood waiting for us.

"Morning, Kev," Tommy called. "How are things at the Landing?"

"Not so bad," the man replied. "I suppose things could be better." He was a man of about sixty-five who walked with a limp and had a nasty looking scar down one side of his face.

Several other people came out of the houses to greet the trader. I noticed there were no young people apart from one toddler of about two carried by a woman who looked as if she could be its grandmother.

"Where is everybody?" Tommy asked, looking around.

"Gone," Kev replied, bitterly. "We was raided couple of weeks ago. The bastards took all the young people. Said they were needed to work for the government." He turned his head and gazed down the road towards the river, probably the direction they had gone.

Tommy shook his head sympathetically. "I've being hearing about a lot of this sort of thing lately," he said. "This is Celeste, my new assistant." He smiled at me. "Her village was raided last autumn then she lost the rest of her friends in another attack only a few days ago. We're keeping our ears open for news. Any idea where they're taking them?"

"Probably Mission. According to what I hear, there's a lot of people there who call themselves *The Government*, although they're not doing anything for anybody but themselves. People keep well away from there. There's been some nasty rumors."

"What kind of rumors?" I asked.

"There's work camps from what I've heard. They keep people locked up and only let them out to work.

They have armed guards—military people—to make sure they don't escape."

"Yes, I've heard something similar," Tommy said. "The rumors may be a bit exaggerated, though. Well, as I said, we'll keep our eyes and ears open. Now, anything you folks need?" He climbed up and unrolled the wagon cover.

"We haven't got much to trade right now," Kev replied.

"What do you need?" Tommy asked. "I'm sure we can come to some sort of terms. We just got some nice honey."

"Honey. That'd be a treat for Kathy," the woman holding the child said. "We could let you have a few eggs I suppose," she continued.

"We've got some smoked fish we could spare too," another woman said. "We could use some salt if you've got any. And I don't suppose you've got any flour?"

"As a matter of fact we have a little. I could let you have a small bag of flour and a few grams of salt for the fish if you'll throw in a hot drink for me and my assistant." He turned to me, "Celeste, would you help these ladies?"

Tommy returned with a bucket of water for the horses, as I was finishing with the customers. I showed him the smoked fish and half dozen eggs we'd received. He nodded his approval, then went to the back of the wagon and pulled out a bottle of clear liquid. "Come on, let's get that hot drink."

We entered Kev's house where we were invited to sit close to the stove and mugs of hot root coffee were put in our hands. Steam rose from our clothes as they began to dry out and, for the first time in days, I felt warm.

Tommy gave the bottle to Kev. "Vodka. On me," he said.

"Thanks," Kev said. He cleared his throat. "Did you go anywhere near Mission?"

"No," Tommy shook his head. "No sense attracting their attention. If those people call themselves 'the government', they might get it into their heads to start making us pay taxes."

Tommy and I continued our journey up the valley, making frequent detours onto side roads to visit scattered communities. The weather warmed up as spring progressed and the fragile veils of sprouting leaves on the trees and hedgerows turned into mantles of rich green. Once it was warm enough, I moved my bed from the cramped space in the wagon to the ground underneath it. Tommy had another tarpaulin, which I used as a ground sheet.

Sometimes, people gave us letters to take to their relatives or friends in other communities, and we frequently carried verbal messages. Tommy had a notebook in which he kept notes, so that he wouldn't forget or mix up the messages.

One afternoon in early May, we saw several armed men on horseback coming towards us. "Quickly, put your hat on," he told me. "And tuck your hair up inside. Now rub some dirt on your face. Remember, you're a boy. Don't speak unless you have to."

"Afternoon," Tommy said when the men stopped in front of us and forced us to stop.

"Who are you?" one of the men asked. He was a beefy, red-faced man wearing a dirty grey cowboy hat with camouflage shirt and pants. He looked about fifty and had a mean face with little, close-set eyes and a small, thin-lipped mouth. He seemed to be the leader.

"Tommy Marcovic, trader," Tommy replied.

"Who's that?" the man pointed to me.

"My son. He's a bit . . . you know." Tommy pointed to his head. "Shock. His mother was killed."

231

"What have you got in there?" the man asked, losing interest in me.

"My merchandise," Tommy answered. "I've introduced myself; may I ask who you are?"

The men laughed, and I'm sure that if they'd been standing close together, they would have nudged one another with their elbows.

"How about we ask the questions?"

The other men laughed again. They certainly had a weird sense of humor, unless they knew something we didn't. I felt an icy tingle down my spine. I could easily imagine them raiding peaceful settlements and carrying off young women.

"Well, since I'm a trader, I just thought you might want to trade," Tommy said mildly.

"Let's see inside the wagon," the leader ordered.

Tommy handed me the reigns and jumped down. Everyone moved to the back of the wagon, and Tommy opened the flap. I could hear them poking around behind me, but didn't dare look for fear of attracting their attention. Every now and then, someone would ask, "What's this," and Tommy would explain.

Finally, I heard the spokesman ask, "Any ammunition?"

"No," Tommy replied. "You know how hard it is to get."

"What's this?"

"Alcohol."

"As in booze?"

"I suppose you could drink it," Tommy said diffidently.

"How about giving us a few bottles?"

"What have you got to trade for it?"

Another burst of laughter.

"Trade?" the ringleader replied. "Let's just call it a tax for allowing you to cross our land without coming to any harm."

"Oh? You own this land, do you?" Tommy asked.

"Don't push it, buddy. And try to get some ammo for next time."

The men rode off with a bottle of vodka hanging from each side of their saddles. When Tommy climbed back onto the box, he was trembling. He picked up the reins and clicked at the horses to start them walking.

"That was scary, Tommy. How could you be so cool? Weren't you afraid?"

"Afraid? I nearly wet my britches, but it doesn't do to let that sort know they can intimidate you. Like all bullies, they get off on scaring people."

"Did they take all the vodka?"

"Most of it, but it was a cheap price to pay."

"You lied about the ammo didn't you?"

"Of course. Can't afford to let it get into the wrong hands."

"I wonder if they have any kidnapped women at their place."

"I wouldn't be surprised."

"God, I feel so sorry for them."

"Not much we can do," he said. "Not yet anyway."

"What do you mean?" I asked.

"Things are bound to change. They're changing already, bit by bit."

In late May, we reached Hope, a town situated at the eastern end of the valley. It was the only community of any size we'd actually gone into. Usually we bypassed towns and just visited smaller outlying communities, but Hope had a different setup from other towns, which were still in a state of relative anarchy. The people of Hope were better-organized under strong leadership, and had some industries to rely on for their economic needs. The main industry was a flourmill driven by the swiftly flowing river at a point where it ran through a narrow gorge. They also had a lumber mill, and a canning plant where they preserved produce brought in from surrounding areas. They had repaired a hydroelectric generator that provided the town with a limited supply of electricity.

When we arrived, Tommy drove directly to a workshop near the hydro plant. He went inside and returned with a couple of men who helped him unload the wagon. They carried some sealed crates into the building and Tommy returned with some papers. He tucked the papers in his notebook and asked me to help him put the stuff back in the wagon.

"What was that about?" I asked.

"One of my most important transactions," he replied, passing a carton up to me. "I brought them some parts they needed."

"But I never saw them."

"I know. I kept them hidden under everything else. Without them, I wouldn't be able to do business. They give me scrip in return which I can spend on flour from the mill and canned goods to trade on the way back."

"Was that the papers you put in your book?"

"That's right."

"Where do you get the parts?"

"That's the hardest part of my job. I have to make a lot of inquiries and do a lot of snooping and bargaining to find them. In the city mostly."

We stayed in a rooming house in Hope for two days, luxuriating in clean bedding, baths, and regular cooked meals until it was time to load up with supplies and start back westward. One night in Hope, we got to see a real video—an old film that had been made several years before the disasters struck. It brought back so many memories of things I had almost forgotten about: streets filled with cars, shops full of goods, and people talking on the telephone, turning on lights, and opening refrigerators. There was one scene in a hospital where everything was so clean and organized with bright lights and people working efficiently with mysterious machines and computers. After it was over, I went back to my room with a feeling of melancholy for all we'd lost. I thought of my father and his computers, driving to the supermarket with Mom, Chris in her nurse's uniform, and all the people who had died.

Our last visit before we left Hope was to the mill where we picked up the cotton sacks of flour for the return journey. We had already loaded the canned food and some other items the day before and the flour filled up the remaining space in the wagon. Once we had finished at the mill, we were on our way. The weather was hot and sunny, so both of us wore shorts with light cotton shirts and hats to protect our heads from the sun.

Chapter 28

I've got a surprise for you," Tommy said after we'd been on the road about an hour.

"What is it?"

"You'll see."

"Oh, Tommy, I hate it when people say that."

"Be patient. You'll find out soon enough."

We had left the highway for a secondary road and I thought we were going back a different way. We called at a couple of communities in the afternoon and were invited to stay for supper at the last. The spring salmon season was underway and we had a delicious feast of Chinook salmon and garden vegetables. They topped it off by serving fresh strawberries for desert. We had picked up a few books in Hope, so I luxuriated in reading before I went to sleep that night. As I was falling asleep, I wondered again about Tommy's surprise.

We set off early next morning on a narrow road that climbed gradually into the hills. It seemed like an isolated area; we only passed one small settlement consisting of a couple of house with five adults and three children. I couldn't imagine how they survived out there by themselves, but when they offered some good quality pelts in trade, I realized they must be trappers. The forests in this area hadn't been so badly damaged by the fires as they had nearer the coast, and what had been destroyed was now replaced with second growth hardwoods—birch and alder. Trees grew luxuriantly over the mountainsides.

The road became steeper after we left the settlement, so we got down from the wagon and walked beside it, pausing periodically to allow the horses to rest and drink from the plastic pail of water Tommy carried in the wagon. The road curved around the hillside and we entered a narrow gorge with a small stream trickling down one side. The climb eventually became less steep and the road opened into a wide flat area with trees and bushes on both sides.

"Nearly there now," Tommy said.

"What about the surprise?" I reminded him.

"You'll see it in a few minutes." He looked very pleased with himself.

Then I noticed smoke rising beyond the trees. "Who lives up here?" I asked.

"You'll see." He started whistling a cheerful tune.

As if it had received a signal, a large collie came charging out of the brush with a joyful bark, its tail wagging furiously.

"Guinn, old girl, what a wonderful welcome. Pleased to see, me are you?" Tommy patted the dog's head and scratched her behind the ears. "I've got a new friend for you to meet. Say hello to Celeste," he said, pointing her in my direction. "This is Guinevere."

"Hello, Guinevere," I said. I patted her on the head, and she licked my hand in response.

"Let's go," Tommy said, pulling gently on the reins.

We continued along the road, which now showed signs of having been repaired. The trees ended and we came out into a large clearing.

"This is the surprise," Tommy said, watching my reaction.

"Tommy, it's beautiful!" I stopped and looked around in amazement. "I can't believe it. Who lives here?"

There was a large meadow with sheep and a couple of cows grazing, and several plots planted with vegetables, but the most striking thing was the buildings. There were seven or eight houses all made of wood, in different styles varying from A-frames to two story chalets, all beautifully finished, with an abundance of glass. Through the houses, I caught a glimpse of sparkling water. People began to leave the houses and gardens and gather by the road as we came out of the trees.

"Tommy!" they greeted him.

"I thought it was about time for a visit from you."

"Who've you brought with you?"

These people seemed to be different from the country people we'd seen down the valley. They seemed somehow more sophisticated, and there was something about them I couldn't quite identify. There was an alertness and self-assurance in their well-groomed appearance. They crowded around the wagon when we came to a stop in the middle of the settlement.

"Who wants to give me a hand unharnessing the horses?" Tommy asked.

Two men responded immediately and led Billy and Jane away after unhitching them.

"Now let me introduce you all. This is my new assistant, Celeste." He went on to tell me the names of everyone in the community, pointing them out one by one.

Ben Oliver invited us into his house, which was one of the large A-frames. Ben was a large man with a grey beard and twinkling eyes. Tommy explained that he was a former law professor at the university. The woman he lived with was Barbara Franklin, a psychologist. They invited us to sit down while they brought some refreshments. I looked around the room in amazement. It was spotlessly clean, with a polished wood floor and vertical wood paneled walls. A large stone fireplace almost filled one of the end walls, the remainder of which was glass. The other end wall was all glass and looked out over the trees towards the distant valley. A staircase curved up one side to a large gallery that overlooked the room. I assumed the sleeping area was up there. The lower parts of the sloping walls were fitted with bookshelves packed with hundreds of books. The furniture all looked handmade and was finished with great care, rubbed to a dull gleam. The floor had some rich-looking oriental rugs as well as a few woven from wool. The coverings on the upholstery looked as if they had been woven by hand too. The whole place reminded me of something out of an old architecture magazine.

"Tommy, this is incredible. It's so beautiful. I can't believe it." I hugged him. "Thank you, Tommy. It's a lovely surprise. But who are they?"

Ben and Barbara came back with a tray containing some glasses and a jug of fruit juice. Barbara had a plate of what looked like cake.

"She wants to know who you are," Tommy said to them. "Want to tell her?"

"What did they call us? Wild-eyed idealists? Dreamers, greens, eco-freaks, ivory tower intellectuals?

"Don't get him started," Barbara laughed. She was a slender woman of about fifty with thick wiry grey hair and sparkling brown eyes.

Several other people arrived and took seats around the room. They were Paris Fisher, a physician, and his daughter Sarah who was about my age. Dr. Fisher looked about forty-five. He was small and slim with curly brown hair; Sarah was petite with straight, dark hair and lovely blue eyes. A couple in their mid-thirties was introduced as Martin Graham and his wife Maggie who was an artist. Martin, an engineer, had thinning brown hair and wore gold rimmed glasses. Maggie was plump with black hair and an easy laugh.

They told me a little of how they had come to this hidden valley to make it their home.

"We got tired of trying to warn people about the disasters that would overtake us if they didn't stop plundering and polluting the planet," Ben said. "They wouldn't listen; they were either too stupid or too greedy to care. Well now they've reaped the fatal harvest."

"That's not really fair, Ben," Barbara interrupted. "All those innocent people dying—they didn't deserve that. Most people felt helpless, they were doing the best they could. They just felt that whatever they did wasn't going to make much difference. They were right in a way. It had gone too far. And we were too accustomed to all the conveniences and luxuries to want to give them up."

"You are correct, my love, as usual," Ben replied. "Anyway, we saw it coming, as the saying goes, so we started looking around for a place to build a new home and discovered this land for sale. All the people living here now were connected in some way with the university, or were friends who believed as we did. We decided to pool our resources and build a community for ourselves and our families where we could be safe from whatever was coming down."

"Don't forget the part about the *guardians of civilization,"* Paris Fisher said with a laugh.

"Oh, yes, mustn't forget that. You see, we didn't know what form the disaster would take exactly and we certainly never expected it to be this bad, but we thought it might be a good idea to collect as many books and stuff . . . the fruits of how many years of civilization?"

"Keepers of the sacred knowledge?"

I turned to see who the new voice belonged to. I don't know how to describe the moment when I first saw him. It was as if I had suddenly recognized the person I had been destined to meet all my life. It was almost as if we had known each other before. I found I couldn't take my eyes off him, and saw he was looking at me with the same astonished expression.

Chapter 29

This is my son, Andrew," Paris Fisher said. "Andrew, this is Celeste."

Of course it is, I thought, as if this meeting was inevitable. He had his sister's dark hair and striking blue eyes, but his hair was curly like his father's and fell to his shoulders. He had his father's wiry build as well, although he was a bit taller.

He came farther into the room to shake hands with me. "Hi, Celeste. Nice to meet you," he said.

I felt as if my insides had turned to liquid, and all I could say was, "Hi." I was sure everyone noticed my face turn red.

Andrew sat down next to me and the conversation continued although I was hearing everything through a fog, aware of no one but the person beside me.

"Would you like me to show you around?" Andrew asked after a while.

"Yes, I'd like that," I replied. "Thank you."

We left Ben Oliver's house and walked across the grassy area in the middle of the village where a few sheep were grazing.

"Our lawn mowers," Andrew commented.

"Where do you live?" I asked him.

"Over there." He pointed out a two-story house with vertical wood siding. The house had solar panels on the

245

roof and shutters folded back from the windows. "Want to see it?"

"Okay."

The interior of the Fisher house was similar to Ben Oliver's having the same paneled walls and hand-made furniture. Andrew led me into the kitchen, which, to my surprise had a refrigerator.

"You have electricity?" I asked him.

"Oh, yes. We've got a generator, but we use the power very sparingly. Mostly it's to run refrigerators and some of the tools and machinery we need. We use oil lamps and candles for lighting most of the time. We've got hot and cold running water, too." He turned a tap on to demonstrate.

"Do you use electricity to heat the water?"

"No. Did you notice the solar panels on the roof?" I nodded. "That's how we heat our water, and in the winter they help heat the house as well. Come on, I'll show you upstairs."

On the second floor were three bedrooms all simply furnished and somewhat untidy with books and clothing scattered about on every surface. "Sorry about the mess," Andrew apologized, picking up some clothes from the floor and stuffing them into a closet. "We get too busy to do much housekeeping."

We went outside again where he pointed out the different houses and told me who lived in each. There were several other buildings apart from the houses. They included a greenhouse, a barn for storing fodder and shearing sheep, a studio for spinning, weaving and other crafts. He took me into the studio where I noticed an easel and some painting equipment in one corner below a skylight, and several paintings hanging on the walls.

"Who's the artist?"

"Oh, that's Martin's wife, Maggie. She was just beginning to get recognition when the trouble started. She's quite good, isn't she?"

I looked more closely at the paintings. They were all done in strong bold strokes and subtle colors. Some of them were obviously portraits of the people who lived in the village. There were also some semi-abstract landscapes in beautiful blends of greys and soft tones of blue-green, gold and violet. On another part of the wall, were some realistic watercolors of plants and flowers.

"Are these hers too?" I asked.

"No, they're my sister's. She's taking lessons from Maggie."

"She's pretty good." I turned to him and was once more struck by his—I almost want to say beauty. The strong attraction I felt left me speechless for a moment. "What do you do?" I inquired to cover my confusion.

"Besides hard labor?" he said with a smile. "I help Ben in his workshop. You could say I'm an apprentice carpenter. Ben's hobby—or what used to be his hobby, it's now his occupation—is furniture making. He made a lot of the furniture in the houses."

"I thought it looked hand-made. It's beautiful."

"Come and see where I work."

He took my hand and led me into the workshop attached to the studio. It was about the size of a four-room house and had workbenches down one side. The air was filled with the aroma of freshly cut wood with an undertone of glue and varnish. There were several pieces of furniture in various stages of completion. The workbench seemed to have every woodworking tool imaginable on its surface or hanging from hooks on the wall above it. Shelves on one wall contained tins and jars of paint, varnish, and glue, as well as boxes of sandpaper and bins of nails and screws. There were racks of lumber along another wall and several saw horses about the floor. Some of the equipment was electrical—I could see power cords leading into a power bar under the workbench.

There was some kind of machine standing on trestles at the back of the room.

"What's that?" I asked.

"It's a pump, or it's going to be. Martin's working on it so that we can pump water from the hot spring."

In a lean-to shed at the back of the workshop was a small furnace and some equipment that reminded me of the blacksmith shop. "This is the foundry where we do metalwork." Andrew informed me

"Come on, I want to show you something. I've been saving the best for last." He smiled as he led me out of the workshop.

We were met outside by two large collies who wagged their tails and licked Andrew's hand. "This is Sir Lancelot and this is his lady, Guinevere."

"I've met Guinevere," I said, giving them each a pat on the head. "What do you call this place? Camelot?"

Andrew laughed. "No, nothing so pretentious. It used to be called *Lost Canyon,* but we just call it *the Canyon.* This way," he added.

We went along a path through the trees. It was cool and shady in the woods and the ground was softened by a carpet of pine needles. Somewhere a woodpecker was busy drilling into a tree and, apart from birds singing and the gentle rustle of the wind in the branches, there was no other sound. We emerged from the trees into a clearing close to the side of the mountain. There I saw a dark pool of water overhung by rocks. Steam was rising from the water carrying a slightly sulfurous smell.

"This is it," Andrew said proudly. "Our own spa!"

"Wow!" I knelt down on a flat rock beside the pool and tested the water with my finger. "It feels perfect."

"Want to try it?"

"Maybe later," I replied, suddenly feeling confused and shy.

"Okay. Want to go back?"

I nodded.

"How did you meet up with Tommy?" he asked on the way back.

"He found me on the road." I told him about our attempt to go back to the city, the attack, and how I had lost my friends.

"Wow, that's rough," Andrew replied. "There's nothing . . . I mean . . . you and Tommy aren't?"

"Oh, no, nothing like that," I replied when I realized what he was getting at. "He's a really nice guy. I like him a lot. I guess I think of him as more of a father figure."

"What about your family?"

"My mother and her companion, Peter, live in a small community west of here. My dad disappeared before we left the city. He went to work one day and never came home. We think he was probably killed by some gang. I used to have a little brother, but he died. My Gran was killed in a raid on the first village we lived in."

"Boy you've had a rough time, Celeste. You must miss them a lot."

I nodded, but I realized guiltily that perhaps I didn't miss Eric as much as I should. I wondered if I had really been in love with him at all. I'd never felt the thrill with Eric that I felt the moment I saw Andrew. Could I have been drawn to Eric because he was the only person available or, even worse, because it was something to do to offset the monotony of our lives? I felt really miserable about what had happened to him and wanted to find out if he was all right, but I didn't really yearn for him. I realized that I rarely thought about him now that he was gone.

251

Andrew put his arm around my shoulder and kept it there as walked back through the trees. We arrived back at the center of the village our moods subdued.

"My mother would love this place," I said for a change of topic.

"What does your mother do?" Andrew asked.

"She's a teacher. She used to teach high school biology. I don't suppose you need a teacher, do you?" I asked half jokingly.

"I don't know. I could talk to the others," Andrew replied, taking me seriously. "What about Peter—is that his name?"

"He used to be a graphic designer. He's sort of a Jack-of-all-trades. He's pretty good at making things work. Oh, and he's a musician. He plays the guitar and writes music."

"A multi-talented sort of guy."

"Where've you been, Andy? We're waiting for you." Sarah was coming across the green towards us.

"I've been showing Celeste around," Andrew replied. "Sorry," he said to me, "I've got work to do, I'll have to leave you now, but I'll see you at supper."

"Is there anything I can do to help?" I asked.

"Don't worry about it. You're a guest." He turned to his sister. "Where's Tommy?"

"He's over at the wagon unloading some supplies," she replied.

"See you later," I said, hurrying away to help Tommy.

Chapter 30

How do you like it?" Tommy asked.

"This is a wonderful place. I wish I could bring my mother here. She'd love it."

"How did you get on with Andrew?"

"He's nice." I felt myself blushing.

"He seemed quite taken with you," Tommy persisted.

"Tommy, I've only just met him."

Tommy gave me a knowing look. "I thought you might like to live here," he said.

"I'd love to, but I have to make an effort to find out what happened to my friends first. And besides, would they even want me here?"

"I can't imagine why not. You're a good worker. Why not keep the option open, just in case?"

"Are you getting tired of me tagging along?"

"No, of course not. I've enjoyed your company, but it can be a dangerous life for a girl—sorry, I mean young woman."

The whole community met for dinner that evening. They had set a long table in the community meeting room in a building I had originally taken for another house. They'd hung several lamps from the rafters to supplement the candles on the table, giving the room a warm, inviting glow. It was a veritable banquet of stuffed trout, roast venison with fresh vegetables, and salad. There was cheese to follow with wine and fresh fruit, but the biggest treat was the bread. It was freshly baked, crusty and still warm from the oven, served with real butter. I hadn't tasted anything so delicious in years.

During the meal, I was re-introduced to the other members of the community. There was Janet who was a nutritionist in her thirties, and her eleven year-old daughter, Jill. Janet and Tommy showed a great deal of interest in each other, and I began to suspect that she was a major part of the attraction the Canyon had for him.

Jeremy was a chemist in his forties with a fifteen year-old son called Kyle. There was Tom, a horticulturist of around fifty, and a woman in her early forties called Vera who had lost her whole family in the epidemics.

The oddest person in such a group was Freddie who was introduced as a former playboy. He was a suave-looking man of around forty with blond wavy hair tied back in a ponytail. He had a devil-may-care attitude and laughed a lot. When I asked him what he did before coming to the Canyon, he said he spent most of his time playing. He drove racing cars, skied, sailed, did some scuba diving and, when he got bored, went skydiving. I wondered how he had been admitted to the community as he seemed to have few useful skills to offer, but I discovered later that he came from a very rich family, and had put up a lot of the money towards developing the Canyon. His companion, who was called Gillian, was in her late twenties. She was slim with curly red hair and pale skin. Gillian was very pretty and seemed a little shy, not saying much, just smiling once in a while. She reminded me of the women in the paintings I'd seen in an art book on the pre-Raphaelite painters. I wondered what kind of work she did. After we'd finished eating, she and Vera cleared up the dishes and took them back to the kitchen. When they returned, Gillian sat down near Freddie and picked up some needlework. I saw she was working some elaborate embroidery on a piece of woolen cloth. Seeing her bent over her work, her hair glowing amber and gold in the lamp light, I was reminded once more of Camelot.

We sat around the table and talked for a while after supper then people started to drift off to their homes, the parents with younger children being the first to leave.

"You can stay the night with me if you like," Sarah offered.

"Thank you, Sarah. I'll get my things." I went out to the wagon and pulled out my pack. As I was crossing to the Fisher's house, I saw Tommy walking towards another house with his arm around Janet.

"All these books," I said inside the house. "I never thought I'd ever see so many in one place again."

"Do you like to read?" Sarah asked.

"Oh yes. We lost all our books when our village was burned."

"How awful. Help yourself, if you want something to read."

I scanned the titles on the spines of the books and chose one on European art. I have always enjoyed looking at art books with their wonderful illustrations. They transport me to another world and time. I wondered if all those pictures are still hanging in galleries somewhere or whether they had been destroyed, knowing I would probably never find out.

Up in her room, Sarah took a thin mattress from a cupboard and unrolled it on the floor. "Here you are. You can put your sleeping bag on this." She stood up and looked at Celeste. "I've got an idea. It's not very late. Would you like to go for a dip in the hot spring?"

"Will anybody else be there?" I asked.

"I doubt it," she replied. "Come on, I'll get some towels."

Sarah used a lantern to light the way through the woods to the spring. No one was there, so we removed our clothes and lowered ourselves into the steaming water. At first, it seemed almost too hot to bear, but after a few seconds of growing accustomed to it, it felt comfortable. It was very soothing and relaxing in the hot pool, and if we hadn't kept up a conversation, I imagine I could easily have dozed off.

Sarah told me about her family, how her mother had been killed in an accident when a bridge collapsed as she was driving over it the year before the epidemics started. How her father had worked around the clock at the hospital caring for plague victims until all the antibiotics had run out and he'd become sick himself. Luckily, he'd survived, but they knew of many health-care professionals who had died. Dr. Fisher had already joined his friends in preparing a new home in The Canyon, and when he realized that there was nothing more he could do to stem the progress of the epidemics, he moved his family out of the city. He felt he had already stayed too long, endangering his children.

"Do you remember what it was like before all the trouble started? When we thought we would grow up and have careers just like our parents?" Sarah asked.

"Yes," I replied. "I wanted to be a computer programmer like my dad. What did you want to be?"

"I wasn't sure. Sometimes I wanted to be a lawyer like my mother, and other times I wanted to be something creative, maybe an architect or designer."

"And now?"

"Well the law's out. I enjoy the workshop, you know, weaving and textiles, that sort of thing."

"I saw some of your paintings. They're good."

"Thank you. What about you? How did you come to be traveling with Tommy?"

I repeated an abridged account of what had happened to my family and friends, and how I couldn't bear to go back and live in Willow Creek.

"God, that's terrible. I don't know how you can bear it," Sarah said when I'd finished. "Was one of those guys that got kidnapped your boyfriend?"

"Sort of. I don't really know how I feel about him now, though."

"Sorry, I shouldn't pry." She stood up and reached for her towel. "Shall we go back?"

"You know my brother's really seems to like you. I've never seen him like that," Sarah said on the way back.

"He's nice, I like him too," I replied.

"The only problem with living out here is the shortage of men," Sarah said.

"There seem to be plenty of men here," I replied.

"I guess there are, but they're either attached to someone else, related, or the wrong age."

"What about Walter? He looks fairly young, and he's certainly good-looking."

"Yes, but he's gay. He and Alan both are."

"Oh."

When we got up the next morning, Dr. Fisher and Andrew were already gone, so Sarah and I made our own breakfast of cold biscuits with fresh fruit and root coffee. After eating, I went to look for Tommy to find out what his plans were. He was sitting on a rustic bench talking with Janet's daughter, Jill. Tyler Graham was playing with a wooden truck in the dirt by their feet.

"Hi! Sleep well?" Tommy greeted me.

"Sure did," I replied. "Are we leaving today?"

"How would you like to spend another night here?"

"Oh, Tommy, I'd love to."

"You're on. Meanwhile, we have work to do." He stood up and walked over to the wagon. "I want you to take everything out and clean the inside while I'm in the workshop."

"Do you want me to put the stuff back afterwards?"

"Not 'til I come back. I'm building some shelves, so that we can organize things better."

We had lunch with Ben and Barbara. Ben seemed to be the leader of the community, whether officially or unofficially, I wasn't sure. Apparently, this valley retreat had been his idea to start with. He also seemed to be the oldest person in the community. Somehow the conversation came around the recent events in my life and I found myself telling the story again.

"What sort of community do you live in now?" Barbara asked me.

I wrinkled my nose. "It's okay, I guess. I mean they're hard working and honest, but it's so boring and restrictive. There are hardly any books in the village outside of bibles and religious books. I don't know how my mother stands it."

"Tell us about her," Ben requested.

So I told them.

"It sounds as if she's out of place there among a bunch of religious fundamentalist," Barbara said sympathetically.

"What about her friend?"

"Peter? He's all right. He seems to have all sorts of talents." I told them about some of Peter's inventions and the gadgets he'd made.

"Well, I suppose we should be getting back to work," Ben said, pushing away from the table.

Tommy and I went back outside and spent the rest of the afternoon fitting the shelves and racks in the back of the wagon and re-packing the merchandise. We'd traded some apple cider and packets of medicinal herbs from the Canyon in exchange for flour and honey.

After we'd finished packing the wagon, I went back to the Fisher's house to wash up, and found Andrew there. This was the first time I'd seen him since supper the previous evening and I was overcome with confusion and uncharacteristic shyness again.

Chapter 31

Hi," he said. "Been working hard?"

"Yep. How about you?"

"Always. What are you going to do now?"

"Nothing, I've finished. I just came in to wash up," I began to climb the stairs up to Sarah's room where I'd left my towel. "I guess we'll be leaving tomorrow," I said over my shoulder.

"Like to go for a walk?" he said behind me.

"Okay. I'll just be a minute. I want to change into something clean."

A few minutes later, I came downstairs wearing clean shorts with a tank top and carrying my bundle of dirty clothes. "Is there anywhere I can wash my clothes?" I asked Andrew.

"I'll show you the wash-house," he replied. "But you don't want to do it now, do you? Let's go for a walk first. You can do your laundry when we get back. It'll dry overnight."

"All right. If you say so."

He showed me where the wash house and I left my bundle of laundry there.

"Where are we going?" I asked.

"Feel up to some climbing?"

"Sure, I'm game."

We went through the woods again, but this time we veered away from the hot spring onto a path that climbed steeply up the mountainside. It was a hot afternoon and I was glad I'd changes into cooler clothes. Andrew was also wearing shorts and after a while he removed his shirt and tied it around his waist. I was able to admire his tanned muscular back and legs as he preceded my up the slope. I realized that I hadn't looked at a man this way before, with such admiration for his physical characteristics.

"Want to rest?" Andrew asked when we'd climbed for a while. He extended his hand to pull me up to his level then sat down on a large rock beside the trail. "Here, sit down for a minute while we catch our breath."

Sitting on the rock next to Andrew, our bare thighs touching, I felt overwhelming desire for him. He was so close I could smell the warm masculine odor of his body and see the sweat glistening in the hairs on his legs. I couldn't believe he was unaware of how I was feeling. He put his left arm round my shoulder and pointed with his right hand.

"Look, down there."

Below us, we could see the tops of houses among the treetops, smoke rising from some of the chimneys. I noticed water glistening through the trees off to one side.

"What's that water?" I asked.

"Oh that's a stream. We've dammed it to form a small lake. More like a large pond, really. I'll show you later." He stood up abruptly. "Want to go on now?"

We climbed steadily for another half-hour without talking, saving our breath for the climb. Every time Andrew offered me his hand to help me over rough spots, a warm glow flushed through me. I wanted to hold onto it forever. When we reached the top, we turned to look at the view. Below us now we could see the entire settlement surrounded by vegetable gardens and meadows with little white blobs that were sheep. The sun reflected off the solar roof panels and greenhouse, and the tear-shaped pond was clearly visible. It took my breath away. It was the most idyllic scene I had ever seen.

"What do you think?"

I thought of the story of Christ on the mountaintop being tempted by Satan, not that I was feeling particularly saintly, but I was very tempted. "I think you're very lucky, Andrew. These last two days have been the happiest I can remember. This is paradise."

"It's pretty special, I must admit, but it takes a lot of hard work." He put his arm around my shoulder again. "You could stay, you know."

I pulled away fearing if I didn't, I'd do something I might regret later. "It's tempting, but you know I can't." I moved further away and turned my head so that he wouldn't see the tears in my eyes. "I have things I must do. I can't just—you know. . ."

"I know, but if you change your mind, I'll be waiting." He sat down on a rocky ledge and gazed at the scene below. "I've never met—I mean. . ."

"Don't, Andrew, please," I begged. "Let's go back down." I knew it would be dangerous to be alone with him much longer.

When we reached the houses, I went to wash my clothes while Andrew left to resume his work. I hung the laundry to dry on one of the lines outside the washhouse. I noticed some of Tommy's things hanging there as well.

There was another communal supper that evening. I overheard Martin Graham say to his wife, "This must be something special, two dinners in one week."

"There's something I wanted to discuss with you all," Ben announced once everybody was served. When he had everybody's attention, he continued, "I was wondering how you would feel about admitting some new people."

Everybody started talking at once.

"One at a time, please," Ben called. "Paris?"

"I assume you mean Celeste's family?" Ben nodded. "From what you've told me, I think they could contribute something to the community. I know Mrs. Colbert with her biology background would be useful to help me with my research into medicinal plants."

All the time they were talking, I was aware of Andrews's eyes watching me from farther down the table.

"And her friend Peter sounds like a useful sort of person. We could use a musician to round out our cultural side." Barbara added. "I hope this doesn't sound too mercenary to you, Celeste. The economics of our

266

situation make it necessary for us to consider what everyone can contribute." She smiled across the table at me.

"I understand." I was thrilled beyond imagining that they were even considering the possibility that we could come to live here. "I forgot to tell you," I added, "There's someone else in our family. Tate."

"Tate? Tell us about him."

"He's—let me see—he's around thirteen or fourteen I think. He's an orphan who sort of adopted us. He's been with us for about five years."

"I see."

"Where would they live if they did come?" Vera asked.

"Nobody's living in the cabin, they could have that," Ben replied. "The cabin is where we lived while our houses were being built. It's not very big, but it's solid and weatherproof," he explained to me.

"Another thing," Ben continued, "Mrs. Colbert is a teacher. It's about time these kids went to school." He beamed at the parents of the younger children.

Fifteen year-old Kyle groaned.

"It'd do you good, young man," his father, Jeremy, said.

"So what's the verdict?" Ben asked. "Should we invite them to come and meet us? That's assuming they'd be interested, of course. We may be taking too much for granted."

"I don't see what we have to lose," Dr. Fisher said.

"How do you feel about it, Celeste?" Barbara asked me.

"I think it's a wonderful idea. They'd love it here and they'd work really hard. I know they would."

"But what about you?"

"I'm not sure. I'd love to live here, but there's something I have to do right now." I didn't want to talk about that subject. It was too emotional for me to deal with at that moment.

"How do the rest of you feel about inviting Celeste's family?" Ben asked.

"It's fine with me," Martin Graham said.

His wife nodded in agreement. Several other people nodded their consent. It looked as if nobody objected.

"That's it then," Ben said.

I saw Andrew looking at me to gauge my reaction. I looked down at the table and picked up my glass and took a sip of water.

We sat at the table talking for a while after we'd finished eating. I heard about the various projects they were working on, experiments with different power sources for running machinery including steam, methane gas, wind, and hydro-electricity. By the time of the epidemics, about half of all motor vehicles had been converted so that they would run on natural gas, but now that the pipelines were no longer delivering, they wanted to find alternatives until they were started up again.

As he had already mentioned, Dr. Fisher was experimenting with medicinal plants. He'd already discovered a few that had proved effective, some of which he traded with Tommy. Several of the people in the community were trying out various vegetable dyes for use in textile manufacture. It seemed to me that there was a great deal of promise for the future in the Canyon.

Chapter 32

Tommy and I left early the next morning. As we rode down the mountain, I felt a pang of regret, already missing the Canyon and the new friends. Especially Andrew.

"Where to now?" I asked.

"We've got a few more places to visit up this way then we head back to the coast."

"How long will it take us to get back to Willow Creek?"

"We should be able to make it in a week. You're dying to tell your mother about the Canyon, aren't you?"

"Uh huh. How come you don't live there?" I asked.

"I could, I suppose, but I think what I do is necessary. I'm sort of their pipeline to the outside world. I bring them the news and things they need." Gripping the reins between his knees, he started to stuff his pipe. "I enjoy life on the road, I guess. One of these days I'll settle down."

"With Janet?"

He peered at me from under his eyebrows and blew a puff of smoke. "Probably."

"Do you keep traveling all winter? It must be awfully cold sleeping outside."

"I usually pack it in around November. I stay up in the Canyon for a few months, then I go back down to the city. I've got a place there. That's where I do a lot of my foraging for the things people need out here."

"What's it like now in the city?"

"Oh it's settled down a bit." He puffed on his pipe. "When were you last there?"

"It was the end of '17. That's when we left," I replied. "Everything was burning then."

"Well, the fires have stopped. A lot of houses were burnt down. Vegetation has taken over a great deal of the city, especially where the buildings were destroyed. It's sort of like a vast park or small forest with a lot of small villages or enclaves. The people have settled in little groups in their own neighborhoods."

"Is there still a problem with gangs?"

"Not so much anymore. The ordinary people got sick of it and started their own vigilante organizations to protect themselves. They're like small private police squads."

"How do people live?"

"Same as we do. Trading, small-scale manufacturing. A lot of little cottage industries have sprung up, and the fishing industry is thriving. There are regular markets all over the city where people bring stuff to sell and trade. I'll take you there, you can see for yourself."

* * *

It was late evening and I had been nodding off in my seat when I became aware of the foul odor that seemed to hang in the air all around us. "God, what a horrible smell?" My skin prickled with fear. I could guess what it was.

"Whoa!" Tommy pulled back on the reins to slow the horses who were acting jittery, as if something was disturbing them.

It was already almost dark, but we had to go on; we hadn't reached the place where we planned to stop for the night. We kept on moving at a slower pace around the next bend. At first, I didn't see them in the shadows, but when I heard Tommy gasp, I followed his eyes. Three trees stood at the edge of an overgrown lot in front of a tumbled house. A grizzly figure was hanging rigidly from each one.

"Don't look," Tommy said. But it was already too late. It's amazing what a lot of details you can take in when your awareness is heightened. The three figures, two men and a woman, looked to be in their twenties. A few rags clung to their emaciated bodies. Then I realized why they were so rigid. They were nailed to the trees, not hanging on ropes as I had first thought. Crucified.

I did look away then, sickened. "Why . . .?"

"Stay here," Tommy said grimly, handing me the reins. He jumped down and went closer to the three bodies.

I saw he was looking at a small board nailed to the trunk above the head of one victim. He rubbed his hands together as if to rid them of something unpleasant as he came back towards the wagon.

"What did the sign say?" I asked.

Tommy grunted and flicked the reins to get us moving. "*This is what happens to food thieves,*" he replied.

"God, that's awful. How long do you suppose they've been there?"

Tommy shrugged. "Days. A week, maybe."

"Shouldn't we bury them or something?"

"It's none of our business," he said coldly.

"Tommy, how did they . . . you know . . .?

"Look, Celeste, I don't want to talk about it anymore. Let's get away from here."

"But. . ." Somehow, I couldn't bear the thought that they had been crucified. It seemed such an awful way to die. No matter what they did.

"Looked as if they'd had their throats cut," Tommy said finally, as if reading my thoughts. "Before they were nailed up," he added.

"Oh." That wasn't much better, only quicker. At least I hoped it was.

We reached Willow Creek five days later. We'd visited a few more communities and I'd met a few more people, but the discovery of the three bodies put a pall on us for the rest of the journey. For a while, every time I closed my eyes, I saw those corpses.

We'd also heard about two more raids on small settlements and the abduction of young people to work for the so-called government. I couldn't understand what this mysterious organization was that called itself *the Government*. They never showed themselves to the people they claimed to govern, nor did they communicate in any way except with their raiding parties. There were all sorts of rumors, of course. The most prevalent, and the one that seemed to have most credence, was that they were a group of rich people who had banded together with some military and former government officials in the town of Mission. Whatever was going on there, people avoided Mission.

Willow Creek didn't appear to have changed at all; there was still a sentry guarding the approach. He waved us on when he recognized us. Several dogs ran alongside, barking at the horses. Tommy made soothing noises to calm Billy and Jane. I recognized Pepsi among the dogs and jumped down from the seat so that she could welcome me properly, which meant I had to endure having my face licked clean. I continued on foot into the village and went directly to the church hall to see if Mother was there. To my amazement and joy, the first person I saw was Pam.

"Pam," I rushed up the steps and hugged her. "Pam, it's good to see you. Are you okay? What happened? Is Eric all right? And Mike? Are they here?"

When she pulled away from me, I noticed a change in her face. It was hard to pinpoint exactly what it was, but she seemed more mature and there was a new sadness in her eyes. "Hi, Celeste, how are you?"

"I'm fine. I want to know about you. Where are Mike and Eric? Are they at the house?"

She shook her head. "No. I came back alone."

Just then, Mother came out into the hallway. She rushed over and hugged me. "Celeste! Welcome back. How was the trip?"

"Great, at least most of it."

"Why? Did something happen?" She glanced from me to Tommy.

"I'll tell you later. I've got some wonderful news as well, but first, I want to know what happened to Mike and Eric." I saw a look pass between my mother and Pam. "What's happened to them? They haven't been killed, have they?" I asked with a hollow feeling.

"No. It's not that bad," Mother replied. "Let me dismiss the kids then we can go to the house and talk. Are you hungry?"

It wasn't hard for her to clear the classroom of children. Once they caught on that the trader was here, they were all eager to go outside and see what he'd brought this time. They didn't have much excitement in their lives, so any visit from an outsider like Tommy was an important event.

I went outside and told Tommy that my friend had returned and I wanted to go home and talk to her. He told me he could manage and he'd be along as soon as he was finished.

"Who were those people that attacked us that night?" I asked Pam while we were walking home. "Did they hurt any of you?"

"Not much," she replied. "I think they were from down south—across the border."

"What makes you think that?"

"Oh, something they said, and the way they talked—their accents."

"What happened?"

A lanky figure appeared from between two houses and flew towards me. It was Tate "Celeste!" he yelled, grabbing me in his arms and swinging me around. "Where've you been?"

"Hey, Tate! How are you?"

He seemed to have grown taller and his voice was getting huskier. His curly hair was bleached light brown by the sun and his skin was tanned to a darker brown. He was becoming a very attractive young man.

"I'm fine. What about you?"

"I'm okay," I said.

"Did Pam tell you...?"

"Let's go home and talk about it while we have something to drink," Mother said.

When we reached the house, I heard the sound of hammering coming from the back. We found Peter working on a piece of furniture he was making outside the kitchen door. After more greetings and explanations, we sat down in the kitchen to a lunch of cold fish and potato cakes with fresh tomatoes and cucumber, which we washed down with tea.

"Okay," I said as soon as the food was served. "Will somebody please tell me now?"

Pam told me about the four men who had surprised us at our riverside camp that night in April. How, when they heard the splash after Eric pushed me down the bank, they thought I might have been swept away in the river and drowned. Until Pam came back to Willow Creek, she hadn't been sure whether I was alive or not.

"I was so relieved when your mother told me you were all right," Pam said.

"What happened then?"

"Like I said, there were four of them—all men, with long hair and beards."

The men knew there had been four of us and they searched for me for a while after tying up Mike, Eric and Pam. They gave up and herded my three friends up the riverbank to the place where they had hidden a covered

278

wagon. They were shoved unceremoniously into the back of the wagon. Two of the men climbed in behind them and told them not to make any noise. The other two sat up front on the driver's box. The wagon, which was pulled by two large horses, had been bigger than Tommy's.

One of the men in the wagon shined a flashlight on the prisoners. "Orientals," he said to his partner. "General'll be pleased. Too bad the other one got away, but maybe this'll make up for it. The gal won't be much good. Looks too frail to work very hard, but we'll find something for her to do," he said, giving the other man a suggestive wink.

"You never know with these dark girls, they're stronger than they look," the other man said.

"Who are you?" Eric demanded. "Where are you taking us?"

"Quiet, boy. Speak when you're spoken to. We'll ask the questions. Go to sleep, we've got a long ride ahead of us—and don't try anything funny. One of us'll be awake all the time."

"Can you untie us so we can get comfortable? How do you expect us to sleep trussed up like this?" Eric asked.

They had their hands tied behind them, with the ropes looped around their necks so that, if they tried to move their hands too much, they would tighten the nooses. One of the men untied the ropes from their hands and re-tied them so that all three were roped together hand to hand and feet to feet with Eric in the middle. At least like that, they were able to stretch out on the floor, which was covered with straw or hay. It was bitterly cold, but the men refused to let them have their sleeping bags, so they huddled together for warmth.

The wagon was still moving when they woke up. It was still dark, but they were able to make out the figure sitting near the opening at the back. His companion was wrapped in a sleeping bag on the floor of the wagon, sleeping.

The three friends struggled into sitting position and tried to coordinate their movements so that they could clean the straw out of their hair and rub their eyes.

"Oh, so you've decided to wake up," the man guarding them said. He was not one of the two men who had been in the back the night before, so they must have stopped and changed places in the night.

"How much longer?" Eric asked. "We need to go to the bathroom."

"You'll have to wait. We'll be stopping soon anyways."

When it got lighter, they saw he was dressed in camouflage fatigues, wore a holstered pistol on his belt and held a rifle in his hand. He was short and stocky, his hair and beard touched with grey.

They scooted round until they were leaning against the boxes in the front of the wagon and sat watching the road unwinding behind them. After another hour or so, the wagon turned off the road into a dense forest. The trail continued through the woods for about a kilometer before coming out into a clearing. They heard a man's voice shout something, and the wagon stopped. The driver said something back and they started moving again. The captives saw they were passing through a gate in a high, barbed wire-topped fence. There was a guard tower beside the gate manned by an armed guard. Another armed man closed the heavy gate after them. Pam had an ominous feeling about the place, as if she were entering a prison, believing this to be their destination.

"All right, you can get out now," the man guarding the back said. He got up and went to untie them.

The other man had woken up when they left the road for the forest trail. He jumped out when they came to a stop and spoke to men outside.

When they descended from the wagon, their legs were so cramped that they could barely walk for a moment and clung to the side for support. They saw they were in what looked like a military compound, or a prison yard. There were long, low buildings on three sides with the fence making up the fourth side of the quadrangle. The buildings were made of cinder blocks, roofed with corrugated aluminum. Several armed men stood around, curious about the visitors, but there was no sign of any women.

Pam, Mike and Eric were herded into what appeared to be a guardroom in one of the buildings. All it contained was a long table with wooden benches. Two men were sitting at the table eating with rifles propped up against the bench beside them. A gun rack hung on one wall filled with an assortment of weapons all chained and padlocked in place. Two doors opened off one end of the room.

One of their captors pushed Pam towards the farther of the two doors and told her it was a toilet. When she came out, the other men had finished eating and left. After Eric and Mike had been to the toilet, the three friends were told to sit at the table then they were served some watery potato soup by a middle-aged woman who entered from the other door. The four men who'd brought them also had a meal, and were given coffee instead of the water that was served to the prisoners.

"Is this where you're leaving us?" Eric asked while they were eating.

"No, this is just a stop on the way," one of the men replied.

"Then where are we going?"

"You'll find out soon enough,"

"Why do you have to kidnap people?"

"Kidnap? Who said anything about kidnapping? You're being recruited. We've got some special work needs doing."

"But you've got no right to just go around grabbing people," Eric said.

"Quiet, Boy."

"But . . ."

"I said shut up." The closest man hit Eric on the side of his head.

"Leave my brother alone," Mike cried.

"You too, boy."

"Let her go, she . . ." Mike continued, pointing to Pam.

"You heard me."

When the meal was finished, they were taken into a hallway behind the kitchen where a door opened onto a concrete staircase. The stairs led down into a cellar that was apparently used for storage. It seemed to run the length of the building and was half filled with boxes and sacks. Shelves down one wall were filled with jars of preserved foods. Some of the wooden crates were marked with stenciled labels indicating that they contained ammunition and explosives.

"Over here." One of the men from the compound unlocked a door and they were shoved inside. It was a small, cell-like room with a cement floor, completely empty and unlit except for a small, slit near the ceiling. The door was shut on them and they heard the key turn in the lock.

"We've got to find a way to escape," Eric said. The three friends sat close together on the cold floor with their backs against the wall.

"How?" Mike asked. "There's not much hope of getting out of here."

284

"I'm scared," Pam said. She was shivering from the cold, and fear.

"They haven't hurt us so far," Eric said. "We'd have a much better chance to escape on the road to wherever we're going. We'll have to be alert for the opportunity, and plan what we're going to do when the time comes."

They discussed escaping for a while longer then lapsed into silence. They even dozed off for a while, but the cold kept them from sleeping very long. Sometime later, they were brought out and taken upstairs to the guardroom, where they repeated the morning's routine of visiting the toilet and having a meal. By the waning light outside, they guessed it was late afternoon or early evening. Their four captors ate with them then three of them went outside with two men from the settlement. One man stayed to guard them, glancing out the window from time to time.

"Outside," the man ordered after a while. He stood up and went towards the door.

In the yard, they were ordered to help load the wagon. When they'd finished, the back of the wagon was more than half filled with sacks and barrels, boxes and sealed jars, leaving a small space for the prisoners and their guard. This time, there was only room only for one man in the back with them. They were tied together again and the ends of the ropes were secured to bars on the side of the wagon. The guard sat opposite them close to the opening with his rifle resting between his knees. It was almost dark when they started out through the woods to the road.

"How far are you taking us?" Eric asked.

"All the way," the man replied.

"I mean how long will it take?"

"You ask too many questions."

"What harm would it do to tell us?"

"None." He turned and spat out the back. "Couple, three days," he said.

"Are we going south?" Eric asked.

"'S right. God's country. Now shut yer mouths and leave me some peace."

Chapter 33

They rode in silence for a while until Pam could no longer contain what she'd been wanting to tell the boys for the last hour. She leaned close to Eric and whispered, "I think I saw Jackie."

"What are you talking about?" he replied.

"When I was in the toilet, the window was open and I peeked out. I saw a girl with red hair. I'm sure it was Jackie."

Eric turned and whispered something to his brother on the other side, then turned back to Pam. "What makes you think it was Jackie? There's lots of girls with red hair."

"It looked like her," she replied.

"Fuck, they could be the bastards who killed Mom and Dad." He turned and spoke to Mike again.

"What are you all whispering about?" the guard demanded. "Don't think you can get away. We won't hesitate to shoot if you try anything."

They fell silent again and soon were asleep. Later, Pam was awakened by a nudge from Eric. He nodded his head towards the guard and Pam saw that his head had sunk to his chest and his grip on the gun was relaxed. He seemed to be sleeping. Eric coughed loudly. The man twitched, but didn't look up. Eric signaled for Pam to draw her legs up so that he could reach the rope around her ankles. He was in the middle with Mike tied to him on his left and Pam on the right, closest to the opening. He worked at the knot for a while, pulling her hand with his because their wrists were tied together. Finally, the rope was loose. They looked across at the guard, but he still hadn't moved. Next, he went to work on the rope that joined his right hand to Pam's left. He pulled at the knot with his teeth until it too was loose. Once their hands were free, he leaned over and untied the knot that bound her right arm to the wagon. She was free.

The man began to stir and they instantly resumed their positions as if still tied up and pretended to be asleep. The guard coughed and changed position. Pam watched him through half-closed eyelids until she was sure he was sound asleep then nudged Eric.

He put his mouth against her ear and whispered, "He's getting restless. He may wake up any minute. I want you to jump out and get away."

"No, I won't leave you. I'm too scared," she whispered back.

"Don't be stupid, Pam. You've got to get away. You don't know what they'll do to you. You're a girl. When I give the signal, jump out and roll into the bushes by the road. Hide, and keep very still until the wagon's gone, then go back to Willow Creek and tell them what happened."

"I can't."

"You've got to. Wait, I want you to take a message for Celeste, if she's there." He paused for a moment then told her what to say to me. "Now, go!"

Pam hesitated for a moment while she untangled herself then she stood up cautiously. Eric gave her a push that sent her over the footboard of the wagon and out onto the road. She landed with a sickening thud on her hands and knees, but still had the presence of mind to roll as he'd told her. She rolled off the side of the road into long grass and weeds then crawled into the bushes and lay still.

Unfortunately, the sudden pain of her landing caused her to cry out. This awoke the guard. She heard him yell and then a shot rang out. The wagon stopped several meters down the road and the other three men rushed to the back.

"I saw them shine a flashlight in the back, and when they saw I was gone, they started to hit Mike and Eric with their rifles," Pam said, tears running down her face. "Then they ran back along the road towards where I was hiding. As soon as the wagon stopped, I'd moved farther back into the bushes."

I put my arm around her. "You were very brave," I said. "What happened after that?"

"They fired a few shots into the bushes then gave up looking for me after a while. There was no way they could find me in the dark, even with their flashlights. I heard them yelling at each other when they got back to the wagon—they sounded pretty mad—and I heard Mike or Eric yell as if he'd been hurt. Then they got back in the wagon and left." Pam stopped talking, trying to suppress her tears.

"You must have been scared to death," I said. "I know I would have been, out there all alone. How did you get back here?"

"I had no idea where I was," she continued. "So I just walked back the way we'd come, hoping I would come to something I recognized."

"Where were you? Do you know now?"

"Not really. Just that it was one of those back roads that lead to the border. It was dark and I didn't see any road signs. I kept walking for hours until I was too tired to go on, then I found a place to hide and went to sleep. It was freezing, but I managed to sleep for a while."

She went on to tell us how she had walked all the way back, stopping for food and to rest at any settlement along the way that looked safe. On her way back to Willow Creek, she acquired some warm clothing and even a pair of boots to replace her worn out shoes.

She was surprised at how hospitable people were to her, but when she heard that some of them had also had people abducted in raids, she understood the reason they made her welcome. It took her about four weeks to get back to Willow Creek, and by then, I had gone with Tommy.

"Are you sure it was Jackie you saw?" I asked, returning to what she'd said earlier.

"I think so," she said. "It was getting dark by then, so I might have been mistaken. There was a garden at the back and that's where I saw her."

"That might be where they took her and Debbie and Lia. Sounds like that kind of place." Unable to wait any longer to hear his message, I asked, "What was it Eric wanted you to tell me?"

"Let's go outside," Pam said, getting up from the table.

I followed her, puzzled. "What's so secret?" I asked her as we closed the door.

"You're not going to like it," she replied. "I didn't want to tell you in front of the others."

"For God's sake, Pam, what did he say?"

"He told me to tell you—he said he never really loved you and—and to tell you you're free now."

I turned cold when I heard this. Tears came to my eyes. I tried to think back, searching for some sign. He had always seemed so loving and tender towards me. He must have loved me, how could anyone fake feelings like that? I remembered how I had questioned my own feelings when I was with Andrew. I had to admit that there had been no magic in my relationship with Eric, not the kind of thrill I felt when I was with Andrew. Could Eric have felt the same way about me?

Then it hit me—he was saying this for me, so that I wouldn't feel tied to him now that he was gone. I sat down on the step and covered my face with my hands to hide my tears. I was overwhelmed with shame, only vaguely aware of Pam hovering nearby.

"I'm sorry, Celeste," she said. "I'm sure he didn't really mean it." She patted my arm.

"I know he didn't, Pam. He just didn't want me to feel I had to wait for him. I think he suspected he wouldn't come back and wanted me to be free." That was all I could say before I lapsed into more tears—tears of shame as well as sorrow.

Behind me the front door opened and Mother stepped out onto the porch. "Is everything all right?" she asked "What on earth's the matter, Celeste?" She obviously hadn't been told about Eric's message.

"It's okay, Mom. I'll be all right." I stood up and wiped my eyes on my shirt hem. I turned to my mother. "Mom, I've got something to tell you. Did Tommy say anything?"

Tommy had quietly joined us while we were eating and listening to Pam's story.

"No. He hasn't said much at all. I hope its good news for a change. Is it just for me, or can everybody hear it?"

"Oh, it's wonderful news. And it's for the whole family," I said, meaning Peter, Tate and Pam as well as Mother.

"Well, let's get them out here to hear what you have to say."

She opened the door and called Peter and Tate to join us. They came out with Tommy in tow, and we all sat on the front steps of the house while I relayed to them the news about Lost Canyon. I saw my mother's eyes light up when she heard about it. She glanced at Peter and he smiled back and took her hand. I could imagine how draining it must have been for them, living in the restrictive atmosphere in Willow Creek.

"It sounds too good to be true," she said. "Are you sure they would welcome us?"

"They all discussed it, Mom, and Ben wants you to come, for a visit at least, to see how everybody gets on."

"Are you coming?" she asked.

"Not right now. I want to go to the city with Tommy first. I'm not sure yet if I want to live there, or keep traveling with Tommy," I replied giving Tommy a sideways look. "That's if he'll have me a while longer."

"It's fine with me," Tommy said with a smile.

"How will we find the place if you're not there to show us the way? How far is it?"

"We can show you on a map," Tommy replied. "It's about one hundred and twenty kilometers give or take, so it would take you about two days on horseback."

"I'm not sure we'd have horses," Peter interjected. "They don't really belong to us. I'd have to discuss it with Joshua. Maybe we could arrange some kind of a trade for them. I think I'll ride over there this afternoon and see if there's anything he needs. You were saying you can get all sorts of things in the city, Tommy?"

"Well, within reason. You don't always get what you're looking for, but sometimes you come across something unexpected that you find useful. All depends. Why?"

"I was thinking maybe you could find something to trade for the horses and then, after we move—if we move—we could let you have the horses."

"I'm sure we could work something out," Tommy replied. "But you don't have to go so far as to part with the horses. I think Celeste has earned something, so maybe we can fit that into the equation."

"Hey! That sounds great," I said.

"What about me and Pam?" Tate asked.

"You can go too," I replied. "If you can drag yourself away from all your admirers."

"Are there any good-looking girls there?"

"A couple, and there's a boy about your age—well, maybe a year or two older. It's a great place, Tate. You'd love it."

"Well, you've given us plenty to think about," Mother said, standing up.

"I don't want to go," Pam said. She had kept very quiet while we were talking.

"Why not?" I asked her.

"It would be too far away from the city. I want to go back and find my dad." She looked from me to Tommy. "Could you guys take me with you?"

Tommy looked at me and I raised my eyebrows questioningly.

"I guess so," he said. "You'd be fairly safe on the road with us, but once we got into the city, you'd be on your own. Any idea where he might be living?"

"If I could get to a temple, I think I'd be able to find him. He was going to live in one of the Indian communities."

"No problem. We could drop you off at the temple then."

"Great." I smiled at Pam. "Thanks, Tommy."

Chapter 34

I'd better get going to see Joshua. I hope he's not off on one of his expeditions." Peter said. He turned and went back into the house.

"Mind if I tag along?" I asked. "I haven't seen Joshua in ages. You don't need me for anything do you, Tommy?"

"I can manage. I'm sure Tate here can give me a hand if I need it."

When we got to Salish, our former home, I was saddened to see how overgrown it was. Our old vegetable garden was a mass of lush weeds, and the burnt out ruins of the houses were covered in brambles with saplings thrusting up through them. Patches of pinky mauve fireweed and bright yellow wild mustard painted colorful streaks across the lush landscape.

Joshua's door was open so we knew he must be around somewhere. His dog—one of Pepsi's offspring—got up from where he had been lying on the porch and greeted us with short sharp barks and a lashing tail. Joshua was nowhere in sight. We dismounted and left the horses to graze then went up onto the porch. Peter called Joshua's name and pushed the door open wider. It took a few seconds for our eyes to adjust to the gloomy interior after the bright sunshine outside.

Joshua was lying on his bed against the wall on the far side of the room, which was uncharacteristically cluttered. Cooking utensils and dishes were piled up by the sink, and a stale, almost rotten smell pervaded the air.

"Don't try to get up." Peter said when Joshua struggled to sit up. "Are you sick?"

Joshua broke into a fit of coughing. "A bit under the weather," he said hoarsely when the coughing stopped.

"How long have you been ill?" Peter said.

"Few days. Didn't count."

Peter looked around the room. "Do you mind if we clean up a bit and get you something to eat?"

Joshua shrugged, then shook his head and lay back on the pillow. He obviously didn't have enough energy to talk. There was an empty cup on a box next to the bed. I wondered how long it had been since he'd had anything to drink.

"Hi, Joshua," I said. "Haven't seen you in a while. Shall I get you something to drink?" Without waiting for his reply, I picked up a pail and went outside to the standpipe, which was still fed with water from our irrigation system.

After giving Joshua some water, I helped Peter tidy Joshua's house. I made some soup for him while Peter helped him out to the toilet then brought him a bowl of water and some clean clothes to change into. I went outside to look around while Joshua got fixed up. Walking over to the garden, I saw that the gravesite had been cleared of weeds. I stood for a moment reading the inscription Peter had engraved on the board, thinking about the people buried there. Poor Gran. My eyes filled with tears. I missed them all so much.

Before returning Joshua's house, I found an empty can and filled it with wildflowers to leave on the grave.

"I think you ought to come back with us, Josh, so that someone can look after you until you feel better." Peter said after Joshua had taken some soup.

"I'll be all right," Joshua replied. He already looked better.

After making him comfortable and feeding his dog, we got down to discussing the purpose of our visit. Joshua said he couldn't think of anything he needed off-hand apart from a rifle and some ammunition, but he was open to suggestions. He told us he hadn't been feeling so strong the past year and was finding it more difficult to tend his traps, so a rifle would make hunting easier for him.

"I don't think it's a good idea to live out here all alone," Peter said. "Have you thought of moving to one of the communities?"

Joshua shook his head. He seemed to be getting tired of making the effort to talk.

"We're tiring you," Peter said. "We should go and let you rest. There's some soup left, but don't leave it too long in this weather, and Celeste has filled your water jars, so you'll have enough to drink for a while. We'll come over again tomorrow to see how you're feeling."

"Bye, Joshua," I added. "I hope you feel better soon."

"I'm concerned about him," Peter said on the ride back to Willow Creek. "He must be nearly eighty. If he had an accident, he could be dead by the time anybody found him."

"I wish we could persuade him to move." I said.

"He's set in his ways. I don't blame him in a way. He treasures his privacy and solitude. Who knows what sort of hostility and discrimination he's had to put up with around here in the past?"

Tommy and I prepared to leave for the city early the following morning. I was excited at the prospect of going back there after being away for three years. Pam didn't have much to say that evening; she seemed anxious and a little depressed. I had no idea how she felt about going back. I couldn't blame her if she was mixed up after what had happened to her, but I could see she didn't want to talk about it anymore.

The following morning, Pam thanked Mom then climbed up beside me and Tommy and we started off towards the city. We didn't stop until we reached a small community located in New Westminster, about twenty-five kilometers from the city center. We had brought a good supply of preserves, cider and smoked game as well as fresh produce to trade with individual people, but Tommy wanted to keep the furs and what was left of the flour for more serious trading in town. The people in this first community were very poor and didn't have much that would be useful for trading, so we didn't stay long.

We took the southern route along the north bank of the river, so that we could take Pam to a temple. I was amazed by the changes that had taken place in the city since we'd left. Vegetation had taken over to a great extent, covering and concealing much of the damage done by the fires. The greenery now dominated everything, scattered here and there with small clusters of buildings. As we continued towards the city center along Southeast Marine Drive, which had trees and shrubs encroaching on both sides, I noticed that most of the side streets where blocked off by natural and man-made barriers. The road, which years ago would have been teeming with all kinds of motorized traffic, was almost deserted. People now seemed to be traveling mostly on foot or bicycles, although we did see a few horse-drawn carts and wagons. The biggest surprise was seeing a few motor vehicles. It wasn't immediately clear to me how they were powered.

We stopped at the first Hindu temple we came to, but although there were signs that someone was taking care of it, there was no one around.

"They probably live nearby," Pam said hopefully. "I'm sure if I look around a bit, I'll find somebody."

"We can't just leave you, Pam," I said. "I want to make sure you'll be all right. What do you think, Tommy?"

"I think the horses could use a rest," he replied. "I'll stay and watch the wagon if you want to go and look around with Pam. You might even find somebody who wants to trade."

It wasn't hard to guess which houses were abandoned and which were occupied. You just had to look at their condition. Abandoned houses were overgrown, had broken windows or were partially dismantled. There were obviously people living in most of the houses on the street behind the temple. We walked slowly along the street until we found a man and woman working in the garden of one house. They were Indian, as we'd hoped. They stopped working when we approached and fixed their dark eyes on us.

"Excuse me," Pam said, moving close to the fence. "Can you help me?"

The man came over to the fence. "What is it you want?" he asked.

"I'm trying to find my father and grandmother. I was wondering if you know them."

"What are their names?" the man asked. He seemed surprised that she would not know the whereabouts of her family.

"My father's name is Narinder Kumari. My grandmother's his mother, Mrs. Kumari"

The man frowned and beckoned his wife to join him. "Kumari," he said. "It's a fairly common name. Have you heard of a Narinder Kumari?" he asked his wife.

She shook her head, then, after a moment's thought, said. "Doesn't your mother have a friend called Mrs. Kumari?"

"I think she does, but it might not be the same person." He turned to Pam and asked, "What's your name?"

"Paramjit," she replied.

"Why are you looking for your father?"

"It's a long story," she said. "I went away to live outside the city with my friends, but they're all scattered now and I want to come back to my family—if I can find them."

"What will you do if you can't find them?" the man asked.

"I don't know," Pam sighed. "I don't know," she repeated despairingly.

"You can come back and live with us," I said. She seemed so sad and lost.

"Do you want to stay here?" the woman offered. "There'll be a meeting at the temple tomorrow; maybe somebody there will know something about your father. My mother-in-law should be there and we can ask her if she knows your grandmother."

"What if nobody knows them?" her husband interjected.

"Well, there are other Indian communities. Someone can take her to another one and she can ask there."

The man shrugged.

"Okay," said Pam. "I've brought some food, so I won't—you know. . ."

"It's all right," the woman said. "My name's Jasbir and this is my husband Rajiv."

"Hi!" Pam said. "I'll get my things. I won't be a minute. Oh—thank you."

"What do you think?" I asked her on the way back to the wagon.

"I don't know," she replied. "Oh, Celeste, what am I going to do? Maybe this isn't such a good idea." She was close to tears.

"Do you want to change your mind?"

"No . . . well . . . I want to see my dad and grandma. I have to find out if they're all right. I'm not sure if I want to live here though."

"At least you won't be called a heathen for not going to church," I said, half jokingly. "I guess we could come back this way when we've finished downtown, then if you change your mind, or if you don't find them, you could come back with us. I'll ask Tommy how long we're going to be in the city and maybe we could arrange some kind of signal for you to use, if you want us to stop and pick you up."

After Pam got her pack from the wagon, Tommy added a packet of flour and some fresh vegetables to it. We said good-bye and I watched sadly until her small figure reached the corner. She turned and waved once before disappearing. Pam and I had been friends since we were seven years old—over ten years. I wondered when I would see her again.

Maybe there'd be a white flag tied to a tree beside the road when we returned in a few days.

Chapter 35

We didn't stop again until we reached our destination early in the evening. The enclave we were to visit was near the university at the western tip of a peninsula bounded on the south by the Fraser River and on the north by the Burrard Inlet. It was on high ground with incredible views of the city, the mountains, and the offshore islands. The houses were large and prosperous-looking although most of them needed a coat of paint, and some had a patched-up look where repairs had been made with materials that didn't match those used originally. All the gardens were under cultivation and many of them sported greenhouses. Most of the people living in this community were old friends of Tommy's, people he'd known before the disasters. I found out later that he himself had once lived in a luxury condominium close by.

Once we had settled the horses, we went down to the beach for a swim with some of Tommy's friends, and afterwards they had a barbecue. For the second time that year, I had the luxury of sleeping in a real bed with fresh linen instead of a mattress on the floor and a sleeping bag.

Next day, Tommy went out early with one of his friends, taking the wagon. The owner of the house we were staying at was a Doctor Levisohn. He had a daughter called Livia who was about eighteen. She offered to show me around the area that, she assured me, was safe as long as we kept our eyes and ears open. We took one of their enormous dogs with us and set off across what had been the university endowment lands. Before the disasters, much of this land had been protected from development and left in its wild state, apart from a few walking trails, but it hadn't completely escaped the fires that destroyed many of the forests along the West Coast. Some of the larger, older trees were gone and had been replaced by second growth, so the area was still very green. We cut across what Livia explained had been the university golf course, but which now was grazing land for sheep and cattle.

"Are these yours?" I asked.

"Yes. I don't know what some of the old members would say if they saw it now," she laughed. "Actually, I do. My father used to be a member. He doesn't mind the animals, as long as he can swing at a few balls once in a while. He says it's a good trade off because he doesn't want to give up eating meat entirely, and they do keep the grass short even if they leave marks of their passing." She stepped neatly around a cowpat.

We followed the trail until we reached the university. Many of the buildings were burned-out shells with broken windows, overgrown with vegetation.

"Does anybody work or study here now?" I inquired.

"Oh, yes. A few diehards from the science departments use the labs, and take on some students, and I believe the engineering department is active as well. Some doctors and health professionals have started teaching in one of the hospitals in town. That's what my father does."

"Did he teach at the University?"

"Yes. Most of the people in our community were professors and they're trying to get some classes going again. They were pretty lucky they had the foresight to barricade the main library and prevent the destruction of the collections there. Some youth gangs tried to break in through the skylights—it's underground, you know—

but they managed to drive them off. It's amazing how destructive some young people became when they're under pressure. You can't blame them I suppose with all that was happening; they had a lot of anger and fear to deal with."

We pushed our way through a thicket towards one of the abandoned buildings and sat down on the steps. The sunlight was hot and the air was fragrant with the smell of vegetation. It was quiet, apart from the sounds made by insects in the weeds.

"I know. That's why we left the city in the end. They were just going around burning houses and attacking people. Not that we were much safer in the country." I told her about what had happened to various members of our group.

"God, you've been through so much. It must be awful, remembering all that stuff," Livia said. "I feel so fortunate, so protected. Nothing really bad has happened to us except some of my relatives and friends died in the epidemics. The only thing I have to complain about is not being able to get an education and have a career as I'd expected when I was growing up."

"I think you can still have a career. It will just be different. We have to learn everything we can, any time we get the chance. There'll be a lot of work rebuilding."

"Do you think it will ever get back to the way it was?" she asked.

"Not exactly. There aren't as many people now, but I think things will improve. I've met people who are working on alternative sources of power and fuels for machinery."

"Yes. That's the sort of thing some of the university people are doing. What do you miss the most from before?"

"I don't know. I haven't given it much thought." I hesitated for a moment to consider the question. "I guess electricity. We used so many things that depended on electricity to run. You know—music, videos, lights, computers, all sorts of machines. I wonder how long it'll take to get the hydro running again."

"Who knows? But it would be great to have it full time. We've got a generator here that gives us power, but not all the time. Sometimes we get together and watch a video or listen to music discs."

"How do you power the generator?"

"We've got several ways. There are the windmills that goes pretty constantly, and if we feel it needs an extra boost, there's a bicycle we can ride in place to turn the dynamo. It gives us a bit of exercise—as if we don't get enough with our work."

"What kind of work do you do?" I asked her.

"A bit of everything. Some gardening, cooking, laundry, weaving. I like weaving, but I hate spinning. We use the sheep's wool. Sometimes I get to go fishing. We've got a small fishing boat that we use to fish in the Strait. Today is like a holiday for me. I'm glad you came with Tommy—gives me an excuse to slack off a bit. I'll probably have to make up for it later," she added ruefully.

"I'll help you if anyone says anything," I offered. "Thanks for showing me around. It's all so interesting. Do you think we should go back now?"

"I guess so. Getting hungry?"

"A little."

"Have you been up to the Canyon?" Livia asked as we walked back.

"Yes, I was there for a couple of days."

"How's Andrew?"

"Do you know him?" I was taken by surprise and wondered if she noticed the color come to my face.

"Yes, they used to live next door to us. How's he doing?"

"He seems okay," I replied, wondering if they had been more than neighbors. I felt a pang of jealousy and was glad when Livia changed the subject.

Tommy was smiling when he returned in the evening. When I asked what he was so happy about, he told me that some people were beginning to use money again, which would make his life easier. For a long time, nobody trusted currency, so it had lost its value.

"But how can they trust it? I mean it's only paper with numbers printed on it."

"I know. As you say, it's a matter of trust. Any exchange of goods and other valuables is like a social contract. There must be a mutual agreement about the worth of the commodities and everybody has to abide by it."

"Like the stock market?"

"Sort of."

"But how do they decide how much something is worth?"

"At first, it's trial and error, bargaining and so on, then it sort of falls into place and a balance is set. If someone thinks the price is too high for something, he won't buy it, so the merchant has to make an adjustment. And, as I said, not everyone wants to take the chance yet. I guess they're waiting to see if it will work."

"Are you going to accept money?" I asked.

"We'll see. Maybe ease into to gradually. One thing's for sure, we won't be able to barter forever. We'll have to find some way of exchanging goods. By the way, I'd like you to come and help me with something tomorrow," he added.

The next morning, we set out on foot. Tommy was carrying a machete-like tool and had a leather satchel on his shoulder.

"Where are we going?" I asked.

"Just a small errand; it's not far. I have to pick up something."

We left the university lands and went down one of the overgrown streets towards the city. Although vegetation had spread out onto the roadway, there was still room to walk down the middle of the street, but Tommy had to chop a way through some of the more tenacious growth occasionally. After about three blocks, we came to the remains of a small townhouse complex, its access almost completely overgrown with brambles and vines.

"This is it," Tommy announced. "What a mess. Looks as if we'll have some work getting into the place."

"Is this where you used to live?" I asked him.

"That's right." He started pushing through the weeds towards the buildings. "It's no wonder the weeds thrive here, all the topsoil and fertilizers we put down." He started to chop at the brambles with the machete, pushing them aside to make a passage for us.

I followed him, puzzled as to why he wanted to return to his old home; the whole place looked a ruin to me, although I could see it had once been quite luxurious. It was another hot day, filled with the drone of insects. Startled birds took to the air with a sudden flurry of wings as we worked our way through their habitat. When we stopped for a moment, we could hear small creatures rustling in the foliage.

Each unit of the complex had a fenced patio paved with square brick tiles. Tommy pushed his way along the outside of the fences until he reached the fourth panel then began to pull away the palings. They came away easily because the wood had rotted and the nails were rusty. When he'd made a gap wide enough to squeeze through, he grunted with satisfaction and beckoned me to follow him inside. The patio doors were broken and the interior of the house looked trashed, but that didn't interest Tommy so much as the patio itself. I watched him count the paving blocks then kneel down and start to pry one of them up.

"Give me a hand, would you?" he said.

I knelt down and tried to get a grip on the edge so that I could add my weight to the effort, but the block wouldn't move—it felt as if it were cemented in place.

"We need a bar or something to pry it with," he said, looking around. Wait here, I'll find something." He went inside the house and I heard him moving around. A few loud crashes and bangs later, he reappeared with a metal bar. "This should do it."

After another short struggle, the paving stone was pried loose. Tommy lifted it and set it aside. Underneath was a metal box wrapped in plastic. He smiled up at me triumphantly. "My secret stash," he said.

"What is it?" I asked.

"Money!" he replied. "I thought it would be useful again one day, and this seemed like the safest place to keep it."

He unlocked the box and lifted the lid to reveal bundles of neatly stacked bank notes. I saw green twenties, red fifties and brown hundreds. It looked like a lot of money to me. He lifted the currency and underneath revealed several gold coins a bit smaller than a dollar. There must have been about twenty of them. It looked like a fortune to me.

"How much is there?" I inquired.

"Not much really, about twenty thousand, not counting the gold, but that's only for extreme emergencies. The banknotes should be enough to get started." He began to pack the bundles of bank note into his satchel, adding two gold coins and leaving the rest in the box. "I brought you along to show you this place. If anything happens to me, I want you to remember this: two north, five west—2N, 5W. That's two tiles in from the north and five from the west. There's another box there. Now, we'd better put this back the way it was. Don't want anybody snooping around stumbling on it."

After we'd tamped the paving block in place and scattered some dry soil around it, we went back through the hole in the fence and Tommy replaced the palings.

"The brambles will soon grow back, so if anyone comes this way, I doubt they'll notice anyone's been here."

Tommy took me with him the next day when he went into the city to trade. Before we left, I saw him tuck a handgun into the space behind the seat.

"Is it dangerous?" I asked.

"Not really. Most neighborhoods have organized their own security and are pretty safe, but there are still a few gangs roaming around though. And we'll be carrying valuable merchandise—don't want to tempt them."

In spite of the lush overgrowth, there was a network of streets throughout the city that had been kept clear, either from frequent use, or the efforts of those who used them. We made our way downhill to the former business district with its ruined office towers but didn't stop there. We continued farther to the east to the area of warehouses near the old railway and bus terminal. Several blocks of Terminal Avenue, east of Main Street under the Skytrain tracks seemed to be the main trading center. Carts and stalls were lined up along its length and more people than I had seen in one place in years were milling around them. At first, the mob of people disoriented and scared me a bit.

Tommy parked the empty wagon at the side of the road and tucked the pistol in his satchel with the money. He hadn't brought all the money or the gold coins with him, but just enough for the day's purchases. Evidently, he'd already gotten rid of most of the stuff we'd brought in from the country the day before, while I was with Livia. We left the horses nibbling on the roadside grass and went on foot to look around. A lot of the merchandise appeared to be recycled goods—repaired and refurbished—from before everything came to a halt, although there were some newly manufactured things. We saw one man who advertised himself as a shoemaker. I stopped to watch him work, deftly cutting a piece of leather and shaping it over his last, then stitching it together with a sharp, thick needle. He looked up and smiled.

"How would you like a pair of new boots?"

"I could use them, but I haven't any money. Sorry."

The shoemaker looked questioningly at Tommy who said, "We'll be back later."

"I could take the measurements and get started," the man suggested. "Only a hundred dollars."

"We'll think about it," Tommy replied. He took my arm and we moved on. "You do need some boots, Celeste, and I owe you some wages. Would you like to have a pair made?"

"It's so much money," I replied. "Maybe we can find some used ones." It was hard to worry about boots in the middle of summer.

We came to another stall, the back of a flatbed cart, selling an assortment of things, many of which were rusty and worn-looking. I noticed an old rifle and pointed it out to Tommy. "Don't forget Joshua needs a rifle.

"That one looks too rusty; it probably wouldn't work. I know a place where we can get a better one." He poked among the old machines and machine parts for a while but didn't see anything worth bidding for.

By midday, we had bought some sacks of salt and a supply of dried fish as well as several bolts of cloth. We stopped to buy a lunch of barbecued meat on skewers with onions and tomatoes from another stall. We washed it down with apple cider, which seemed to be in good supply. After lunch, we continued to browse, stopping to look through a table of books, many of which had public library stamps in them. Tommy had given me some money to spend, so I bought a couple of books. I also looked through some used clothing and found a shirt and pair of jeans that fitted me. Tommy was more interested in buying things he could sell or trade up the valley, but I did notice him looking through a table of women's and children's clothing, probably looking for something for Janet and Jill.

At one end of the market was a large bulletin board on which people advertised things they wanted to sell or trade. They didn't put their addresses, but each advertiser had a number so that anyone interested in something could leave a note in a box by the board to arrange a meeting. Tommy looked carefully at the notices and wrote down a couple of numbers—one for a rebuilt generator and another for ammunition. He then wrote notes and deposited them in the box.

"I asked them to meet me here tomorrow or the next day," he said as we walked away.

We bought some homemade medical supplies and cosmetics, things like shampoo, hand lotion and antiseptic ointments, then packed up and returned to the university.

Chapter 36

The wagon was stocked with merchandise and we were ready to depart ten days later. As we were saying good-bye, Livia asked me to take her regards to Andrew.

We returned the same way we had come in case Pam wanted to go back with us, slowing down as we went by the temple. We carefully examined the trees and bushes beside the road in case she had left a sign. When we didn't see anything, we assumed she'd decided to stay on in the city. The rest of the day was spent meandering through various enclaves on the outskirts, doing a little trading and searching for things we hadn't found in the city. We reached Willow Creek the following afternoon after camping for the night in a park near the river.

When the people in Willow Creek heard that they could now use money to trade, many of them went back to their houses and returned with the bank notes they had been saving for such a day.

"Have you decided?" I asked Mother later when we sat down to have a meal.

"We were just waiting for you to get back. Did you find something to trade for the horses?"

"Yes," Tommy replied. "We found him a good hunting rifle and a small wind-powered generator. How is Joshua, by the way?"

"He seems better now. He's up and around, but not as active as he used to be. He's just getting old. I've arranged for someone from Willow Creek to go over and check with him while we're away. I wish he'd come into the village, but he's determined to hang on out there."

"We thought we'd leave as soon as you got back, so that we can return in time to help with the harvest," Peter said.

Mother told us how she'd arranged to swap one of the two stallions for a year-old filly from Willow Creek. They'd agreed to the deal because they thought they owed her something for teaching the children. It was good news because now we would be able to breed more horses. Both stallions were getting old and might have to be put out to pasture permanently before long.

I still felt pretty mixed up about what I wanted to do. I was thinking about Andrew all the time, but also feeling guilty about Eric. The urge to rush back to the Canyon and stay there was compelling, but I knew I shouldn't give into it without taking time to work out my feelings, so I asked Tommy if he would mind if I accompanied him for the rest of the season. He seemed pleased with the idea, so the next day, after giving Peter and Mother detailed directions for finding Lost Canyon, we ventured eastward again.

* * *

We reached Hope in the middle of August and stayed a couple of days then we went directly to the Canyon where we stayed two more days before heading back to the city. There was time for me to take a couple of walks alone with Andrew, one to the far end of the canyon, and one to the top of the hill where we'd been the last time. My feeling when I was near him seemed even more intense than before, if that was possible. It was hard to resist him. When he looked at me with such burning intensity in his eyes, or caressed my cheek with his fingertips, I almost melted with desire, but I wouldn't let myself give in to it. Yet.

When I told him about Livia's message, all he said was, "How's she doing?" His face reddened slightly, though.

"You'll come back, won't you, Celeste?" he urged when we said good-bye. "Promise? I'll have to come and find you if you don't"

"I'll be back," I said.

We visited many communities in the valley on our way west, but made a wide detour around Mission.

"Have you ever tried to trade there?" I asked Tommy.

He shook his head. "Not until I know more about them. Never know what they might decide to do."

The idea of using currency for trading was beginning to be accepted. By the time we finished for the year, almost half the people we visited were willing to use money. Another change or sign of progress was the increasing number of manufactured goods available. It seemed that once people were assured of having enough food, they started to create little industries to improve their economic situation. We knew of several potters; furniture, barrel and box makers; spinners and weavers; smiths who worked in iron, and even a glassmaker. There were manufacturers of patent medicines, soap and candles, leather goods—shoes, belts, and bags; wheels and carts; clothing, and all sorts of devices for powering generators and small vehicles.

In the city, we saw dozens of small, motorized vehicles—some running silently on batteries, others shaking and chugging along under some other sort of power. It was an exhilarating time for me with signs of recovery everywhere and people seemingly less afraid of one another, more open and friendly.

Chapter 37

Tommy, have you ever thought of going farther south on one of your trips?" I asked as we rode into the city.

"Why? Do you have an interest in something down there?" he replied.

"In a way." I wondered how to ask him without sounding manipulative. "If you ever do decide to go that way, I would like to go with you and see if I can find the place Pam was telling us about—where they stopped before she escaped."

"It sounded like a survivalist camp. Might be dangerous. What do you hope to achieve by going there anyway?"

"I thought they might tell us where they were taking Mike and Eric, and if there was any chance of them coming back. I'd be afraid to go there myself because they might not let me leave, but if I was with you . . ."

"You think you'd be safe because I'm a trader?" He looked at me sideways, but he was grinning.

"I guess so." I felt a bit foolish. I certainly didn't want to endanger him after he'd been so good to me, but I had to know if there was any chance of Eric returning— either by escaping or being released. "It's all right if you don't want to go there. I don't want you to take any unnecessary risks."

"I'll think about it," he replied. "I haven't been down there in over a year; it might be worth a trip to find out if there's anything new to trade. I'm not promising anything—it'll depend on the weather. Don't want to delay too long."

We stayed for two weeks with Dr. Levisohn and went to the various trading centers every day, loading up for the return journey.

Returning to the university area on the last day before leaving, I caught sight of a familiar figure standing with a group of people on a street corner. My heart lurched. "Tommy, stop, stop," I cried. As the wagon slowed down, I jumped off and rushed towards the corner. I saw him turn away from the other people and begin to walk in the other direction. When he disappeared around the corner, I broke into a run. I raced around the corner and as I caught up with him, I called, "Dad?" The man turned round and I saw it was not my father after all, although he looked so much like him. Tears of disappointment welled up. "Sorry," I mumbled, "I thought you were. . ." I turned and walked back to where Tommy was waiting, wiping my eyes with my sleeve.

"What was that about?" he asked gently.

"I thought I saw my father. Sorry," I told him dejectedly.

Tommy put his arm around my shoulder and squeezed. He flapped the reins and the horses started walking again.

When we left the city the next day, instead of taking our usual route eastward, we crossed the Oak Street Bridge over the river and took the old freeway south towards the border.

"You decided then?" I said.

"Might as well," Tommy replied, looking up at the clear sky. "The weather looks good; I think the rain will hold off for a while." We'd been hearing the rumble of thunder and clouds were starting to gather low on the western horizon. "I'm curious to see if there have been any new developments since I was last down this way."

"Do you think we'll be able to find the place?"

"Oh, I know where it is."

"You do?" I was surprised. "Have you been there before?"

"No. I thought it prudent to give them a miss last time. Things have changed a bit in the past year; it shouldn't be too risky now. I think I can convince them they have more to gain by doing business with us than by being hostile."

"Tommy, Pam said she thought she saw one of our friends who was kidnapped from Salish. What shall we do if we see her—or any of the others?"

"It would be best—for you and for her—if you stay cool. Pretend you don't know each other if you can. We'll have to play it by ear—see what happens. We certainly don't want to give them the idea that we're planning to run away with any of their women."

"But what if they want to go with us?"

"As I said, we'll have to see what happens. Don't forget they're heavily armed and we'll be on their territory, not to mention being outnumbered." He turned to me. "I also think we should introduce you as my daughter—we don't want them to get any ideas about keeping you there." He must have noticed that I'd filled out a bit since we met. It would have been foolish to continue trying to pass me off as a boy.

The highway we were on was formerly a freeway— six lanes wide with a divider down the middle. Although we could see houses and small communities in the distance, there was nothing directly off the freeway. Vegetation almost covered the two outside lanes, but there was still one clear lane along which we could move unimpeded. We saw a few horse-drawn wagons like our own, the occasional individual on horseback or bicycle, and a couple of motorized wagons.

We didn't stop until we had almost reached the border crossing where we turned off the highway onto a narrower road going east. Once off the highway, we let the horses rest and ate our lunch beside the road. After lunch, we went on past overgrown fields and ruined houses. The suburbs had spread all the way to the border here, but the area had kept some of its rural characteristics, having small subdivisions scattered among agricultural fields, horse farms, and golf courses.

"It's not far now," Tommy said about an hour after lunch. "Don't forget, pretend you're my daughter. And act reticent; let me do the talking. Whatever you do, don't mention Eric until we know how things lie."

"Yes, Daddy," I replied with a grin that belied the nervousness I felt.

We soon reached the woods Pam had described, and started to look for the trail leading to the camp. I always thought of it as a camp for some reason. Probably because Pam's description made it sound like a prison camp.

"There's an opening," Tommy said, pointing to a gap in the trees. He slowed down to take a better look then steered the horses onto a well-worn trail that disappeared into the woods.

The trees completely cut off the sunlight making the air chillier on the gloomy track. I shivered and pulled my sweater closer around me, wishing I had a heavier one. I pushed my hands into my pockets. Tommy checked his handgun and tucked it inside his jacket, then pushed the rifle down behind the seat and tucked a burlap sack around it.

After a while, we saw sunlight ahead and came to a clearing in front of the gates. They must have heard us coming because there was a reception committee waiting for us when we entered the clearing—about fifteen men dressed in khaki, all armed with rifles. A tall bearded man wearing a black knitted toque stood in front of the group. He held his hand up, palm towards us

"That's far enough," he said.

We stopped the wagon and waited for their next move. They didn't seem overtly hostile—the expressions on their faces were bland, and they seemed relaxed. Why not? They were armed and greatly outnumbered us.

"Who are you? What do you want?"

Tommy climbed down and held up his hands to show he meant no threat. "Alexander Marcovic," he said, holding out a hand towards the tall man. The man ignored it so Tommy continued; "I'm a trader. I thought you might like to do some trading. Oh," he added, gesturing towards me, "this is my daughter, Julie." I was surprised he didn't use my real name then I realized that, if my friends were here, these people might have heard it and Celeste is not a very common name. Clever Tommy!

The leader moved back into the group and held a short conference with the other men then he went to the back of the wagon.

"Show us what's inside," he ordered.

Tommy pulled back the flaps for the man to look at the interior of the wagon.

"All right. Pull the wagon into the yard." He signaled to a guard to open the gates.

Tommy returned to his seat and the horses slowly pulled the wagon through the gate. The group of men split up and stood on either side as we passed through, then followed us in. The gate closed behind us. We sat where we were, waiting to see what the men wanted us to do before making a move.

"All right, let's see what you've got," the tall man said.

The men surrounded the wagon, watching intently, as if it were the wooden horse of Troy and they expected a concealed army to jump out and attack them. Tommy climbed down and gestured for me to go with him. We walked to the back of the wagon and folded back the flaps. Tommy let down the tailgate and beckoned them forward to look inside.

Chapter 38

Can we get some water for the horses?" Tommy asked. He walked forward and loosened their harnesses.

Now that the men were confident we were what we said we were and not a threat, they became friendlier. They invited us into the building that Pam had described to us—the guardroom—where they offered us tea. I stayed close to Tommy and kept quiet as he'd suggested. I didn't like the way some of the men eyed me and didn't want to be alone with them.

We sat down at the table and one of the men—a short thin man with a bristly haircut—disappeared into the adjoining kitchen where I heard him issuing orders. I looked towards the door just as a girl appeared carrying a tray. She started in surprise when she saw us, spilling some of the tea out of the mugs on the tray. I realized with shock that it was Lia. I took a breath, but the slight shake of her head and the fearful look in her eyes stopped me in time. Her hand trembled as she placed the mugs on the table. I saw her glance fearfully at the man who'd followed her in from the kitchen.

"Do you have a toilet I could use?" I asked, hoping this would give me an opportunity to speak to her alone.

"I'll show you," she replied, gesturing towards the farther door.

I stood up and followed her to the small wash room.

She went inside ahead of me and as soon as she was out of sight of the men, she put her finger on her lip and shook her head. "Don't say anything," she whispered. "I'll have to bring you some water," she said aloud. She picked up the empty bucket and left me alone.

I was shocked by the change in her appearance. Her lovely glossy hair was now dull and lank. She wore it drawn back severely and tied at the back of her neck. She had on a loose-fitting grey dress of a coarse cotton material. Her skin looked sallow and pasty and her eyes no longer glowed with life. Her movements were sluggish and awkward, and her shoulders slumped, as if she barely had enough energy to get around. The only

333

positive change I could see was that her body had filled out.

When she returned with the water, I grabbed her hand. "Lia, I'm so glad to see you. Are you all right?"

Tears filled her eyes. "I have to talk to you," she whispered. "When are you leaving?"

"Later, after we've done some trading. Half an hour to an hour, maybe."

"I have to go," she said anxiously. "I'll see you later." She peered through the opening in the door then turned back to me. "That man you're with . . . is he okay?"

"Yes, he's very nice."

"What's going on in there?" a man yelled. "You're taking enough time . . ."

Lia jumped, fearful, and hurried away. After she'd gone, I wondered how she intended to talk to me. There didn't appear to be any way of escaping the vigilant eyes of the men. I looked out of the window of the wash room at the garden Pam had told me about, hoping to see Chris or Debbie or Jackie, but there was no one out there.

We spent almost an hour trading with the people in the camp. The only women who came out were two middle-aged matrons who seemed to have a bit of

Fatal Harvest

influence with the men. Their clothing was a little more colorful than Lia's. I guessed they were probably wives as opposed to captured women like Lia, who appeared to be hardly more than a slave. After we had stowed away the merchandise, I finished tying down the flaps on the back of the wagon with fumbling fingers while Tommy prepared the horses to leave. It was late afternoon by the time we left the camp and entered the woods bordering the site.

"That girl who served us tea was Lia—one of the girls who was kidnapped from Salish," I said to Tommy as soon as we were outside the camp.

"I thought there was something strange about her behavior," Tommy replied. "She looked so jumpy. Did she say anything to you?"

"Not much. She didn't want anyone to find out she knew me. She said she wanted to talk to me, but I guess she didn't get a chance." I sighed. "I wish we could do something to help her—and the others. She looked so miserable."

"Maybe another time, if we can gain the trust of those men. I'd hate to try anything now; it would probably leads to open warfare. They've got us outnumbered and outgunned."

335

"I was wondering if we could ask them to—I don't know—let them go or something. . ." I trailed off, the idea not quite formed.

"I doubt that would do any good. It would only alienate them more."

"Did you find out anything about Eric and Mike?" I asked, changing the subject.

"A little. It was tricky. They're very touchy about being asked questions." Tommy replied

"Well, what did they say?" I asked.

"There's a group down south working on some sort of scientific or technological project. They needed more people to work for them. My guess is they have a few scientists who survived, but not enough to do whatever it is they're doing. They needed new people they can train to help them and carry on with the work. I think it was sheer chance they took your friends. They probably weren't even looking for anyone, but just took advantage of the opportunity when they came across you."

"But what made them think *we* would be useful to them when they attacked us?"

"Who knows? They probably listened to you talking for a while before they attacked. You can tell a lot about people by their conversation, especially whether or not they're intelligent and educated."

"I wonder what they're working on."

"Your guess is as good as mine. Knowledge is power, though, and the group that has the most advanced technology dominates."

"Do you think there's any chance Mike and Eric might get away and come back?"

"I've no idea." Tommy replied

"I sure hope they treat them well."

"I imagine they will. They're not going to get much useful work from them by mistreating them. They'll probably enjoy the work; it's a bit different from the manual labor everybody has to do nowadays. Did either of them have an interest in science?"

"Oh, yes. Eric was always studying science books. Mike too."

"Well, there you are. Apart from being separated from everyone they care about, they'll probably be reasonably contented."

"I hope so. I still feel as if I owe it to them to do something to help them. Do you know what I mean?"

"I think so."

Our conversation was cut short by the appearance of two figures on the road ahead of us. They had slipped out of the trees as we came along and stood waiting for us to reach them. One of them was Lia, and by the red hair, I knew the other must be Jackie. Tommy brought the horses to a stop when we reached them.

The two girls looked up at us—Lia with tears running down her face.

"Help us to get away, Celeste," she begged. "I can't bear it here anymore."

"Climb up here and get in the back out of sight," Tommy said holding out his hand towards Jackie. "We'll talk about it, but we must keep moving."

I helped Lia climb up onto the wagon. She followed Jackie inside through the canvas flaps. Tommy got the horses moving again, then turned to the girls and asked them, "How did you get away. Will they be coming after you?"

"We went out the back way to pick mushrooms so they won't miss us for a while," Lia replied.

"You mean they let you go outside the compound alone?" Tommy asked.

"No, one of the men came along to watch us."

"What happened to him? How did you get away?"

"Chris. She was with us. She said she'd keep him occupied. She told us to go away while she . . . so they could . . ." Lia's explanation ended in a sob

"This guy's always after Chris, but she doesn't like him. She usually manages to avoid him." Jackie added.

"Who's Chris?" Tommy inquired.

"She was the nurse. Remember? I told you about her." I turned round to speak to Lia. "Won't she get into trouble when they find out?"

"She wanted us to have a chance to escape." Lia said tearfully. "She'll be punished, but she's important to them, being a nurse."

"Poor Chris. What will they do to her?"

"Probably lock her in the cellar without any food for a few days. Sometimes they beat us, but I don't think they'll hurt her. One of the head guys is kind of—you know—likes her."

"Well they'll be after us as soon as they realize you're missing. And it won't be too hard for them to guess who you're with, so we'd better get a move on."

"You mean you'll take us with you?" Jackie asked, her tone rising as if she could hardly believe it.

"Can't very well send you back to that," Tommy replied gruffly.

He pulled to a stop and jumped to the ground, then went around and opened the back. After rummaging around for a moment, he walked to the side of the road carrying a coil of wire. I watched curiously as he tied one end to a tree, then crossed to the opposite side and tied the other end to another, pulling it tight, so that the wire was strung across the road about chest high.

He jumped up onto the box and jerked the reins. "That might stop them for a little while," he said. "As long as they don't see it in time."

I peered around the side of the wagon and looked back, but was unable to see the wire in the semi-twilight of the forest. I pulled aside the flap and looked at Lia and Jackie. They were huddled together shivering—not entirely from cold, I was sure.

"Is my dad all right?" Lia asked.

This completely floored me. She didn't know he'd been killed! How could I tell her?

Sensing my dismay, she asked, "What's the matter, Celeste? Has something happened to him?"

"I'm sorry, Lia, I thought you knew."

"What? Tell me?"

"They killed him. In the raid."

She let out an anguished wail. Jackie put an arm around her and I took her hand. "What raid? You mean . . .?"

"Yes. When they kidnapped you. They killed everybody there except Tate. He managed to hide."

Lia sobbed noisily for a while. Her weeping gradually subsided into muffled gasps then she wiped her wet cheeks and closed her eyes, leaning back against the side of the wagon, exhausted. My own eyes were filled with tears. I had never felt so helpless, seeing that much pain and not knowing what to do to help.

"How's Debbie doing, and the baby?" I asked, hoping to avoid talking about anything that would cause them more distress.

"Debbie's dead," Jackie replied.

"What? How?"

"She caught something and got sick last year. I don't know what it was—maybe the new flu. Anyway, she died. I don't think she wanted to live."

"Poor Debbie. Who looks after the baby?"

"Chris. One of the other women—a wife—tried to take her, but Carol-Anne screamed every time she came near her."

"It must have been pretty awful for you, living there," I said.

Jackie snorted. "Awful doesn't describe it," she said bitterly.

"Do you want to tell us about it?" I asked.

"Maybe later. I just want to forget it right now. What happened to you? How did you and this guy . . .?" She nodded towards Tommy.

"I should introduce you, I'm sorry. This is Tommy. He's a trader. He travels around trading goods with different communities all through the valley. I've been traveling with him this summer, helping out." I turned to Tommy. "These are my friends, Lia and Jackie." I felt a little silly introducing them after the conversation we'd just had, and the possible trouble Tommy was risking having the two girls with us.

"Thanks, Tommy, for not making us go back." Lia said.

"How could I send you back to that place? We're not out of the woods yet, though. Excuse the pun. They might be coming after us right this minute."

We had actually left the trail through the woods and turned eastward on the highway.

"Luckily for us the horses are rested, so we'll be able to keep going for while even though it's getting dark."

The sky had clouded over and twilight was falling early. Tommy urged the horses to move a little faster. I kept my ears open for any sign of pursuit.

"If we do hear them," Tommy said to the two girls, "You'll have to jump down and hide in the bushes. We'll try to convince them you aren't with us. We'll let them search the wagon and hope they leave us alone."

"What about the wire you tied across the road?" I asked. "Won't they know it was us?"

"We'll say we don't know anything about it. Convince them the girls must have done it if we can."

We rode on in silence until it was completely dark. There was still no sign of pursuit.

"Are we going to stop for the night?" I asked Tommy.

"Soon," he replied. "I want to put as much distance between us and them before the horses get too tired."

About fifteen minutes later, we heard the sound of horse's hooves behind us. Tommy stopped the wagon.

"Out, out. Hurry," he said, holding out his hand to help the girls down. "Quick up there, behind those bushes. Lie down flat and don't move."

Lia and Jackie scrambled up the bank and disappeared from sight behind some scrawny bushes. They must have been terrified—I know I was. We listened for a moment to the approaching hoof beats. They weren't galloping, as we would have expected, but cantering at an easy trot. Tommy urged our horses to start moving again at a slow pace to show we weren't in a hurry. The hoof beats finally caught up with us and pulled ahead of the wagon. We waited tensely for the encounter.

Chapter 39

Hi there!" The man's voice sounded friendly. "Lousy night to be out."

"You've got that right," Tommy replied. "Live around here?"

"Not far. Been visiting my wife's family, showing them the new baby." Tommy stopped the wagon and the two riders also halted. They turned their horses towards us and I saw that one of them was a woman. She had a bundle strapped to her front, which I assumed was the baby.

"It's a bit late to be out with a baby," Tommy said.

"I know," the man replied. "We ran into some trouble back there. Held us up for a time."

"What sort of trouble?" Tommy asked.

"Nothing serious. Bunch of men looking for some thieves. Least that's what they said. Looked like they were from that survivalist place. Didn't like the looks of them one bit. Dangerous."

"I know what you mean," Tommy continued "What did they say when they stopped you?"

"They wanted to know if we'd seen a man and some girls in cart going towards the coast. A wagon like this I guess. They said they'd been to their camp and stolen some stuff. We told them we hadn't seen anything." He looked at his wife then back at us. "You see anything?"

"No. My wife and I are moving to a village in the interior." Tommy replied. "She's not been feeling too good, so we had to stop and rest this afternoon; it's made us a bit late." What an accomplished liar Tommy was turning into!

"Sorry to hear that, Hope you're feeling better, ma'am."

345

I nodded.

"Best be on our way then," the man said. "Have a safe journey."

"You too." Tommy replied.

The two riders took off. Tommy let out a long breath, releasing the tension. We waited until the riders were out of sound range, then Tommy climbed down and went back up the road to where the girls were hiding. When they returned, he helped them up onto the wagon. They were both shaking, breathing in quick gasps that sounded almost like sobs.

"Phew! That was scary." Tommy said. "Wrap some blankets around you," he said to Lia and Jackie. Celeste'll help you find them."

I helped my friends get reasonably comfortable as we set off again. After another hour, we pulled off the road into a wooded lane. We went along the lane for a while then Tommy guided the horses off the path onto a grassy clearing surrounded by trees and bushes. We jumped down and loosened the harnesses so that the horses could graze.

"We won't unharness them," Tommy said, "I'll bring them some water. Will you get something ready for us to eat? We can't light a fire so it'll have to be a cold supper."

Lia and Jackie woke up when the rhythmic jolting of the wagon stopped. They looked out through a gap in the canvas to see what was happening.

"We're stopping here to rest," Tommy informed them. "Mainly for the horses. When they've rested, we'll go on. They've probably given up looking for you now that it's dark and gone back home. One advantage we have is that they don't know which way we went."

After we'd eaten, the two girls and I went into the bushes to relieve ourselves.

"Are you and Tommy—you know . . .?" Lia asked when we were out of earshot.

"No." I answered. "He's a good friend, my employer too."

"How did you meet him?" she asked on the way back to the wagon.

"It was after Eric and Mike and Pam were kidnapped. He rescued me."

"What?" they exclaimed in unison, coming to a standstill.

"There's so much to tell you, I don't know where to start. How about we leave it till morning? We must get some rest now." I replied and started walking again.

As we emerged from the bushes, we felt the first drops of rain. Tommy was waiting for us. He handed me a sleeping bag. He'd spread a tarpaulin on the ground under the wagon.

"You'll have to sleep outside tonight," he said. "The girls can sleep in the wagon."

I usually slept in the front of the wagon when it was cold or raining, but there wasn't room for me and the two girls. We should probably have had Lia and Jackie sleep away from the wagon, but it was so wet and cold, it would have been cruel to add to their misery. I said good night to them and spread my sleeping bag under the wagon beside Tommy's. He'd disappeared into the bushes and by the time he returned, I was cocooned inside my bag ready to sleep, wearing all my clothes except for my boots.

"We'll not be staying long," Tommy said as he pulled his sleeping bag around him. "I want to be away from here before it gets light. Get some sleep, Celeste. Goodnight."

It seemed as if I'd only just fallen asleep when Tommy shook me awake. "Come on, time to get moving."

It was still dark and a light steady rain was falling. I put on my boots and dragged myself groggily from under the wagon, rolled up my bedding and threw it inside. I turned my face up to the sky, allowing the rain to wash it then rubbed with my wet hands, hoping the makeshift shower would refresh me. After we had folded and stowed the tarpaulin, Tommy and I tightened the harnesses and did a quick survey of the area to make sure we'd left nothing lying around then we climbed onto the wagon.

A flick of the reins got the horses moving, somewhat reluctantly. We turned back the way we had entered from the lane and were soon on the highway again. I heard Lia and Jackie stirring behind me and pulled the flap aside to look in.

"What time is it?" asked Lia, yawning.

"About five o'clock." Tommy replied. "Are you hungry?"

"A bit," she admitted.

"How about breaking out some biscuits, Celeste? There's some apple juice we could wash them down with."

"Would one of you like to change places with me so that I can find them?" I asked.

"I will," said Lia, poking her head through the opening.

After I'd found and shared out the food, Lia went back inside the wagon and I resumed my place beside Tommy. While I was fumbling about inside, I had pulled out a couple of empty plastic sacks to cover our heads and shoulders against the rain, which looked as if it had set in for the day.

By the time it started to get light and we could see something of our surroundings, we were in the midst of an area crisscrossed with roads and lanes, abandoned commercial buildings, and housing developments: Surrey. The poor light and misty rain made it hard to see very far, so we couldn't tell if any of the buildings were still occupied.

"If this weather keeps up, we might make it," Tommy commented.

"I don't understand why they haven't come after us," I said. "They could ride much faster on their horses than we can go in the wagon."

"Maybe it's because they're looking in the wrong direction," Tommy said with a grin. "I told them we were on our way to the coast instead of away from it—I didn't want them to know too much about our business. There's plenty of roads in that direction for them to search. It may fool them long enough to give us time to get away."

We turned north towards the river at the first passable road we came to and plodded onward. We only saw one other vehicle—a wagon similar to ours that crossed the road in front of us going from west to east. After what seemed like hours, Tommy pulled the wagon off the road into the parking lot of an abandoned shopping center. We went around the back, out of sight of the road and came to a stop.

"Time for another break," he announced. "It should be safe here for us to light a fire and heat some food. Your friends can get down and stretch their legs." He unhitched the horses and led them to a drainage ditch filled with water.

Lia, Jackie and I started searching for some wood to light a fire. We found some dry twigs under the shrubbery that surrounded the lot, and after a bit more scrounging, uncovered some old wooden fruit crates. We lighted the fire in an alcove formed by the buildings. It was out of sight of the road, and sheltered by an overhanging roof.

The activity drew us out of our lethargy and we began to liven up a little. I think it was just starting to sink into Lia and Jackie that they were free and, in spite of the dismal weather and additional bad news they'd heard from me, they were beginning to feel more hopeful.

It was hard to believe it was only a little over a year since the raid, so much had happened, and we'd all changed in some way. Jackie and Lia had been thirteen and fourteen when they were taken from our home in Salish. Jackie, who had been barely past childhood, had grown taller. Her face was thin and gaunt with shadows under her haunted eyes. Her mouth looked small and pinched, and she had permanent worry lines creasing the center of her forehead. I wondered what dreadful things she'd had to endure in the past year.

Lia had also grown taller. She looked equally pale and careworn, but she seemed to be a bit thicker around the middle and chest. That was apparent even with the thick clothing. "They must have fed you well, Lia, You've put on a bit of weight," I commented.

She jumped up from her seat near the fire and turned away from us, but not before I'd seen her tears. I stood up and followed her, putting my arm around her shoulder.

"I'm sorry, Lia. What's wrong?"

"It's not the food, I'm pregnant," she sobbed, turning to me. I pulled her close and put my arms around her. "Oh, Celeste, what am I going to do? I'm so miserable, I wish I was dead."

"Shh, Lia. You'll be all right. You've escaped from them. We'll take care of you. You'll be safe now." I stroked her head, shocked at the latest revelation and embarrassed that I hadn't realized. I wondered what we were going to do about Lia and Jackie. It was all very well for Mom and Peter and Tate to move to the Canyon, they'd been invited, but would they accept two more—one of whom was going to have a baby? Poor Lia. How awful it must be for her.

"When . . .? Do you know?"

"February or March, I'm not sure."

"What about the father?"

She shrugged. "I don't care about him, whoever he was. I hate them all. One day, I'm going to kill every one of them."

"You mean there was more than one?"

"Oh yes," she said bitterly. "Anyone who felt like it could have a go at us. We were there for their pleasure. Even the married ones. Then their wives took it out on us, as if we could stop them. Fucking pigs." Her shoulders shook with renewed sobbing.

"I'm sorry, Lia. I don't know what to say. It must have been so terrible. I can't imagine. . . I'm so sorry. Come on; let's finish our lunch, okay?" I didn't know how to handle my friend's distress.

We went back and sat with the others. Jackie took Lia's hand to comfort her. I thought about the hell they'd been through. It's no wonder they looked so much older than their years. Tommy looked at me and raised his eyebrows. I shook my head, not wanting to discuss it with him in front of them.

We finished eating and packed up our things. After kicking the ashes around to eliminate our fireplace, Tommy and I went to bring the horses back from where they were grazing by the ditch.

"What was all that about?" he asked.

"Lia's pregnant," I replied.

"Oh, God, the poor kid. I thought she looked bit . . . I thought it was the bulky clothing." He shook his head. "How old is she?"

"Fifteen, I think."

Tommy shook his head. "Bastards!"

We resumed our journey northward, reaching the bridge over the river before nightfall. Once across the river, we finally felt confident that we were out of danger. There were just too many different routes for the pursuers to search; the odds were against their picking this particular one.

We continued uphill from the bridge to the grounds of an abandoned hospital where we set up camp for the night. It was still drizzling, but we found a sheltered spot among the big evergreens to make camp. After another hot meal, we settled down for a good night's sleep. In the light from the fire, I caught a smile from Lia as she lay down and wrapped the blankets around her. The three of us snuggled close together for warmth and comfort, leaving Tommy alone under the wagon.

The next morning, leaving Lia and Jackie to start the fire, Tommy and I went to find the horses. They had wandered away in the night. They hadn't gone too far and we soon found them happily munching the lush grass under some trees near an artificial pond.

"Tommy," I said, searching for a way to say what was on my mind, "I hope we aren't being a burden for you. I mean, you didn't bargain for this . . . three of us and all. And you could have had real trouble if those guys had caught us. I'm sorry; I know you were doing me a favor by going there and now..."

"Hmmm. Now that you mention it. . ." He grinned at me. "What kind of a person would I be if I refused to help those poor kids?"

"You're such a good guy, Tommy." I gave him a hug.

"I know. The problem now is, what are we going to do with them?"

"It is a problem, isn't it?" I agreed.

"We'll work it out. Come on; let's get this show on the road."

"Are we going to stay at Willow Creek tonight? I wonder if Mom and Peter will be there."

"Yes. And we'll see when we get there," he replied.

Chapter 40

It took us all morning to reach Willow Creek. We didn't stop to do any trading because Tommy thought it best to avoid the risk of anyone seeing Lia and Jackie. It was still raining when we turned into the narrow road leading to the village, and we didn't see the sentries until we were almost on them.

We had tucked the canvas cover to one side so that Lia and Jackie could see where we were going over our shoulders.

"What is this place?" Lia asked.

"Willow Creek. Remember? Where we used to get our honey? It's the place we moved to after the raid on Salish. There were only the seven of us left and we didn't think we could make it alone, and we were scared of another raid, so we moved here. They gave us an empty house to live in and Mom has a school for the kids."

When we pulled up by the church, the Reverend Eikhart came out of his house. "There's no school today," he said. Turning to me he added, "Your mother's at the house."

"Thank you," I replied

"We'll go straight to the house and trade later, after we've had a chance to dry out a bit," Tommy said. "How are things going?"

"Very well, praise the Lord!" the Reverend replied. "I understand we're going be losing our teacher though. We'll be sorry to see her go; she's been a great help." He peered into the wagon behind us. "I see you've picked up some passengers, "he said.

"Yes," Tommy replied. "These are two of the young women who were abducted in the raid on Salish. They managed to escape from their captors, so we brought them back."

"Where are they going to live?" asked the minister.

"We don't know yet. They've had a rough time, as you may imagine. They're in pretty bad shape at the moment and need time to recover before we decide."

"Let me know if there's anything I can do to help."

"Thanks, we will. We'll see you later." With that, Tommy gave the reins a flick and we moved on.

"Who was that?" asked Lia

"Reverend Eikhart. He's the minister at the church. He's sort of the head guy around here."

"He looks a bit—you know—stuffy."

"He's all right. They're pretty strict about religion and stuff, but they're okay."

A few people waved to us as we went down the street. When we rounded the corner, our house came into sight, smoke rising from the chimney and a light glowing in the window. As if they sensed the journey was coming to an end, the horses picked up their pace a little. When we pulled off the road into the driveway, the side door opened and Tate rushed out with Pepsi, then Mother and Peter appeared in the doorway.

Tate came over to help with the horses. When he saw the two girls behind us, he stopped. His mouth fell open. "Lia? Jackie? Is it really you?"

I climbed down from the wagon and looked up at the two girls. "Come on inside. Everything's okay now."

Mother and Peter had joined us to wait as Jackie and Lia came out of their cubbyhole and climbed down from the wagon. Mother immediately enclosed them in her arms, kissing them and stroking their heads while they wept and clung to her.

Mom and I ushered the two girls into the house leaving Tate and Peter to help Tommy with the horses. We took off our wet jackets and hung them to dry near the stove.

I saw mother give Lia a startled look when she took off her bulky sweater. She looked at me questioningly.

"Mom, Lia's pregnant," I said. She had obviously guessed, but I wanted to save Lia having to explain.

This brought on a fresh flood of tears from Lia.

Mother put her arm around Lia and pressed her to her side. I noticed tears glistening in her eyes. "Oh Lia, I'm so sorry." Sensing Lia's acute discomfort, she continued, "I know you've been through a terrible experience. You don't have to talk about it now if you don't want to. You're here, safe, that's what counts." She pulled away and stroked Lia's hair. "Would you like to go to the bathroom and freshen up?"

Lia nodded.

"Celeste will show you the way while I get you something hot to drink."

When we returned from the bathroom, we huddled close to the stove for warmth while mother put out some mugs and bowls for the soup and coffee that were already heating up.

The men came in and sat at the table and before long we all had bowls of soup and mugs of coffee in front of us.

"Tommy was telling us about how you escaped. Boy, I wish I'd been there." Tate said, his eyes glowing. "What happened to you?"

Seeing Mother's warning glance, he looked down at his bowl. "Sorry," he said.

"It's okay Tate," Lia said. "It's just . . . We don't feel like talking about it right now. I'm glad to see you again. You've really grown up, hasn't he, Jackie?"

"Yes, I hardly recognized you," Jackie said, blushing.

Tate's complexion had turned a shade darker too. "So have you," he replied. He went on with his meal, sneaking looks at Lia and Jackie from time to time. They both seemed equally taken by him, as were most girls who met him. I wondered how things would work out, and if one of these two would end up with him, even though they were older.

"So, you went to the Canyon, did you?" I asked Mom.

"Yes. We got back two weeks ago. It's just as wonderful as you described. They really are nice people. I think we could do some useful work there. We've told the Reverend we might be moving on, haven't we, dear?" She put her hand over Peter's.

"Yes. We were planning to go up there next week. We've found a small cart to carry our things."

"That's great," I said.

"Let's talk about it later," Mother said, glancing at Lia and Jackie. "I bet you girls would like some exercise after being cooped up in that wagon all that time." They nodded. "Tate, why don't you take them out and show them around when you've finished eating?"

After lunch, Tate and the girls put their jackets on and left the house. Peter and Tommy went outside to do something with the wagon, so mother and I were left alone to talk, as I'm sure she had intended.

"I suppose this'll change things," I said as I helped clear the table.

"I guess it will," she replied. "How did you ever end up finding them?"

I told her how I had asked Tommy if we could try to find out what had happened to Eric and Mike, and how Lia had appeared unexpectedly. When I had finished, she sighed, wiped her hands on a dishtowel and sat down at the table.

"Did they tell you anything about what happened to them there? They look ready to fall apart."

"I know. They told me a little bit, but it's hard for them to talk about it. Apparently, they were—any man could—you know . . ."

362

"Jesus! They're only kids. What kind of animals could do something like that?" She rested her elbows on the table and covered her face with her hands. "We'll have to keep them with us. They're going to need a lot of care if they are to come out of this. . . "

"Does that mean we'll take them with us to the Canyon?"

"I don't think it would be fair to the folks there to take any extra people. We'll have to stay here, I suppose. At least until the baby's born. When is she expecting it?"

"In February or March, she doesn't seem sure."

"God! Well, we'll have to do what we can. We can't abandon them." She must have caught the disappointment on my face. "You can go with Tommy if you want to. You don't have to stay. By the way," she added with a smile, "we met Andrew. He sent his regards,"

I felt my face turning red. "Thanks."

"Celeste, is there something you'd like to talk about? You seem to have something on your mind."

I hadn't realized I was so transparent. I sighed. "I feel so mixed up. You know, about Eric and stuff."

"Do you want to talk about it?"

"I guess so. It's—I feel as if I owe something to Eric, but I don't. . ."

"You mean you think you should wait for him?"

I nodded, ashamed of the way I felt. "Uh huh. I don't even know how I feel about Eric now." I looked down at my hands on the table. "Maybe it was because he was the only one around . . . and . . . I don't even know if I'll ever see him again."

"I understand. And now you've met someone else you want to get to know better and you feel guilty about that?"

I nodded again.

"Did you find out anything about Eric while you were at that place?"

"Yes. They said they've been sent to a place across the border where they might be doing some kind of scientific work."

"It sounds as if that would suit Eric."

"I suppose so." I looked up at her. "Do you know what Pam told me?"

"Not unless you tell me."

"She gave me a message from Eric saying he didn't really love me and that I was free."

"Do you believe that?"

"No. I think he was just saying it in case he never came back."

"Is that why you feel guilty about Andrew?"

"In a way. I wish—I don't know. If I could just be sure Eric would be happy there. It's not knowing . . ."

"I can see your dilemma. It won't do much good tormenting yourself over it. I don't know what advice to give you—that is, if you want advice."

"I guess I just want to know that I won't be an absolute monster if I forget about Eric and go with Andrew."

"I don't think so. It takes time to accept that someone is gone and you can continue your life without him. Don't think it was easy for me when your father disappeared. I didn't know for sure that he would never return. I felt as guilty as hell about my relationship with Peter." A little smile played around her lips.

"I bet my attitude didn't help much." I smiled, remembering the bratty way I'd acted. "I'm sorry, Mom. I understand how you must have felt now."

I suddenly remembered the incident in the city the last time I was there. "I thought I saw Dad one day in the city and went running after him, but it wasn't him. I felt like such a fool."

She took my hand. "Feel better now?"

"Yes. Thanks, Mom."

There was a flurry of stamping feet outside the door then Tate entered the kitchen with Lia and Jackie. I noticed that the girls' faces were flushed and their eyes looked less dull and lifeless than they had earlier.

"Did you have a good walk?" Mother asked.

They nodded and began to remove their jackets and boots.

"We'll have to see about finding you places to sleep before it gets too dark," Mother continued. "Come along."

They followed her out of the room and I heard them going upstairs. I think Mother wanted to have a chance to talk to them alone.

"So, what's new?" I asked Tate.

"Not much. Hey that Canyon's a real cool place."

"I know. What do you think? Want to go and live there?"

"I. . ." He shrugged. "I haven't decided yet. What do you think Jackie and Lia will do now?"

"I don't know. Mom says she and Peter will have to stay here and look after them for the winter."

"Why? Are they sick?"

"No. I mean—it was pretty awful at that place. They need somewhere safe to recover with people who care about them. And Lia's going to have a baby."

"I know." Tate looked down at the floor as if the thought of Lia being pregnant embarrassed him. "What about you? Are you staying here?"

"I'll probably go on with Tommy—to the Canyon, I mean."

"I bet I can guess why," Tate said with a grin. "He's a cool guy."

"Who?" I retorted, blushing.

"Andrew. Don't pretend he's not the reason you want to go up there."

"How about all your female admirers? Are you going to break their hearts by leaving?"

He decided to change the subject. "What happened to them at that place? Jackie looks so—I don't know how to put it—lost, I guess."

"They had a pretty bad time. They were used like slaves. We'll have to be very patient and understanding with them. It could take a long time for them to get better. I remember when I . . ."

"What?"

"Oh, nothing." I had almost blurted out the story about the punks. Although he knew something happened at the time, I was still reluctant to discuss it. "We'll just have to show them we care about them and don't judge them if they sometimes act a bit funny."

I was saved from further conversation along this line by the reappearance of Mother with Lia and Jackie.

"Well, that's squared away. I think you'll be comfortable for the time being. We may be able to get an extra mattress from someone in the village if you two don't mind sharing it," Mother said. She walked over to the dresser and lighted another lamp then she sat down at the table, glancing at the clock on the wall. It was almost four thirty and starting to get dark. "I wonder where Peter and Tommy have gotten to."

"They were doing some trading when we came in. As soon as the people heard Tommy was here, they all wanted to come and see what he'd brought," Tate replied.

"I almost forgot—how's Joshua?" I asked.

"He seems to be getting on all right," Mother said.

"Does someone go and visit him once in a while?" I asked.

"Yes, about once a week. I still worry about him out there all alone."

"It's what he wants. He's happy," Tate said.

"I know, but all the same. . ."

The door opened, letting in a blast of damp, cold air. Peter and Tommy had returned.

Chapter 41

The next day, Tommy and I set out for the Canyon where we both planned to spend the winter. We left behind some extra food for the family to help feed Lia and Jackie. Tommy was very generous about the whole situation. I knew I was very fortunate to have him as a friend. I also intended to pay him back one day.

The night before, after we'd finished supper, we sat around the stove and brought Jackie and Lia up-to-date. We went to bed early, exhausted from the stress of the past couple of days.

As soon as we were on the road, I started to fantasize about seeing Andrew again. My discussion with my mother had clarified things a little for me and I now felt less guilty about letting go of Eric. That and the normal hopefulness of an eighteen-year-old lightened my mood considerably.

We stopped a few times on the way to visit some of Tommy's regulars, delivering messages and things they had ordered. It took ten days for us to reach the Canyon this time. The rain had stopped falling the day we left Willow Creek, but the sun didn't come out until we turned off onto the road to the Canyon.

By the time we pulled into the clearing, the sun had set behind us. Everything looked so warm and inviting. Golden light radiated from the houses, and smoke curled up from the chimneys. The dogs came trotting across the clearing and were soon joined by several people. I looked eagerly to see if Andrew was among them, but there was only Ben and Barbara, Martin, Janet and Jill. Tommy climbed down and went to hug Janet and ruffle Jill's hair. Another figure emerged from behind one of the buildings and started running towards the wagon. When he was close enough to recognize, I jumped down and ran to meet him. Without giving a thought to the appropriateness of my action, or whether it would be welcome, I ran into his arms.

"Hey! What's this?" he said, laughing. "I was beginning to wonder if you'd ever come back." He stopped talking and kissed me on the mouth.

I responded enthusiastically this time instead of trying to push him away. "It's so good to see you again, Andrew," I said when we paused for breath.

"Welcome back," he replied. "How are you? When are your folks coming? How was your trip?"

"Which question would you like me to answer first?" I laughed.

"None of them. What I really want to know is, are you going to stay this time?"

"I guess so. For the winter at least."

"I suppose that'll have to do for now. At least I'll have all winter to persuade you to stay longer."

I pulled away from him and looked back at the group around the wagon. "I'd better help Tommy with the horses," I said.

"I'll give you a hand." Andrew took hold of my hand and we walked back to the wagon.

"Where are you staying?" Andrew asked once we had freed the horses and taken them to the stable.

"I don't know. I never thought about it," I replied. "Do you think I should stay in the cabin where Mom and Peter were going to live?"

"Why? Aren't they coming?"

"Not for a while. Something came up and they have to stay there for the winter. They'll probably come in the spring. They loved it here by the way."

"That's too bad. Their not coming, I mean. Anyway, I don't think you'll want to stay alone in that old cabin without any running water or electricity. You could stay with us if you like. I'm sure Sarah won't mind you sharing her room."

"We'll see. Right now I want to get indoors out of this cold."

"Come on, let's go." He put his arm around me and we walked back to Ben's house where everybody seemed to have gathered. Before opening the door, he turned to face me, lifted my chin with his finger and kissed me once more. "I'm really glad you came back. I missed you," he said.

When Ben and Barbara offered to let me use their spare bedroom, I accepted. I thought it was preferable to inconveniencing Sarah, and I knew the proximity to Andrew would probably drive both of us crazy if I stayed at his house. At first, he pretended to be hurt, but in the end, he had to agree that it was probably the best arrangement.

It was a heady time for me. For the first time in many years, I felt comfortable and safe. The warmth and kindness of everybody in Lost Canyon were remarkable. I understood that Tommy belonged there—he was truly one of them. I felt as if I had come home at last after years of wandering, lost and lonely. I don't want to downplay the happy times we'd had in Salish before the raid, but life had been difficult there, we'd suffered many hardships and had few comforts. Here in the Canyon, it was more like before the disasters.

* * *

Not long after we arrived, there was discussion at one of the weekly meetings as to what role I could play in the community. Everyone was encouraged to have expertise or skills in some special area of knowledge.

"Couldn't I just help with the cooking and gardening? There must be plenty of work to do," I said.

"That's true," Barbara said. "But is that all you want to do? Most of the people here have some kind of specialty that they pursue, and everyone helps with the labor anyway. We don't want you to get bored and stagnate."

"But I don't know anything else."

"You could learn something. There's plenty of talent for you to pick from and I know any of us would be happy to share what we know with you. Isn't there something you'd like to do? Some special interest?"

I stared down at my hands while I thought this over. She had a point. I tried to recall what my ambition had been when I was little. Something to do with animals, and then computers, which would be useless here.

"I'm sort of interested in helping people—you know—nursing or something like that," I said, hoping nobody would laugh at the triteness of it.

"Why not go for medicine?" Andrew offered. "I'm sure Dad could use some help."

"You mean become a doctor?" I said, astounded at the audacity of the idea.

"Why not?" Dr. Fisher said. "There's going to be a great need for new doctors. Somebody'll have to take over."

"But. . ." I stammered. "There's so much to learn. I don't know if I could do it. I might not be smart enough."

"You won't know unless you try. We'll all help you."
Dr. Fisher replied. "And next spring, you could go to the
university to see what you can pick up there. The
training would be a bit piecemeal at first, but it's worth a
shot."

And that's how I entered the medical profession. I
did help with the cooking and looking after the
livestock—gardening had stopped for the year, apart
from the greenhouses—but I also started studying the
books Dr. Fisher gave me. He would give me a chapter to
read, then we would discuss it, and after that, he would
sometimes give me a test to see if I had retained
anything. Occasionally, one of the others would help me
with certain subjects: Janet with nutrition, Walter—
Alan's partner—with chemistry, and Barbara with
psychology. I also helped Paris—as he soon insisted on
being called—in his research lab where he was
experimenting with medicinal plants.

I didn't have too much free time to spend with
Andrew, but we did manage to get together fairly
regularly. I was still very shy about intimacy with him
and avoided being alone with him too much. I was afraid
of losing control I suppose. I don't know why I felt it was
so important to keep such a tight rein on my feelings.
Maybe I suspected that once I gave in to them, I wouldn't
be able to stop. The temptation was there all the time,

and I could see in his eyes that he felt it too, but he didn't try to rush me. Not until the day his father was called away to an emergency in one of the small settlements below the Canyon. Sarah had gone with him because she had more experience than I at that time.

Andrew said he wanted to make supper for me and told me to be at his house at seven. Before leaving, I spent half an hour in the hot tub at Ben and Barbara's, then put on my newest clothes: an ankle-length skirt and light sweater. When I arrived, I found the table set with candles, and a most delicious aroma coming from the kitchen. Andrew sat me down in a comfortable chair and handed me a glass of wine. He seemed a little nervous. I realized the occasion was important to him.

"It smells delicious. I didn't know you could cook," I said.

"It's a secret family recipe," he said with a laugh. "The only thing I know how to cook is spaghetti only we don't have any pasta, so we'll have to eat it with. . ."

"Let me guess. *Potatoes*!" I cried.

"What else?" he replied. He took a sip of his wine, then came over and kissed me. "I love being with you, Celeste," he said.

"Why, thank you. I like you too."

"Come on it's ready." He reached pulled me out of the chair and led me to the table. "Sit here and I'll bring it in. I hope you like it," he added anxiously.

It was quite good—a blend of various vegetables and morsels of meat seasoned with herbs in a tomato sauce. He'd baked the sliced potatoes in fat so they came out crispy and brown. We finished off a bottle of wine with the meal—something I'm not used to—so by the time we were done, I was feeling a bit light-headed. After we finished eating, Andrew led me into the sitting room where he had laid out a fire in the fireplace. All he had to do was light it and before long, the room was suffused in a warm glow. He took some cushions off the sofa and put them on the floor in front of the fireplace. We sat, dreamily watching the flames, holding hands. After a while his arm went around me and kissed me. I didn't feel any urge to hold back, although I knew what would inevitably follow. I responded wholeheartedly.

Andrew pulled away and looked into my eyes. "How are you feeling?" he asked.

"Wonderful," I replied dreamily.

He brushed his hand over my sweater. "Pretty sweater," he said. "Pink suits you." He kissed me again. This time his hand crept under the sweater. After that, it didn't take long for us to shed our clothes and come

377

together in the most incredible sexual experience I'd ever had. Until then, I hadn't known just how pleasurable the relationship between a man and a woman could be, but after it happened, I knew I couldn't give it up for anything.

We lay side by side afterwards—we may even have dozed for a few minutes until the room began to chill and Andrew roused himself to add another log to the fire.

I sat up, suddenly anxious, and pulled his shirt over my lap. "Won't your father and Sarah be back soon?" I asked.

"Don't worry, my love. They're staying down there tonight."

"So, you had this planned all along. Pretty sneaky," I said, kissing him on the corner of his mouth.

"Of course. Do you mind?" He reached out and caressed my breast.

"No. It's fine with me."

"I love you, Celeste." He looked into my eyes as he said this.

"I think I feel the same about you," I replied.

"You're not sure?"

"Yes, I'm sure."

"Wait here," he said, jumping up. "I'm going to fetch some blankets. We can sleep down here by the fire tonight.

"You're taking a lot for granted, aren't you?" I said lightly. "Won't Ben and Barbara be expecting me?"

"Don't worry about it, they'll understand."

I felt exhilarated. I was sitting naked in front of a glowing fireplace, waiting for my lover to return. He came back in no time with a couple of blankets, shivering from the cold.

"That'll teach you to run around in the middle of winter with no clothes on," I teased him. "Come here and get warm."

Chapter 42

I was awakened the next morning by the warmth of sunlight on my face. A stabbing pain crashed through my head like a bolt of lightning when I opened my eyes. I snapped them shut again. I moaned.

Andrew moved beside me. "What's the matter, love?" he said anxiously.

I opened my eyes a crack, shading them with my hand, and saw him resting on his elbow, looking down into my face. Trying to smile, I replied, "It's my head. God, it feels as if it's going to burst."

He tried to kiss me, but I flinched—I couldn't bear anything touching my throbbing head. "Poor Baby; sounds as if you've got a hangover."

"Is that what it is? I'll never drink wine again, I swear," I groaned.

"I'll get something for it," he said. He pushed aside his side of the blankets that covered us and pulled on his long underwear and socks then he stood up and put on a pullover. It was chilly in the house in spite of the bright sunshine outside.

I heard him rattling with the wood-stove in the kitchen, then the sound of running water. From the noise of clattering dishes and cupboard doors banging, I assumed he was clearing away the dishes from the previous night's dinner. In spite of feeling guilty about not helping him, I had no inclination to move. I couldn't remember ever feeling this rotten before. The light hurt my eyes, my stomach churned, and every time I moved, the pain in my head pounded harder.

Andrew returned with a steaming mug, which he placed on the floor while he helped me into semi-sitting position. He held it to my lips and urged me to try a few sips. After the first sip, I bunched up my mouth and shuddered.

"Ugh! It's bitter."

"It'll help, believe me. Come on, drink some more."

I managed to drink most of it then lay down again. After a while the pain began to recede until it was merely a dull throb. While I was waiting for the medicine to take effect, Andrew cleaned out the fireplace and lit another fire. At last, I felt I could safely get up.

"Feeling better?" he asked, smiling down at me.

"A bit. What was that?"

"Something Dad concocted from bark. One of his native medicines. Speaking of Dad, we'd better get moving, they could be back any minute.

I sat up and looked around for my clothes. I found my long johns and undershirt in front of the sofa and put them on, then crawled around looking for the rest of my things. My socks were over by the window, and my skirt and sweater were behind the sofa. *Must have been quite a night!* I thought ruefully.

We rushed around, clearing up all traces of the previous night's revelry before his father and sister got back. When everything looked more or less in order, I put my boots on and picked up my jacket, thinking it better not to be there when Dr. Fisher and Sarah arrived.

When I returned to Ben and Barbara's, all Barbara said was, "Did you have a good time?" I assured her that I did.

* * *

Andrew and I began to look for more ways we could be alone together, but it wasn't easy in such a small community, especially while he was living with his father and sister and I was boarding in someone else's home. We decided to fix up the cabin in our spare time—cleaning it and scrounging pieces of furniture and bedding. We weren't able to bring a water line into the cabin because of a shortage of pipe and the freezing weather outside, so we had to carry buckets of water from the other houses or the workshops. The cabin did have a primitive outhouse up against the back wall of the building near the back door. In a way, it felt as if we were playing house, but it seemed right in light of how we felt about each other.

Finally, after cutting a stack of firewood and stocking up with some food and borrowed cooking utensils, we decided to try it out for a night. Andrew went in and lit the fire while I was still working with his father, so that when I got there, it was fairly warm, and some of the dampness had dissipated. The cabin was a three-room affair, a large living room-kitchen, and two smaller sleeping rooms. There was no bathroom. The cooking was done over an open fire in the main room. We closed off the two smaller rooms and set our bedding out in a corner near the fireplace.

"This must have been how the pioneers lived," I said as I cut up some vegetables and meat to throw into the stew pot.

"We are pioneers really. In that case I suppose I should be out hunting," Andrew replied, coming up behind me and putting his arms around me.

I pulled free so that I could finish my work. "How about putting a pot of water on the fire to make some tea?" I suggested. "Isn't this wonderful—our first home?"

"Do you mean that, Celeste?"

"It's what I want, if you do. I really do love you. I think we're a good match." It just popped out without my thinking. I felt a little nervous after saying it in case I was assuming too much. I didn't want to drive him away by being too possessive.

"Me too," he replied to my relief. "I'm willing to give it a try."

383

"Something bother's me though, Andrew. What about birth control? I mean I could get pregnant, you know. "

"We'll have to see what happens, I suppose. I don't mind being a father."

"Yes, but I want to finish my training. How can I become a contributing member of the community if I don't learn to do something useful?"

"Why not ask Dad if he can recommend anything?"

I did bring it up with Paris the next time I saw him. He'd already let me know that he was pleased about my relationship with his son, so I felt more or less comfortable discussing it with him.

"There aren't many options open to you now, Celeste. We used to have a good supply of condoms, but unfortunately, rubber doesn't have a very long shelf life, so they're not much good now. There's the so-called rhythm method where you avoid intercourse during the period around ovulation. It's not foolproof, but it works for some. If you take your temperature every day, you will see a slight increase when you ovulate. Some of the people at the university have been experimenting with a small ocean sponge soaked in spermicide that women can insert before intercourse, but I'm not sure how that's going."

"What do they use for a spermicide?" I asked.

"They're trying out a couple of plant extracts from aboriginal folklore."

I didn't feel much wiser after this discussion. I would just have to hope for the best.

There was a lot of snow that winter and I had my first white Christmas. It was a beautiful holiday with music, presents, lots of food and wine, and trees decorated with hand-made ornaments. The only damper on my happiness was that my family couldn't be there to share it.

* * *

Andrew and I lived most of the time in the cabin by then, preferring to rough it together in spite of the cold and inconveniences. We bathed at the hot spring, where a small shed had been built with a little wood stove, so that we could dry off and dress in relative comfort afterwards. We spent most of the day apart, helping with the work of the community, but we were together in the evenings, studying, reading and having endless discussions until bedtime.

The whole community gathered together once a week in the community building for a communal meal followed by a discussion of any problems or policies that needed working out. After the business meeting was concluded, we had a party, playing games, listening to music and dancing. Sometimes, they showed a video-drama, laughing or groaning about the way people lived before the disasters. After watching videos, everyone was subdued, and a few had tears in their eyes.

Inevitably, the subject of the epidemics came up during my sessions with Paris Fisher. My having lived through them was probably a contributing factor to my interest in medicine.

"I can't understand why all those diseases suddenly hit at the same time all over the world," I said one day when we were reviewing the immune system

"It wasn't really as sudden it seemed. Epidemics had been cropping up for years everywhere," he replied. "One human characteristic that doesn't seem to have much survival value is the refusal to accept reality in the face of disastrous events. It's called denial. The World Health Organization and the Centers for Disease Control knew for the last forty or more years that mutated strains of some of the deadliest microbes known to man had been cropping up in various places—not just the so-called third world countries either. And that many of those microbes were resistant to every known

386

antimicrobial on earth. As fast as new antibiotics were developed, the bacteria developed defenses against them. They warned governments, but there wasn't the political will to do anything about it, and pharmaceutical companies saw no profit to be made from investing in research for new disease-fighting drugs. They said it wasn't sexy."

"But that's so stupid. Didn't they realize what would happen?"

"It's very complicated, Celeste, but I agree it was insane. One factor was that most of the people falling ill and dying were the poorest of the poor. It wasn't affecting the people with power and money. The attitude seemed to be that it would never happen here—wherever or whatever here happened to be. The richest countries, which could have helped prevent some of the devastation, saw the problems as affecting other places, Asia, Latin America or Africa. The problems eventually became so overwhelming, they wouldn't have known where to start even if they'd wanted to do anything. Small, dedicated groups of people were out there doing what they could, but without the government backing, both at home and in the countries they worked in—well, it was like trying to stop the ocean tides with piles of sand.

"Here at home, governments were cutting back on social programs—trying to balance budgets—so of course public health funding for immunization and primary health care dropped substantially. Also, assistance to poor families—the majority of which consisted of the elderly, women and children—was cut back, which meant that millions of children were not getting proper nutrition. This weakened their immune systems and increased the risk of disease.

"Most of the progress against disease that had been made in the first three quarters of the twentieth century was reversed in the last quarter and the beginning of this one. By then the population of the world had increased enormously—from around two billion in 1900 to over six and a half billion in 2000—putting a severe strain on resources and increasing the proportion of people living in poverty. Not to mention the ecological damage we had done to the planet and the inevitable changes that brought about. We cannot ever deny that, whatever the causes, the epidemics were man-made—the widening gap between the very rich and the poor—do you know that in 1995 three hundred families controlled fifty percent of the world's wealth?"

"Wow, that's incredible."

"Yes. Added to poverty was the lack of enough resources to go around—especially when the Europeans and North Americans monopolized more than forty percent of what was available. Pollution and erosion, loss of thousands of biological species, overuse of antibiotics, the list goes on. Most of the world's population lived without proper roads, sewage facilities, potable drinking water or proper health care," he sighed and wiped his forehead. "Sorry, got carried away there."

"It's appalling. And now we're paying for it. I wonder how many people died—in the epidemics, I mean."

"I don't know. Even in the closing years of the last century, millions were dying every year of diseases that had been curable twenty years earlier: tuberculosis and malaria, for example; and millions from new microbes such as Ebola virus, Lassa fever and the most infamous of all, HIV. In the 1970s, scientists discovered that bacteria and viruses had the ability to exchange and share bits of genetic material, which meant that when an antibiotic-resistant strain met a non-resistant bacterium, it could pass on its resistance. That's one of the ways they managed to mutate faster than man could discover new antimicrobials. In the fight between microbes and man, the microbes won, hands down."

Paris gave me a book to read. It was called *The Coming Plague,*_written by a woman called *Laurie Garrett.* Written in the early 1990s, it was a fascinating and horrifying account of man's losing battle with disease, and the great heroism of some of the scientists fighting the battle, as well as the stupidity and perversity of governments and politicians. In light of the information contained in this book, I can't understand why nothing was done before it was too late. And I felt a lot of anger and resentment that we had been left to pay such a bitter price.

Chapter 43

Winter finally came to an end and the snow began to melt, making it easier for people to travel once again. In early March, Tommy started preparing for his first trip of the year. I had discussed it with Andrew and Paris, and reluctantly decided to go with Tommy one more time. I'm sure Tommy could have managed without me, but I wanted to get back to Willow Creek and find out how the rest of the family was doing. I was eager to see Lia's new baby, which would have been born by then. Another reason I wanted to get back to the city was to investigate the prospects of studying at the university.

I think everyone in the Canyon was feeling a bit restless after being cooped up all winter and several of them were planning trips of one sort or another. Paris and Sarah were also going to the city to check out the university, both from the point of view of Sarah studying there and Paris re-acquainting himself with old colleagues and arranging for me to become a student. Andrew wanted to go too, hoping that we could meet there, but other members of the community pointed out that if everyone left, there would be no-one to prepare for planting the spring crops, so he reluctantly agreed to stay behind.

Finally, well wrapped up against the cold, Tommy and I were ready to leave. Andrew and I hugged each other long and hard before sharing one last kiss.

"Be careful," Andrew said, "I want you back in one piece. And don't stay away too long."

"I'll miss you every minute," I replied. "And I'll come back as soon as I can. I love you."

"Me too."

I climbed up onto the wagon where Tommy was waiting patiently to go. He gave a flick of the reins, which the horses ignored. They were treading restlessly in place, shaking their heads and snorting, annoyed by the unaccustomed harnesses after being free of them for the past four months.

"Come on, let's move," Tommy said, slapping the reins down on their backs.

It was only when Andrew and Ben pulled on their bridles that they reluctantly started to walk. I took one last look around the Canyon where most of the snow had melted. The trees were still bare and there was little green evident apart from the dark, almost black color of the evergreens. Smoke was slanting sideways from the chimneys, and a lineful of laundry flapped in the breeze. I waved to the small group of people who were seeing us off, then turned to face ahead.

The tiny, almost unnoticeable stream that ran down beside the track through the narrow canyon had turned into a raging torrent, threatening to engulf the entire roadway. The track itself was rutted and bumpy where the melting snow had washed away the loose soil and gravel from around the larger stones making it a very uncomfortable ride in spite of the wagon's springs and the padding in the seat.

Our first stop before we headed west was Hope where we stocked up on flour and canned goods. We were surprised to meet some other traders there. Tommy talked to a couple of them and found out that one was from farther north, up the Fraser Canyon, and another covered communities to the east. There was also one trader who covered the valley between the city and Hope as we did. He said he'd just started the year before and kept to the southern region, along the border.

We spent the night in Hope, leaving after breakfast the next day. After making our regular stops on the way, we reached Willow Creek eight days later. We went directly to the house instead of stopping on the main street to trade. We were tired and cold, and there would be plenty of time to do some trading later.

Someone must have been looking out of the window because the door flew open before we reached the driveway and Lia came out on the doorstep—a slimmer Lia than last time—with Mother behind her. I was relieved to see them looking reasonably happy, taking it as a sign that nothing terrible had happened in my absence. As soon as the wagon stopped in the driveway, I jumped down and ran to the house.

"Hi, Mom! Lia what did you have?

"Come on, let me show you." She grabbed my arm and pulled me into the kitchen. "Here he is."

The sleeping baby was bundled up in a basket near the stove. All I could see of him was his thick black hair and one tiny fist curled up by his cheek. His little lips pursed and relaxed as he slept.

"Oh, Lia he's so beautiful. What's his name?"

"I called him Anthony after my father," she replied. "His name was Antonio, but . . ."

I looked at her more closely and saw she had regained her beauty. Her long wavy hair was glossy and her deep brown eyes glowed. She looked almost happy again, although I detected a hint of sadness underneath. I knew she would always carry the scars of her ordeal with the survivalists, but at least she was free of them now and had a chance of making a happier life for herself and her son.

"I'm so happy for you, Lia." I hugged her. "He's a beautiful baby. Did you have a hard time?"

"It was pretty awful." She grimaced. "I thought I was going to die, but as you see . . ." She glanced at the baby. "I guess it was worth it, in one way."

"Who help with the delivery?"

"Your mother and a woman from the village. Mrs. Stewart—I think she used to be a nurse—she acts as a midwife now, too."

I recalled the soft-voiced, dark-haired woman who had three children of her own—a large family in those days. "That's right, I'd forgotten about her." I turned to my mother. "How are you, Mom?

"I'm fine. What about you? You look as if you've got a secret you're just dying to tell."

"Oh, Mom, I'm so happy," I replied, hugging her.

"Could this have anything to do with a certain young man?"

"Andrew? Yes, I guess so."

The door opened and Tommy stuck his head in. "Is anyone going to help me with these horses?"

"Oh, Tommy, I'm sorry. I was so excited about Lia's baby, I forgot all about you." I went to the door, then turned back to speak to mother and Lia. "I won't be long. When I get back, I want to hear all the news."

Soon, we were all soon sitting comfortably at the kitchen table, sipping hot coffee.

"Where are the others?" I asked. I caught a look passing between Mother and Lia. "Has something happened?"

"It's nothing serious," Mother replied.

"Tate and Jackie left," Lia blurted.

"Where? When?" I asked.

"They said they wanted to go back to the city," Mother replied. "We couldn't *make* them stay," she added defensively.

"I think they got sick of all the religious stuff," Lia added. "Always being corrected and told they would end up in hell if they didn't change their ways. Besides, it's pretty boring here."

"Why? What were they doing?" I asked.

"Nothing, really. Just being normal adolescents," Mother said.

"They were sleeping together," Lia said.

"I hope they'll be all right," was all I could think of to say.

"Speaking of. . . What's happening with you and Andrew?" Mother asked.

"Oh, Mom, he's wonderful. We're so happy. We fixed up the cabin and have been living in it for a couple of months. "

"Well, I'm happy for you," Mother replied.

"Where's Peter?" Tommy asked.

"Oh, he's off somewhere helping the men," Mother said. "What about you, Tommy? When are you going to settle down?"

"Soon, I hope, but I'll have to carry on until I can find someone to take over. There's a real need for this kind of service. I expect there'll be more traders before long though, giving me some competition. We've already seen signs."

"What else is new?" I asked.

"Joshua died," Lia said.

I went cold inside. I had grown very fond of the old man and it felt like losing a loved relative. "Oh, no! What happened?" I asked, fighting back tears.

"Peter rode over to Salish on his regular weekly visit and found him. He'd died in his sleep. I guess he was just worn out. He was quite old. And it wasn't much of a life for him with all his people gone. Poor old man. I don't know how we'd have survived without his help those first two years."

I suppose it was a better way to go than the long drawn-out death from some disease or accident. Nevertheless, it was a blow to know that I'd never see him again. Mother was right; the fact that we'd been able to make a go of it in Salish was largely due to his knowledge and skills.

"Where was he buried?" I asked.

"We buried him next to the other graves," Mother said. "Reverend Eikhart insisted on everyone going to the funeral and having the whole religious ceremony. It was a good send off, I suppose, even if these same people hadn't done much to help him while he was alive. I still miss him," she added.

"So, there's just you and Peter and Lia left now," Tommy said.

"Don't forget Anthony," Lia said.

As if to underscore what his mother had said, Anthony opened his eyes, gave a little cry, and started beating the air with his arms. Lia jumped to attention instantly.

"He must be hungry," she said. "Or wet." She picked up the little bundle and unwound it until she reached his undershirt and diaper. Once set free, his legs began to kick in time with his waving arms, while his dark eyes darted around, looking at everyone. When Lia spoke to him, he smiled.

"He looks like a happy baby. Look at him smiling," I said. "How old is he?"

"Let's see. Five weeks, I guess. He was born at the end of January." She picked him up and held him against her shoulder with one hand under his rump. "He's wet all right, aren't you, you rascal?"

Lia seemed to have taken well to motherhood even though she was not yet seventeen. She handled the baby well and judging by his disposition and appearance, she was doing a good job. I'm sure she had plenty of help from Mother as well.

Having a baby in those circumstances wasn't easy; there were diapers to wash, diseases to worry about now that there were no vaccination programs and few doctors, and no pre-packaged baby foods. All clothing that couldn't be obtained through barter had to be made by hand. When I saw Lia hand washing the baby's clothes and bedding, then hanging them out on a clothesline to dry, I didn't envy her so much. There weren't any waterproof pants to keep moisture in the diapers, so when the baby wet, it soaked through all his bedding as well, often tripling the amount of laundry.

I helped my mother prepare the evening meal while Lia and her baby took a nap. It was exhausting for such a young girl to have to take care of a baby, especially when she was breast-feeding, and Lia tired easily, so Mother encouraged her to sleep for a while in the afternoon. While we worked, I told Mom about my plans to become a doctor. She was delighted.

"How are you going to pay for the education?" she asked.

"Paris—Dr. Fisher—explained how they work at the university. They'll accept whatever I can pay—either in cash or goods—and I'll have to work while I'm there. You know, helping out with whatever needs doing to keep things running. And after finishing a level, students have to help teach the newer students what they've learned— with supervision, of course. It would be disastrous if they passed on misinformation."

"That sounds like a good idea. I'm glad to hear they've got things so well organized. How long do you think it will take?"

"I'm not sure. Each student goes at his or her own pace. When an instructor thinks somebody is ready to go on to the next level, they do. Oh, and I almost forgot, after we graduate, we are expected to donate a year or two to the U, either that or pay for our tuition, or a bit of both."

Peter came in while we were having this conversation, so, having finished cutting up the vegetables and putting the pot on to heat, we stopped and sat down to have some tea.

"Are you guys going up to Lost Canyon soon?" I asked.

"Probably at the end of the month," Peter replied. I want to give them a hand here first preparing the ground for planting. I feel we owe them that."

"What about Lia?" I asked.

"I don't suppose they'd mind if we brought her with us, that's if she wants to come," Mother said. "They were prepared to accept Tate. What do you think?"

"I'm sure it would be all right," I answered. "How's she really doing, Mom? She seems all right, but the last couple of years. . ."

"I think the baby makes her happy. I was afraid she might reject him, given the way she became pregnant, but she seems fine with him. She's got someone of her own to love—she's lost everyone else. She still has problems though, gets depressed and won't talk to anyone, and she has nightmares. We hear her moaning and crying out sometimes at night, and sometimes she's afraid to go to sleep; she just sits there and stares at nothing."

"Poor Lia. Maybe she'll be happier in the Canyon. Hey, I just remembered—there's a really nice boy about her age. You know, Tommy—Jeremy."

"He's a bit young," Tommy replied.

"He's sixteen, isn't he? So's Lia."

401

"Well, it's up to them anyway. We'll see what happens. She may not even want to go up there."

"It's nice to see you want everyone to be neatly paired off," Mother laughed.

"Well. . ." I said. "You know how it is."

"You're happy," she replied.

I nodded, smiling.

Spring had already come to the city when we arrived. Trees everywhere were resplendent with pink and white blossoms. Those that didn't have blossoms were covered in a haze of delicate green leaves. The air was clean and sparkling, filled with the energetic chirp and chatter of birds. I felt exhilarated as we rode through the quiet streets towards the university. For the first time, I was hopeful about the future—optimistic that we were finally making progress rather than just struggling to survive.

We reached the home of Tommy's friends just as the sun was setting and found Paris and Sarah already there to greet us.

Chapter 44

During the next few days, while Tommy was taking care of business, Paris and Dr. Levisohn took me to meet the various members of the medical faculty. The hospital was several kilometers from the university so we rode in Dr. Levisohn's small horse-drawn buggy. The ingenuity people used in improvising ways to get around was amazing. The buggy was somehow put together with parts from old cars. It had two wheels with rubber tires, springs, and two comfortable automobile backseats— one behind the other—that were each big enough for two people. They must have discarded the heavier metal parts because it was light enough to be pulled by one horse. I sat in the back seat and the two doctors sat in front.

It was probably an exaggeration to call it a medical faculty at that point, as there were only four members. There were three practitioners of so-called conventional medicine: David Levisohn who was formerly a heart surgeon; Carolina Melendez, a young obstetrician; and Jack Faraday, a specialist in internal medicine. The fourth member was Harvey Lee, a practitioner of traditional healing, acupuncture, naturopathy and so on.

I was surprised when we arrived at the hospital and I saw where they had set up shop. "Why are they using this old building instead of the newer ones?" I asked. The largest and most modern building had been opened in the early 2000s.

"The new buildings are useless. They need air-conditioning and we have no way of running the elevators to reach the upper floors. It's a shame, all that space and equipment, useless." Dr. Levisohn replied. "What we've done is gather all equipment we can use and brought it over here. We don't need a large hospital; there aren't that many patients."

"I thought there was a hospital at the university," I said.

"There was, but we decided it would be more useful to the community to use this one because it's more central, easier to get to. Would you like to look around?"

"Yes, that would be great," I replied.

"I wouldn't mind a tour myself if I'm going to be joining you," Paris added.

"Right, then. I'll get one of the students to take you." He looked at his watch. "I've got a class in five minutes." He stopped a young woman who was walking down the hallway carrying a tray full of instruments. "Georgie, have you got a minute?"

"I can spare about fifteen minutes, but I really have to study for this afternoon's test after that," she replied.

"Good," he said. "I'd like you to meet Dr. Fisher and Celeste—er. . ."

"Colbert," I prompted.

"Yes. Celeste Colbert. She's thinking of joining us as a student. And Paris—Dr. Fisher—is probably going to join the faculty. I wonder if you'd mind giving them a quick tour."

"Sure. I could show them around."

"Well, I'll leave you two in her good hands. See you later. Must run. Take them to the lounge when you've finished."

"Hi, Georgie," I said. "Are you a student?"

"First year," she replied. "Come this way. Shall we start at the top?"

We went through a door at the end of the corridor and climbed two flights of stairs. At the top of the stairs, we entered another corridor.

"This is the third floor. It's used mostly for storage and staff. Those doors at the other end are student dormitories. Come on, I'll show you one. Will you be staying here, Celeste?"

"Probably. I'm not sure yet."

The hallway had hard terrazzo floors and a tall window at each end. It widened out halfway along with elevators on one side and an open area behind a counter opposite. Several smaller rooms about the size of closets surrounded this space. This had been a nurses' station at one time, but now it was piled up with cartons of supplies and miscellaneous equipment.

Georgie opened the door to one of the student rooms to allow us to see inside. There were two single beds, a closet, a sink, and a chest of drawers. The students who lived in this room were not very neat. There were clothes on every piece of furniture, and the beds, which were unmade, were strewn with books.

"Sorry about the mess," she apologized. "We don't have much time for housekeeping."

"What's in those other rooms?" Paris inquired.

"Down at that end it's mostly equipment and supplies." She opened another door. "Bathroom. And that's the student lounge," she added pointing to the one across the hall. "We study and sometimes eat in there."

"What kind of supplies have you got?" Paris asked.

"There's plenty of dressings and stuff like that, glassware and instruments. Anything made of metal. But we're really short of disinfectants and soaps, antiseptic solutions. I'd show you, but it's all kept locked up."

"That's all right," Paris said. "How about bedding and linens?"

"We've got enough. We have a bit of a problem with laundry though. Everything has to be done by hand and hung up to dry. It's an awful lot of work." We had reached the staircase. "Let's go down and look at the second floor. That's where we have in-patients."

"What kind of problems do the patients have—the ones who are admitted?" he asked.

"It's mostly injuries and accidents. And we get some terrible burns sometimes."

"Do you get any infectious diseases?" I asked.

"Not many. We have a small area on the ground floor that we use for isolation."

We reached the second floor and entered a hallway identical to the one above except for the amount of activity. Several patients were moving along the hallway, one with a heavy bandage on his leg walking with crutches, another had her arm in a sling, and a third—a child—was in a wheel chair. The nurses' station was manned by a woman and a man dressed in green cotton trousers and tops. We went there first and Georgie introduced us to them.

"Dr. Fisher and Celeste, this is Karen and Jeff. They're second year students. How's it going?" she asked them.

"Not too bad this morning," Karen replied. "Good to meet you Doctor, and you Celeste. Are you going to be joining us?"

"Probably," Paris replied.

"Yes," I said. I looked around. "Where are the nurses?"

"You're looking at them," Jeff replied. He was a tall thin man in his early twenties with dark hair and glasses.

"But—I thought Georgie said you were second year . . .?"

"That's right. The faculty decided to train everyone together because of the shortage of instructors. Everyone gets the same training, medicine and nursing combined. We have one nursing instructor. Claudia. I guess you haven't met her yet. She has a masters' degree in nursing and teaches first and second year. We work at whatever level we have reached in our training and right now, Karen and I are nurses. We can stop at this level or go on to be paramedics or full-fledged doctors."

"How much work do you have to do compared to studying and classes?" It sounded like a lot of work to me.

"It's split up about forty-sixty—classes and on-duty time. That means we actually spend more time working than we do in class, but we are still learning as we work. There aren't many trained nurses around who can afford to work for nothing, or next to nothing," Karen replied.

"What kind of work do new students do if they have no training?"

"Ah! That is where you get to prove you've got what it takes," Georgie said with a grin. "We get to do the laundry and cooking and cleaning." She glanced at the clock on the wall. "Look, I have to get going soon. Do you want to see the patient rooms?"

"That's okay," Paris replied. "We'll have a chance to see them soon enough, I'm sure. "Thank you for the information, all of you, I'm sure we'll be seeing more of one another."

"Thanks," I added. I still had hundreds of questions to ask, but I knew they would be answered in the coming days.

"Okay," Georgie continued. "These are treatment rooms, patient lounge and dining room. A lot of the patients are ambulatory and don't need to eat in their rooms. Patient bathrooms, linen and supply cupboard—locked, of course."

She continued her catalogue of the facilities and then led us down to the ground floor. "This is outpatients. They treat a lot of minor illnesses, aches and pains, here. There aren't many doctors working from their own offices so most people come here." She pushed through a swinging door. "Next to that is emergency."

There were several curtained cubicles along one wall, and a row of chairs near the outside door. A woman with a small child sat waiting on one of the chairs, looking scared and nervous. From one of the cubicles came the howls of another child. A man came from behind the curtain carrying some blood stained rags and instruments on a tray. He was wearing blue cottons. He handed the tray to a woman in greens. "Get rid of these, Val, and would you mind sterilizing the instruments please?" he said. He turned to the mother. "He's got a nasty gash on his leg. I had to put some stitches in, that's what all the noise was about."

"Can he go home?" the mother asked.

"I'd really prefer to keep him here overnight to make sure the cut isn't infected," the man replied. "You have to be very careful these days. An infection could turn into something really nasty."

"I don't know how we could pay, that's the problem. I brought this," she added, producing a jar of fruit from her bag. "We've hardly got any money. . ."

"Don't worry about it Ms Warren. Could you maybe come and help us out for an hour or two? We could always use help with some of the work around here."

I smiled to myself as the transaction continued. They seemed to have arranged a way to help people and get the work done. I was dying to discuss it with someone, but I could see Georgie looking anxiously at the clock again.

"I think we'd better let you get on with your studying," Paris said. "If you'd like to point us in the direction of the lounge David mentioned. . ."

She took us back through the swinging doors into the corridor. "Right at the other end, past the kitchen," she said. "You can't miss the kitchen—you can hear the pots clattering from here. It's been nice meeting you. I'll see you again soon." With that, she turned and made for the stairway door.

Later, while we were having lunch, I asked Dr. Levisohn about the uniforms the staff wore.

"When we started gathering together all the supplies, we discovered that there were plenty of green 'scrubs' for the OR and the blue ones they used in maternity, but hardly any white uniforms and lab coats, so we decided to use the blues and greens for the students. Second years wear the green, and the blues are worn by third and fourth years."

"I'm surprised there was anything left at all after all the looting," Paris said.

"This hospital is a very elaborate complex," Dr. Levisohn replied. "You remember the tunnels that join the buildings underground, where the old morgue and a print shop used to be, and the hospital laundry and stores? Somebody had the foresight to block off some of the tunnels when the hospital was finally abandoned. It was a devil of a job getting into them again, but it paid off. Everything above ground was stripped bare, but we found enough stuff in the basement to keep going. An added touch was to hide all the pharmacy supplies in the morgue. People were scared to death of cadavers and wouldn't go near a dead body. The funny thing was, there were no bodies in the morgue at all; the name on the door was enough to scare people off."

412

"How's the drug supply?" Paris inquired.

"Not good, I'm afraid. We've no antibiotics at all. Not many analgesics either. There's a bit of local anesthetic, and some general anesthetics—not nearly enough. We seem to have plenty of drugs for chronic diseases like diabetes, cancer and heart disease, but a severe lack of patients with those diseases. I guess they all died off during the epidemics." He finished off the rest of his chowder and took a sip of coffee. "Funny thing, Paris. This hospital used to be full of elderly people with chronic ailments, now it's mostly young people with acute illnesses, and accident victims. There's not much for a heart surgeon like me to do any more except teach I suppose."

"I hope to be able to put some of my work with traditional medicines into production soon. The problem is testing them." Paris said. I stopped listening to the conversation and looked around at the people in the cafeteria. Most of them were dressed in ordinary street clothes—jeans and shirts, and had books open on the tables as they ate. I saw Karen and two more people in greens and four in blues. While most of the people in street clothes were young, a few appeared to be in their thirties and forties; too old to start studying medicine, I would have thought. I commented on this later to Dr. Levisohn and he told me that the families of some of the patients worked in the hospital for a few hours to help pay for their treatment. They did mostly cleaning, laundry, and cooking. I was impressed by the way they had organized things.

I learned that a nearby building was used for teaching. It had some labs and several rooms for lectures. They even had a generator providing power to run the small portable X-ray machine and some other equipment, but they had to manage without any high-tech apparatus.

After Tommy left on another trip up the Valley, I presented myself at the hospital administration office and was allotted a room on the third floor, which I had to share with another girl. As a parting gift, Tommy presented me with a large sack of flour and a whole carton of canned fruit so that I could make a down payment on my tuition.

My roommate's name was Davina Jackson. She was short and energetic with frizzy, sandy-colored hair. Davina, or Dave as everyone called her, was nineteen. Her home was across the inlet on the north shore.

When I discovered that the program had only been running a year and a half, I was puzzled by the fact that there were second and third year students. I soon learned that some of them had been studying medicine and nursing before the disasters, and others had learned so quickly that they had been advanced to a higher level. Everyone entering the program was tested to assess their level of knowledge, and those with more advanced knowledge were allowed to enter at a higher level. However, if they only had medical training, they had to take the nursing part of the program first. Former nurses who wanted to get more training could also join at the appropriate level.

The small amount of studying I had done with Paris wasn't enough to allow me to start anywhere but at the bottom. The day after I arrived, I was told to present myself at the other building where I was sent to one of the classrooms. There were seven other students there, including Dave. We sat down around two tables and waited for the instructor. Dave introduced me to the other students, four men and two women. The class was evenly split between men and women.

Chapter 45

A tall, stately Afro-Canadian woman entered the room and greeted everyone. She was Claudia Mbatha-Cartier, RN, M.Sc. Everyone called her Claudia. She had the three people at my table wait a few minutes while she gave assignments to the other five. When she came to our table, she introduced herself and gave us an outline of what we would be learning.

"The first thing you will learn is the principle of asepsis. Now, what does that mean?" She looked at each of us in turn.

My first day was spent learning how to wash my hands properly, how to sterilize instruments and equipment, and the principles of what causes contamination and how it is spread. Classes started at seven a.m. We had a break at ten-thirty and were dismissed at 1 p.m. After lunch, we had to work. A schedule had been made up for the first year students allowing them to rotate weekly from one type of work to another. I was relieved to see that I would spend the first week cleaning. I was given a cart of cleaning materials, a mop and bucket, and told to clean the ground floor rooms.

One morning of the second week, I got up with a very queasy stomach. I went to the bathroom then returned to my room to wash up ready for class. I was still feeling pretty sick and the thought of eating anything only made me feel worse, even the smell of food was unbearable. I got myself a cup of coffee in the cafeteria and sat down with Dave and another girl.

"Is that all you're having?" Dave asked.

"I'm not feeling too good," I said. "I seem to have lost my appetite."

"You're looking a bit pale. You'd better check it out," Dave continued. "You might be coming down with something."

"I'm sure I'll feel better in a little while. It's nothing serious." I took a sip of coffee. As soon as it hit my stomach, the nausea overwhelmed me. I got up and darted from the room to the nearest bathroom where I threw it up. Once I had been sick, I felt better. I washed my mouth out with water and returned to the cafeteria. On the way to my table, I picked up a piece of corn bread.

"What happened?" Dave asked.

"Nothing. I just got sick. I feel much better now."

"I still think you should have it checked."

Feeling so much better the rest of the day, I forgot about the morning nausea. Until the following morning when it hit again. I remembered how sick my mother had been in the mornings when she was pregnant. *Oh no,* I thought, *not that.* I had to speak to someone about it; I needed to know for sure so that I could decide what to do. *Damn! Why now?*

417

I went to outpatients after breakfast. Dr. Melendez was usually there with some of her students in the mornings. When I found her, I asked if I could have an appointment to see her and she told me to come back just before lunch. She had classes in the afternoons and saw patients in the mornings, unless there was an emergency or a delivery.

I asked to be excused early and dashed across to outpatients. Dr. Melendez was just finishing with her last patient, a woman who looked as if she was ready to give birth any day. When the woman had gone, the doctor invited me into her office and shut the door. She was a pretty, dark-haired woman—short and rather plump, with warm brown eyes. She took down my name and age, and other vital statistics, then asked me why I wanted to see her.

"I'm not sure. I've been nauseated the last two mornings and yesterday, I threw up. I was wondering if I might be pregnant. My mother was sick in the mornings when she . . ."

"Do you think you might be? I mean have you been having sexual relations with someone?"

"Yes. My—the man I was living with. We tried to— you know—pick safe times, but that last night before I left . . . I . . . we. . ."

"I understand," she said with a smile. "When was your last period?"

I tried to count back. It was difficult to keep track of dates without calendars. "It must have been four and a half weeks ago."

"So you think your period was due this week or last?"

"I think so."

"All right. I'd like to examine you. Come with me." She led me out of her office and into one of the curtained cubicles. "Take your clothes off and put this on," she said handing me a pale green cotton gown. "You can keep your socks on if you like, but take everything else off. Sit up on the examination table when you're ready. I'll be back in a minute." She left me alone, pulling the curtains close behind her.

After the examination, Dr. Melendez told me there were of signs of pregnancy: cervical swelling and breast tenderness, but since they had no way to do pregnancy tests, we'd have to wait to be sure. If my period didn't start soon, I might as well resign myself to having a baby. She went on to tell me that I was healthy and I shouldn't have any problems.

"I've just started my medical training and hate to give it up," I told her. "How will I be able to continue with a baby to look after?"

"Well, you can still work for the next six or seven months. You can learn a lot in that time. What about the baby's father?"

"He's back in the interior where we live."

"I meant are you—is it a permanent relationship?"

"I think so. We love each other very much. He's Dr. Fisher's son, Andrew."

"I see. If you are pregnant, will you go back up there to have the baby? Or can Andrew come here to be with you?"

"I don't know. I haven't had time to think about it very much. I'll have to let Andrew know somehow."

"I think that's enough for today. Do you have any questions?"

"Is it all right for me to go on doing the heavy work—I mean . . .?"

"It won't do you any harm as long as you don't do anything silly. The human embryo is extremely difficult to dislodge once it is embedded in the uterus. Don't worry."

"Thank you, Doctor Melendez."

Before she turned to go, she added, "I might call on you from time to time for teaching demonstrations, that's if you don't mind. We don't have that many expectant mothers for the students to work with."

I didn't like the sound of that at all. The thought of having fellow-students examining me and prodding my body didn't appeal to me at all. When I didn't reply, Dr. Melendez left me to finish getting dressed. I would have to come up with a good excuse for not agreeing to her request before I saw her again. As if I didn't have enough to worry about.

I hadn't seen Paris around the hospital for several days and I wanted to discuss my situation with him, so on my next day off, I hitched a ride home with Dr. Levisohn. To my surprise, Paris was preparing to leave for the Canyon.

"Aren't you going to teach at the hospital?" I asked him.

"Yes, I am. I just have to go back and fetch the rest of my notes and medicines. I also think I should tell the others that I'm planning to be away for a while. I'm glad you came up today, now I'll have a chance to say good-bye. Any messages you'd like me to take?" he added with a knowing smile.

"Can we go outside?" I asked. "There's something I need to talk to you about?"

"Surely. Nothing wrong, I hope?"

I shook my head.

We put on our jackets and left the house. It was a clear windy evening with the sun low in the sky beyond the trees. We walked down a path that led through tangled undergrowth to the cliffs above the inlet. The ocean was a pale silvery turquoise with streaks of cobalt where the wind ruffled the surface. Towards the west, it was tinged with peach and violet.

"So, what did you want to talk about?" Paris said, turning away from the view to face me.

I looked at his face and saw a look in his eyes that reminded me painfully of Andrew. I turned away and looked towards the sea again. "I think I'm pregnant," I blurted out.

"I see," he said. "It sounds as if you're not absolutely sure."

"I'm almost sure. I've been getting morning sickness for about a week, and my period's overdue. I went to see Dr. Melendez the other day and she thinks it's likely."

I must have sounded pretty forlorn because he put his hand on my shoulder. "Hey, cheer up! It's not the end of the world. What do you want to do?"

I turned my back to him and wiped my eyes. "That's just it," I said. "I don't know what to do. I wanted to do this training so badly and now it looks as if I'll have to give it up. And Andrew's so far away. It's going to turn his life upside down too."

"I see. You want to finish your training, and you want to be with Andrew because of the baby?"

I nodded.

"Well, we'll have to work something out, won't we? I'm sure we can come to some arrangement."

"How do you think Andrew will feel about it?"

"I'm sure he'll be delighted. He thinks a lot of you, Celeste. I know that."

"What about you? How do you feel?"

"Quite frankly, dear, I'm delighted. I didn't expect to be a grandfather quite so soon, but I'm happy for you both."

This cheered me a little and I began to see it from another perspective. Less of an obstacle and inconvenience, more of bringing a new life into the world—my own child. I hoped it would cement the bond between Andrew and me.

"Will you take a letter to Andrew? I suppose I should write to my mother as well. I wonder if she's left for the Canyon yet."

"I'd be happy to. We'll have to work out some way for you to go on with your training at the hospital. You will be able to work until . . . when is it due?"

I did a quick calculation from the time we left the Canyon. "December, I guess"

"A long time yet. Do you want Andrew to come down and be with you?"

"Oh, that would be wonderful. Do you think they'd mind?"

"I'm sure he'd be more than happy. He's under no obligation to stay there. I think his place is with you and I'm sure he'll be able to find something useful to do here. It might do him good to take some courses himself."

"I feel better already. But what about after I have the baby? How can I look after it and go to school at the same time?"

"We'll think of something. Andrew will be able to help." He put his arm around my shoulder. "Come on, let's get back. Supper will be ready." He chuckled to himself. "I'm dying to see his face when he hears the news."

"I wish I could be there," I said ruefully.

The next morning, before saying good-bye to Paris, I asked him about morning sickness while it was on my mind. "It's awful, Paris. I hate it. I can't eat any breakfast or anything."

"I know. It won't last too long, if that's any comfort. It's caused by high levels of HCG in the bloodstream. Once the embryo is safely embedded in the endometrium, the level of HCG will drop."

"Oh," I replied. Paris never lost an opportunity to teach me something. "But what's HCG?"

"Human chorionic gonadotropin. It's a hormone secreted by the chorion, the outer layer of the amniotic sac that holds the embryo. It keeps the embryo from being aborted before it can become firmly established in the endometrium—the lining of the womb."

"I see. I always wanted to know that," I laughed. "But how do I deal with the nausea?"

"We used to have drugs for that sort of thing, but I doubt if we'd be able to find any now. My wife used to drink a glass of water with some honey as soon as she woke up, then she'd go in the bathroom and throw up, and that would be the end of it, for that day at least."

Strangely, I felt much better after talking to Paris. I seemed to have more energy too, so I offered to help in the garden and spent my day off setting out some of the seedlings that had been germinating in the cold frames. I slept well that night and returned to the hospital the next morning much lighter of heart than when I'd left.

Two more weeks passed, one of them on evening shift. First year students alternated between afternoons and evenings. There was not much need during the night for the type of services we provided, so we were not called upon to work night shift. When we worked evenings, we had the afternoon off to study and catch up on our laundry and so on. By the end of the second week, I was sure that I was pregnant. My period hadn't come, and my breasts were swelling.

Chapter 46

The weather was improving so much we were able to sit outside during our time off. The trees were completely covered in bright green, and most of the blossoms had disappeared. Sometimes I caught a sweet floral fragrance on the breeze—lilac or hyacinths, I wasn't sure, but it was familiar and somehow reminded me of my grandmother.

One afternoon, I was sitting out on the hospital steps with the other two students who had started at the same time as I—Melanie and Colin. We were quizzing one another—studying for our weekly biology test—when I saw a familiar figure enter the grounds from the street. I felt my heart jump and instantly forgot what we were talking about. I stood up and dashed to meet him. As soon as he saw me, he stopped and held his arms open wide, waiting for me to rush into them. When we collided, his arms went around me and he picked me up and swung me around.

"Andrew!" I cried. "Wow, what a surprise." I was laughing and crying at the same time. "Put me down. Be careful."

He did, and then he started to smother me with kisses. "Oh, Celeste, my sweet, darling love. I'm so happy to see you. How are you feeling?" He placed his hand on my still flat abdomen.

"Andrew! Everyone can see us. Let's go somewhere more private." I took his hand. "God, I'm so glad to see you."

"Where can we go?"

"Let's go to my room. I think my room-mate is working this afternoon."

We went into the building and raced up both flights of stairs to the top floor. Arriving at my room breathless, we flung open the door and flopped down on my bed. I was relieved that I had made the bed before going outside. Unfortunately, Dave hadn't made hers and I suddenly felt self-conscious about the general messiness, although I didn't usually notice it.

Andrew got up and closed the door, then came back to the bed where he rolled on top of me and started kissing me again until I struggled free and sat up. "We'd better cool off a bit," I said. "Someone might come along and catch us. I'm not even sure if we're allowed to have men in our rooms."

He grinned at me. "But I'm not just any man. I'm the father of your child." He put his arm around me. "How's it going, love? I missed you."

"I missed you even more," I replied. "I feel okay, except for the morning sickness. What are you doing here, anyway?"

"If you don't want me here, I can always go back."

I punched his arm. "Don't be silly. Of course I want you. I meant what are you going to do?"

"As soon as Dad gave me your letter, I couldn't wait. I had to come and be with you." He suddenly looked serious. "You are pregnant still, aren't you?"

"Of course, silly. How do you feel about it? Are you glad?"

"I'm ecstatic. I think it's wonderful. As long as you're all right. I don't want anything to happen to you, my love. How about you? Are you happy?"

"I was upset at first." I replied. "It seemed too soon, and it wasn't the most convenient time, but I'm happy. Especially now that I know how you feel. What are you going to do? Are you planning to stay?"

"Of course I am. Dad says it'll be born in December. Do you want to have it here or at home?"

I liked the way he said *at home*. "It would be nice to have it up there, wouldn't it? With all our friends and family. But I don't know if it would be safe for me to travel in an advanced state of pregnancy. I don't want to leave here until the last possible moment so that I can take as much of the course as I can before I have the baby."

"There's no hurry to decide. We'll see how you feel when the time comes. We could leave it until October or November before deciding. In the meantime, I have to find some work to do."

"Do you have anything in mind?" I asked.

"I thought I might buy up some old furniture to repair and refinish, then I could try to sell it at the market. Dad was thinking I should try to learn something at the U as well while I'm here. I was thinking of maybe trying engineering. There's going to be a big demand for engineers when we start trying to restore the infrastructure."

"Where are you going to live?"

"I'd like it to be somewhere with you."

"Well, I'm pretty sure you can't stay here. Maybe we could find a house nearby that we could fix up." I caught a glimpse of the clock on the dresser and jumped up suddenly. "God, look at the time. I have to work this evening. I'd better get down to the cafeteria and have my supper."

"I don't suppose I could eat with you?" Andrew asked forlornly.

"I don't know. Maybe if we could find some work you could do in payment . . .," I thought for a moment.

430

"Let's go and see the administrator, she might have an idea."

Mrs. Erlichman, the administrator, had the unenviable job of coordinating all the activities of the hospital and keeping everything going. She had an office on the ground floor of the school building. The walls of her office were always covered in large charts and white-boards with different colored writing to indicate different activities or departments—I was never sure which. She somehow managed to ensure, by whatever ingenious methods she could muster, that almost as many resources came into the institution as were expended. She was packing up for the day when we arrived, loading piles of papers into a leather case— preparing to take them home and do more work, I was sure.

After we explained our minor dilemma to her, she quickly came up with a partial solution: there was plenty of broken furniture scattered about the hospital that Andrew could fix up. In return, he could eat with me in the cafeteria. He would have to provide his own tools for the work, though. As far as accommodation was concerned, she couldn't help us, but would keep her ears open. Sensing that she was in a hurry, we thanked her and left for the cafeteria.

After eating, I reluctantly said good-bye to Andrew then put on the ragged hospital gown I used as a coverall, and carried our dishes into the kitchen. My job that evening was to clean up the cafeteria and kitchen and wash all the dishes that had been used for supper by patients and staff. Having nowhere else to sleep, Andrew had gone back to the U to stay with his father's friend, Dr. Levisohn, promising to return the next afternoon.

We weren't able to find a place to live near the hospital so Andrew resigned himself to staying at the U where he'd decided to give engineering a try. It wasn't quite as bad as having him far away in the Canyon, but it was painful enough—having him so close, but not being able to see him every day. I continued my habit of going up to stay at the Levisohn's on my days off, and Andrew managed to visit the hospital every few days. He continued to do odd jobs to earn an occasional meal, and when I was free, we went for walks, or stayed in my room. Dave was very understanding and left us alone when Andrew was there.

* * *

My studies continued to go well and my pregnancy progressed normally. By June, my abdomen had swollen enough to make wearing my regular clothes a problem. I could no longer get my jeans on and started wearing drawstring skirts or pants with loose shirts. The weather became very hot and there was scarcely any rain the whole months of July and August. We kept the windows open at the hospital and created a cross draught by leaving doors open.

Once the students found out I was pregnant, I was bombarded with questions and requests to listen to the fetal heartbeat or palpate my abdomen. In spite of my resolve not to cooperate with Dr. Melendez's request to use me as a teaching subject, I found it difficult to resist her warm, charming manner when she pleaded with me to help out. Every so often, I received a call to present myself to her class in order for her to illustrate some point she was teaching. Once I got over my shyness, I appreciated the opportunity to learn—usually, maternity wasn't studied until the second year. It wasn't as if the hospital had no other maternity patients. Two or three babies were born there every month, but most women preferred to have their babies elsewhere. Many young people still associated hospitals with plague and death and were afraid of going to them.

At the end of August and beginning of September, all the students and staff were given a week off—not all at the same time, but half one week and half the next.

This was to enable us to help with the harvest at home, for those who had homes. Those who were too far from home, or didn't have a home to go to, went with friends. I had my break the first week of September and returned to the U to help Dr. Levisohn's community. It was wonderful to be with Andrew all the time instead of stolen moments here and there.

By the end of the week, my back was aching and my skin burned a deep tan. Andrew's hair was lightened to a rich auburn by the sun. After one afternoon of picking beans, we put down the full baskets and flopped down in the shade of a tree. Andrew rolled onto his stomach and stroked my swollen abdomen. As if sensing this, the baby gave a violent kick.

"Ouch! I felt that," Andrew exclaimed. He looked at me. "Energetic little fellow isn't he?"

"What makes you think it's a boy?"

"What do you think it is?"

"We'll have to wait and see, won't we?" I leaned over and kissed him. "How do feel about becoming a daddy?"

"Hmmm. Proud, I guess. I'm proud of you too. Have you thought of any names?"

"I thought maybe, if it's a girl, we could call her Dawn. What do you think?"

"It's okay, I guess. But I still think it's a boy. What's the last name going to be? Yours or mine?"

"Both. I think Fisher-Colbert has a nice ring to it, don't you? Dawn Fisher-Colbert."

"I've always like the name Lance for a boy," Andrew said.

"Lance! Ugh, it sounds like some comic book hero," I replied.

"All right. What do you like?"

"Something traditional like Robert or Charles."

"No way. They're too old fashioned."

"It's going to be a girl anyway," I said stubbornly. "But if it is a boy, would you mind if we called him Paul after my little brother?"

"I guess that would be all right. Have you made up your mind about whether to stay here or go home to have the baby?"

"I think I'd rather go home. I want to be in our own home, not in borrowed rooms."

"Good. I think that would be better. Do you think you'll be able to manage the journey all right?"

"I think so. I don't know about riding horseback though. I wonder if we could find a wagon or trap like Dr. Levisohn's."

"I've got a better idea. Why don't we go back with Tommy?"

Chapter 47

Tommy had turned up at the end of October. He was planning to return to the Canyon a few days later. I'd only seen him once since we'd arrived together in March. In July, his return to the city had coincided with one of my days off from the hospital. That time, he and Andrew had borrowed a boat and we'd gone for a trip across the inlet to the north shore. The journey had taken us around the small peninsular that had once been the city's downtown core, but now contained only the skeletons of former office towers and high-rise apartment buildings. We had gone around the heavily wooded Stanley Park on the point that jutted out into the Inlet like a thumb and under the old suspension bridge which had turned orange with rust. The new bridge hadn't fared much better.

"I'll be glad of some company," Tommy said when we suggested returning with him. "I can't promise you a very comfortable ride—well you already know what it's like."

"I'll be all right," I replied. "It'll be like old times."

"Yes. I didn't realize how much I'd gotten used to having company on my travels until you were gone. I've missed you."

"Can't you find someone else to go with you?"

"Young Kyle has been begging me to let him come, but his dad's not too enthusiastic about the idea."

"When are we leaving?" Andrew asked.

"Well, if you'd like to come and give me a hand, I can finish up tomorrow and we can leave the next day. I just hope the weather holds out for a few more days."

We started out at sunrise two days later. The sky was clear when we left the university, but clouds were rising on the horizon behind us. I noticed that Tommy had a new horse paired with Jane in place of old Billy.

"What happened to Billy?" I asked.

"Poor old boy's getting too old. He's all right, but he can't make these long journeys any more. I think he's got a touch of arthritis."

"But where is he?"

"He's up in the Canyon. He can still help out around the place with lighter loads. This one—we call her Alice—is a two-year-old. She's a better match for Jane."

The rising sun made a rosy haze of the smoke coming from home fires. The trees still had some their autumn foliage, just waiting for one last windstorm to finish stripping them bare for winter. I shivered and wrapped my wool coat more snugly around me. It would have seemed like old times, sitting up on the box next to Tommy, if I hadn't been feeling so cumbersome and awkward. In my ninth month, there seemed to be no way I could be comfortable for long, whatever position I tried.

Andrew, who was riding on horseback beside us, came up beside me and asked, "How's it going? Feeling okay?"

I nodded and smiled.

When we reached the edge of the city and stopped for a break, I asked if I could try riding the horse for a while.

"Are you sure it's all right?" he asked.

"Of course. You know I always feel more comfortable sitting astride a chair. It seems to help support the weight of the baby better. Let me try it and if I'm not comfortable, I'll switch back. It's not as if I'm going to gallop away."

Andrew helped me down from the wagon and up into the saddle. I straightened up and took the reins, immediately feeling much more comfortable. I smiled at the two men and kicked the horse's sides gently to start him moving. Looking back, I saw the wagon start to follow, Andrew sitting beside Tommy watching me.

Because of my condition, we had decided to go directly to the Canyon, only stopping at a few friendly communities to rest at night. This meant no detours to places like Willow Creek. We stopped the first night at a small community near the river where I was given a bed in one of the houses. Andrew and Tommy slept on the floor. The clouds that had been building up when we left the city caught up to us the second day and made the weather gloomy and threatening, but at least it was not so cold.

We made good progress the third day, Andrew and I taking turns to ride the horse. It was already getting dark and we still had a way to go to reach the farm where we planned to spend the night. We turned off onto a narrow road, Andrew riding the horse and I sitting on the wagon beside Tommy. Suddenly Tommy pulled sharply on the reins and stopped the horses.

"Damn. A tree across the road," he said.

Andrew, who had been riding beside us, went ahead and dismounted.

"Andrew. Watch out! *Get down!*" Tommy yelled. I felt him push something cold and hard into my hand.

A shot rang out; I saw a flash and Andrew fell to the ground. I screamed, "Andrew. No, *no*, NO . . ." What happened next was confusing—everything seemed to happen at once, in a blur. Tommy had disappeared from the seat beside me. Shadowy figures appeared from the bushes beside the road. I saw flashes and heard more shots. The figures fell. I realized that the gun in my hands was suddenly hot, pointing towards where they'd fallen, and I was screaming.

"Hold your fire," a man's voice said. "We're friends. We've got them, don't shoot."

"*Celeste!*" Andrew's voice brought me back to reality. "Celeste. Are you all right?" I felt his hands on mine, trying to loosen my grip on the handgun. "It's all right, love, it's all right. Let go." I let him take the gun from me. I was still shaking with fright. He reached up his arms and helped me down from the wagon.

I clutched him tightly, sobbing, "I thought you'd been shot. Oh God, I thought you were dead, Andrew."

He stroked my hair and pressed his lips on my head. "It's all right, love. When I heard you scream, I thought they'd got you. I was never so scared in my life."

"What happened? Where's Tommy?"

I became aware of the urgent voices and movement on the other side of the wagon. I went around to see, refusing to let go of his hand, pulling him along with me. In the light from a lantern hanging from the side of the wagon, I saw two men kneeling on the ground. Looking past them, I saw Tommy's still form lying silently on the ground, his clothing soaked in blood on one side. His eyes were closed.

"Oh, God, Tommy. Tommy's been shot. Is he dead?" I cried.

One of the men turned to me. "He's hurt bad, miss, but he's not dead."

"Let me look," I said, pushing past them to kneel beside my old friend.

"Best not touch him, miss, we'll take care of him."

"Let her have a look," Andrew said. "She's got some medical training. She might be able to do something for him."

"Tommy, can you hear me? It's Celeste. Tommy?" His eyelids flickered and he groaned, so I knew he wasn't unconscious. "I'm going to take a look at you to see how badly you're hurt." I started by checking Tommy's vital signs. His breathing was rapid and shallow, his pulse weak and quite fast and his skin was cold and clammy. Shock. I ran my eyes over him, looking to see first of all where he was injured, and how badly. Most of the blood seemed to be coming from his upper left arm. I turned to Andrew. "Get me some of the Vodka, will you? And some clean towels."

I opened Tommy's jacket and shirt. The cloth was torn and blood soaked on his right shoulder "I'll need some scissors," I said. The blood seemed to be seeping from the outer aspect of his arm. The bleeding was copious, but not pumping out, so I guessed that the shot might have caught a small artery, not a major one. Someone handed me a pair of scissors and I cut away his shirt and jacket sleeve, exposing a large ugly wound. It looked as if a large chunk of muscle had been blown away. We'd had a few gunshot wounds while I was working at the hospital and I'd seen how sometimes the exit wound was worse that the entry. If the slug had gone through him, this was probably the exit wound and he must have been shot in the back as he turned to give me the gun. The first thing I had to do was stem the bleeding. I took one of the towels and poured some vodka on it, then pressed it against the wound. "Can somebody hold this? Keep it pressed firmly, I want to turn him over." A hand appeared beside me and held the towel.

"I thought you wanted the vodka for him to drink," one of the men said.

"No. That would be the worst thing you could do when someone's in shock. I wanted something that would sterilize the dressing so that it doesn't cause an infection, and alcohol's the only thing we've got. All right, I'm going to roll him onto his right side so that I can see the back. Gently now."

Andrew knelt beside me, ready to help me move Tommy.

"Wait a minute. I forgot something," I said. I ran my hands gently down Tommy's body, his arms and then his legs, feeling to see if there were any other injuries I had overlooked. It was a good thing I did because when I came to his legs, I found the right one strangely twisted. "Damn," I said. "Looks as if he hurt his leg when he fell. We'll have to splint it before we move him. Can somebody find a straight board or piece of wood?"

It was completely dark by then and we were working in the dim light of a lantern. Nobody could find anything strong or straight enough to use for a splint, so we had to make do with strapping two rolled blankets around his leg. When we turned Tommy over, we discovered a small hole in the back of his arm where the bullet had entered. There was a long contusion along the side of his rib cage, so I assumed the bullet must have hit the side of his body and then gone into his arm through the triceps muscle and out through the biceps. I just prayed that it hadn't hit the bone. He had a nasty wound and was losing a lot of blood. The worst danger now, as long as the bleeding stopped and the bone wasn't splintered, was infection. We had no antibiotics. I dressed the wound with another towel and secured both dressings with bandages made from a torn sheet. When I had done everything I could for the moment, we wrapped Tommy in blankets. He seemed to be sleeping, so I dabbed some grazes on his face with a little alcohol to clean them up.

I had been so engrossed in my work that I hadn't paid much attention to the men who had helped us. Holding onto Andrew's arm, I pulled myself up and looked at them for the first time. There were two of them, an older man and a young man who looked enough like him to be his son.

"Thank you," I said. "If you hadn't come along, we would probably all be dead by now."

"Maybe not, miss. They probably only planned to rob you."

"Who were they?" Andrew asked. He walked down the road and looked at one of the bodies.

"I don't know, but we've had our eyes on them for a couple of days now. We knew they were up to no good and when we saw them knocking that tree over the road, well . . . It's too bad we weren't quick enough to stop them shooting him."

"They look half starved," Andrew said as he turned away from the bodies of the ambushers. He looked at Tommy lying on the ground. "How are we going to move him?" he asked.

"Don't worry; Jake's gone to fetch an old door. We can use it for a stretcher. He won't be long," the older man said. He lifted his cap and scratched the back of his head, then held out his hand to Andrew. "Simpson, George Simpson. And this is my youngest son, Rick."

"Hey you're the people we were going to see," I said. "So you know Tommy?"

"That's right, miss. That was pretty impressive work you did there. Especially in your condition." We heard a horse approaching. "This must be Jake now with that door." George Simpson said.

While Mr. Simpson and I secured Tommy to the makeshift stretcher, Andrew cleared a space in the back of the wagon for him. The two Simpson boys went to move the fallen tree.

"What are we going to do with these guys, dad?" one of them asked.

"Leave them in the ditch for now. We'll bury them tomorrow. Let's get these folks home so they can have something to eat and get some rest."

We rode past a bend in the road and into a long driveway that ended at a cluster of buildings. Lights were glowing from the windows of the central building, so Andrew pulled the wagon up to the door.

"You go on inside. We'll take care of the horses," George Simpson said.

He told his two sons to carry Tommy on the stretcher into the house while Andrew helped me down. My back was aching badly, but at least the baby was not kicking. I waddled slowly into the warm embrace of the farmhouse, using Andrew's arm for support. The two women inside the house took our coats and pressed mugs of hot sweet tea into our hands.

I don't remember too many details of the rest of the night. We ate, I think I checked on Tommy and gave some instructions to our hosts then we slept.

I started awake in the middle of the night, my heart pounding. The baby was kicking again, but that wasn't what awakened me. I think it was delayed shock. Suddenly I found myself trembling with chills. I went over the events again and felt a pang of pity for the men who had attacked us, one of whom *I* might have killed. Who knows what had brought them to such desperate action? From the comments I'd overheard, they had been starving.

I started to worry about Tommy and knew I wouldn't be able to get back to sleep unless I checked on him again. I was in a room off the main living room and I could see the glow of the fire through the open door. I slid out of bed and wrapped my sweater around my shoulders, then crept out of the room. Tommy's stretcher, now padded with two sleeping bags and a pillow, was on the floor near the fireplace. I could see his skin shining in the firelight. Kneeling beside him, I wiped his face then took his vital signs again. His breathing and pulse had slowed down a little, but he felt hot. I had no thermometer to take his temperature, so I could only guess, but it didn't seem dangerously high. I pulled back his covers and looked at the dressing. There was no fresh blood on it since I last checked, so the bleeding was must have stopped, at least at the front. I eased my fingers under his shoulder. The towel was still a little damp, but no worse than before. I checked his leg. His ankle was starting to swell badly, so I loosened the bindings slightly. I wished I could see better. I wanted to be sure he wasn't hemorrhaging under the skin. His toes felt cold to the touch, another bad sign. I sighed. If only I had some ice to put on the swelling.

Sensing a movement behind me, I turned and saw Andrew.

"What are you doing?" he asked. "Is he all right?"

"I was awake so I thought I'd check up on him. We'll have to get him back to the Canyon as quickly as we can so that your father can look at him. I'm worried about his leg, and I'm afraid the bullet might have damaged the bone in his arm. I think the leg's broken, but I don't know what to do. Oh, Andrew, this is so awful." I buried my face in his shirt.

"Come on, love, back to bed. You need some rest too." He put his arm around me and drew me back to the bedroom.

The next morning, I was awakened by voices and movement out in the living room. Seeing that Andrew was gone already, I got out of bed and put my clothes on, then pulled open the door and went out. Andrew was sitting by the stretcher with Tommy propped up on his arm, holding a cup to his lips.

"Morning," I said. "Tommy. I'm glad to see you're awake. How do you feel?" I noted the pallor of his skin and the dark shadows under his sunken eyes. The side of his face was badly scraped and bruised.

"Well, I'm alive, thanks to you," he said in a weak, shaky voice. "Other than that, I won't kid you—terrible. How bad is it?"

"You've got a gunshot in the shoulder, but the bullet went right through and I'm hoping it didn't do too much damage. And you may have a broken leg or ankle. We're going to try to get to the Canyon by tonight so that Paris can do something for you, if you think you can stand the journey."

He groaned as Andrew lowered his head onto the pillow. "Let's go for it," he said. "I'll be all right." He closed his eyes.

"Has he eaten anything?" I asked.

"Just I bit of broth from the stew, and a few mouthfuls of mashed potato. Speaking of food, you ought to have some yourself."

George Simpson's wife, Angela, gave me a large bowl of stew and some root coffee with milk, then sat at the table and chatted with us.

After eating, we put Tommy into the back of the wagon and waved good-bye to the Simpson's. So that he wouldn't stray, Andrew tied his horse to the wagon with a piece of rope and then we were ready to leave. I was incredibly grateful for all the Simpson's did for us, but I was so preoccupied with Tommy and the imminent birth of my baby that I'm afraid I may not have thanked them as much as they deserved.

Chapter 48

The journey must have been hell for Tommy; the road was rough and bumpy and the weather blustery and wet, but we needed to hurry, as there was a lot of ground to cover if we were to reach the Canyon before nightfall. We heard him groan whenever we went over a rough spot. I wished I had thought of clearing a space for me to sit with him because we had to keep stopping so that I could check his injuries. After an hour or two, when I could not endure the discomfort of the wagon seat any longer, I rode the horse.

We stopped around noon to rest the horses and heat up some broth for Tommy. We had invented a quick way of heating up small amounts of food or water. We would make a fire with twigs and wood chips in a perforated two-liter can and rest the pot or kettle over it. There was just enough heat to warm up the food before the fire burned out.

When he'd finished eating, I realized I hadn't taken into consideration that Tommy might need to go to the bathroom. I mentioned it to Andrew.

"Don't worry, it's been taken care of," Andrew replied. "A bottle."

"Oh. Good. Thanks."

"Do you think we could make a space in the back so that I can sit with him? That way, we wouldn't have to keep stopping."

"I don't see why not."

I made myself a little nest next to Tommy on a pile of blankets and bolts of cloth. Not that I expected to be comfortable for long; that would have been asking too much. Tommy seemed to be sleeping, but when I took hold of his hand, I felt an answering squeeze. The swaying of the wagon and steady clop of the hooves lulled me to sleep for a while. When I woke up, Tommy's hand was still clasping mine. I thought about what Dr. Lee had told us about the healing effect of touch and hoped that it would work on Tommy.

"Celeste," Tommy said. "I owe you a lot." He gasped and groaned as we hit a bump.

"How are you feeling?" I asked, automatically checking his temperature with my hand on his forehead.

"I'll live, I think," he replied. "How are you?"

"I'm fine, thank you. Let me check your pulse for a minute." I took his wrist and looked at my watch, counting. "It's a bit better. Does it hurt when you breathe?" I noticed he was still taking quick, shallow breaths.

"A little bit."

"Let me listen to your lungs." I put my ear against his chest and listened while he took a breath, but it sounded fine. "At least your lungs seem all right. The bullet creased your side along the rib cage, so I expect that's what makes it painful when your ribs expand— that and being in such a cramped position."

I felt a stab of pain in my back and flinched, drawing in a sharp breath.

"What is it?" Tommy asked.

"Nothing," I replied, "Just a cramp. I think I've been sitting in the same position too long. I need a change. I tell you, Tommy, being pregnant is no picnic. *Andrew*!" I called. "Can we stop for a minute?"

He stopped the horses and came to the back of the wagon. "What's the problem, love?"

"I'm getting too cramped. I think I'll ride the horse for a while."

"Is Tommy all right?"

"As well as can be expected," I said, trotting out the standard hospital terminology. "You'll be okay for a while won't you, Tommy?"

"I could use a drink," Tommy said.

After giving Tommy some water, I climbed up into the saddle and rode behind the wagon for about an hour. I'd left the back flap open so that Tommy and I could see each other. We seemed to be making good time. From the scenery, I knew we'd be reaching the turnoff before long. If the threatened rain held off, we should be able to make it the rest of the way without any more delays. When we came to the turnoff from the highway onto the narrower road that led to the Canyon, the sky in the west had taken on a pinkish glow. Behind the clouds, the sun was setting. We stopped for a snack before it became completely dark, allowing the horses to rest, then we continued. We were traveling much more slowly by this time. The horses were getting tired. Finally, we came to the steep climb through to the canyon; Andrew got down to walk beside the wagon. I stayed on the horse in spite of my aching back. Walking wouldn't have made much difference, so I thought I might as well save my energy. Mercifully, Tommy was sleeping—it was a rough ride.

Alerted by the dogs, people started to leave their houses and run to meet the wagon. They must have been alarmed that someone was arriving so late at night. I recognized Janet who had probably been waiting for Tommy, and Sarah Fisher then my mother appeared followed with Peter and Lia.

"Where's Tommy?" Janet asked as we came to a stop.

"Get Dad, will you, Sarah? Hurry," Andrew said, urgently then he came to help me dismount.

"Celeste!" My mother was hugging me. "Let me look at you. How are you feeling?"

"What's happened to Tommy?" Janet asked with a touch of panic in her voice.

"It's all right, Janet. He'll be okay," Andrew replied.

"Yes, but where is he?" she insisted, her voice rising.

"He's in the back."

Everyone rushed to the back of the wagon. Janet lifted the flap and tried to climb in. Andrew gently pulled her back to make room for his father who had arrived with his medical bag.

"What happened, Celeste?" Paris asked.

"We were held up on the road. Tommy was shot in the left shoulder and I think his leg may be broken from when he fell off the wagon. His vital signs are stable, and I think the bleeding's stopped. I did what I could, but. . ." I finished with a sob.

"She was terrific, Dad. A real professional," Andrew said, squeezing my hand.

"We'd better get him inside so that I can examine him properly. Do you want to give me a hand?"

"You must be tired, Celeste. They'll take care of him now. Why don't you come and get something to eat and rest?" my mother urged, her arm still around my shoulder. "Come on."

I gave in thankfully and allowed myself to be led away to the warmth of the cabin. When we got inside, Mother helped me take off my coat and boots then brought me a hot drink. I took a sip and burst into tears. "It's all right, darling. It's all over now. You're safe,"

Mother comforted me. "It must have been a terrible ordeal. It sounds as if you handled it very well. Come on now, eat some stew."

I didn't even think about Andrew, who had gone to help carry Tommy. I finished eating and let Mother lead me into one of the bedrooms where she helped me undress and get into bed. Before I had a chance to think about anything, I was asleep. I woke once in the night to find Andrew curled up behind me with his arm around me. Even the baby was still. I sighed contentedly and went back to sleep.

Chapter 49

Andrew, what was your mother's name?"

"Why do you want to know?"

"Well, I thought, if it's a girl—and I'm sure it will be—we could name her after your mother. I mean, if I like the name. I don't want to call her Agatha or Gertrude or anything like that."

He laughed. "It was Camille."

"I like that. It's a beautiful name. Camille Fisher-Colbert. How does that sound?"

"It's okay. What about a second name? And what happened to *Dawn?*"

"Oh that's too corny. I was thinking of it being like the dawn of a new age. Isn't that dumb?" He grinned. "I haven't thought of a second name. How about my grandmother's name? Sandra?"

"It's okay."

"Just okay?" I punched his arm. "We'd better get up, it must be almost noon. I want to see how Tommy's doing."

The rain, which had held off the previous day, was now falling steadily. I got out of bed and realized I didn't have any clean clothes to put on. Thinking they must still be in the wagon, I wrapped Mother's old woolen robe around me and walked into the living room. The first thing I saw was the little boy sitting on the rug before the fireplace, playing with some colored blocks. He stared at me with big grey eyes and smiled. He had glossy, curly dark hair just like Lia's. I knew immediately it was her son Anthony. The sound of dishes clattering around the corner told me that someone was in the kitchen area.

"Mom? Lia? Anybody home?" I called.

"In here," Lia called from the bedroom next door. "I'll be right out."

Mother appeared from the kitchen. "Good morning. Have a good sleep?"

"Wonderful. What time is it?"

"Almost eleven-thirty. Do you want something to eat?"

"Yes, please, Mom, but first, I need to pee," I put my coat on over the robe, then pulled on my boots and went to the door. I had to tug hard to get it to open because the damp had made the wood swell, and when I did, a blast of damp, icy air hit me in the face. The outhouse was freezing as well so I did what I had to and rushed back indoors. Mother had put a bowl of hot water in the kitchen sink so that I could wash my hands and face.

"Save that for me, love." Andrew came out of the bedroom fully dressed except for his jacket, and went out the kitchen door. He was back about a minute later, blowing on his hands. "God, it's cold. I think it's going to snow." He washed his hands in the water I'd used.

"Here, come and eat something, you two," Mother said. She put two bowls of soup on the table then went to the stove to pour us some coffee. After she'd served us, she sat down at the table with us, sipping a mug of coffee and watching us eat. "You're looking healthy, Celeste. How do you feel?"

"I feel great, a bit uncomfortable, but otherwise, everything's fine"

"It won't be long now by the look of it."

"Are you ready to be a grandmother, Kate?" Andrew asked her with a smile.

"I'm looking forward to it. I think it's wonderful."

Lia came over with Anthony and sat down with us. "Hi, Celeste. It's your turn, I see."

"Hi, Lia, How's it going? Anthony sure has grown. He's so handsome."

The baby smiled and banged on the table with his block. A shadow passed over Lia's face then she smiled. "Did you see anything of Jackie and Tate while you were down there?" she asked.

"I didn't really have much time to look for them," I apologized. "Next time we're there, maybe we could put a notice up at the market to try and get in touch with them. They'll be okay. It's much safer now. How do you like this place?"

She shrugged. "It's all right. The people are great; I really like them."

"But . . .?"

"It's a bit boring. You know what I mean?"

I'd never found it boring. Everyone seemed so fascinating to me, and they were always doing something interesting. I thought so anyway. And I loved having access to so many books. But Lia was not a book person. She liked people and excitement, so I could understand her point of view.

When I stood up, I felt a sharp pain in my back. I flinched and drew in a breath.

"What is it?" Andrew jumped up and came to my side.

"It's nothing, love, just a little twinge in my back," I put my hand on his arm. "I'm always having these little aches and pains. I probably need more exercise. You know what I would really like right now? A hot tub."

"Well, let's go, I'll get your clothes."

We put on our coats and boots, and Andrew picked up my bag, which was sitting on the floor by the front door. As soon as Anthony saw us at the door, he struggled down from Lia's lap and crawled across to us. Holding up his hand to us, he said, "A-aa, a-aa."

"Oh, bless him, he wants to go out," Mom scooped him up. "Auntie Kate'll take you out for a walk in a few minutes." She nuzzled his neck.

"Thanks for the bed and breakfast, Kate. You can have your room back tonight. We'll stay at Dad's"

"Thanks, Mom. " I kissed her cheek. "I'll come back and see you later and return your robe. Bye, Anthony, Bye, Lia."

"I wonder how Tommy's doing," We walked across the soggy ground to Ben and Barbara's house. They had the biggest hot tub and we knew they wouldn't mind us using it.

"He should be fine with Dad taking care of him. Let's have the bath first and then go and see him."

When we got to the Fisher house, we found Tommy lying on the sofa near the fireplace. Janet was kneeling on the floor beside him, trying to persuade him to drink something from a glass. Paris was standing behind the sofa, watching.

"Come on, Tommy, You have to finish it all."

He made a face. "It tastes so awful. All right, give it to me."

"Hi, Tommy, how are you?" I asked. "What's that you're drinking?"

"Some foul concoction the doctor made up," Tommy replied. "Other than feeling as if a rock slide landed on me, I guess I'm not too bad. If this stuff doesn't poison me, I think I'll live."

"You sound better," I said. "What's the damage?" I asked Paris. I noticed Tommy's arm had new dressing. His right leg was resting on a cushion, newly splinted and bound up to the knee.

"The bullet wound seems clean enough. It's hard to tell whether or not the bullet damaged the humerus without an x-ray. I didn't see any bone fragments when I cleaned the wound, so I'm hoping it missed. The bleeding's stopped. I've packed the exit wound with a sterile dressing for the time being. I may have to suture it closed as soon as I'm sure it hasn't become infected. That awful concoction Tommy's moaning about is the best I can do in the way of an antibiotic. It's that plant extract from the two plants the Indians used to use."

"How's the leg?"

"He seems to have a badly sprained ankle with some torn ligaments—it must have turned sideways when he landed—and maybe a small fracture. Again, without an X-ray it's hard to tell. We'll have to keep it immobilized for a few days. Think you can make some crutches, Andrew?"

"Sure. Do you want to tell me the specs?"

Paris gave Andrew some instructions for taking measurements, so that Andrew could make them the right size.

"When do you want me to be up?" Tommy asked.

"As soon as we get the crutches. The sooner the better. In fact, I think you should be sitting up properly now instead of lying there like an invalid. What do you think this is? A holiday resort?" Paris smiled. "And when you get up, you'll need a sling for your arm."

"Right, boss," Tommy replied. "How am I going to manage crutches with my arm in a sling?"

"You'll have to manage with one. Fortunately, your injured leg is on the opposite side, so it shouldn't be too hard."

Paris put his arm around me and led me to a chair. "You did a good job out there," he said. "Tommy was lucky to have you along."

"When did you do the dressings?" I asked.

"Last night. I wanted to make sure the wounds weren't starting to get infected. You should have heard the racket when we took the dressings off."

"Poor Tommy. What happened?"

"They had stuck to the wound so we had to soak them off, but there was still a bit of pulling." He turned to face me. "What about you. How are you coming along?"

"I'm fine except for occasional pain in my back. I wish it was over though."

"Would you like me to examine you and see how close you are?"

"Maybe later, when things settle down a bit. Thanks, anyway."

The rain turned to snow that evening. It continued for the next two days leaving the whole valley cloaked in a crystalline white blanket. After the snow stopped, the clouds passed on and the sun shone again in a vivid blue sky. Andrew and I went for walks together, sometimes taking Anthony on a sled. He loved the fluffy white stuff, crawling and rolling in it and picking up handfuls to toss in the air, squealing with delight then howling with rage from the hurt when his hands became too cold.

Andrew had resumed his routine of working in the workshop and helping with other jobs around the community. Nobody seemed to want me to do anything, but I felt the need to keep busy, so I helped with the cooking and looking after Tommy.

Tommy had gone to Janet's house to recover. Awkward at first, he soon got the knack of walking with a crutch. I'm sure the fact that he was moving around helped accelerate the healing process. A couple of days after we arrived, as soon as Paris was reasonably sure there was not going to be any serious infection, he put a few sutures in the shoulder wound to draw the flesh together so that it could heal properly, although there was going to be an ugly scar. The wounds were still slightly inflamed, but to our relief, seemed free from infection. The hard part was trying to persuade Tommy to exercise the arm when any movement was excruciatingly painful.

Paris gave us his bed to sleep on in Andrew's room and took Andrews narrower bed for himself. Although the house was quite chilly away from the fireplace, it did get some warmth from the solar panels on the roof. It was certainly more comfortable than any other dwelling in which I'd lived in the past five years, except for Dr. Levisohn's house, that is.

There were still some preparations to be made for the birth of my child. Between us, we designed a birthing chair, which Andrew built with help from Ben. Instead of a seat, it had a concave, padded arm on each side for me to kneel or rest the backs of my thighs on. The back was also padded with bars jutting out behind it for me to grip. The idea was to sit or kneel facing the back and use it for leverage, leaving the space underneath for the delivery of the baby. Everything was ready and now all that was left was to wait. There was an air of excitement in the community. Everyone was caught up in the anticipation. This would be the first child born there, and being so close to Christmas seemed to give it added significance. More than one person mentioned that it would be a wonderful Christmas present.

I started to have pains a couple of weeks after we got back, but it turned out to be a false alarm. There was no way I could get comfortable anymore; sitting, standing, lying down, it was all the same. Sitting backwards astride a chair might have been the best position except that the bulk in front of me meant that my tail-end was over the edge behind me. I'm sure Andrew was getting tired of all my fidgeting and longed just as much as I for it to be over with.

One day I realized that the pressure on my ribs and diaphragm wasn't as bad as it had been. The baby seemed to be lying lower in my abdomen. It was also resting more quietly and not kicking and squirming so much. I got up one morning a few days later and suddenly felt like cleaning the house and washing all our dirty laundry. I seemed to have more energy than usual. Hardly aware of the tiny twinges I was getting from time to time, I went about the work with gusto. After a while, however, I could no longer ignore them and their significance dawned on me.

Andrew and Sarah were out somewhere and I was alone in the house with Paris. I knocked on the door of his study and poked my head in. "I think something's happening," I told him.

Chapter 50

He closed his book and came to the door. "All right. What's happened so far?"

"I've been getting some contractions, not very strong. They're fairly regular—oh, I'd say about fifteen or twenty minutes apart." I grabbed the doorjamb and took a deep breath. "Another," I said.

"Shall we take a look?" he asked. I nodded. "All right get yourself ready while I go and wash my hands."

Paris had an examination couch in his study. I climbed onto the couch and lay down. I felt a little uncomfortable having Andrew's father examine me and had to remind myself that, in this situation, he was a doctor, the only doctor for that matter. I ran my palms over my abdomen trying to imagine what was happening in there under the skin. I felt the muscles tighten and relax again.

"Ready?" Paris came into the room rubbing his hands together. "All right let's take a look. Sorry if my hands are a bit cold." He raised my skirt and began to palpate my abdomen with the fingers of both hands, shaping them around the fetus and nodding to himself. "Here give me your hands," he said. He placed my hands on both sides of a round, firm little mound just above the pubis. "Feel that? That's the back of its head. It's ready to enter the birth canal now." He then guided my hands over a larger mound above the head. "The back," he said. "It's facing the right way, thank goodness. All right, I'm going to listen to the fetal heartbeat next." He took his stethoscope and moved it around until he found the right place, then listened for a moment. "Sounds good. Everything's fine by the look of it, but it'll be quite a while yet."

"What about checking the cervix?" I asked.

"No need to do that yet. I haven't got any rubber gloves, so I want to keep the risk of infection to a minimum. I'll have to check closer to the delivery, but for now. . . You can get up and go on with whatever you were doing. Don't tire yourself too much; you're going to need all your energy for later. Up you get." He pulled down my skirt and helped me into sitting position.

"Thanks, Paris. Do you think everything will be all right?"

"I'm sure it will. You're a healthy young woman and everything seems to be normal."

"How long do you think it'll be?"

"It's hard to say, but it's a matter of hours now, if that's any comfort. Scared?"

"A bit," I replied. "But I'm sure you'll take good care of me."

"And don't forget, I've got a vested interest in this. It's my grandson, or granddaughter. You'll be fine." He smiled and patted my shoulder.

"Do you think I should get Andrew?"

"It's up to you. He'll probably drive you crazy with nervousness once he finds out. First-time fathers usually do."

I finished making the bed with clean sheets then I put a couple of fresh logs on the fire. After that, I couldn't hold off telling Andrew, so I put my boots on, wrapped up warmly and went out to look for him. I found him in the workshop with Ben.

"Hi, Celeste, what's up?" He came over and kissed me.

"Good morning," Ben said. "How are you?"

"Fine," I replied. As if to belie my response, a painful contraction started. I gasped and squeezed Andrew's arm.

"You okay?" His expression was comical, a mixture of alarm and joy. "Are you . . .? Is it time?"

I nodded. "I think it is, this time. Your dad examined me and he says this is the real thing."

"Wow! Are you sure you're all right?"

"I'm fine Andrew. How about you?" I added with a grin.

"Wow!"

"Andrew. Let's keep it quiet, okay? I don't want everybody to start making a big fuss. You don't mind do you Ben, if I ask you not to tell anyone yet?"

"Of course not. I think I understand. But you will let everybody know as soon as the baby's born, won't you? So that we can all celebrate."

"Of course," I said. "I'm going back now, Andrew. I just wanted to let you know." I started for the door.

"Wait, I'm coming with you," he replied, grabbing his coat. "See you later, Ben."

Everything was ready. The birthing chair was placed on a clean sheet near the fireplace, clean towels were laid out, and the scissors and gut for cutting and tying the umbilical cord were sterilized. All that remained was the long and at times painful wait. I paced, sat down, climbed the stairs and came back down again. When the contractions grew stronger and closer together, I took a warm bath. The membranes ruptured at dusk with a rush of warm amniotic fluid. That's when I changed into a clean cotton nightgown and put a shawl around my shoulders. Paris sent me into his study again, telling Andrew to stay where he was. I climbed up onto the table and waited. Paris soaked his hand in alcohol for a couple of minutes then did a pelvic examination to check the dilation of the cervix.

"Eight centimeters. Not long now," he said when he was finished. "You'll have to keep up the panting for a while longer, but you'll soon be in the third stage. Think you can handle it?"

Just at that moment, another big contraction started. I panted until it was over. "Ouch," I let out my breath and relaxed. "I'll have to, won't I?"

"You're doing fine," he said. "Are you sure you don't want your mother here?"

I nodded. "We'd better get back to Andrew before he thinks something's wrong," I said.

Our daughter was born a few minutes before ten o'clock that evening, which, as best we could calculate was December 19, almost exactly two years to the day since Mother had lost her baby. As soon as I was cleaned up and comfortably ensconced on the sofa, I sent Andrew to tell my mother. While I waited, I examined my daughter, holding her up in front of me, in wonder at the miracle of her being. She was quiet and alert with her eyes wide open and her little fist curled up beside her mouth. She had a downy fuzz of dark hair and deep blue eyes. Her skin was bright red with a fuzzy, peach-like texture. As I gazed into her eyes, she looked back into mine.

"Hi, baby!" I murmured.

When her mouth made a rooting movement towards her fist, I felt a tingling sensation in my breasts and wondered if I should try to nurse her. Paris was sitting close by, watching us with a smile on his face.

"Do you think she's hungry?" I asked him.

"No, not yet," he replied. "But put her to your breast and see what happens."

I loosened the neck of my gown and put her face to the breast. She rooted around for a moment as if she wasn't sure what to do, then suddenly latched onto the nipple and began to suck. An incredible sensation shot through my body followed by a strong contraction in my uterus. It was painful, but there was an unexpected element of pleasure in it too. I stroked her head as I watched her little cheek moving and her fist clenching as she sucked. After a moment or two, she let go. She had fallen asleep.

We called her Camille after Andrew's mother, but decided she didn't need a middle name. She was a good baby, given more to smiling than crying, and she thrived in the nurturing atmosphere of the Canyon where, being the youngest member of the community, she received lots of attention.

Chapter 51

One morning in April, mother came over to the Fisher house carrying Anthony on her arm. "Have you seen Lia?" she asked.

I shook my head. "When did you see her last?" I asked.

"Last night, I suppose, at bedtime. She wasn't in her room this morning. I heard poor little Anthony crying so I went in and found him alone in his cot. The way she's been acting, I'm worried, Celeste."

I had noticed that Lia had seemed to be more despondent recently. Even Anthony didn't seem to raise her spirits. She spent a good deal of time lying in bed or taking solitary walks. She wasn't eating well and was becoming pale and lethargic.

"Maybe she's gone for a walk," I suggested. "Come in, I was just going to give Camille her bath." I gave Anthony a carrot to chew on and some empty baking pans to play with then spread a towel on the kitchen table. Filling a bowl with warm water, I put it next to the towel. Camille was lying in her basket, burbling and shaking her rattle. I picked her up, laid her on the towel and started to undress her. She waved her arms and smiled at me.

Anthony came over and stuck his nose over the edge of the table. "Ba'y!" he said, pointing at Camille.

That's right, Anthony; baby," I replied.

"Ba'y!" he repeated, clapping his hands and laughing. As soon as he let go of the edge of the table, he sat down with a bump and turned his attention to something else.

I noticed my mother watching with a look of longing on her face. "Do you want to do it, Mom?" I asked.

"I'd love to. Do you mind?"

"No. Of course not." I moved aside and let her take over. "Grandma's going to bathe you today, you lucky girl," I said to Camille.

"About Lia. It's not very likely she would be out walking that early. I can't understand it." She gently lowered Camille into the water. "I think we should look for her."

"Are you worried because she's been depressed?" I asked. "You don't think she'd . . .?"

"I don't know. I thought she was getting a little better, but the scars are still deep."

"Surely she wouldn't do anything to herself, not with Anthony." It's hard to imagine any mother abandoning her baby.

"We'll have to get everybody out looking for her." Mother replied. "She might have had an accident and be lying somewhere all alone." She lifted Camille out of the water and wrapped her in a towel. Handing her to me, she added, "I must do something. I'll go and talk to the others. Can you look after Anthony?"

"I'd love to. Maybe she's at the hot spring."

Mother put on her jacket and boots and left. I saw her through the window making her way to Ben and Barbara's house. After I finished dressing Camille, I sat down near the fire to feed her. Seeing me sitting with my baby, Anthony abandoned his pans and came over to lean against my knee with his thumb in his mouth. He was fourteen months old and had just started to walk. He had a vocabulary of cryptic words, which could only be understood by the accompanying gestures and hand signals.

He poked a finger into Camille. "Bay's!" he said.

"Baby. That's right."

He pointed to the door. "Mama!"

"Mama's coming soon," I said, stroking his head. "Do you want to sit up here with us?"

I finished feeding Camille and put her to sleep in her basket, then cleaned up the kitchen. After that, I warmed up some milk for Anthony and some coffee for myself. Mother came in just as we were finishing.

"Did you find her?" I asked.

"No," Mother replied. "But I think we've found out where she's gone. Any of that coffee left?"

"Sure. Help yourself. Don't keep me in suspense. Tell me where she's gone."

"It was Kyle who saw her. He'd gotten up early to check on the lambs. He saw her carrying a bundle going towards the road. I think she's left."

"Didn't he ask her where she was going?"

"Apparently not. I don't think he likes her very much; I don't know why. He said he just saw her as she disappeared into the trees."

"I wonder where she's going. How could she leave Anthony behind like that?"

"I don't know. I talked to Barbara and she said Lia's showing typical signs of posttraumatic stress and postpartum depression and they've probably compounded each other. I think she's right. I know Lia was lonely here. She didn't seem to make any friends although people tried to be friendly. Lately, she seems to have been getting even worse. You keep forgetting she's only a kid. Seventeen! God, when I was that age, all I was thinking about was having fun, dating and going to the mall or the beach. My biggest concern was whether I could persuade my father to let me use the car. She's lost her entire family and been used as a virtual slave and God knows what else by those . . ."

"But she seemed so happy when I saw her last March, just after Anthony was born."

Hearing his name, Anthony started tugging at my skirt. "Mama?" he said.

"Come to Auntie Kate," Mother said, scooping him up into her lap. "Here, finish your milk." She put the mug to his lips and he took a sip then pushed her hand away.

"Mama!" he demanded. He struggled free of her arms and slid to the floor. He went over to the front door and banged on it. "Mama!" he repeated then he started to cry.

"Don't cry, sweetheart, Auntie Kate's here. Come on." Mother picked him up and tried to soothe him. "I think he's getting tired. I'm going to take him home for a nap. I don't know what's going to happen if she doesn't come back."

"I'll bring Camille over when she wakes up, unless you want to come over here for lunch."

"No. You come to the cabin and I'll make lunch."

A few days later, a boy came to the Canyon with a note from Tommy. Tommy had recovered from his injuries although his ankle still gave him problems and his arm was still a bit stiff. He'd left the week before, saying he would be going to Hope first as usual and then heading for the coast. The note said that Lia had been waiting for him at the road from the Canyon when he came back from Hope. She said she wanted to go to the city and no amount of persuasion on his part could change her mind. He had agreed to take her only when he realized how determined she was and because he didn't fancy her chances if she traveled alone. He'd paid the boy from a nearby community to bring us the message because he knew we'd be worried about her.

"How could she leave her baby like that?" I asked.

"Don't be too hard on her; she wasn't thinking or feeling, normally. And she knows we'll take care of Anthony," Mother replied. "I don't really blame her. She's had a rough time. Maybe she's hoping to find Rick."

I'd almost forgotten about her brother who'd left home shortly after his mother died in 2015. He'd be twenty-six now, *if he was still alive*—a postscript we always added when referring to people we hadn't seen for a long time.

That spring brought a burgeoning of new life and hope. I had my baby, lambs and calves were born, Guinevere gave birth to a batch of puppies, and the filly

Mother and Peter had brought to the Canyon had a foal. The peeping of chicks was heard in the poultry yard, and yellow ducklings followed their mothers in orderly formation across the pond. By the end of April, rows of fragile green shoots filled the vegetable garden, and the trees had shed their blossoms, replacing them with mantles of green.

I had decided to stay on all summer and devote myself to Camille, planning to keep up my studies, using books, so that I could go back to the hospital the following year. I was able to study psychology and biology with Barbara and my mother, so that's what I concentrated on. In addition to that, I helped with the gardening and livestock. As the days became warmer, life settled down into a pleasant, peaceful routine, a perfect atmosphere for raising a child.

* * *

Andrew was enormously proud of his daughter and used every excuse he could to be with her. Until the day in May—two days before my twentieth birthday—when he broke the news, he was planning to leave for a while. We were sitting by the pond with Camille who was propped up in her basket, trying to grab two butterflies that were circling around her.

480

"Why do you have to go?" I asked.

"I want to go on with the work we were doing at the university. I think it's an important project and I could learn something useful."

"But. . ." I started.

He put his finger across my lips to keep me from saying it. "Shh! Listen, Celeste, things are changing. If I want to have a part in building the future, I have to have some skills and education. I don't want to be a laborer for the rest of my life. The work we're doing at the U with fuel cells and alternative power resources will give me that chance. I've already missed six months; I'll be left behind if I don't go back soon. You're going to go on with your education, aren't you?"

"Of course, at least I hope so," I replied. "I understand, Andrew. It's just that I'll miss you so much. I wish I could go with you, but I don't want to take Camille all that way at her age. Couldn't you at least stay for my birthday?"

"Of course I won't leave before your birthday, silly. Dad's going back in a few days and I thought I'd go with him, so that he doesn't have to travel alone. I'll be lonely without you both, but it's something I have to do."

Ten days after Andrew and Paris left, Tommy returned. The first opportunity I had, I asked him about Lia.

"She was adamant," he said. "She said if I didn't take her with me, she'd go anyway and take her chances. It's as if she didn't care what happened to her. No amount of persuasion would sway her."

"Where did she go? Do you know?" I asked.

"I took her with me to the university to show her where she could get in touch with us, and the next day when I went into town, I showed her the hospital. She said she was going to try to find her brother, and then she took off."

"Poor Lia. I hope she finds him." I noticed how wan Tommy looked. Even his tan didn't hide the pallor. "How are you feeling Tommy?"

"Not as strong as I used to." He sighed ruefully. "My arm's still painful and stiff; that takes a lot out of me.

"You were badly hurt and lost a lot of blood. Maybe you didn't take enough time to recover properly. I think you should stay here and take it easy for a while."

"Yes, doctor," he said with a grin. "I may stay for a couple of weeks. I think you're right."

"I didn't mean to lecture you. I'm concerned about you, that's all. When are you going to settle down, anyway?"

"Ah, Celeste, believe me, I appreciate your concern. You've turned out to be a good friend. I think the time is coming when I will have to think about retiring and finding a new occupation. If it hadn't been for you, I might not be here at all."

"Tommy. . ." I said, turning my head away to hide my tears. "I think you're exaggerating a bit."

"Nevertheless. . ." He put his arm around my shoulder and gave it a squeeze.

Part Three - The Turning Point

Chapter 52

The barking of the dogs warned us of the approach of a stranger. We'd learned to distinguish between their happy yaps that announced friends and the more agitated barking when a stranger was coming. Ben and Freddie came running with their rifles and several others looked out of their doors or came from the gardens and workshops, ready to help if necessary. A man on a horse emerged from the trees with the dogs yapping and running around him. He stopped and raised both his hands in the air. Freddie whistled to call off the dogs while Ben went to meet the man.

I went to the edge of the garden near the trail and rested my arms on the fence while I watched and listened.

"Do you mind if I dismount?" the man requested. "I'm alone. My name's Greg Archer by the way."

Ben nodded. "Is there something we can help you with?"

The man climbed down from his horse and took the reins to the front so that he could lead it, then he and Ben started walking towards the houses. Freddie fell in behind them after first looking down the trail to see whether anyone else was coming. Archer was a tall, husky-looking man in his early forties with reddish brown hair and a ginger beard. He looked familiar—maybe I'd met him while I was traveling with Tommy.

He caught sight of Tommy's wagon, which was standing in a grove of trees. "Is Tommy here?" he asked.

"Yes," Ben replied. "Did you come to see him?"

"Not just him; I want to talk to all of you. I've come with some news and an invitation."

"I bet you could use a drink," Ben said. "Sit on this bench in the shade."

"I'll get it," I offered.

"It's Celeste, isn't it?" Greg Archer asked.

"That's right. You remember me?"

"Of course. You came by our place a couple of times the year before last. Have you given up traveling?"

"Yes. I have a baby to look after now." I said.

"Congratulations!"

"Thank you. I'll get the drinks."

When I got back with a large pitcher of water and some glasses, most of the people in the community had gathered around the bench, sitting on the ground or leaning against tree trunks.

". . . then we thought we could get all the representatives to meet in a sort of regional assembly," Archer was saying.

"What do you hope to achieve?" Ben asked.

"Well, a number of things. If we could get this organized, we could work together—combine our resources to start working on restoring the infrastructure. You know, get the power lines repaired so that we can have electricity, establish some sort of transportation and communications systems."

"Sounds like a good idea," Freddie said. "I'm surprised you haven't thought of this already, Ben."

"Of course I've thought about it," Ben replied in mock irritation. "I just hadn't worked out all the details, that's all.

"Spoken like a true lawyer," Tommy said.

"Another advantage of forming a regional council or assembly would be our ability to present a united front to those people in Mission. While we were just a bunch of isolated communities, they could pretty much come and go as they pleased, and we couldn't do anything about it if they raided us. They claim to represent the government, but haven't shown any sign of doing anything for the people they claim to govern, so I think it's time we showed them what a real government is."

"Do you think we'd be able make them release the people they've taken from other communities?" I asked.

"At least we should be able to send a delegation to ask for their release," Ben said.

"Do you plan to ask them to send delegates to the assembly?" Peter asked.

"I think that's something we'll have to discuss once the assembly convenes," Archer replied. "It would depend on how they react when we approach them. If they want to take over, well we may not want them."

The discussion continued for a while longer until Greg Archer said he had to leave.

We had a dinner meeting in the community building the next evening. After the meal, we went on to discuss how we would go about nominating and electing a representative. We decided that everybody would write a nomination on a piece of paper and put it in a box. The nominations would be counted and the one with the most votes would be elected—that is if he or she was willing. In the event of a tie, we would have a vote to choose between the two candidates. It came as no surprise to anyone that Ben received the largest number of nominations.

"Thanks for the show of confidence," Ben said. "I know I didn't ask for this dubious honor. A famous American politician once said, 'if nominated, I will not run; if elected I will not serve,' or something like that. I think that was a cowardly attitude, although I don't know the circumstances. However, when I decided to become a lawyer, the last thing I had in mind was politics. In the recent past, it's been a scurrilous, self-serving business at best. Maybe we can do it better this time. I hope so. For now, I'll do what I can, but one of you younger folks will have to be ready to take over before long. I was looking forward to a peaceful retirement, not getting into politics." He sat down again amidst cheers and laughter.

No one traveled alone if he could help it—we were still unsure of our safety—so, when Ben left for the first meeting of the regional assembly in Chilliwack, he was accompanied by Freddie. When they returned, we had another meeting to discuss what the assembly had come up with. The meeting was held in the afternoon, out of doors this time. We sat on the grass while the children played around us and Ben made his report.

"It was an interesting meeting," he began. "We covered a lot of ground, but only made two resolutions for the time being. The first one was to formalize the assembly and set out the rules for elections and meetings and so on. The other resolution was to take a census."

"Whatever for?" Martin Graham asked.

"The main reason is to assess what skills we have amongst us. So far, we've been working in isolation, probably having several people throughout the valley working on the same problem, not knowing what others are doing in the field. Look at us for example: we have you, Martin, working on fuels and generators and other power sources. There's a couple of fellows in Hope doing the same thing, not to mention what's being done at the university, and probably others scattered around in different places. Think what you could accomplish together."

"Yes. I think we'd make much better progress by cooperating," Mother said. "What about schools, Ben?"

"We talked about that. We wanted to wait until we know how many teachers there are, and where they're located, before making any decisions. It wouldn't be feasible to set up a school in every little settlement, but we might have some traveling teachers who can visit several communities on a rotation basis. Perhaps you can think about it and give me some suggestions."

"What about security? It's still not completely safe to travel. Look at what happened to Tommy last year," Peter said.

"That was the foremost concern of all the delegates. We're hoping to form some kind of militia to police the valley, but we wanted to get feedback from our home communities before going ahead and organizing anything. One of the problems is that such a force would require able-bodied men—the very people who are most needed by their communities to do the work that keeps them alive. It's possible we could do it on a reserve basis, where they rotate every week or month or whatever, so people won't have to be away from home for long periods. Again, we welcome suggestions."

"They'd have to be on the road a lot I suppose?" Barbara said. "How would they communicate? I mean, how would they know when they are needed to deal with a situation?"

"That shouldn't be too much of a problem. They can communicate by radio. There are plenty of two-way radios around; all we need is batteries. That reminds me of something else. We're hoping that each community will start monitoring radio signals to see what we can pick up. It might be possible to communicate and exchange information with other areas. We should be able to get enough short wave sets. What do you think, Tommy?"

"I'm sure there'll be some in the city. It's a great idea; I'm surprised we didn't think of it before."

"Some people did. There's a fellow in Hope. He's picked up quite a bit of traffic, some from as far away as Mexico and Russia. The problem is understanding what they're saying."

"Nothing closer to home?"

"Oh yes. He's found one place he thinks is south of the border judging by the accents, but a lot of the traffic's in code. He keeps a log, which we might find useful. It takes a lot of listening time and luck. You can easily miss something while you're scanning the different frequencies searching for signals."

"This assembly is only for the eastern part of the valley, isn't it?" Allan asked. "What about the west and the city? Do you think they'll be getting organized as well?"

"They probably are. In any case, we're sending a delegation to communities outside the area to find out. If they are organizing, we may have a larger regional assembly before long. That's our goal in any case, within the next year."

"You know what would be a good idea?" Jeremy said. "Starting a postal service. It could run from Hope to the city with relay points along the way for communities off the highway. You'd only need one or two people to run it, and each community could be responsible for picking up its own mail from the relay station."

"Another good idea would be to have a coach service for people who want to travel in safety. Something like the old fashioned stage coaches." Vera added.

"Great ideas," Ben replied. "It would take a bit of organizing and cost something to set up. Actually, the two could be combined. I'll certainly bring it up at the next assembly."

"When is the next meeting?" Barbara asked.

"Next week." Ben replied. "Well, I don't know about the rest of you, but I've got work to do. Or should I say *meeting adjourned?"* he added with a grin, rising from his chair.

* * *

By the end of July, the census was finished, and people with similar skills and interests were getting together with one another to talk about what they were working on and to share information. The assembly was talking about setting up a marketing board to facilitate the distribution of goods more efficiently. It would be in a central location—probably in Chilliwack, the largest town in the area—where people could go to trade or sell their produce and buy other things they needed. They had also ironed out the matter of patrols. To everyone's surprise, Freddie volunteered to organize it. "Might as well make myself useful," was how he put it, although he worked as hard as anyone.

For me, it was a fairly uneventful summer, although there was a lot of exciting things happening outside our peaceful community. I watched joyfully as my baby grew into a toddler. She seemed to become prettier every day. Her baby fuzz turned into blond curls, but her eyes stayed the same deep blue. The only thing that kept it from being a perfect time was Andrew's absence. He was missing crucial stages in his daughter's development:

learning to crawl, and her first words, which were unintelligible to everyone but me. By the time Andrew returned in October, she was pulling herself onto her feet and walking around the furniture.

One day I heard the dogs barking and knew somebody was coming through the gap. I picked up Camille and went outside. The moment the first rider emerged from the trees, I started running across the green. Andrew dismounted and walked towards us, leading his horse by the reins. His father followed more slowly on the other horse.

Chapter 53

Andrew, welcome back! It's so wonderful to see you."

Andrew wrapped us both in his arms, hugging us tight, then stood back and looked at Camille. "Who's this pretty girl?" he asked, chucking her under the chin.

She pouted and buried her face in my shoulder

I turned Camille around to face him again. "This is your daddy, Camille."

She put a finger in her mouth and gazed at him solemnly, not quite knowing what to make of the strange man.

"She's grown so much, I hardly recognized her." Andrew said.

"Isn't she beautiful?" I replied.

"She certainly is," Paris came to join us. "How are you, Celeste?"

"We're both fine. Welcome home."

"Thank you. It's great to be here, and to see my lovely granddaughter again." He stroked Camille's head then turned to Andrew. "You go ahead to the house; I'll see to the horses."

Andrew handed the reins to his father, then removed the saddlebags and slung them over his shoulder. When we got indoors, he dropped his backpack and bags on the floor. I put Camille down so that we could embrace properly. This time the kiss was longer and more passionate.

"God, this feels good," Andrew said, burying his face in my hair. "I've missed you so much. If I wasn't so grimy, I'd drag you upstairs this minute."

"Well you can soon remedy that," I replied. "How about a dip in the hot-spring?"

495

"Fabulous. Shall we take Camille?" He bent down and picked her up. "How's my little girl?" he said, rubbing noses with her. She reached out her hand and pulled his nose, then looked at me to see if I approved. "I see you've got some of your mother's ways," Andrew said.

The door opened and Paris entered. He dropped his pack next to Andrew's and took off his jacket. "Think I can join in this celebration?" he asked with a smile. "How about letting me hold my granddaughter?"

"Would you like some tea? Are you hungry?" I suddenly remembered my manners.

"Tea would be great," Paris replied. "But nothing to eat until I've cleaned up a bit."

I went into the kitchen to make the tea and warm up some apple juice for Camille. When the tea was ready, we sat at the table to drink it. Paris, who had Camille on his lap, tried to get her to drink some juice, but she was much more interested in his beard.

"We're going to the hot-spring, Dad, do you want to come?" Andrew put down his empty cup.

"No, I don't think so. I'll take a shower here. You two run along, I can watch Camille."

We took some clean clothes and towels and set off hand-in-hand through the trees to the spring. I was hoping there would be no one else there. After taking off our clothes, we lowered ourselves into the steaming water. Andrew sat on a rocky ledge under the water and I positioned myself astride him with my arms around his neck, savoring the blissful feeling of being in his arms again.

"Welcome back," I said, placing a kiss firmly on his lips.

"Now this is what I call a real welcome," he replied, holding me tightly.

That night at supper we caught up on all the news. We'd invited Mother and Peter to join us with Anthony along to keep Camille company.

"So what's happening in the big city?" Peter asked.

"Some progress," Paris replied. "Although there was a minor setback this summer. Another mini-epidemic, if that's not an oxymoron."

"What do you mean?" Mother asked. "How bad was it?"

"It was bad enough. A lot of people got sick, but only a few died, as far as we know."

"What kind of disease was it?" I asked

"Some sort of virus, probably a new strain of the flu virus. It's a good thing you and Camille stayed here. It hit young children the worst. Most of those who died were babies—under three years old—although there were a few old people too."

"Oh God," That's all we needed just when we seemed to be making progress. "I bet the hospital was busy."

"We were swamped. We turned one floor of the teaching building into an emergency isolation ward, only admitting those most at risk, but there wasn't much we could do other than treat the symptoms. We had to send older children and adults home with instructions for taking care of them.

"It's over now?" I asked.

"For the time being." Paris sighed.

"What else is happening? Did you see Lia?" Mother asked.

"We did, as a matter of fact," Paris replied. "She came by the hospital to see if she could contact somebody to bring back a message."

"How is she? What did she say?" I asked.

"She looked a bit wan, as if she's not been feeling well or getting proper nutrition. I'm worried about her. She has that lack of affect that people get when they're chronically depressed. It's not surprising, after everything that's happened. I wish we could have done more for her while she was here."

"Do you know what her plans are?" Mother inquired. "What was the message she wanted you to bring?"

"Oh, she said she'd met someone and she'll come and get the baby once they've got things organized. I have doubts about whether she can care for a baby properly given the state she's in."

"That poor girl. And poor little Anthony," Mother sighed.

She turned and looked behind her at the two toddlers. I automatically followed her eyes and saw Anthony throw a soft ball at Camille. He laughed when Camille, taken by surprise, fell over. Once she'd recovered from the surprise, she joined in the laughter, clapping her hands together. He ran and picked up the ball and threw again, this time missing her by inches. When the ball landed near her, she grabbed it and tried take a bite out of it.

"He's such a happy little guy. I'd miss him if she took him now." She turned back to Paris. "I wonder if she found her brother, Rick."

"She didn't say anything about it," Paris replied.

When Tommy arrived in November, he brought with him a short wave radio receiver and transmitter. "Cost me a small fortune, this did," he said. "I think someone must have liberated it from the coast guard station. How's the power situation?"

"Oh, it's coming along nicely," Peter replied. "With some of the technology Andrew picked up at the U, we've improved the generator and made some more storage cells. There should be enough to run the radio. We'll have to put an antenna on top of the hill though. We'd have a hard time receiving much down here surrounded by mountains the way we are."

Tommy and Janet announced that they were going to be married in November. I was happy to hear the news, hoping he would give up the grueling work on the road and settle down. We had no legal method of formalizing marriages, so they asked Ben to officiate. Paris acted as best man and Janet's daughter, thirteen year-old Jill was bridesmaid. The ceremony took place in the community meeting room and was followed by a buffet and dancing. An old CD player was hooked up to a battery and loaded with everyone's favorite dance music, some of them going back to the nineteen sixties, which Ben swore was the golden age of popular music. It was pretty good, I have to admit.

While Janet was dancing with Andrew, Tommy came and sat by me, massaging his foot. He was still having trouble with his ankle. It seemed to have healed all right, but it sometimes gave him pain when he was on his feet too much.

"Does this mean you're going to give up trading and settle down?" I asked him.

He gave me a wry grin and shrugged. "Looks like it."

"What made you decide to get married now?"

"It's as good a time as any. Besides, we're going to have a baby."

"Tommy, that's wonderful! Congratulations." I leaned closer and kissed his cheek. "I'm so happy for you. When?"

"June, I guess. It must have happened when I was here at the end of September."

"What are you going to do if you give up trading?"

"I've been planning to set up a trading center in the valley. Janet likes the idea, although she'll be sorry to leave here. It's a way we can be together at least."

"Are you talking about me?" Janet came and sat next to Tommy on the bench. She was wearing a pale blue matching blouse and skirt and looking radiant. Her glossy dark hair was pinned up in a very flattering style, held in place with an ornamental gold comb.

"I was just telling Tommy how happy I am for you," I said. "I know you'll be happier when he gives up traveling all over the place for months on end."

"You're so right." She took his hand and smiled into his eyes.

Early on, when I'd first come to stay in the Canyon, I had talked to Janet about my traveling with Tommy. I wanted to assure her that I was not threat to her relationship with him. It was an awkward conversation that embarrassed both of us, but I think we came away from it feeling less anxious, if not exactly friends. She probably resented my just being with him, having his company when she was stuck at home without him, even though she knew there was nothing between us other than friendship and respect. It must have been a great relief for her when I took up with Andrew.

I noticed an almost imperceptible change in Andrew. It was not anything I could put my finger on. He seemed to be restless and preoccupied at times and spent a lot of time in the workshop or going for solitary walks. Usually, when he went out walking, he took a rifle and one of the dogs with him, and sometimes he returned with some game. He was as affectionate as ever with me Camille and me, but I felt something was bothering him.

"Is anything wrong?" I asked him one day.

"No, Why?" he replied.

"I don't know—you just seem a bit restless sometimes."

He took my hand and pressed it to his lips. "It's nothing." He stood up and walked over to the window with his hands in his pockets. "I just feel as if I'm wasting time. There's so much to do out there." He waved his hand towards the window. "I think it's these long winters, just hanging around waiting for spring; they're getting to me."

"Do you think we should move to the city?"

"That might be an idea. You want to go back to school, don't you?" He turned to face me.

"Yes, of course. I think Camille is old enough to make the journey now. We could maybe find a place to live and stay there, until I finish school at any rate. Let's think about it."

We celebrated Camille's first birthday, and then Christmas, but after that, we fell into the same routine as before, waiting for the winter to end so that we could start traveling again. I began to understand how Andrew felt.

It was not impossible to leave the Canyon in winter, but the trail was often covered with deep snow, which was difficult to clear. The steepest, narrowest part of the trail ran for about half a kilometer before leveling off slightly and widening out. It was fun to toboggan or ski down, but a lot of work getting back up, so we didn't go down very often. If someone really felt the need to go somewhere, riding on horseback was the easiest way.

In January, a militia was organized to police the region which became known as the East Valley, and all able-bodied men in our region were required to put in a month's service once a year. They received their training in Chilliwack, where headquarters were set up at an abandoned military base. Chilliwack was close to the center of the territory they would be covering, and looked as if it was going to be the regional capital.

* * *

There was still the problem of what to do about Mission. The Assembly had sent a messenger to deliver a proposal for a meeting, but he'd returned empty handed. I wondered if they were as perplexed and apprehensive about us as we were about them.

504

Andrew's turn to go on patrol came in the middle of February. He would be away until the middle of March, although he would probably be able to visit us when his rounds brought him into our area. The militia usually went out in pairs with three teams out in the field at any one time. They kept in touch with one another and their headquarters by radio. Each community of any size had a radio transmitter-receiver so that if a problem came up, they could reach a patrol.

We had set up a radio room in a small storeroom off the workshop where we took turns monitoring broadcasts. We also had the short wave receiver in there so that whoever was on duty could also search the dial for signals. I got into the habit of going to the radio room and listening to the traffic at least once a day when I wasn't busy, hoping to hear Andrew, or news of his whereabouts.

One morning, Ben came to the lab where I was preparing some plants to make a tincture. He'd been working in the workshop and overheard what he thought was a strange transmission from the militia.

"What did they say?" I asked.

"It sounded as if one of the teams had gone off the air after calling the others for assistance. It seems that one moment they were calling in to say they had a

505

problem, and the next, their radios went dead. It sounds as if it was Andrew and his partner, Jerry Brodnick who were having the trouble."

I put down the jar I was holding and grasped the edge of the bench, feeling myself turn cold. *Not now,* I thought, *I can't lose him. Not on top of everything else. Please, not Andrew.*

Ben put his hand on my shoulder. "I'm sure he'll be all right. Maybe the battery went dead. Don't worry, Celeste, they've sent the other patrols to find out what the problem is. I just thought you should know."

"Where were they? Do you know?" My voice came out shaky.

"I'm not sure. It sounded as if they were somewhere close to the river, in the Mission area."

"Oh, God, Ben, we've got to do something. Let's get everybody together. We'll have to go and find him." I got down from my stool and started for the door.

"Wait, Celeste. Let's not get carried away. We need to keep listening until we find out what happened before we start taking action."

Ben was right, I knew. I and pushed my hair back. "I'm going to the radio room to listen. Who's on right now?"

"Kyle," he replied. "Don't worry, he won't miss anything."

"I know, but I want to be there," I turned to go. "I can't just sit around doing nothing."

I stood in the doorway listening to the crackle of static from the radio interspersed with occasional burst of barely comprehensible talk. After a few minutes, I offered to take over.

"Sure," Kyle replied, "Thanks, I could do with a break. Sorry about Andrew." He got up from the chair and went past me out the door. He turned round and asked me, "Do you want me to send someone else to relieve you? I think it's Walter's turn next."

"Okay. I'll have to feed Camille in about half an hour."

When he was gone, I sat down and fiddled with the knobs, trying to get the signal to come in more clearly. A burst of static was followed by a distorted voice: "Guardian Angel, this is Angel Four, come in Guardian Angel, over." Guardian Angel was militia headquarters.

I sensed somebody behind me and turned to see Ben standing in the doorway. I turned back to listen.

"This is Guardian Angel, go ahead, Angel Four, over."

"We've checked all the side roads . . . last known location . . . to report, over to you Guardian Angel." The message was broken by bursts of static.

"Thank you Angel Four. Continue searching . . . south, but don't . . . Mission. Stay clear of . . . Report if you see anyone, but don't make con . . . know who they . . . Over."

I was so tense with the frustration of not being able to hear what they were saying that my fingernails were making grooves in the bench. Piecing together the various pieces of broken messages between headquarters and the two patrols, I assumed they were searching the area around Mission, but were not to make contact.

Before long, it became clear that Andrew's patrol had encountered a group from Mission and had probably been taken into the town.

When Walter came to relieve me, I went straight to Mother's to get Camille for her lunch.

Chapter 54

Any news?" Mother asked. By now, everyone in the settlement knew about the missing men.

"No. They've probably been taken to Mission." I said gloomily. Anthony was playing on the floor alone. I looked around for my daughter. "Where's Camille?"

"She fell asleep. I put her in Anthony's cot. Poor little thing, her teeth were bothering her all morning, so I let her sleep."

"I'm sorry, Mom, I hope she's not giving you too much trouble."

I peered into Anthony's bedroom and saw her curled up fast asleep, a slight frown on her face and her cheeks red from teething. I quietly closed the door and returned to my conversation with Mother. "I was going to take her for lunch. I don't want to disturb her, so I'll go and get my own lunch. Maybe she'll be awake by the time I've finished."

"Why don't you stay here?" Mother suggested. "I was just going to have a bite to eat, and I'm sure Anthony's ready for his lunch."

"Thanks, Mom. Can I do anything?" I asked, distractedly, my mind still on Andrew. I was just going through the motions, trying to act as if things were normal.

"Bring Anthony and put him in his chair, I've got everything ready."

Hearing his name mentioned a second time, Anthony trotted over to the table. "Din!" he said, patting the seat of his chair. "Anty din."

"Yes, Anthony's going to have his dinner," Mother replied.

I lifted him up and put him in his high chair. He picked up a spoon and drummed on the table until Mother put a bowl of soup in front of him, then he started picking out the vegetables with his fingers and popping them in his mouth.

"Mom, I have to find out what's happened to Andrew. I can't bear sitting around, not knowing anything." I took a bite of my sandwich and put it back on the plate. I had no appetite.

"I'm sure they'll do everything they can to find him," she replied. "What can you do?"

"I don't know. I just know I have to do something."

"If they have taken him to Mission, they're bound to let him go before too long. They must know by now that they're dealing with an organized community, not just a few isolated settlements." She poured some coffee into our mugs. "Aren't you going to eat that sandwich?" she asked.

"Bwed," Anthony said, pointing at my plate. He'd finished picking out all the solid lumps in his soup and wanted something else to have fun with. I broke off a piece of sandwich and gave it to him. He dumped it into the soup bowl, then picked it up dripping with broth and put it in his mouth.

"I'm not hungry. I think I'll go back and listen to the radio for a while." I gave Anthony the rest of the sandwich, then stood up and took my plate to the sink. Picking up the mug of coffee, I moved to the door. "Do you want to call me when Camille wakes up? I'll come and take her for her lunch."

By nightfall, we still hadn't learned any more about the fate of Andrew and his partner. The two patrols that had been out looking for them had packed up for the night and returned to headquarters in Chilliwack. They'd been replaced by three other teams which, we gathered from listening to the radio traffic, had been assigned to their regular patrols, not specifically searching for the missing men. In fact, they had been cautioned to avoid going across the river near Mission.

"Why don't you go home and get some rest?" Ben urged me. "There's nothing you can do now. We'll let you know the moment we hear anything."

I was very tired. I'd fed Camille and put her to bed an hour earlier and rushed back to the communications room, leaving her with Paris and Sarah. "I think I will," I yawned. "What about you?"

"I'm going too. I'll walk over with you."

We said goodnight to Martin, who was manning the radio, and left the workshop.

"What are we going to do if they don't come back?" I asked as Ben and I walked across the green.

"I'll go down to Chilliwack tomorrow to discuss the next move."

"I want to go with you."

"There's no need for that; there's nothing you could do. You'd be better off staying here. What about Camille?"

"Mother can take care of her." We had reached the Fishers' house and paused outside. "I'll go crazy if I don't do something."

"Let's talk about it in the morning. Try to get some sleep. Goodnight, Celeste." He patted my shoulder again and walked away.

I sighed impatiently, clenching my fists, then opened the door and stamped inside.

The next morning, I was awake at dawn in spite of having to get up in the night with Camille. I let her sleep while I had some breakfast, then got her up and fed her. As soon as we were both ready, I took her over to Mother's. On the way, I checked the corral to make sure Ben hadn't left early without me. None of the riding horses was missing apart from the one Andrew had taken, so I knew he hadn't left.

I knocked on the door of the cabin and walked in. "Morning!" I took Camille's sweater off and put her down on the floor. "Ben's going down to Chilliwack today and I want to go with him. How do you feel about having Camille for a couple of days?"

"Are you sure that's a good idea?" Mother looked up from her breakfast. "What could you do down there?"

"I don't know. I do know I'm going crazy waiting. If you don't want to look after her, I can take her with me."

"Calm down, Celeste. I didn't say I wouldn't take her. Of course you can leave her here if you insist on going."

I flopped down on a chair and burst into tears. "Oh, Mom, I don't know what to do."

She came and crouched beside me, putting her arm around me. "Go and sit by the fire. I'll pour you a cup of coffee and we can talk about it."

Seeing me crying, Camille started to wail. I picked her up and sat down with her on the sofa by the fireplace.

Peter cleared his throat and started putting on his boots. "If you'll excuse me, I've got work to do."

"I'm sorry, Peter, I didn't mean to drive you out of your own house."

"Don't worry about it, I was ready to leave anyway," He kissed Mother. "I'll see you later. Take care." Peter put on his jacket and went out the door.

He was working on building an extension to the cabin so that they could have a bathroom and a larger bedroom. Some of the other men were helping Peter cut down some trees to provide the lumber. They had already put in the plumbing for running water the previous year.

"Now, let's talk about it," Mother put a mug of coffee on the end table and sat down beside me on the sofa.

As a result of talking it over with my mother, I decided to stay home with Camille for the time being, but if Andrew didn't turn up within a week or ten days, I would go and see what I could do. I think I had a romantic idea of myself as some sort of latter-day Joan of Arc, rallying the people to rescue my man.

Andrew returned two days later.

The Assembly decided that the best way to deal with the situation was by a show of force. They called up as many men as they could rally on short notice, telling them to bring their weapons with them. They all put on the uniform of the militia: a fluorescent yellow vest of the type formerly worn by school crossing guards. It was a cheap and simple way of identifying them, and the vests seemed to be quite plentiful.

Once all the men were assembled, they mounted their horses and rode across the bridge and up the road towards the town of Mission. Situated on the north shore of the river about half way up the valley, Mission has the advantage of being easy to defend. At this point, the range of mountains behind the town is close to the river and there is only one road in. The road runs parallel with the river, going through the town from the west to east. Our militiamen halted when they were challenged by uniformed sentries as they approached the town. Freddie, who had gone along as their commander, and representative of the Assembly, dismounted and told the guards the purpose of their presence. Asked to wait while they checked with someone in town, our men watched with amazement as one of the guards went into a shack beside the road and picked up a telephone.

Through the window, they saw him talk animatedly for a moment, then replace the telephone and leave the shack.

"Somebody's coming to talk to you," the sentry told Freddie.

Some of the militia dismounted. Holding their rifles at the ready, they spread out across the road. The soldiers and our militiamen eyed one another warily as they waited. Our men outnumbered the Mission guards at least four to one. After about ten minutes, they heard hoof beats and the sound of a noisy engine coming along the road from the town. A jeep came around the bend followed by about twenty men in military uniform on horseback. An officer wearing the uniform of a colonel was riding in the jeep.

I don't know the details of the discussion that followed as I only heard second hand reports about it later, but apparently, when faced with a superior force, the commander agreed to release our two men. He claimed that they had been treated as guests of the people of Mission, and had not been harmed. He refused to allow the militia into the town and asked them to wait where they were while somebody went to fetch Andrew and the other man.

"They just kept asking us questions about what we were doing and what was happening outside," Andrew reported. He was giving an account of his captivity at a family dinner. He and his teammate had spent a day in Chilliwack being debriefed, as they called it, and now he had a couple of day's leave before going back to finish his patrol rotation.

"What do you make of them?" Peter asked.

"I got the impression they were scared."

"What do you mean?" Mother looked up, surprised.

"Well, they'd dug themselves in there, isolated from the outside world, as if they thought someone was going to come and rob them of everything and probably murder everyone. That was the impression I got from the kind of questions they asked."

"What was it like in the town?"

"They kept us locked up most of the time, but from what we could see from the windows it didn't look too bad. The streets were clean and the houses seemed to be in good shape."

"What about that jeep? Were there any other motor vehicles?"

"A few. Like I said, we didn't get to see much. On the way out of town, when they let us go, I saw a gas station with a couple of cars outside. I don't know if they were running or not, but they didn't look like wrecks. I think there must have been some electric cars too; we sometimes heard the sort of humming noise they make."

"Where did they keep you? You said they locked you up," Paris asked.

"In a house. They locked us in a bedroom upstairs. I think some soldiers lived there, we only heard men's voices and it was always soldiers who came to get us for questioning or to take us to the bathroom."

"I heard they've got electricity," Peter said.

"That's right. All the places I saw had electric lights. I don't know how they do it; they wouldn't answer any of our questions. Mission is more like the way it was before the disasters than any other place I've seen so far."

"What were the people like?"

"We only got to meet the soldiers who were guarding us and the people who interrogated us. The soldiers asked us all sorts of questions about what was happening out here. I got the impression they weren't too happy there, but had been told it was much worse outside. The group that interrogated us was mainly some older men and the army colonel. There was one woman. She was about sixty, very strong—at least she seemed to have a lot of authority. She was very sharp and got impatient with the men when she thought they said something stupid. I got the impression that she might have been in charge."

"Now that we've got their attention, we intend to follow up and force them into some sort of dialogue," Ben said. "We told them we'll be sending a delegation to talk to them about opening up a bit and joining the outside world."

"But what about all the people they're supposed to have kidnapped?" Mother asked. "Aren't we going to try to find out about that?"

"Of course. We'll insist that they account for them. We've set up an office in Chilliwack for people to register missing relatives and neighbors they think might have been abducted. Once we have that done, we'll be able to ask about specific individuals. I suspect that once we know exactly who's missing, we'll find that there aren't so many as we think. There were a lot of rumors and exaggeration going around, facts getting blown out of proportion through fear. At least, I hope that's how it turns out."

Andrew's capture and subsequent return from Mission seemed to mark another turning point in the events of this time. It was the beginning of an opening up, a time of growing trust among the different communities and a lessening of fear and suspicion. It had taken the courage of intelligent, imaginative people like Tommy to start the process of communication and healing, and now it was up to all of us to make sure that it continued. I feel immensely privileged to have been a part of it.

Chapter 55

Freddie was part of the delegation that finally went to Mission to try to bring them out to join the community at large. He wasn't surprised to find that he knew some of the people there. Just as everyone had suspected, a number of wealthy families from the coast had taken refuge in Mission, and a few of them were among his acquaintances from his more carefree days. Their recognition of Freddie contributed greatly to their trust of our delegation and the validity of our claims. In order to convince them further, Freddie invited a couple to visit the Canyon to see for themselves.

Jeffrey and Samantha Parkinson arrived on horseback one sunny afternoon accompanied by Ben and Freddie. They were both in their mid forties—a tall, slim, look-alike couple with greying dark brown hair, his a little thin on top. They dismounted near Ben's house and looked around nervously. I don't know what they expected. They probably had visions of a bunch of wild mountain men in dungarees with long beards, living in primitive log cabins. They weren't what I'd expected either. I suppose I'd had the idea, probably from old videos, that rich people were arrogant, always putting on airs and looking down their noses at everyone else. Jeff and Sam, as they preferred to be called, were subdued, almost timid until they got to know us a little. I had to remember that they had spent the past seven years in a small community with little contact with outsiders and that this was a big step for them.

I hadn't worked out at the time that they were no longer rich. I found out later from Tommy that most people's wealth was on paper in the form of investments, usually shares in large corporations, and once the corporations went out of business, they had nothing. Many of them also owned land and real estate, which they had some hope of recovering as long as the land title records were still intact. They'd probably have to wait until somebody got the computers running again to find out how things stood in that respect. The trend over the thirty or more years before the disasters had been towards investing in large urban development projects such as shopping centers, office complexes, and convention centers. Investors in these types of projects faced enormous losses unless they could find some way of revitalizing them, which seemed very unlikely given the changed economy and the complexity of the investment structures themselves. The paper economy had collapsed like a straw house in a storm, and the rich were no longer rich, they were just like the rest of us.

Freddie smiled as he stood beside the two visitors and watched them look around. "Not quite what you expected, eh?"

"It's beautiful," Samantha replied.

"You've done quite well for yourselves," Jeffrey added. "But not everywhere is like this, surely?"

"No, I'm afraid it isn't," Ben put in. "Like you, we were well prepared here. Most people were caught by surprise and had to make do as best they could with what they could scrape together." He turned towards the house. "Come inside and get warm."

The three of them disappeared into Ben's house leaving Freddie to take care of the horses, and that was the last I saw of the visitors until the community dinner that evening. During the course of the evening, we got to hear a little more about Mission.

"Everyone was so afraid of you people," Tommy said. "Even I made a wide detour around Mission."

"It was our way of defending ourselves," Jeffrey replied, somewhat shamefaced. "We were afraid hordes of people would come and take everything we had. Not that we had that much for anyone to steal. Most of us had to work damned hard to survive."

"But what about the raids on neighboring communities?" Andrew asked. "Why did you have to kidnap people and steal things from them?"

"Andrew!" Paris interrupted.

"It's all right," Jeffrey looked around the table at all the attentive faces. "I don't know if you know this, but there were three factions in Mission, and we didn't always see eye to eye. I'm not trying to make excuses; we're all to blame to some extent." He turned and looked at his wife who was listening to the interchange.

She took over. "You see, when things started to get too hot on the coast, some of us began to buy property in Mission, just places we could go in the summer during the worst of the heat and fires. Then when the epidemics started, we moved there permanently." She stopped to take a drink, glancing towards Jeffrey.

"Then some of our politician friends heard about it and decided to join us," Jeffrey went on. "Some of them were invited, I have to admit. They insisted on bringing in some military people, 'just in case', as they put it. So, in the end there were the politicians and their families, us, and the military, all vying for power. We felt, because we were the first to settle there, that we should be in charge, but the politicians, being politicians, thought they should run things. The army said it was an emergency situation, and they ought to be in control. If it hadn't been for Anita, I think it might have disintegrated into a self-destructive power struggle."

"Anita?" someone asked.

"Sorry. Anita Shawcross." Jeffrey explained. I saw several people nod, as if they recognized the name. "She used to be the CEO of Bower and Western Logging until it went under. She's a strong woman and a powerful negotiator. She managed to keep the balance of power by using a lot of common sense and knowing when to compromise." Jeffrey smiled at his wife. She smiled back at some shared memory. "It was wonderful to watch her at work. It seemed as if she had something on every one of the political hacks. She had probably made some of their careers with her support. When one of them started getting on his high horse, she'd smile at him and say, 'You don't really want to insist on that, do you, Jack?' or whatever his name was. But she was fair. There was no point in alienating them; she just wanted to keep them in line. The army was a bit harder to handle, but fortunately, she knew Colonel Hunter's family and could usually persuade him to be reasonable."

"I can understand that, but it still doesn't explain the raids," Andrew said.

"Right. As I said, we had to make compromises to keep the peace and the military people were hard to control. We needed them to protect us, or so we believed. Most of the enlisted men—all of them really—were away from home, and only a few had their wives with them. We were afraid they would just leave and probably rob us into the bargain, so we had to turn a blind eye sometimes. It was they who made the raids. They needed women and went out looking for them."

"Couldn't their officers control them?" Ben asked.

"There weren't many officers and NCOs, not enough to go up against the men if they mutinied, and they couldn't very well send for back-up. They also informed the men that it would be a lot worse for them on the outside, claiming they'd heard reports of much worse situations in other parts of the country. They have a short wave radio."

"We made sure they treated the women well," Samantha interjected. "Some of them even got married. We didn't know they were robbing people as well."

"The politicians tended to support the military when it came to a confrontation," Jeffrey added. "So, as you can see, it was a precarious situation."

"I still don't understand why you claimed to be the government," Andrew said.

"Most of us didn't know about that. It may have been an idea the soldiers got from the politicians. They probably used it when they went on a raid to give themselves some legitimacy and to prevent retaliation."

"It will be a relief not to have those political types around. I can't believe how slimy they turned out to be, and to think, we were the ones who put them in power," Samantha said.

"I'm curious about how you managed to have electricity," Martin said.

"Oh well, we were fortunate in that the military unit was a part of the Corps of Engineers. The hydro sub-station wasn't damaged and the lines only needed some minor repairs, so they fixed them and kept it running. I don't understand much about that sort of thing, so I can't tell you the details. It worked though, and that's what counts."

"That's good news. We'll be able to use them to help with restoring power to other areas," Ben said.

"Do you mind if I ask a question?" Jeffrey said, glancing around the table.

"Please. Go ahead. Sorry if we've been grilling you," Ben replied.

"Have you any idea how many people there are left in this area?"

"It's hard to make more than an educated guess," Ben replied. "We've done a rough census in the eastern part of the valley—from Hope to Chilliwack—and there's about forty-five thousand. The western valley, excluding the city is more heavily populated, so I'd guess about a hundred thousand there. The city and North Shore are harder to estimate, but there's probably another one or two hundred thousand."

Samantha gasped. Her hand went to her mouth and I saw the shine of tears in her eyes. Even I was surprised at the low estimate of the number of survivors.

"My God, I can't believe it was that bad," Jeffrey said. "What happened to them all? There must have been three million people before. . . They can't all have died of the plague."

"No, you're right," Paris replied. "I guess the plague killed around sixty to seventy thousand, all told, but other epidemics followed that: Cholera, and a number of unknown or mutated viruses that proved to be quite deadly. They accounted for far more deaths than the plague."

"Thousands of people evacuated," Mother added. "I don't know where they went; they just packed up and fled from the city."

"Then there was the famine," Paris continued. "There was no way to feed a large city once transportation broke down. Riots, gang killings, exposure—a lot of people died in the aftermath."

"But so many," Samantha said. "It's horrible. Do you think we'll ever recover?"

Chapter 56

When spring came, Andrew and I were impatient to leave the Canyon and return to the city. Once he'd finished his tour with the militia, we packed as much of our stuff as we could carry on horseback and set out. We weren't traveling alone; Paris and Sarah were also leaving, so we would have some help with Camille. At the age of fourteen months, she had just started to walk and when she was forced to sit in one position for any length of time, she tended to squirm a lot. Trying to keep her still while she was riding up front in the saddle was quite tiring, so we took turns riding with her.

When we reached the city, I was met with quite a few surprises. There had been some changes since I'd left a year and a half earlier.

"Stop please. Right here!" Two men with red armbands stood in the middle of the road, barring our way.

As usual, we'd traveled as far as the city limits by the old freeway. Once in the city, we would take one of the major east-west arteries to the university—either Twelfth Avenue or Broadway. The two men stopped us just as we exited from the freeway. They didn't look unfriendly, so we weren't alarmed.

"What's the problem?" Paris asked.

"No problem. We'd just like to find out who you are and the purpose of your journey. Have you got any identification?"

"No. What sort of ID?" Paris dismounted from his horse and held the rein.

"Everyone in the city has been issued with identification papers. If you're from out of town, you probably haven't heard about it."

"No, we're from up the Valley. What's it all about?"

Andrew got down and joined his father. Camille started to squirm the minute she saw the men dismount and I had a hard time controlling her.

"The new district council wants to keep track of who lives in the city, and who comes in from outside. What's the purpose of your visit?"

"We're going to the university. The three young people are students, and I'm an instructor at the medical school."

"I see," the spokesman replied. "Are you a doctor, sir?"

"Yes. And my daughter-in-law is a medical student."

"That's fine. How long are you planning to stay?" The other man was writing something in a notebook.

"We may decide to stay permanently," Andrew replied.

"All right. You'll have to go to City Hall to register. You know where it is?"

"Near the hospital?"

"That's right. Some of it was burnt down, but they've set up shop in the annex. It's not hard to find." He turned to the man with the notebook. "We'll just take down some information and you can be on your way."

They asked us our names, where and when we were born, where we would be staying in the city, and a few other things, then they let us go.

"Seems a bit drastic, doesn't it, Dad?" Andrew commented as we rode away.

"It must be their way of getting things under control and finding out who everyone is and what they're doing. Kind of like our census. You must realize that everything is pretty chaotic; nobody knows who's alive, how many people there are and what they do. They have to create some kind of order so that they'll know what's required in the way of services. It must be a logistical nightmare, trying to get everything going again."

"I wonder if they'd come after us if we don't register," Sarah said.

"It's hard to say. Depends on how much manpower they have—probably not a lot. But I don't see any reason not to register."

The second surprise was the increase in the number of motor vehicles, especially two-seater electric cars.

"Have they got the electricity back on?" I asked.

"They must have," Andrew replied.

It was the middle of the day, so there was no other evidence of electrical power apart from the cars. The traffic lights were not working—they weren't really necessary with so little traffic.

As we got closer to the city center, we saw more people on the streets, moving with purpose and seeming much more at ease than they had the last time I was there. Some of the streets and buildings seemed to have been spruced up a bit too, although most areas still remained overgrown and wild. That's how it would be for a long time. With the population so diminished, the city was more a like cluster of small villages than the metropolis it had once been.

We discovered that evening that the hydro-electric power had been restored, although it was still subject to breakdowns and power outages every once in a while. This development was exciting because it meant that the hospital would have access to more equipment, making some of the work easier. I couldn't wait to get back there and take up my studies again, but first we needed to find a place to live. There was some discussion about whether we should all live together as we had done in the Canyon, but when Paris discovered that the people who had been living in his old house were planning to move out, the decisions was made for us. It was a large enough house that we could all live there and have a reasonable amount of privacy.

I had another surprise when I arrived at the hospital a few days later—well, several surprises really. Another building had been opened up, one that was larger and more modern. Emergency, outpatients and in-patient departments had been removed to the new building where they occupied the three lower floors. The student dorms were on the higher floors—the administration must have felt that students wouldn't mind climbing the extra stairs. The new building had an X-ray department, a small operating room and a laboratory. The two old buildings were used for administration and food preparation, and also had classrooms and labs for students.

The second surprise was the size of the faculty and student body. The faculty had increased to fifteen, and there were a lot more students, probably five times as many as the first year I was there.

Because I had no money of my own, I would still have to work for my training—at least at the beginning. Once Andrew found a way of earning money, he would be able to help me. Being away from Camille for the first time was upsetting for me—and for her—although I could return home whenever I was free. I was usually so exhausted from carrying a full load of courses and working at the same time that, when I did get home, I often fell right into bed and slept for about ten hours. I had entered my second year of training and also worked as a nursing assistant on the in-patient wards.

Andrew decided to go into the home renovation business, with a friend he had met at the university. There was plenty of work for them with all the damaged houses and people returning to the city needing places to live. When Andrew started to be away from home working most of the day, we found an older woman to take care of Camille while I was at the hospital.

The cash economy was picking up, although many people still bartered for goods and services. Some enterprising businessmen had even opened a couple of small banks. These had nothing to do with the former big national banks, but were private, local institutions run along the lines of credit unions. The center of business activity, what there was of it, had moved from the downtown core with its useless office towers to empty buildings on Twelfth Avenue and Broadway around city hall, no doubt to be close to government services. They took over and renovated empty houses and small apartment buildings, and before long, the area was booming.

Chapter 57

The weather was very hot and I was glad to exchange days off with one of the other students who had a wedding to attend. She had agreed to work for me and let me take a couple of days before she left.

I hitched a ride back to the university, hoping that Andrew would be home so that he and I could take Camille to the beach to cool off. When I reached home, I found the front door open and heard the murmur of voices from the back of the house. I put my bag down on a chair in the hall and walked back to the sunroom to see who was there.

Maybe I should have called out or made a noise, but I don't think it would have made much difference. The first thing I saw was Livia, wearing nothing but a man's shirt unbuttoned down the front, sitting astride Andrew who was lying on the couch. Their shorts and a pair of sandals lay on the floor nearby. Livia had her head thrown back and her eyes closed. An empty bottle and two wineglasses stood on the table. I stood paralyzed with my hand covering my mouth. Livia must have sensed my presence because she opened her eyes and saw me. At first, she looked shocked then an expression of amusement took over.

Andrew's eyes they shot open as Livia's sudden tension communicated to him. "Oh shit!" He jumped up, spilling Livia on the floor.

I was frozen in the doorway, unable to comprehend what I was seeing. I wanted to go out and come in again and find it wasn't happening.

"Celeste—it's not . . ."

"What?" I was suddenly filled with rage. "What? It's not what I think it is? Well what is it then?" I picked up the closest thing I could reach, which happened to be a bowl of freshly picked raspberries, and flung it at them. "Get that bitch out of here!" I screamed.

Squashed berries and juice spattered everywhere and the bowl shattered on the wall behind them. They flinched and ducked, looking at me as if I had gone crazy.

Livia picked up her shorts and stood up casually, a look of amused scorn on her face. She still hadn't closed the shirt, as if flaunting her nakedness. Andrew was struggling to put his shorts on, the expression on his face a mixture of guilt and fear.

Livia laughed nervously. "Grow up, Celeste. It's not as if he's married to you."

Not wanting them to see my tears, I turned and ran out of the house. I ran blindly until I was out of breath, then I stopped out of sight amongst the trees at the edge of the golf course. I dropped to the ground and sobbed. As long as I could cry, I didn't have to think about it, but inevitably, the tears stopped. The worst thing was the feeling of betrayal, the breaking of the trust I had believed existed between Andrew and me. And I had thought Livia was a friend. We weren't particularly close, but we did move in the same social circle. I sat up and wiped my face with the tail of my shirt. What was I going to do now? Was it over between us? Did he love her? Confused, angry and hurt, I rose to my feet and started walking back.

When I reached the house, Andrew was in the sunroom trying to clean up the mess I'd made. I walked past the doorway without a word and went into the kitchen to pour myself a glass of water.

"Celeste," He was standing in the doorway holding a stained rag.

I said nothing. Pushing past him, I went to the stairs and started to climb.

"Celeste, don't turn away from me. What can I say? I'm sorry."

"There's nothing to say Andrew. I'm taking Camille and leaving." I continued upstairs. "Is she still at the sitter's?"

"No, I picked her up. She's taking a nap." He started up the stairs after me. "Can't we talk about it? I don't want you to leave."

"It's too late." My voice was rising. "You should have thought about it before you started . . ." I went into our bedroom and slammed the door.

Andrew knocked on the door. "Celeste, *please.*"

"Go away!" I screamed.

The noise woke Camille and she started howling in the room next door. "Mommy! Mommy!"

I flung the door open and saw Andrew going into her room. "Stay away from her," I shouted, rushing in to pick her up. "There, baby, don't cry. Mommy's here." She buried her face in my neck and gave a final shuddering sob. I pushed past Andrew and took Camille into our room, closing the door firmly behind me."

I changed into my swimsuit and put a large shirt over it then I took Camille back to her room and changed her. Andrew had gone back downstairs. Picking up a towel from the linen cupboard, I took Camille down the stairs and out the front door, determined that we would not be deprived of our afternoon at the beach.

When we returned to the house, Paris was eating his supper alone in the kitchen. To my relief, there was no sign of Andrew. Camille was feeling cranky, so I fed her and put her to bed then I showered and changed into clean clothes. I returned to the kitchen and automatically made myself something to eat, even though I wasn't hungry.

"Where's Andrew," Paris inquired. "I thought he was with you."

"No. I don't know where he is." My voice sounded dull and lifeless.

"Is everything all right?"

"It's fine. I'm just tired. I think I'll go up to bed." I scraped my food into the compost bin, rinsed my plate and fork, then poured a glass of water and went back upstairs.

I didn't want to discuss what had happened with Paris or anyone. Although I was curious about where Andrew had gone, I wasn't eager to see him. It was still light outside; the sun was shining with that special golden light that comes at the end of the day. I could hear birds singing. Life was still going on out there even though, for me, it seemed to have stopped. I lay on the bed, trying to decide what to do. How could this man that I adored so much have betrayed me? I had been so sure of his love. What did it mean? Had we been living a lie? I rolled over onto my face so that my tears would soak into the pillow instead of running down my neck. "Damn!" I sat up and punched the pillow.

The important question seemed to be: should I leave him, give him up, or should I fight for him? For Camille's sake, maybe I should at least hear what he had to say. I wondered how long he'd been seeing Livia. Had they been lovers before he went to live in the Canyon? And had they picked up where they left off, or was it an isolated incident?

It was no use; I was too angry and mixed up to sleep. Glancing at the clock, I saw it was only nine-fifteen. I went to the door and listened. The house was silent. I went downstairs and out the front door to avoid Paris, who was probably reading in the sunroom as he often did in the evening. Outside, I sat on the front steps and watched as the light disappeared from the sky, then I stood up and started walking, my mind replaying the scene I'd come upon in the sunroom. I don't know how long I walked; I was oblivious to everything but the thoughts going round in my head. Eventually, I turned back and let myself into the house. All the lights were out, except for the one in the hall. When I got back to my room, the bed was empty.

The following morning, I got Camille up and gave her breakfast. While Paris was getting ready to leave for the hospital, I debated whether to get a lift with him and start looking for somewhere else to live, but decided I should at least give Andrew the chance to have his say. Where could he have been all night? Surely not at Livia's.

I spent the morning working in the garden, picking vegetables. Camille, who was two and a half, was helping. Her way of helping was to pull off half the plant when she picked a bean pod or a tomato, and emptying the basket of vegetables on the ground when it got full to make room for more. She also enjoyed tasting everything, taking one bite before dropping it into the basket. She was happy so I didn't try to stop her. How could anyone want to stop such obviously joyful activity?

"Celeste."

I turned quickly, taken by surprise. Shading my eyes, I looked up at Andrew. He looked rumpled and in need of a shave. There were dark blotches under his eyes, signs of tension and fatigue.

"Daddy!" Camille jumped up, overturning the basket again, and ran to Andrew.

He scooped her up and kissed her, then turned back to look at me. "Celeste, can't we talk?" There was pleading note in his voice.

I began to pick up the things that had spilled out of the basket, giving myself time to think. "I'll be there in a minute."

He sighed, then turned and carried Camille towards the house. When I'd finished picking up the spillage; I followed, my heart pounding.

"Celeste, would it do any good to say I'm sorry?" Andrew was sitting at the kitchen table drinking iced tea. Camille was in the sunroom playing with some toys on the floor.

"It depends, doesn't it?"

"On what?"

"Your explanation and whether I believe it."

"Boy, you're really making this hard for me." Andrew blew out a breath.

"How do you think it is for me? Do you think I'm enjoying this?" I could hear my voice was rising in spite of my resolve to stay calm. "How long has it been going on?"

"Yesterday was the only time, I swear."

"But why? That's what I don't understand. Are you tired of me? Don't I satisfy you anymore?" I sat down, putting the table between us.

"It's not that. I love you. I don't know why it happened. I guess we had too much wine to drink or something. I swear it won't happen again. She means nothing to me."

"I wish I could believe you." I looked down at my hands, which were twisting, together in my lap. "How do I know it won't happen again?"

Andrew stood up and came around the table to where I was sitting. He put his hand on my shoulder, touching me tentatively. When I tensed, he took it away. I looked up at his face and saw the glitter of tears in his eyes. He turned away and wandered over to the window. "I'd give anything for this not to have happened, Celeste. Will you forgive me?"

I stood up and went to him. Moving close so that our bodies touched, I leaned against him and felt his arms wrap around me. "I don't know, Andrew. I feel so hurt. Let's see what happens, all right?"

He let out a long breath. "I couldn't bear to lose you." He pressed his lips on the top of my head.

"You need a shower." I pulled away, wiping my eyes with the back of my fingers.

When we were lying in bed that night, Andrew suggested we should be married.

"Not right now, let's wait a while," I wanted to be sure before committing myself.

Chapter 58

I was working the evening shift in emergency when he was brought in. At first, I didn't pay any attention because I was too busy behind another screen working on a patient. I vaguely heard another student ask his name.

"John Colbert," a familiar voice replied.

I froze. My heart started to thud and I suddenly found it hard to breathe. The voice sounded older and thinner than I remembered. "Excuse me a moment, I'll be right back," At least I had the presence of mind to say something to my patient before leaving the cubicle.

I peered around the screen of the next cubicle. He was lying on the examination table with a bloody rag around his leg. I looked at his face. His hair and beard were completely grey and the hair was almost gone from the top of his head. His eyes were sunken in his tanned, wrinkled face.

"Daddy?" I moved closer to the top of the examination table.

His eyes focused on me and I saw a look of bewilderment pass over his face, then he smiled. "Celeste?" He raised his hand towards me.

"Daddy. It really is you? I—we thought we'd never see you again." Tears ran down my face. I grasped his hand. "What happened to you?"

"I hardly recognized you. You've grown up." He held my hand tightly, tears welling up in his eyes.

It was nine years since my father had disappeared.

Realizing that something important was happening, my fellow student, Nathan, continued to quietly work on my father's leg, cutting away the trouser leg and removing the bloody bandage. Seeing him doing his job finally brought me back to the present and I remembered I had left a patient in the next cubicle.

"Dad, I have to go and finish up with a patient. I won't be long and I'll come right back. Don't go away." I squeezed his hand and went back to my patient.

My father had injured his leg in an accident with a chain saw, but it was not serious enough for him to be hospitalized, so once he was patched up, he was ready to leave. It was then I met Ariel, the woman who has been waiting for him in the waiting room. She stood up when she saw Dad limping out of the treatment room with his arm around my shoulder for support. The concern on her face left no doubt in my mind that she cared a great deal for him. She was small and slender like my mother, but she had brown eyes and long grey hair plaited in a single braid at the back. I stood for a moment, looking at her.

"Ariel, honey, this is my daughter, Celeste." He cleared his throat. "Celeste, this is Ariel. Ariel's my—we live together."

She came forward, smiling, and held out her hand. "Celeste. I'm so glad you're all right. Your father was very worried about what might have happened to you."

I took her small slender hand. "Hi." I couldn't think of anything else to say. I didn't even know how I felt at that moment; so many emotions were vying for attention.

"Can you go home now, John?" Ariel asked.

I gave him a final hug and kiss on the cheek. He held onto me for a moment and then let go and went to Ariel.

She took his arm and supported him as they walked towards the door. When they reached the door, he turned back to look at me. "You will come soon, won't you?" He'd already given me his address.

"I will, Dad, I promise."

I went through the rest of my shift in a kind of daze, hardly aware of what I was doing. Fortunately, the work was routine and I don't think I harmed anyone. At the end of the shift, I signed off and changed into my street clothes. Dad and I had only exchanged the briefest information while he was being treated. There was too much to talk about for us to know where to begin, but I did get his address and he had mine. As I walked out of the hospital, I had the urge to go straight to his house, but I curbed my impatience and went back to my rooms.

Camille and I were sharing a house with another student and her five-year-old son. My feelings for Andrew had started to change after the episode the previous summer, and by the end of the year, we were drifting apart. That's when I started looking for a new place to live closer to the hospital. I found a fellow student, Amalie Tresco, who was looking for someone to share a three-bedroom house about two kilometers south of the hospital. So far, it had worked out well for us. We rented out a suite in the basement to a woman in exchange for looking after the children when we were at the hospital.

I rode my bicycle home, getting off and pushing it when the road became too steep. The house was close to what had once been beautiful Queen Elizabeth Park. It was still beautiful, but in a different, wilder way. Whereas before it had been very cultivated with magnificent flowerbeds, it had now gone wild. Many of the flowers, especially the bulbs, had survived, but they were almost overrun by more tenacious wild plants. The grass was uncut and scattered with bushes and saplings, and the paved pathways were broken and overgrown. There was a spectacular view of the downtown area of the city from high on a hill in the center of the park. It was a good place to take the children on our days off.

I didn't get a chance to see my father until three days later. As soon as we'd finished breakfast, I strapped Camille into the child seat on the back of my bicycle and took off. When I reached my father's house which was about three kilometers to the east of where we lived, I stopped and stayed astride the bicycle with my feet on the ground, suddenly feeling nervous. It was a small bungalow that showed signs of recent repairs. The garden was neatly kept, and the windows were clean. I noticed a large tree beside the house that had recently had some of its branches trimmed off. I suppose that's what he was doing when he got hurt. As I stood there, a small face peered out of one of the windows, then instantly disappeared.

A moment later, Ariel opened the front door. I got off the bicycle and wheeled it up the path to the door then I unstrapped Camille and put her on the ground.

"Come in, Celeste. Your father's resting his leg. He's in there." She pointed towards the room where I'd seen the face at the window. "Is this your little girl?"

"Yes, this is Camille." I picked her up. My father was sitting in a comfortable chair with his foot up on a hassock. "Hi, Dad. How are you?" I put Camille on the floor and went over to kiss him.

"Celeste. God, I can barely believe I'm seeing you." He started to rise from the chair.

"Don't get up, Dad."

He settled back and turned his attention to Camille who was standing staring at him with a finger in her mouth. "So this is my granddaughter. She's—she looks like you. How old is she?" His eyes shiny with unshed tears.

"She was three in December." I turned to my daughter. "Say hello to your Grandpa, Camille."

"Hello, g'ampa." She turned and buried her face in my lap.

"Sit down. I'll bring some tea," Ariel said.

"How's your leg?" I sat in a chair opposite my father.

"It's sore, but it's healing okay." He rubbed the leg as if to confirm what he'd said.

"I thought I saw a child looking out of the window," I said.

"Yes, that's our son." He looked at me almost apologetically. "Dane, where are you?" he called. "Come and meet your sister."

"How old is he?" I asked.

"Seven. He'll be eight in June." The boy came into the room. He looked so much like my dead brother Paul, it broke my heart. He was small with pale skin, dark hair and brown eyes. "Say 'hi' to Celeste," Dad told him. "She's your sister."

"Hi. Are you really my sister?"

"Yes. I guess I am. I'm very happy to meet you."

"But you're so old. How come?"

I laughed. "I suppose I grew up too fast."

Camille stood in front of Dane, looking up hopefully at his face. "Boy play?" she said.

"Who's she?" Dane asked.

"This is my daughter. Her name's Camille. She wants to play with you."

"But she's a baby."

"Don't be mean, Dane." Ariel came in with a tray and put it down on a table near Dad's chair. "I bet we could find something for her to play with. Come along with us, Camille." She held out her hand. Camille looked at me for approval, then took Ariel's hand and went out with her and Dane. As they went, I heard Ariel say, "You're her uncle, did you know that?"

I picked up one of the mugs of tea and sat back. We looked at each other for a moment.

"How's . . .?"

"I'm . . ."

We both started to talk at once.

"Go ahead," I said.

"I was going to ask how Kate—your mother—is."

"She's fine. She's living in the interior with . . ." I hesitated.

"Go on."

"I'm sorry, Dad. After you disappeared and we couldn't find out what had happened to you—we were afraid you'd been killed—well. . . You remember Peter?"

"Hetherington?" He looked surprised.

"Yes. Well he and Mom are living together now." I took a sip of tea, waiting for his reaction. He rubbed both hands over his face, but said nothing. "What happened to you, Dad?"

"Is she happy with him?" he said, ignoring my question.

"Yes. They get along very well. They're happy."

"I'm glad. It's not good to be alone these days." He paused for a moment. "I'm trying to piece it together, what happened. Let's see, we had just left the dump and were going back for another load—God it seems a long time ago. Anyway, we were ambushed. They shot both of us, then dragged us out of the truck and dumped us by the roadside. Louie was dead, but I somehow survived."

"Where were you shot?" I asked.

"Here." He fingered a spot on the side of his head. "The bullet creased my skull, but it didn't penetrate. I was unconscious, for a while. Anyway, somebody came along and found I was still alive, so they carried me to their place. Fortunately, they had some medical knowledge—Ariel used to be an emergency paramedic, and another woman was a nurse. They took care of me and I survived."

"But why didn't you let us know?" I asked.

"I couldn't remember anything. When I regained consciousness, I couldn't even remember my name. It was months before things started to come back and I was still having a problem getting around as well. As soon as I could, I sent a couple of the men to find you and tell you where I was, but you'd already gone. By the time I was able to start looking for you, you'd disappeared. I had no idea . . ."

"I left a note for you when we moved out of our house, in case you came back. Did you find it?"

"No. The house was burnt down when I got there. I was afraid you'd all been. . . Where did you go?"

I started to tell him about our moves, first to the townhouse complex, and then to the country. We were interrupted once when Ariel came to tell us lunch was ready. After lunch, she offered to take Camille and Dane out for a while so that we could talk. She seemed to be a thoughtful, understanding woman. I was glad he'd found someone like her.

While Ariel and the children were out, Father and I continued our discussion. At one point, he stopped to light a fire in the fireplace. Seeing him flinch when he tried to kneel to position the kindling, I told him to sit down and let me do it.

"It's hard to believe all those people are gone," he said at one point. "Edward and Emily, the Harrises, Marvin, and the children. So many casualties. It's a miracle any of us survived."

"I know." We sat in silence for a moment, watching the flames.

"And you're going to be a doctor." He looked at me.

"I hope so. If I can get through the course; it's hard work."

"I'm proud of you, Celeste. You seem to have come out of it in one piece."

"Thanks, Daddy. What are you doing these days?"

"Guess."

"Not computers?"

"Well, somebody has to get things going again. Don't forget, most of the essential information of the old society was stored on computers."

"I guess so. I'm happy for you. I know how much the work meant to you. Did you know I wanted to go into some sort of computer work when I was younger?"

We heard footsteps on the porch then the front door opened. Ariel and the children were back. Camille ran in and leaned her elbows on my knees. She was holding a bunch of wild flowers with very short stems.

Her eyes were shining and her cheeks red from the fresh air. "Mommy, I bwought you some f'owers."

"Thank you, darling, they're beautiful." I lifted her onto my knee. "I think it's time to go home now, give Grandpa a rest."

Epilogue - Reunion

What's that, Mommy?" Camille pointed to the buzzing white object in the sky that was growing larger and noisier the closer it came.

"It's an airplane." I shaded my eyes with my hand and gazed at the approaching aircraft, feeling a flutter of anxiety and excitement.

"What's a nairplane?"

"It's like a bus that flies through the sky."

"Can people ride in it?"

"Yes."

"Can I ride in one?" She held my hand and jumped up and down.

"One day. Not today, though, we're just meeting someone."

"Who?"

"An old friend of Mommy's."

The plane touched down on the far end of the runway and taxied towards us. It was a small turbo-prop aircraft with room for about twenty passengers. Although we were at the main airport, we were waiting at the edge of the field by a group of hangars, not in the large terminal building, which we could see in the distance, girdled by the rusting hulks of massive airliners.

The aircraft came to a stop and two men ran out from the hangar to wedge chocks under the wheels. When the door opened, portable steps were wheeled up so that the passengers could disembark. I watched anxiously, looking for the familiar faces. There they were! I darted forward, pulling Camille by the hand and stood waiting for them to reach the bottom of the stairs.

"Eric!" I rushed into his arms. "It's great to see you. How are you?" I stood back and looked at his face. The new lines around his eyes were magnified by his glasses and his hair was a little thinner, but otherwise, he was the same old Eric.

"Celeste, you look wonderful." He kissed me on the cheek. "I want you to meet my wife, Tina." He put his arm around the shoulder of a petite, dark haired woman with luminous brown eyes and a bright smile. She looked as if she might be Latin American.

Vicki Wootton

"Hello, Tina." I shook her hand.

"Hi, Celeste," she said with a shy smile. "I've heard a lot about you. I feel I already know you."

I moved over to Mike who was standing behind his brother. "Mike, how are you?" We hugged each other. "This is my daughter, Camille." I brought her forward.

Once the greetings and introductions were over, we stowed their luggage and piled into the bus that was waiting take us into the city.

"Who all is here?" Eric asked.

"Dad, Lia." I noticed Mike's interest perk up when I mentioned Lia. "Tate and Jackie, Pam and her father— her grandma died, you know. We're still waiting for Chris, and Mom and Peter should be here tomorrow. They'll be bringing Lia's son, Anthony, and Chris will bring Debbie and Don's daughter, Carol-Anne. Oh and Tommy and his wife and children are coming too."

"Who's Tommy?" Mike asked.

"I forgot, I met him just after you were taken. He's a very good friend. I worked for him for a while."

It was to be the first reunion of all the survivors of the group that had started out together, a project I'd been working on for a year. I had just received my preliminary degree, which gave me the right to practice medicine and call myself doctor, even though I still had a long way to go before I would be qualified to practice independently. I had to put in at least two years of supervised work in the hospital and community yet. Now that I had completed the first and major stage, I felt this reunion was a fitting way to celebrate. Most of the work setting it up had been done by mail.

Once things were more organized, most communities compiled and published lists of survivors which were then circulated to other areas, so that people could locate lost friends and relatives. It was possible to go to city hall and look at the lists from various areas. That's how I discovered that Mike and Eric were living in a university community three hundred kilometers to the south. As soon as I located them, I wrote to Eric and started an exchange of letters between us in which we brought each other up-to-date.

The men who had snatched them that night by the river had been on a routine trip to get supplies and had seen an opportunity to make an extra profit when they came across the four of us. They knew that certain groups were looking for extra workers and thought they could sell us to one of them. Mike and Eric were taken on at a university in a relatively unpopulated area. They were well treated and given work to do on some interesting projects concerned with environmentally

Vicki Wootton

friendly power sources. According to Eric, it was the best thing that could have happened to them. Eric met Tina there and after a couple of years, they were married. Mike, it seems, had become something of a lady's man, playing the field rather than settling down in a permanent relationship. Maybe he was afraid to commit himself to a relationship for fear of having it taken away from him after all the losses he'd suffered.

I'd already met Chris who had finally been released from the survivalist camp two years earlier. Deciding how to approach the survivalists had been one of the many problems the new civil authorities had to deal with and, because it was not a serious problem, they'd taken some time getting around to it. But after receiving a number of complaints, they went into action. It was much like the approach taken by the East Valley against Mission—a show of force. It wasn't easy and could have turned into a blood bath, but they must have known that they couldn't win if it came to an all-out battle. They were surrounded by superior numbers, and they knew they couldn't hold out once they ran out of ammunition. After a four-day siege, they called a truce. Once the siege was over, they were forced to free anyone who wanted to leave. One of those freed was Chris who brought Carol-Anne with her.

I remembered Chris as a cheerful, golden-haired young woman in her early thirties. I felt like weeping when I saw the husk she had become. Her hair was completely grey; her skin was leathery and lined. She seemed to have shrunk, and her eyes were dull and expressionless. I was reminded of descriptions I'd read of people being released after long imprisonment. She had been robbed of her youth—I couldn't imagine anything much worse. Carol-Anne was a pale, placid little girl, listless and overweight.

Chris had no idea what she was going to do after she was released, so I had suggested that she go to the Canyon which had become something of a resort for people—friends mostly—who needed a place to recover. I was looking forward to seeing her again, hoping she was adjusting well.

The university was still one of the best places for people to stay; especially now since they had renovated some of the old dorms, so we had arranged to accommodate everybody there for the reunion. I watched with tears in my eyes as my old friends and family got re-acquainted. When Mother and Peter arrived with the rest of the band from the Canyon, I saw her look at my father who was waiting with Ariel and Dane. As they walked towards each other, they had tears in their eyes. I felt as if I was intruding on an intensely private moment when they came together and embraced.

"Kate. My God . . . ."

"John!"

I looked around at the others. Peter was staring at the ground. Ariel was holding tightly to Dane's hand, biting her lip, her eyes focused somewhere off to the side. My parents turned from each other and gestured for their respective partners to join them. Peter and my father shook hands. I saw Mother say something to Ariel, then bend down and speak to Dane. She looked so sad, probably thinking, as I had, of Paul.

I wiped my eyes and looked away. Andrew was coming across the grass, holding Camille by the hand. He'd had his hair cut a little shorter and looked a bit more muscular, tanned and as handsome as ever. I felt a pang of regret for what might have been. Neither of us had found a new partner.

- END –

About the Author

Vicki Wootton was born and educated in England but has spent most of her adult life in North America. She currently resides in British Columbia.

Among her many occupations, she has been a mother, galley girl on a fishing boat, law office accountant, and a government contractor. She is now a full-time writer and book designer.

She is a vegetarian and a Jesusonian and enjoys balcony gardening. As a reward for working hard, she likes to do online jigsaw puzzles.

ℬℭ

Thank you for reading these books. It would mean a great deal to me if you could find the time to leave a review on amazon. Thank you.

Other Books by this Author

NOVELS

Where Have All the Young Girls Gone?

At War with Terror

Forbidden World

Reluctant Warriors

NON–FICTION

Names of the World